A
Thornton Wilder
Trio

A
Thornton Wilder
Trio

THE CABALA
THE BRIDGE OF SAN LUIS REY
THE WOMAN OF ANDROS

Introduction by
MALCOLM COWLEY

CRITERION BOOKS NEW YORK

Contents

Introduction

THE middle 1920's were famous years for American writing. A group of powerful novelists, who had started as idol breakers, at last had been accepted by the public. They would become idols themselves, but first they were producing their mature and most characteristic work as if in a burst of collective energy. *An American Tragedy, Arrowsmith, Dark Laughter, Barren Ground,* and *The Professor's House* all appeared in 1925. So did *Manhattan Transfer* and *The Great Gatsby,* but these belonged in another category, for Dos Passos and Fitzgerald were younger men who pictured what seemed to be a different world. Soon the picture would be enlarged by other members of the postwar generation. Hemingway's first book of stories, *In Our Time,* was also published in 1925, and *The Sun Also Rises,* his first novel, in 1926. That same year Faulkner came forward with *Soldier's Pay,* and Hart Crane with *White Buildings,* a first collection of poems that carried a first introduction by Allen Tate. E. E. Cummings published *Is 5,* not a first book of verse but his wittiest, and Edmund Wilson wrote a series of critical dialogues, *Discordant Encounters.* In 1926 a new galaxy of writers was taking shape, with its novelists, poets, playwrights, and critics.

That was also the year when Thornton Wilder published *The Cabala*. I was lucky enough to be sent an advance copy —a young book for a young reviewer—and it became a personal discovery for me as for many others. From the opening sentence—"The train that first carried me into Rome was late, overcrowded, and cold"—it announced a new writer who was not a novice, who knew how to set a scene without useless furniture and how to make simple words stand cleanly on a page. "It was Virgil's country," he said at the end of the first paragraph, "and there was a wind that seemed to rise from the fields and descend upon us in a long Virgilian sigh." That had the authority of rightness; nobody could improve it by changing words or the order of words; and it also hinted that the story, although set in the present, would have something to do with the past. A circle was closed when the shade of Virgil appeared in the last chapter and spoke to the young traveler on his way back to America. The book had form, and hardly anyone doubted from the first that Wilder would be an important member of the new galaxy.

But did he really belong to it, in any sense except that of being the same age as the others and hence of having lived, in many respects, the same sort of life? . . . He was born in 1897, a year after Dos Passos and Fitzgerald, two years before Hemingway and Hart Crane, and like those others he was born in the Middle West. He was the second of five children, two boys and three girls. His father, Amos P. Wilder, was a devout Congregationalist from Maine who had taken a doctorate in economics at Yale and then had bought a newspaper in Madison, Wisconsin. As a publisher Dr. Wilder also played a part in Republican politics, and during Theodore Roosevelt's second administration he was sent to China, where he served as consul general at Shanghai and Hong Kong. He tried to instill a sense of duty into all his children and to pick a career for each of them; for example, Amos, the elder son, was designed to be a theo-

logian and later he carried out his father's plan; he is now
a professor at the Harvard Divinity School.

About Thornton's future there was more doubt. He read
wildly, wrote plays for his sisters to act in cheesecloth robes,
and used the margins of his schoolbooks for taking literary
notes. "Poor Thornton, poor Thornton," his father used to
say, "he'll be a burden all his life." It was decided to make
him a teacher, on the theory that he would fail in any other
profession. He went to a missionary school at Chefoo, on
the China coast, and then to a high school in Berkeley,
when the family settled in California. After being graduated
from the Thacher School, at Ojai in the same state, he was
sent East to Oberlin College for two years, because his
father thought that Yale was too worldly for an underclass-
man. In 1917 he enlisted in the Coast Artillery, rising, he
said, "by sheer military ability to the rank of corporal."
From 1918 to 1920 he was at Yale, writing for the *Lit* and
reading his one-act plays to classmates who crowded his
room. In 1920–21 he was studying archaeology at the Amer-
ican Academy in Rome. Then his father summoned him
home with a cablegram: "HAVE JOB FOR YOU TEACHING NEXT
YEAR LAWRENCEVILLE LEARN FRENCH." Thornton knew
French already, having always been quick with languages,
but he set about learning to teach it.

He was launched on the profession that had been picked
out for him, and he enjoyed it—at Lawrenceville, the boys'
preparatory school near Princeton where he taught for six
years, as later at the University of Chicago and briefly at
Harvard. He is a born teacher, and in that respect he bears
more resemblance to the writers of a succeeding generation
than to those of his own. Sometimes he remains a teacher
even when he is writing plays and novels. At Lawrence-
ville, where he was a housemaster as well as an instructor,
his only time for literary work was "after the lights of the
House were out and the sheaf of absurd French exercises
corrected and indignantly marked with red crayon." Then,
writing in a bound ledger with a fountain pen, he might

set down the first draft of a three-minute play for three actors—he wrote more than forty of these, and the best of them were later collected in a volume called *The Angel That Troubled the Waters*—or he might work on a more ambitious project growing out of his year in Europe and called in its first state *Notes of a Roman Student.*

He became a novelist as if by request. Friends from the Yale *Lit* wrote and asked him, "Why haven't you published a book when you were the most brilliant in your class and all your friends have published." His answer was to copy out from the *Notes* about a hundred pages of manuscript, which afterward became the first three chapters of *The Cabala.* He finished the book during a summer at the Mac-Dowell Colony in Peterboro, New Hampshire; almost always he does his writing away from home, during three or four months spent in some new corner of the globe. Then, having read galley proofs of *The Cabala* not too carefully—the first edition was full of misspellings—he wrote the first sentence of a new novel: "On Friday noon, July the twentieth, 1714, the finest bridge in all Peru broke and precipitated five travelers into the gulf below."

From its publication in November 1927, *The Bridge of San Luis Rey* was a success with the public. There were six new printings in the one month of December. In May it received the Pulitzer Prize, and during the year after publication it had a sale of three hundred thousand copies, without benefit of book clubs or cheap editions. It was popular in England too, and was soon translated into most of the European languages. Its success—still a little hard to understand, for the best qualities of *The Bridge* are not those usually regarded as being popular—was one of the accidents or miracles that sometimes happen in the lives of young writers, and that happened a little more frequently in the 1920's, though seldom on this grand scale. One day the author was a housemaster in a boys' boarding school with a passion for writing in his spare time, to please himself. The next day he could read with a little incredulity that he had

"already attained to the front rank of living novelists," and that his book was quite simply "a work of genius." The critic was William Lyon Phelps, of Yale, who had always been given to superlatives, but in England Arnold Bennett agreed with him. "The writing," Bennett said, "has not been surpassed in the present epoch. It dazzled me by its accomplishment."

Wilder resigned his post at Lawrenceville and spent most of the next two years traveling in Europe. His third novel, *The Woman of Andros*, was started in England (where parts of it, he says, were thought out during church services) and was continued on the Riviera, at New Haven, where he was planning a house in the suburbs—"the house that *The Bridge* built"—and at Oxford, Paris, and Munich. For a pastoral novel about Greece in the last century before the Christian era, it appeared at an unpropitious moment— a year after Black Thursday, in a month marked by bank failures, by apple sellers at street corners and stockbrokers jumping out of high-story windows. In the *New Republic* Wilder was scolded for his indifference to the sufferings of fellow Americans; he was called "the poet of our genteel bourgeoisie" and "this Emily Post of culture." Though many readers and a few critics came to his defense, even violently, it was evident that they had been less impressed by his new book than by *The Bridge*. Perhaps that was the beginning of a long coolness that has existed between Wilder and the critics; it is as if they nodded distantly or even respectfully when they passed in the street, but never stopped to talk. For more than twenty years his work has received less critical attention than the work of any other major American writer.

2

His life until 1930 had resembled, in most respects, the lives of other Americans born at the turn of the century who were also becoming famous novelists. It was distin-

guished from those other lives chiefly by the fact that some of his boyhood years had been spent in China—an experience that had more of a negative than a positive effect on his work—and by his professional interest in teaching. Everything else seems on the surface to be part of a familiar picture: the early delight in reading, the literary reputation gained in college, the wartime service in the Army (although it was his older brother, the future theologian, who went abroad with the ambulance corps, like so many postwar writers), the year in Europe as a spectator of greatness and decay, the critical recognition of a first book, and the popular success of a second, followed by more wanderings abroad; all the novelists of his generation have been great travelers. On the Riviera in 1928–29 he was one of the young writers who often met at Gerald and Sara Murphy's; some of the others were Hemingway, MacLeish, Dos Passos, and Scott Fitzgerald, whose next novel, *Tender Is the Night,* would be dedicated to the Murphys. The novel was praised even less than Hemingway's books of the same period, while Faulkner, then writing his best work, was condemned or passed over in silence. Thus, even the attacks on Wilder in the early depression years were part of a pattern in many lives.

Yet under the surface there was an essential difference between his life and those of the others, a difference not so much in events as in the quality of experience, and it helps to explain a quality in his work. As immensely varied as that work has been, in fiction, drama, and criticism, with each new book presenting a different period and place—from the Ice Age to the Atomic Age, and from Peru to the isles of Greece, passing through Omaha and Grover's Corners, New Hampshire—still it has been animated from the beginning by the same spirit, and by one that is almost unique in our time and country. Perhaps, by contrasting Wilder with the other novelists of his generation, we can find at least an approximate statement of what the spirit is.

Most of the others had a geographical starting point, a

sort of rock to which their early books were attached like a colony of mussels. One thinks of Hemingway's Michigan woods, of Faulkner's county in Mississippi, of Wolfe's Asheville (or Altamont), and of Summit Avenue in St. Paul, the scene of so many stories by Scott Fitzgerald. With this generation a strong sense of place re-entered American literature for almost the first time since Hawthorne and Thoreau. But the place that most of them cherished was the country of their childhood, where they had felt at home. They were always thinking back on it, or saying good-bye to it (like Glenway Wescott in *Good-bye, Wisconsin*), and often they complained, like Wolfe in the title of his last book, that *You Can't Go Home Again.*—In all his travels Wilder never had this sense of being exiled or expatriated, because there was no one place that he regarded as home. Perhaps that was the chief result of his boyhood years in China; they did not make him a citizen of the world, but they took him away forever from Madison, Wisconsin. He ceased to be a Midwesterner, and he did not become a Californian in spite of his schooling. Today he is a little more of a New Englander, but chiefly he is an American, whose home is wherever he opens a ledger, uncaps a fountain pen, and begins writing about people anywhere.

The others had a home place, but no longer had a family. That doesn't mean they had quarreled with their parents; the days of tears and final separations had ended for writers with the First World War. Now the young men simply went their way, but it was so different from the parents' way, there was such a gulf between generations, that sons couldn't talk sincerely with their fathers and be understood. They had rejected the standards by which the fathers lived. —There was no such rejection in Wilder's early career. He never belonged to a conspiracy of youth, leagued in a moral rebellion against middle age. He had worshiped in his father's church and followed the profession his father picked out for him. In a way he represented continuity and tradition, so far as they existed in American society.

The others lived in a new world, but not one they had fashioned for themselves. They were disillusioned by the war, cynical about politics, hostile to the institutions of society, and pessimistic about the future, while having a good time in the present and feeling a little guilty about it, or hung-over. Some of them were becoming connoisseurs of decay. Fitzgerald called them "all the sad young men."—Wilder describes himself as "fundamentally a happy person." He likes to find the goodness or greatness in people and books. He is optimistic by instinct, in the fashion of an older America.

The others were new or at least tried to be new; they made experimental forays in all directions. Each of them wanted to write what might have been the first novel since the beginning of time, from a fresh vision of life, in a new language. Some of the minor writers, now forgotten, would have liked to abolish all literature before Joyce or Baudelaire or whoever might be their idol of the month. I have heard a toast drunk to Caliph Omar for burning the library at Alexandria.—Wilder is devoted to books, the older the better, and he says that his writing life has been "a series of infatuations for admired writers." He likes to acknowledge that most of his plots are borrowed and to specify their sources, as in a note that precedes *The Woman of Andros:* "The first part of this novel is based upon the *Andria,* a comedy of Terence, who in turn based his work upon two Greek plays, now lost to us, by Menander." But he transforms the borrowed material, with a richness of invention that would be rare in any age, and becomes original through trying not to be.

Each of the others had an ideal of art that was allied to symbolism, or to naturalism, or to impressionism, or was a mixture of all three. In any case the ideal was an outgrowth of the romantic movement, and some of the writers tried to make their lives romantic too, most often Byronic or Baudelairean.—Wilder holds to the classical ideal of measure and decorum. Most of his infatuations have been for classi-

cal authors, including Sophocles, Catullus, Virgil, Mme. de
Sévigné, and La Bruyère, as well as the severely classical
Noh drama of Japan, although he has also taken lessons
from Proust and Joyce. Among his models he makes little
distinction of time or place, for he remembers what he was
told by an admired professor at Oberlin: "Every great work
was written this morning." Perhaps his tastes are more
Roman than Greek, and more English Augustan than Ro-
man. Yale in his day was a center of eighteenth-century
studies, and there has always been something of that cen-
tury in his habit of mind; possibly he is the one contem-
porary author who would subscribe to most of the axioms
that Pope advanced in his *Essay on Criticism:*

> Like Kings we lose the conquests gain'd before,
> By vain ambition still to make them more;
> Each might his sev'ral province well command,
> Would all but stoop to what they understand.

> Those RULES of old discover'd, not devis'd,
> Are Nature still, but Nature methodiz'd.

> Regard not then if Wit be old or new,
> But blame the false, and value still the true.

> Men must be taught as if you taught them not,
> And things unknown propos'd as things forgot.

Pope's ideal, and Wilder's, is to restate in new, but not
shockingly new, language "What oft was said, but ne'er so
well express'd." I doubt that any other writer of his gen-
eration would exclaim, as Wilder did to a reporter from
Time, that "Literature is the orchestration of platitudes."

3

But there is a more fundamental difference between his
work and that of his contemporaries. The others write novels

about a social group—sometimes a small group, as in *Tender Is the Night*, sometimes a very large one, as in *U.S.A.*—or they write about an individual in revolt against the group, as in *A Farewell to Arms*. The central relationship with which they deal is between the many and the one. Very often—to borrow a pair of terms from David Riesman—their theme is the defeat of an inner-directed hero by an other-directed society. They feel that the society and its standards must be carefully portrayed, and these writers are all, to some extent, novelists of manners.—Wilder is a novelist of morals.

Manners and morals are terms that overlap, sometimes confusingly, but here I am trying to use the two words in senses that are easier to distinguish. Manners would be the standards of conduct that prevail in a group, large or small, and hence they would change from group to group and year to year. Morals would be defined as the standards that determine the relations of individuals with other individuals, one with one—a child with each of its parents, a husband with his wife, a rich man with a poor man (not *the* rich with *the* poor)—and also the relations of any man with himself, his destiny, and his God. They are answers found by individuals to the old problems of faith, hope, love or charity, art, duty, submission to one's fate . . . and hence they are relatively universal; they can be illustrated from the lives of any individuals, in any place, at any time since the beginning of time.

The characters in Wilder's novels and plays are looking for such answers; his work is not often concerned with the behavior of groups. An outstanding exception might be *Our Town*, in which the Stage Manager speaks with the voice of the community. But the community hasn't much to say about itself and will not admit to having local color; it might be any town, a fact that explains the success of the play in towns all over this country, and other countries. The events portrayed are coming of age, falling in love, getting married, and dying; in other words they are not truly

events—except for the characters, who are not truly char-
acters—but rather they serve as examples of a universal
pattern in human lives; and they are not greatly affected,
in the play, by the special manners of this one community.
The Cabala also starts by dealing with a group, but very
soon the young American narrator shifts his attention to its
separate members, explaining that he is "the biographer
of the individuals and not the historian of the group." The
statement applies to the author himself, and in a more posi-
tive form: Wilder is not a historian. In Rome he had studied
archaeology and had learned to look backward and forward
through a long vista of years; that sort of vision is a special
quality of all his work. But what he sees at the end of a
vista is what the archaeologist often sees, that is, fragments
of a finished pattern of life, in many ways similar to our
own. It is not what the historian tries to see: a living com-
munity in a process of continual and irreversible change.

The other novelists of his generation are all of them his-
torians. Their basic perception was of the changes in their
own time, from peace to war, from stability to instability,
from a fixed code of behavior to the feeling that "It's all
right if you can get away with it." For them the First World
War was a true event, in the sense that afterward nothing
was the same. All of them were "haunted fatally by the
sense of time," as Wolfe said of his autobiographical hero.
His second novel was *Of Time and the River*. Hemingway's
first book was *In Our Time*, and he left it to be understood,
". . . as in no other time." Faulkner saw his time in the
South as one of rapid and violent decay. Dos Passos tried
to put thirty years of American life into one big novel. He
invented a device called the Newsreel: it consisted of quo-
tations from Chamber of Commerce speeches, newspaper
headlines, and the lyrics of popular songs, and it was in-
tended to convey the local color of each particular year.
Fitzgerald put the same sort of material into the body of his
stories: he wrote as if with an eye on the calendar. *The
Great Gatsby* belongs definitely to the year 1923, when the

Fitzgeralds were living in Great Neck, Long Island, and *Tender Is the Night* could have ended only in 1930; no other year on the Riviera had quite the same atmosphere of things going to pieces. Both books are historical novels about his own time, which is so accurately portrayed in them, from such a long perspective, that the books are permanent.— Wilder would never attempt to draw such a picture of his time. He is our great unsocial and antihistorical novelist, the artist of the anachronism.

Like Dos Passos he gives us a newsreel, or rather two of them, to introduce the first two acts of *The Skin of Our Teeth*. The contrast here is complete. Where Dos Passos recalls episodes like the capture of the bobbed-hair bandit, the Florida real-estate boom, and the suppression of a revolt in Canton (to the refrain of "I'm Dancing with Tears in My Eyes"), Wilder presents another order of phenomena. Before the first act, when the lights go out, a picture flashes on the screen and we hear the Announcer's voice:

> The management takes pleasure in bringing to you —the news of the world! (*Slide 2. The sun appearing above the horizon.*) Freeport, Long Island. The sun rose this morning at 6:32 A.M. This gratifying event was first reported by (*Slide 3*) Mrs. Dorothy Stetson of Freeport, Long Island, who promptly telephoned the Mayor. The Society for Affirming (*Slide 4*) the End of the World at once went into a special session and postponed the arrival of that event for *twenty-four hours* (*Slide 5*). All honor to Mrs. Stetson for her public spirit.
>
> New York City. (*Slide 6, of the front doors of the theatre.*) The Plymouth Theatre. During the daily cleaning of this theatre a number of lost objects were collected, as usual, (*Slide 7*) by Mesdames Simpson, Pateslewski, and Moriarity. Among these objects found today was (*Slide 8*) a wedding ring, inscribed: To Eva from Adam. Genesis 2-18. The ring

will be restored to the owner or owners, if their credentials are satisfactory.

Wilder's news of the world is first what happens every day, and then what happened at the beginning. In all his work—except for this hint of the Creation—I can think of only one event that marks an absolute change; it is the birth of Christ, announced on the first and last pages of *The Woman of Andros*. That other Christian event, the Fall, is never mentioned; perhaps it plays no part in his theology. Everything else in his plays and novels—even the collapse of a famous bridge—is merely an example or illustration of man's universal destiny. Nothing is unique, he seems to be saying; the Ice Age will return, as will the Deluge, as will Armageddon. After each disaster man will start over again—helped by his books, if he has saved them—and will struggle upward until he is halted by a new disaster. "Romes existed before Rome," the shade of Virgil says at the end of *The Cabala*, "and when Rome will be a waste there will be Romes after her." Wilder does not think of history as an irreversible process or a river in flood; he thinks of it—at least in his work—as a series of recurrent patterns, almost like checkerboards set side by side.

4

At this point I think we are beginning to see a design that unites his work. Wilder has written a dozen books, each strikingly different from all the others in place, in time, in social setting, and even more in method; yet all the books embody or suggest the same feeling of universally shared experience and eternal return. *Everything that happened might happen anywhere, and will happen again.* That principle explains why he is able to adopt different perspectives in different books, as though he were looking sometimes through one end of a telescope and sometimes

through the other. In *The Ides of March* a distant object is magnified, and Rome in 45 B.C. is described as if it were New York two thousand years later. In *Our Town* he reverses the telescope and shows us Grover's Corners as if it had been preserved for two thousand years under a lava bed and then unearthed like Herculaneum. He has many other fashions of distorting time. There is a one-act play in which he presents a Christmas dinner that lasts for ninety years, with members of the family appearing from a bright door and going out through a dark door, to indicate birth and death. In *The Skin of Our Teeth* he epitomizes the story of mankind in three acts and four characters: Adam, Eve, Lilith, and Cain. They are living in Excelsior, New Jersey, when the glacial cap comes grinding down on them. At Atlantic City, just before the Deluge, they launch an ark full of animals two by two from the Million Dollar Pier.

Because Wilder denies the importance of time, his successive books have proved to be either timely or untimely in a spectacular fashion—and in both cases by accident. *The Bridge* exactly fitted the mood of the moment, and nobody knows exactly why. *The Woman of Andros* was published thirty years too late or too soon. *The Skin of Our Teeth* had a more complicated history. Produced on Broadway in 1942, it was a success largely because of Tallulah Bankhead's so-jolly part of Lilith, or Lily Sabina. Hardly anyone said that the play expressed the mood of the moment, more than that of any other moment. But when it was produced in Central Europe after the war, it was not only a success but a historic success, for any cast of actors that played in it. The Germans and Austrians felt that it was a topical drama written especially for them, to soften their defeat and give them strength to live.

The Skin of Our Teeth is derived in part from *Finnegans Wake,* as *The Woman of Andros* is based in part on Terence's *Andria,* and as the plot of *The Bridge* was suggested by one of Mérimée's shorter plays. There are many other acknowledged derivations in Wilder's work, from authors of

many times and countries, and together they reveal another aspect of his disregard for history. He feels that a true author is independent of time and country, and he also feels, apparently, that there is no history of literature as a process of change; there is only a pattern of literature, consisting of books that continue to live because they contain permanent truths. Any new author is at liberty to restate those truths and to borrow plots or methods from older authors, so long as he transforms the borrowed material into something of his own. Not only was every great book written this morning, but it can be read tonight as on the first day. That principle, in two of Wilder's plays, becomes a metaphor that is a masterpiece of foreshortening. In a one-act play called *Pullman Car Hiawatha,* and again in the third act of *The Skin of Our Teeth,* the great philosophers are presented as hours of the night. One of the characters explains: "Just like the hours and stars go by over our heads at night, in the same way the ideas and thoughts of the great men are in the air around us all the time and they're working on us, even when we don't know it." Spinoza is nine o'clock, Plato is ten, Aristotle is eleven, and Moses is midnight. Three thousand years of human thought are reduced to four hours, which pass in less than two minutes on the stage.

This foreshortening of time becomes an opportunity for the novelist as well as for the dramatist. When history is regarded as a recurrent pattern rather than a process, it becomes possible to move a character from almost any point in time to almost any other. In *The Bridge* Mme. de Sévigné reappears in Peru as the Marquesa de Montemayor. Keats is presented in *The Cabala,* with his genius, his illness, and his family problems; he dies in 1920, among a group of strange characters who might be resurrected from the *Memoirs* of the Duc de Saint-Simon, or who also might be classical gods and goddesses in modern dress. People can be moved backward in time as well as forward. Edward Sheldon, the blinded and crippled dramatist who lived for

thirty years in retirement, dispensing wisdom to his friends, appears in *The Ides of March* as Lucius Mamilius Turrinus; and one suspects that Cicero, in the same novel, is a pre-incarnation of Alexander Woollcott. As for the hero of the novel, he is not a historical character but a model or paradigm of the man of decision, as such a man might exist in any age. Wilder has called him Julius Caesar, just as Paul Valéry called his man of intellect Leonardo da Vinci, and just as Emerson gave the title of "Plato" to his essay on man as philosopher.

The mention of Emerson reminds us that he was another writer who denied the importance of groups or institutions and refused to think of history as a process. When he discussed Montaigne and Shakespeare, it was not against the background of their times, but rather as "representative men" whom he might meet at the next dinner of the Saturday Club. Wilder, in the brilliant series of lectures that he gave at Harvard in 1950–51, started with Emerson and the other classical American writers, notably Melville and Whitman. What he tried to deduce from their works was the character of the representative American, but what he actually presented was, I suspect, partly a reflection of his own character. Here are some of his statements:

> From the point of view of the European an American is nomad in relation to place, disattached in relation to time, lonely in relation to society, and in-submissive to circumstances, destiny, or God.

> Americans could count and enjoyed counting. They lived under a sense of boundlessness. . . . To this day, in American thinking, a crowd of ten thousand is not a homogeneous mass of that number, but is one and one and one . . . up to ten thousand.

> Since the American can find no confirmation of identity from the environment in which he lives,

since he lives exposed to the awareness of vast dis-
tances and innumerable existences, since he derives
from a belief in the future the courage that animates
him, is he not bent on isolating and "fixing" a value
on every existing thing in its relation to a totality, to
the All, to the Everywhere, to the Always?

These are perceptive statements, but I would question
whether they apply to most Americans today, or to many
American novelists since World War I. Their primary appli-
cation is to Emerson and to the big and little Emersonians
—including Whitman, the biggest of all. In our own day
they apply to Wilder himself more than to any other living
writer. If on one side he descends from Pope and Addison,
or at least has something of their attitude toward the art
of letters, on the other side he is an heir of the Transcen-
dentalists. His work has more than a little of the moral
distinction they tried to achieve, and like their work it deals
with the relation of one to one, or of anyone to the All, the
Everywhere, and the Always. Like theirs it looks toward
the future with confidence, though not with the bland con-
fidence that some of the Emersonians displayed. "Every
human being who has existed can be felt by us as existing
now," Wilder said in another of his Harvard lectures, as if
to explain his foreshortening of history. "All time is present
for a single time. . . . Many problems which seem insoluble
will be solved when the world realizes that we are all bound
together as the population of the only inhabited star."

5

The present volume contains Wilder's first three novels,
two of which have been out of print and rather hard to find,
while *The Bridge* has been available only in paper covers.
They are not his most ambitious works, but each of the
novels is a special achievement, different in its own fashion
from any other novels written at the time, or since.

The Cabala is a young man's book and the only one in
which Wilder sometimes—but not often—yields to the florid
taste of the 1920's; there is some display of learning for its
own sake, as well as a few precious adjectives and two or
three witty remarks that might have been saved for after
dinner. But what a rich and finished book it is, for all its
minor faults, and what a collection of extraordinary people!
Even the suggestion in the last chapter that the members
of the Cabala are really ancient gods come back to earth
again is handled with discretion. Another novelist might
have spelled out the comparisons: besides the narrator as
Mercury there would be Miss Elizabeth Grier as Minerva,
the Duchess d'Espoli and James Blair as Venus and Adonis,
Marcantonio as Pan; and the Cardinal might be Jupiter
himself, grown weary of being worshiped. But already in
his first book Wilder knew when to stop; he had a sense of
measure that left these parallels unformed and imprecise,
among other echoes hanging in the Roman air.

The Bridge of San Luis Rey is the first book written with
the ease and grace of his mature style. It is notable for its
creation of a Peru that never existed, yet is a real country,
and notable too for the portraits of the Marquesa de Monte-
mayor and of that indubitably great actress the Perichole.
As an essay on the ways of providence—for that is one aspect
of the book—it comes to no definite conclusion and leaves
us feeling that the author felt God's wisdom was inscrutable.
But still the victims of the disaster, except the two children,
have this in common, that they were hopelessly in love, the
Marquesa with her daughter, Esteban with his dead twin
brother, Uncle Pio with the Perichole; and they left behind
a legacy of love, so that the Abbess was heartened to con-
tinue her work for the poor. Even the Perichole, who had
been selfish all her life, became an assistant in that work,
and perhaps the successor for whom the Abbess was seek-
ing. In the end the book is more concerned with love or
charity than it is with providence.

The Woman of Andros is Wilder's closest approach to

writing a historical novel, because the story exists in relation to the birth of Christ, which is the one decisive event in any of his books. Chrysis and Pamphilus are premature Christians, and if they had been born in the Christian era—so the author implies—they would have led happier lives. Because of its historical theme, I suspect that the book did not engage his deepest feelings, and it ends rather hastily, with the heroine and her child killed off in a sentence. The rest of the story, however, is a Greek pastoral as beautifully handled as the figures on a Greek vase. It contrasts with *The Bridge*, which is a fable (perhaps more Buddhist than Christian in its feeling), as much as with *The Cabala*, which is an album of boldly depicted characters. All three novels, different as they are from one another, have something in common besides their economy of statement and their felicity of style. Perhaps it is the quality that was praised by Henry James in his little book on Hawthorne. There he said, speaking of *The Scarlet Letter*, "It has about it that charm, very hard to express, which we find in an artist's work the first time he has touched his highest mark—a sort of straightness and naturalness of execution, and unconsciousness of his public, and freshness of interest in his theme." These books have that quality too, and they ask to be reread.

MALCOLM COWLEY

The
CABALA

To my friends at the American
Academy in Rome, 1920–1921
T.W.

My companion sat reading a trodden copy of the London Times, real estate offers, military promotions and all. James Blair after six years of classical studies at Harvard had been sent to Sicily as archaeological adviser to a motion picture company bent on transferring the body of Greek mythology to the screen. The company had failed and been dispersed, and Blair thereafter had roamed the Mediterranean, finding stray employment and filling immense notebooks with his observations and theories. His mind brimmed with speculation: as to the chemical composition of Raphael's pigments; as to the lighting conditions under which the sculptors of antiquity wished their work to be viewed; as to the date of the most inaccessible mosaics in Santa Maria Maggiore. Of all these suggestions and many more he allowed me to make notes, even to the extent of copying some diagrams in colored inks. In the event of his being lost at sea with all his notebooks—a not improbable one, as he crosses the Atlantic on obscure and economical craft, not mentioned in your paper, even when they founder—it would be my confusing duty to make a gift of this material to the Librarian of Harvard University where its unintelligibility might confer upon it an incomputable value.

Presently discarding his paper, Blair decided to talk: You may have come to Rome to study, but before you settle down to the ancients you see whether there aren't some interesting moderns.

There's no Ph.D. in modern Romans. Our posterity does that. What moderns do you mean?

Have you ever heard of the *Cabala?*

Which one?

A kind of a group living around Rome.

No.

They're very rich and influential. Everyone's afraid of them. Everybody suspects them of plots to overturn things.

Political?

No, not exactly. Sometimes.

Social swells?

Yes, of course. But more than that, too. Fierce intellectual snobs, they are. Mme. Agoropoulos is no end afraid of them. She says that every now and then they descend from Tivoli and intrigue some bill through the Senate, or some appointment in the Church, or drive some poor lady out of Rome. Tchk!

It's because they're bored. Mme. Agoropoulos says they're frightfully bored. They've had everything so long. The chief thing about them is that they hate what's recent. They spend their time insulting new titles and new fortunes and new ideas. In lots of ways they're medieval. Just in their appearance for one thing. And in their ideas. I fancy it's like this: you've heard of scientists off Australia coming upon regions where the animals and plants ceased to evolve ages ago? They find a pocket of archaic time in the middle of a world that has progressed beyond it. Well, it must be something like that with the Cabala. Here's a group of people losing sleep over a host of notions that the rest of the world has outgrown several centuries ago: one duchess' right to enter a door before another; the word order in a dogma of the Church; the divine right of kings, especially of Bourbons. They're still passionately in earnest about stuff that the rest of us regard as pretty antiquarian lore. What's more, these people that hug these notions aren't just hermits and ignored eccentrics, but members of a circle so powerful and exclusive that all these Romans refer to them with bated breath as The Cabala. They work with incredible subtlety, let me tell you, and have incredible resources in wealth and loyalty. I'm quoting Mme. Agoropoulos, who has a sort of hysterical fear of them, and thinks they're supernatural.

But she must know some of them personally.

Of course she does. So do I.

One isn't afraid of people one knows. Who's in it?

I'm taking you to meet one of them tomorrow, this Miss Grier. She's leader of the whole international set. I catalogued her library for her—oh, I couldn't have got to know her any other way. I lived in her apartment in the Palazzo

Barberini and used to get whiffs of the Cabala. Besides her there's a cardinal. And the Princess d'Espoli who's mad. And Madame Bernstein of the German banking family. Each one of them has some prodigious gift, and together they're miles above the next social stratum below them. They're so wonderful that they're lonely. I quote. They sit off there in Tivoli getting what comfort they can from one another's excellence.

Do they call themselves the Cabala. Are they organized? Not as I see it. Probably it never occurred to them that they even constituted a group. I say, you study them up. You ferret it out, the whole secret. It's not my line.

In the pause that followed, fragments of conversation from the various corners of the compartment flowed in upon our minds so recently occupied with semidivine personages. I haven't the slightest desire to quarrel, Hilda, muttered one of the Englishwomen. Naturally you made the arrangements for the trip as best you could. All I say is that that girl did *not* clean off the washstand every morning. There were rings and rings.

And from an American-Italian: I says it's none of your goddam business, I says. Take your goddam shirt the hell outta here. He run, I tell you; he run so fast you don't see no dust for him he run so.

The Jesuit and his pupils had become politely interested in the postage stamps and the Japanese attaché was murmuring: Oh, most exclusively rare! The four-cent is pale violet and when held up to the light reveals a watermark, a seahorse. There are only seven in the world and three are in the collection of the Baron Rothschild.

Symphonically considered, one heard that there had been no sugar in it, that she had told Marietta three mornings running to put sugar in it, or bring sugar, although the Republic of Guatemala had immediately cut them, a few had leaked out to collectors, and that more muskmelons than one would have thought possible were sold annually at the corner of Broadway and 126th Street. Perhaps it was

in revulsion against such small change that the impulse first rose in me to pursue these Olympians, who though they might be bored and mistaken, had at least, each of them, "one prodigious gift."

It was in this company then, and in the dejected airs of one in the morning that I first arrived in Rome, in that station that is uglier than most, more hung with advertisements of medicinal waters and more redolent of ammonia. During the journey I had been planning what I should do the moment I arrived: fill myself with coffee and wine, and in the proud middle of the night, run down the Via Cavour. Under the hints of dawn I should behold the tribune of Santa Maria Maggiore hovering above me like the ark on Ararat, and the ghost of Palestrina in a soiled cassock letting himself out at a side door and rushing home to a large family in five voices; hurry on to the platform before the Lateran where Dante mixes with the Jubilee crowd; overhang the Forum and skirt the locked Palatine; follow the river to the inn where Montaigne groans over his ailments; and fall a-staring at the Pope's clifflike dwelling, where work Rome's greatest artists, the one who is never unhappy and the one who is never anything else. I would know my way about, for my mind is built upon the map of the city that throughout the eight years of school and college had hung above my desk, a city so longed for that it seemed as though in the depth of my heart I had never truly believed I should see it.

When I arrived finally, the station was deserted; there was no coffee, no wine, no moon, no ghosts. Just a drive through shadowy streets to the sound of fountains, and the very special echo of travertine pavements.

During the first week Blair helped me find and fit out an apartment. It consisted of five rooms in an old palace across the river and within stone's throw of the basilica of Santa Maria in Trastevere. The rooms were high and damp and bad eighteenth century. The ceiling of the salon was mod-

estly coffered and there were bits of crumbling stucco in the hall, still tinted with faint blues and pinks and gilt; every morning's sweeping carried off a bit more of some cupid's curls or chips of scroll and garland. In the kitchen there was a fresco of Jacob wrestling with the angel, but the stove concealed it. We passed two days in choosing chairs and tables, in loading them upon carts and personally conducting them to our mean street; in haggling over great lengths of gray-blue brocade before a dozen shops, always with a view toward variety in stains and unravelings and creases; in selecting from among the brisk imitations of ancient candelabra those which most successfully simulated age and pure line.

The acquisition of Ottima was Blair's triumph. There was a trattoria at the corner, a lazy casual talkative wineshop, run by three sisters. Blair studied them for a time, and finally proposed to the intelligent middle-aged humorous one that she come and be my cook "for a few weeks." Italians have a horror of making long-term contracts and it was this last clause that won Ottima. We offered to take on any man she recommended to help her with the heavier work, but she clouded at that and replied that she could very well do the heavier work too. The removal to my rooms must have arrived as a providential solution to some problem in Ottima's life, for she attached herself passionately to her work, to me, and to her companions in the kitchen, Kurt the police dog and Messalina the cat. We each winked at the others' failings and we created a home.

The day following our arrival, then, we called upon the latest dictator of Rome and found a rather boyish spinster with an interesting and ailing face, fretful birdlike motions and exhibiting a perpetual alternation of kindness and irritability. It was nearly six when we walked into her drawing room in the Palazzo Barberini and found four ladies and a gentleman seated a little stiffly about a table conversing in French. Madame Agoropoulos gave a cry of joy at seeing Blair, the absent-minded scholar to whom she was so at-

tached; Miss Grier echoed it. A thin Mrs. Roy waited until something had been dropped into the conversation about our family connections before she could relax and smile. The Spanish Ambassador and his wife wondered how on earth America could get on without a system of titles whereby one might unerrably recognize one's own people, and the Marquesa shuddered slightly at the intrusion of two coarse young redskins and began composing mentally the faulty French sentence with which she would presently excuse herself. For a time the conversation blew fitfully about, touched with the formal charm of all conversation conducted in a language that is native to no one in the group.

Suddenly my attention was caught by a tension in the room. I sensed the tentatives of an intrigue without being able to gather the remotest notion of the objectives. Miss Grier was pretending to babble, but was in reality quite earnest, and Mrs. Roy was taking notes, mentally. The episode resolved itself into a typical, though not very complicated, example of the Roman social bargain, with its characteristic set of ramifications into religious, political and domestic life. In the light of information received much later, I call your attention to what Mrs. Roy wanted Miss Grier to do for her; and what Miss Grier asked in return for her services:

Mrs. Roy had narrow eyes and a mouth that had just tasted quinine; while she spoke her ear pendants rattled against her lean clavicles. She was a Roman Catholic, and in her political activity a Black of the Blacks. During her residence in Rome she had occupied herself with the task of bringing the needs of certain American charitable organizations to the attention of the Supreme Pontiff. Slander attributed a diversity of motives to her good works, the least damaging of which was the hope of being named a Countess of the Papal States. The fact is that Mrs. Roy was pressing audiences in the Vatican with the hope of inducing His Holiness to commit a miracle, namely to grant her a divorce under the Pauline Privilege. This consummation,

not without precedent, depended upon a number of conditions. Before taking any such step the Vatican would ascertain very carefully how great the surprise would be in Roman Catholic circles; American cardinals would be asked in confidence for a report on the matron's character, and the faithful in Rome and Baltimore, without their being aware of it, would be consulted. This done, it would be well to gauge the degree of cynicism or approval the measure would arouse in Protestants. Mrs. Roy's reputation happened to be above reproach, and her right to a divorce indisputable (her husband had offended under every category: he had been unfaithful; he had lapsed from a still greater faith; and he had become an *animae periculum*, that is, he had tried to draw her into an irreverent argument over the liquefaction of the blood of St. Januarius); but the Protestant *imprimatur* was needed. Whose opinion would be more valuable for this purpose than that of the austere directress of the American Colony? Miss Grier would be approached—and both women knew it—through channels exquisite in their delicacy and resonance; and if an uncertain note were sounded from the Palazzo Barberini, the familiar verdict Inexpedient would be returned to the petitioner, and the question never reopened.

Mrs. Roy, having so much to ask from Miss Grier, wanted to know if there were any service she could render in return.

There was.

No Italian work of art of the classic periods may leave the country without an enormous export tax. How then did Mantegna's "Madonna between St. George and St. Helen" ever arrive at the Alumnae Hall of Vassar College without passing through the customs? It was last seen three years before in the collection of the poor Princess Gaeta; it was so ascribed in the reports of the Minister of Fine Arts for the following years, in spite of the rumor that it was being offered to the museums of Brooklyn, Cleveland and Detroit. It changed hands six times, but the dealers, savants and curators were so taken up with the problem as to whether

or not St. Helen's left foot had been retouched by Bellini
(as Vasari affirms) that it had never occurred to them to
ask if it had been registered at the border. It was finally
bought by a mad old Boston dowager in a lavender wig
who, dying, bequeathed it (along with three spurious Bot-
ticellis) to that college with which her vicious spelling alone
would have prevented her association in any capacity save
that of trustee.

The Minister of Fine Arts at Rome had just heard of the
donation and was in despair. When the thing became
known his position and reputation would be gone. All his
vast labors for his country (*exempli gratia:* he had ob-
structed the disinterment of Herculaneum for twenty
years; he had ruined the façades of twenty gorgeous
Baroque churches in the hope of finding a thirteenth cen-
tury window; etc., etc.) would avail him nothing in the
storms of Roman journalism. All loyal Italians suffer at the
sight of their art treasures being carried off to America; they
are only waiting for some pretext to rend an official and
appease their injured honor. The Embassy was already in
agonies of conciliation. Vassar could not be expected to give
up the picture, nor to pay a smuggler's duty. Tomorrow
morning the Roman editorials would picture a barbarous
America stealing from Italy her very children, and refer-
ences would be made to Cato, Aeneas, Michelangelo,
Cavour and St. Francis. The Senatus Romanus would sit
on every bit of delicate business that America was endeavor-
ing to recommend to Italian favor.

Now Miss Grier, too, was a trustee of Vassar. She had a
flattering position in the long processions that formed in
June among the sundials and educative shrubs. She was
ready to pay the fine, but not until she had placated the
city fathers. This could be done by obtaining the favorable
votes of the committee that was to sit that very evening.
This committee was composed of seven members, four of
whose votes she already commanded; the other three were

Blacks. For the matter to be dropped in the interest of the Princess Gaeta a unanimous verdict was necessary.

If Mrs. Roy descended at once to her car, she would have time to drive to the American College in the Piazza di Spagna and confer with dear omniscient Father O'Leary. Marvelous are the acoustics of the Church! Before ten that evening the three Black votes would be decently cast for conciliation. It was Miss Grier's task over the tea table to convey this long exposition to Mrs. Roy and to intimate the ineffable return she, Miss Grier, would be able to make for any favors. This was complicated by the necessity of making sure that neither Mme. Agoropoulos nor the Ambassadress (men don't matter) suspected the least collusion. Fortunately the Ambassadress could not understand rapid French, and Mme. Agoropoulos, being sentimental, could be continually distracted from the main issue by little sops of prettification and pathos.

Miss Grier played these several cards with the economy and precision of a faultless technique. She had that quality which is a peculiar part of the genuine that invests great monarchs, and which we see notably in Elizabeth and Frederick, the power of adjusting threats to just the degree that stimulates, yet does not antagonize. Mrs. Roy understood at once what was expected of her. She had been packing committees and conciliating soured Papal chamberlains and Italian political *dévotes* these many years; trading in influence was her daily portion. Moreover joy can exert the happiest sort of influence on the intelligence and she felt her divorce was at hand. She rose hastily.

Will you excuse me if I run? she murmured. I told Julia Howard I would call for her at Rosali's. And I have an errand in the Piazza di Spagna.

She bowed to us and fled. What emotion is it that lends wings to such matter-of-fact feet and blitheness to such thin dispositions? The next year she married a young French yachtsman, half her age; she settled down in Florence and gave birth to a son. The Blacks no longer talked votes when

she entered their drawing rooms. Vassar retains the painting and in its archives a letter from the Italian Secretary for Foreign Affairs which reads like a deed of gift. The influence of a work of art upon the casual passer-by is too subtle for determination, but one has faith to believe that the hundreds of girls who pass beneath the Mantegna daily draw from it impulses that make them nobler wives and mothers. At least that is what the Ministry promised the College.

When the others had gone, Miss Grier made a face after them, lowered the lights and bade us talk about New York. She seemed to take some pleasure in such exotic company as ourselves, but her mind strayed until suddenly jumping up, she smoothed out the folds of her gown and bade us hurry off, dress, and come back to dinner at eight. We were surprised but equal to it, and dashed off into the rain.

At once I harried Blair for more facts about her. He could give me little; the portrait of her mind and even of her features lies in the following account of her ancestry that I made out for myself by reading between the lines and by studying the photographs of a history of the Griers, written by a second cousin, for considerations.

It seems that her great-grandfather had gone to New York in 1800, suffering from ill-health. He took an old house in the country and intended spending his days like a hermit, studying the prophetic passages of the Bible and encouraging the multiplication of four pigs that he had brought across the water in a basket. But his disposition improving with his affairs, he soon discovered himself to be married to the heiress of Dawes Corners, Miss Agatha Frehestocken, the death of whose parents, ten years later, united two farms of considerable extent. Their children, Benjamin and Anne, were brought up with such education as fell to them on rainy afternoons at the caprice of their father. Our Miss Grier's grandfather, a crafty single-minded country boy, disappeared for many years into a whirlpool of obscure activity in town, becoming in turn potboy, newspaper devil and restaurant manager. At last he revisited his parents and

forced them to permit his using their land as security for some railroad investments. We have his picture at this stage: the daguerreotype of the Dutch yokel with the protruding lower lip and grinning pugnacious eyes is reproduced in any history of the great American fortunes. Probably the gentle art of horsewhipping one's parents was revived that Sunday evening at Dawes Corners for Anne intimates that she was directed to take her knitting into the feedhouse and sit on sacks until she was recalled. The old father cursed the son roundly from the imprecatory psalms and had his curious revenge: the worm of religious introspection was stirred in the brain of Benjamin Grier and a strain of ill-health in his body. Success came of it; he became a deacon and a millionaire at about the same time; he was presently directing five railroads from a wheel chair. His parents died in a Washington Square mansion, unforgiving to the end.

Benjamin married the daughter of another magnate, a girl who in another age and faith would have retired to a convent and eased the poverty of her mental and spiritual nature in a perpetual flow of damp unexplainable tears. She bore a sickly son to the world of brownstone, a son in whom the æsthetic impulse stifled during so many generations of Griers and Halletts, attained a piteous flowering, a passion for the operas of Rossini, and for things he fondly took to be Italian, garish rosaries, the costumes of the peasant of Capri, and the painting of Domenichino. He married a firm sharp woman, older than himself, who had deliberately chosen him in the vestry of the Presbyterian Church. They were incredibly wealthy, with that wealth that increases in the dark and, untended, doubles in a year. With the affiliation of this determined Grace Benham one last offspring was made possible to the Grier line—our Miss Grier. To the score of governesses that trod sobbing on one another's heels, she appeared a monster of guile and virulence. She was dragged without rest from New York to Baden-Baden, from Vevey to Rome, and back again; and she grew up

without forming any attachment to place or person. Her parents died when she was twenty-four and finally sheer solitude did what exhortation could not do: her character softened in an attempt at piteously luring people to talk to her, live with her, to fill somehow the moneyed emptiness of her days.

Such an account of her extraction, if she read it, would have neither interested her nor embarrassed her. Her mind lay under the hot breath of a great fretfulness; she lived to ridicule and insult the fools and innocents of her social circle. In this fretfulness floated all the enthusiasms and frustrations of her line: her great-grandfather's gloom, her grandfather's whip and his dread of the Valley of Bones, her grandmother's red eyes and her father's repressed loves for the Normas and Sémiramides of the Academy of Music. She was restless too, with the masculine capacities inherited from her grandfather, the capacities of a business magnate, that given her sex and situation could find their only outlet in a passion for making women tremble and a mania for interfering in the affairs of others. She was with all this a woman of intelligence and force; she ruled her eccentric and rebellious parish with acrid pleasure and at her death the drawing rooms of Rome resounded with a strange wild murmur of muted joy.

Her portrait is not complete without an account of her strangest habit, due partly to the sleepless nights of a lifetime of illness, and partly to the fear of ghosts instilled in her by governesses when she was a girl. She was never able to sleep until the coming on of dawn. She feared to be alone; toward one in the morning she could be found urging her last callers to stay a little longer; *c'est l'heure du champagne,* she would say, offering them that untimely inducement. When finally they went away she would devote the rest of the night to music, for like the German princes of the eighteenth century she maintained her own troupe of musicians.

These sessions before dawn were not vaguely and sentimentally musical; they were to the last degree eclectic. In

one night she would hear all the sonatas of Scriabin or the marches of Medtner; in one night both volumes of the Well-tempered Clavichord; all the Handel fugues for organ; six Beethoven trios. Gradually she won away from the more easily appreciated music altogether and cultivated only what was difficult and cerebral. She turned to music that was interesting historically and searched out the forgotten rivals of Bach and the operas of Grétry. She paid a group of singers from the Lateran choir to sing her endless Palestrina. She became prodigiously learned. Harold Bauer would listen meekly to her directions on phrasing Bach—he averred that she had the only truly contrapuntal ear of the age—and the Flonzaleys acceded to her request to take certain pages of Lœffler a little faster.

In time I encountered a number of people who for one reason or another were unable to sleep between midnight and dawn, and when I myself tossed sleepless or when I returned late to my rooms through the deserted streets—at the hour when the parricide feels a cat purring against his feet in the darkness—I pictured to myself old Baldassare, in the Borgo, former Bishop of Shantung, Apostolic Visitor to the Far East, rising at two to study with streaming eyes the Church Fathers and the Councils, marveling he said, at the continuous blooming of the rose tree of Doctrine; or of Stasia, a Russian refugee who had lost the habit of sleeping after dark during her experience as nurse in the War, Stasia playing solitaire through the night and brooding over the jocose tortures to which her family had been subjected by the soldiers of Taganrog; and of Elizabeth Grier listening the length of her long shadowed room to some new work that d'Indy had sent her or bending over the score while her little troupe revived the overture to *Les Indes Galantes.*

When we remounted the steps an hour later, then, we found the guests already arrived and awaiting their hostess. Among other privileges Miss Grier had long reserved to herself a prerogative of royalty, that of being the last arrival at

one's own parties. In the hall the maître d'hôtel gave me a note reading: Please take in Mlle. de Morfontaine, a high Merovingian maiden who may invite you to her villa at Tivoli. In a few moments Miss Grier had slipped in and was greeting her guests in a hurried zigzag across the room. She was dressed after a costume plate by Fortuny, conceived in salamander red and black. About her neck hung a rare medal of the Renaissance, much larger than any other woman would have ventured to wear.

As this woman wanted to be in a position to hear every word spoken at her table, Rome had long had good reason to complain of the crowded arrangements of her dinners; we were packed together like the hurried diners at Modane. But she had still other conventions to challenge; she discussed the food; she reversed the direction of conversation from the right to the left hand at the least convenient opportunities; she talked to the servants, chattily; she shifted the conversation from French to English or Italian capriciously; she referred to guests who had been invited but had not been able to come. One suddenly became aware that she was not eating the courses that were served to us. She began with a little bowl of bread crumbs and walnuts; to this she added later—while we confronted a *faisan Souvaroff* dressed with truffles and *foie gras* and graced with that ultimate dark richness which it is the privilege of Madeira to confer on game—and American cereal, soaked in hot water and touched with butter. Nor could she restrain herself from teasing her guests in a dangerous way, and with almost inspired precision: a political duke on his dull speeches; Mrs. Osborne-Cady on the career as a concert pianist that she had sacrificed to a more than usually disappointing home life. For a moment at the beginning of the meal her electric eyes paused at my place and she began to murmur ominously, but thinking better of it she ordered the servant to offer me some more *œufs cardinal* adding with a sort of insolence that they were the only *œufs cardinal* that one could eat in Europe and that Mémé (the

elder Princess Galitzine) was a little fool to vaunt her chef,
who had received his training in railway stations, etc., etc.

The high Merovingian maiden at my left was Made-
moiselle Marie-Astrée-Luce de Morfontaine, daughter of
Claude-Elzéar de Morfontaine and Christine Mézières-
Bergh; her grandfather Comte Louis Mézières-Bergh had
married Rachel Krantz, the daughter of the great fi-
nancier Maxi Krantz, and had been the French am-
bassador to the Vatican in 1870. She was then, excessively
rich, for she owned, they said, more shares in the Suez Canal
than the Rothschilds. She was tall, large-limbed and bony,
without somehow being too thin. Her high white face,
framed between two carnelian ear pendants, recalled some
symbolical figure in a frieze of Giotto, out of drawing, but
radiating gaunt spiritual passions. She had a hoarse voice
and a rapt manner, and for the first ten minutes said many
foolish things because her mind was afar off; one felt
vaguely that it would come around in its own time. This it
presently did and with considerable impact. She outlined
to me the whole Royalist movement in France. She seemed
to believe as passionately in its aim as she despised its prac-
tice. There can be no king in France, she cried, until cathol-
icism has had a great revival there. France cannot be great
save through Rome. We are Latins; we are not Goths. They
are forcing alien systems upon us. Eventually we shall find
ourselves, our kings, our faith, our Latin hearts. I shall see
France return to Rome before I die, she added, clasping
her hands before her chin. I replied faintly that both the
French and Italian temperaments seemed to me singularly
unrepublican, whereupon she laid her long pale hand upon
my sleeve and invited me to come that week end to her
villa.

You will hear the whole argument, she said. And the
Cardinal will be there.

I asked which Cardinal. The pain on her face showed me
that at least for the circle in which she moved there were
not seventy cardinals, but one.

Cardinal Vaini, of course. The College at present is singularly free of uninteresting priests, but surely the only cardinal with learning, with distinction, with charm, is Cardinal Vaini.

I had so often encountered learning, distinction and charm (to say nothing of piety) in the lower reaches of the Church that I was shocked to learn that these qualities were so rare higher up.

Besides, she added, what other is friendly to France, the rebellious daughter? You have not yet met the Cardinal? Such knowledge! And to think that he will not write! If I may say it without disrespect, His Eminence is afflicted with a sort of—inertia. The whole world is waiting for an explanation of certain contradictions in the Fathers; he is the only man who can do it; yet he remains silent. We beg him with prayers. It is in his power to effect the re-entry of the Church into literature. Perhaps he might singlehandedly carry through the cause we all have so at heart.

I asked shyly what cause this might be.

She turned toward me with some surprise. Why, the promulgation of the Divine Right of Kings as a dogma of the Church. We hope to have an Ecumenical Council called for that purpose within the next twenty-five years. I thought that of course you knew; in fact I assumed that you were one of our workers.

I replied that I was both an American and a Protestant, an answer that I felt relieved me of the burden of being a catholic royalist.

Oh, she said, we have many adherents who at first glance would appear to have no interest in the movement: we have Jews and agnostics, artists, and, yes, even anarchists.

I now felt quite sure that I was sitting beside an insane person. They don't lock you up when you have millions, I said to myself. The idea of trying to collect a council, in the twentieth century, to give crowns a supernatural sanction and to enroll the sanction among the articles of obligatory belief, was no mere pious revery; it was lunacy. We were

prevented from returning to the subject that evening, but several times I found her spacious half-mad glance resting on me with greater implication of intimacy than I was quite ready to acknowledge.

I will send the car for you at eleven, she murmured as she passed me in leaving the table. You must come. I shall have a great favor to ask of you.

On returning to the drawing room I found myself beside Ada Benoni, daughter of a popular senator. Although she seemed almost too young to go out in the evening, she had that soft cautious sophistication of well brought up Italian girls. I asked her almost at once if she would tell me about the Cabala.

Oh, the Cabala's only some people's joke, she answered. There is no Cabala, really. But I know what you mean. And the young girl's eyes carefully estimated the distance between us and the company on all sides. By Cabala they mean a group of people that are always together and have a lot in common.

Are they all rich? I asked.

No . . . she answered thoughtfully. We mustn't speak so loudly. Cardinal Vaini can't be rich, nor the Duchess d'Aquilanera.

But they're all intellectual?

The Princess d'Espoli isn't intellectual.

Then what have they in common?

Oh, they haven't anything in common except . . . except that they despise most people, you and me and my father and so on. They've each got one thing, some great gift and that binds them together.

Do you believe that they work together and plan trouble here and there?

The girl's forehead wrinkled and she reddened slightly. No, I don't think they mean to, she said softly.

But they *do?* I insisted.

Well, they sit over there in Tivoli and talk about us and somehow, without knowing it, they then *do* something.

How many of them do you know?

Oh, I know all of them a little, she replied quickly. Everybody knows all of them. Except, of course, the Cardinal. I love them all, too. They're only bad when they're together, she explained.

Mlle. de Morfontaine has asked me to spend the week end at her villa in Tivoli. Will I see them there?

Oh, yes. We call that the hotbed.

Is it all right? Have you any advice to give me before I go?

No.

Yes, you have.

Well, she admitted, drawing her eyebrows together, I advise you to be . . . to be stupid. It's hard. You must expect them to be very cordial at first. They have a way of getting very excited about people and then getting tired of them and dropping them. Except every now and then they find someone they like and they adopt him or her for good, and there's a new member of the Cabala. Rome's full of people who went through the rapids and didn't stick. Miss Grier's especially that way. She's just met you lately hasn't she?

Why, yes—just this afternoon.

Well, she'll have you around every minute of the day for a while. She's coming over in a minute to ask you to stay to her midnight supper. She has famous midnight suppers.

But I can't. I was here to tea and immediately asked to dinner. It would be ridiculous to stay to midnight. . . .

It's not ridiculous in Rome. You're just getting into the rapids, that's all. Everybody cultivates their friendships in rushes. It's very exciting. Don't try and fight against it. If you do that you lose the best of everything. Do you want to know how I know about your being in the rapids? Well I'll tell you. My fiancé was to have come to the dinner tonight, and an hour before, a note was brought to his house asking him to come next Friday instead and go to the Opera

also. She does that often and it only means that she has found some new friend she insists on keeping by her that evening. Of course the second invitation, the consoling one, is always bigger and more showy than the first, but we get angry.

I should say so. I'm sorry I was the one to prevent. . . .

Oh, that's all right, she answered. Vittorio's out waiting for me in the car now.

So it was that when Blair and I presented ourselves before Miss Grier to take our leave, she drew me aside with an irresistible vehemence and standing against my ear said: You are to come back here tonight. There will be some people in to a late supper whom I want you to meet. You can, can't you?

I made some show of protest, and the effect was appalling. But, my dear young man, she cried, I'll have to ask you to trust me. There is something of the first importance that I want to put to you. The fact is I have already telephoned a very dear friend of mine. . . . Please now, just as a favor to me, put off what you have planned. There's a very great service we want to ask you.

Of course with that I fairly folded up, as much with surprise as compliance. Apparently the whole Cabala wanted me to do favors.

Thank you, thank you so much. About twelve.

It was then about ten. Two hours to kill. We were about to go to the Circus, when Blair exclaimed:

Say, do you mind if I drop in and see a friend of mine for a minute. If I'm going Tuesday I ought to say good-bye and see how he is. Do you hate sick people?

No.

He's a nice fellow, but he hasn't long to live. He's published some verse in England; one of the thousand, you know. It got an awful rap. Maybe he's quite a poet, but he can't get over that diction. He's awfully adjectival.

We climbed down the Spanish Steps and turned in at the

left. On the stairs Blair stopped and whispered: I forgot to tell you that he's watched over by a friend, a sort of water-colorist. They're dead poor and it's all they can do to get a doctor. I meant to lend them some more money—what have you with you?

We assembled a hundred lire and knocked at the door. Receiving no answer we pushed it open. There was a lamp burning in the further of two mean rooms. It stood beside a bed and cast its light on the remorseless details of a barricade built during the last stages of consumption against a light vaulter; bowls and bottles and stained cloths. The sleeping invalid was sitting high in bed, his head turned away from us.

The artist must have gone out for a minute to look for some money, said Blair. Let's stay around a bit.

We went into the other room and sat in the dark looking at the moonlight that filled the Fountain of the Boat. There were fireworks on the Pincian Hill in memory of some battle on the Piave and the tender green of the sky seemed to tremble behind the Chinese blooms that climbed the night. A friendly tram entered the square at intervals, stopped inquiringly, and bustled out again. I tried to remember whether Virgil had died in Rome . . . no, buried near Naples. Tasso? Some piercing-sweet pages of Goethe, the particular triumph of Moissi who brings to them his wide-open eyes and elegiac voice. Presently we heard a call from the next room: Francis. Francis.

Blair went in: I guess he's gone out a minute. Can I do something for you? I'm going in a day or two and I called around to see how much better you are. Would it tire you if we sat with you a bit? . . . Come on in, say!

For the moment Blair had forgotten the poet's name and our introduction was slurred over. The sick man looked his extremity, but his fever gave to his eyes an eager and excited air; he seemed willing to listen or to talk for hours. My eye fell upon a rough penciled note that lay on the table beyond the invalid's reach: Dear Dr. Clarke: He spat

up about two cupfuls of blood at 2 P.M. He complained so of hunger that I had to give him more than you said. Be back at once. F. S.

Have you been able to write anything lately? Blair began.

No.

Do you read much?

Francis reads to me. He pointed to a Jeremy Taylor on his feet. You're Americans, aren't you? I have a brother in America. In New Jersey. I was to have gone over there.

The conversation lapsed, but he kept staring at us, smiling and bright-eyed, as though it were swift and rare.

By the way, are there any books you'd like us to lend you?

Thank you. That would be fine.

What, for instance?

Anything.

Think of one you'd like especially.

Oh, anything. I'm not particular. Only I suppose it would be hard to find any translations from the Greek?

Here I offered to bring in a Homer in the original and stammer out an improvised translation.

Oh, I should like that most of all, he cried. I know Chapman's well.

I replied, unthinkingly, that Chapman's was scarcely Homer at all, and suddenly beheld a look of pain, as of a mortal wound, appear upon his face. To regain control of himself he bit his finger and tried to smile. I hastened to add that in its way it was very beautiful, but I could not recall my cruelty; his heart seemed to have commenced bleeding within him.

Blair asked him if he had almost enough poems for a new book.

I don't think about books any more, he said. I just write to please myself.

But the insult to Chapman had been working in him; he now turned his face away and great tears fell upon his hands. Excuse me. Excuse me, he said. I'm not well, and I seem to . . . to do this about nothing.

There was a search for a handkerchief, but none being found he was persuaded to use mine.

I don't want to go away without seeing Francis, said Blair. Do you know where I might find him?

Yes, yes. He's around the corner at the Café Greco. I begged him to go and get some coffee; he'd been here all day.

So Blair left me with the poet, who seemed to have forgiven me and was ready for the hazards of further conversation. Feeling it was better I did the talking, I began to discourse upon everything, on the fireworks, on the wild flowers of Lake Albano, on Pizzetti's sonata, on a theft in the Vatican library. His face showed clearly what matter pleased him; I experimented on it, and discovered that he was hungry for hearing things praised. He was beyond feeling indignant at abuses, beyond humor, beyond sentiment, beyond interest in any bits of antiquarian lore. Apparently for weeks together in the wretched atmosphere of the sickroom Francis had neglected to speak highly of anything and the poet wanted before he left the strange world to hear some portion of it praised. Oh, I laid it on. His eyes glowed and his hands trembled. Most of all he desired the praise of poetry. I launched upon a history of poetry, calling the singers by name, getting them wrong, assigning them to the wrong ages and languages, characterizing them with the worn epithets of an encyclopedist, and drawing upon what anecdotage I could—all bad, but somehow marshaling the glorious throng. I spoke of Sappho; of how a line of Euripides drove mad the citizens of Abdera; of Terence pleading with audiences to come to him rather than to the tightrope walkers; of Villon writing his mother's prayers before the great picture book of a cathedral wall; of Milton in his old age, holding a few olives in his hand to remind himself of his golden year in Italy.

Quite suddenly in the middle of the catalogue he burst out fiercely: I was meant to be among those names. I was.

The boast must have revolted me a little and my face

have shown it, for he cried again: I was. I was. But now it's too late. I want every copy of my books destroyed. Let every word die, die. When I'm dead I don't want a soul to remember me.

I murmured something about his getting well.

I know more about it than the doctor, he replied, staring at me with stern fury. I studied to be a doctor. And I watched my mother and brother die, just as I am dying now.

There was no answer for that. We sat silent. Then in a gentler voice he said:

Will you promise me something? My things weren't good enough; they were just beginning to be better. When I am dead I want you to make sure that Francis does what he promised. There must be no name on my grave. Just write: Here lies one whose name was writ in water.

There was a noise in the next room. Blair had returned with the water-colorist. We withdrew. The poet was too sick to see us again and when I came back from the country he had died and his fame had begun to spread over the whole world.

Book Two: Marcantonio

THE Duchess d'Aquilanera was a Colonna and came
from the conservative wing of a family that cannot forget
its cardinalitial, royal and papal traditions. Her husband
had come of a Tuscan house that had received its illustra-
tion by the thirteenth century, was praised in the histories
of Machiavelli and execrated in Dante. Neither family had
counted a misalliance in twenty-two generations, and even
in the twenty-third incurred only such stigma as attaches
to marriage with an illegitimate Medici or a Pope's "niece."
The Duchess could never forget—among a thousand similar
honors—that her grandfather's grandfather, Timoleo Nerone
Colonna, Prince of Velletri, had carried many an insulting
message to the ancestors of the present King of Italy, the
old but apologetic house of Savoy; and that her father had
refused a grandeeship at the court of Spain because it had
been withheld from his father; and that through herself she
carried to her son the titles of Chamberlain of the Court of
Naples (if there were one), Prince of the Holy Roman Em-
pire (if that superb organization had only survived), and
Duke of Brabant, a title which unfortunately reappears
among the pretentions of the royal families of Spain, Bel-
gium and France. She had the best of claims to an altesse,

48

and even to an altesse royale; at least to the Sérénissime, for her mother had been the last member of the royal family of Craburg-Hottenlingen. She had the largest cousinage outside the Buddhist priesthood. The heralds of the European courts bowed to her with a particular distinction realizing that by some accident many diverse and lofty lines converged in her odd person.

She was fifty when I met her, a short, black-faced woman with two aristocratic wens on the left slope of her nose, yellow, dirty hands, covered with paste emeralds (an allusion to her Portuguese claims; she was Archduchess of Brazil, if Brazil had only remained Portuguese), lame with the limp that pursues the Della Quercia, just as her aunt had been epileptic with the epilepsy of the true Vani. She lived in a tiny apartment in the Palazzo Aquilanera, Piazza Aracœli, from the windows of which she watched the sumptuous weddings of her rivals, ceremonies to which she had been invited, but dared not attend, foreseeing that she would be assigned to places that fell below her pretensions; to accept a humble seat would be to admit that one had relinquished the whole bundle of vast historic claims. She had left many a great function abruptly on discovering that her chair was behind some of those Colonna cousins who had cast away all right to aristocratic distinction by marrying theater women or Americans. She refused to be seated behind pillars among dubious Neapolitan titles—in the shadow of her own family tombs; to be left among the footmen at the door of a musicale; to be invited at the eleventh hour; and to be kept waiting in antechambers. For the most part she clung to her ugly stuffy rooms, brooding on the disregarded glories of her line and envying the splendors of her richer relatives. The fact is that from the point of view of a middle-class Italian she was not really poor; but she was too poor to afford the limousine and livery and great entertainments; to be without these and yet invested with her pretensions was to be poorer than the last nameless body fished out of the Tiber.

Recently however she had begun to receive unexpected and thrilling recognitions. Little though she went out, when she did appear in society, her austere face, her majestic limp, and her strange jewels carried conviction. People were afraid of her. The arbiters of precedence in Rome dared at last to intimate to the Odescalchi and Colonna and Sermoneta that this almost shabby little woman whom they snubbed and shoved like some half-wit poor relation, had every right to precede them at a formal function. French circles, such as had not lost all seigneurial deferences under the sponge of republicanism, recognized her ultramontane alliances. She was the first to notice the improvement in her reception, and if a bit bewildered it did not take her long to set her sails to the unexpected breeze. She had a son and daughter to advance and it was for them that she now resolved to immolate her pride. From the earliest signs of her rehabilitation she forced herself to sally out into the world, and finding that her stock was higher in the international colony she stooped distastefully to call upon the American peeresses and on the South American representatives. Eventually she found herself at Miss Grier's midnight suppers. The reflection of the consideration she received in such places finally reached her own people and she was gradually spared the more obvious humiliations.

It became necessary for her now to drop her former friends, the dull soured old women, more plaintive than herself, and with less reason, with whom she had been accustomed to fret away the long afternoons and evenings behind the drawn blinds of the Piazza Aracœli. She was obliged likewise to abandon a sordid habit that linked her no less surely to the previous centuries, namely that of rushing into lawsuits. The innate capacity for affairs which abounded in this woman had found during the days of her obscurity this extraordinary outlet. She went about scenting out old claims and deeds, the slips of tradesmen and the subtle omissions of lawyers. She was always protecting her shyer friends from imposition, and she was always success-

ful and often made a good deal of money. She employed
obscure boy-lawyers and when she was called upon as a
witness, relying on her distinctions to prevent her being in-
terrupted, she used the occasion as an opportunity to sum
up the whole case. The middle classes seeing in the morn-
ing paper that S. A. Leda Matilda Colonna duchessa d'Aqui-
lanera was attacking the City of Rome over the valuation
of property near a railroad, or contesting the bill of some
popular stationer or fruiterer on the Corso, suffered will-
ingly the inconvenience of holding a seat in court for hours
in order to see the malignant resourceful woman and to hear
her trenchant sarcasms and her irresistible accumulation
of evidence. Yet her relatives had always sneered at this
passion, failing to see that she represented more clearly than
themselves the qualities that had always gone to charac-
terize the aristocracy.

It was this woman then whom we confronted when we
returned at midnight for our third engagement that day in
the old palace. Supper was served in a larger, brighter
apartment than I had yet seen. As I entered the huge door-
way my eyes fell upon a strange figure that I knew at once
must be a Cabalist. A short, dark, ugly woman holding a
cane between her knees was staring at me with magnificent
fierce eyes. With the boticed dress and eagle's head I be-
came aware of her jewels, seven huge lumpy amethysts
strung about her neck on a golden rope. I was presented to
this witch who at once, and by the blackest art, made one
like her. On hearing that Blair was leaving Rome shortly
she centered her attention on me.

For a moment she sat before me, sliding the end of her
stick nervously about on the floor, drawing in her upper lip,
and gazing hard into my eyes. She asked me my age. I was
twenty-five.

I am the Duchess d'Aquilanera, she began. What lan-
guage shall we speak? I think we will talk English. I do not
talk it good, but we must be plain. It must be so you must

understand me quite perfectly. I am a great friend of Miss Grier. I have often talked over with her a great problem—a sorrow, my young friend—that is in my home. Suddenly tonight at seven o'clock she call me up on the telephone and told me she have found someone who could help me: she mean you. Now listen: I have a son of sixteen. He is important because he is somebody. How you say?—he is a personage. We are of a very old house. Our family has been in the front of Italy, everyone in her triumph and in her trouble. You are not sympathetic to that kind of greatness in America, not? But you must have read history, no? ancient times and the middle times and like that? You must realize how important the great families are . . . have always been to . . . countries. . . .

(Here she grew nervous, and blew several bubbles and expended herself in those splendid Italian gestures denoting difficulty, perhaps futility, and resignation before the impossible. I hastened to assure her that I had great respect for the aristocratic principle.)

Perhaps you have and perhaps you haven't, she said at last. In all events, think of my son as a prince whose blood contains all sorts of kings and noble people. Well, now I must tell you he has fallen in bad ways. Some women have got hold of him and I do not know him any more. All our boys in Italy go that way when they are sixteen, but Marcantonio, my god, I do not know what is the matter with him and I shall go crazy. Now in America you are all descended from your Puritans, are you not, and your ideas are very different. There is only one thing to do, and that is: you must save my boy. You must talk to him. You must play tennis with him. I have talked to him; the priest has talked to him, and a good friend of mine, a cardinal, has talked to him and still he does nothing but go to that dreadful place. Elizabeth Grier says that most boys in America at your age are just . . . naturally . . . good. You are *vieilles filles;* you are as temperate as I do not know what. It's very strange, if it's true, and I do not think I believe it; at all

events it's not wise. At all events you must talk to Marcantonio and make him stay away from that dreadful place or we shall go mad. My plan is this: next Wednesday we are going for a week to our beautiful villa in the country. It is the most beautiful villa in Italy. You must come with us. Marcantonio will begin to admire you, you can play tennis and shoot and swim and then you can have long talks and you can save him. Now, won't you do that for me, because no one has ever come to you in such trouble as I have come to you in today?

Hereupon, in sudden fear that all her efforts had been in vain, she began waving her stick to attract Miss Grier's attention. That lady had been watching us from a corner of her eye and now came running up. The Duchess burst into a flood of tears, crying into her pocket handkerchief: Elisabetta, speak to him. Oh, my god, I have failed. He not want us and all is lost.

I was divided between anger and laughter and kept muttering into Miss Grier's ear: I'd be glad to meet him, Miss Grier, but I can't lecture the fellow. I'd feel like a fool. Besides what would I do with a whole week. . . .

She's put it to you wrongly, said Miss Grier. Let's not say anything more about it tonight.

At this the Black Queen began rolling about in her chair, the motions preparatory to rising. She rammed her stick against my shoe for leverage on the polished floor and stood up. We must pray to God to find another way. I am a fool. I do not blame the young man. He cannot realize the importance of our family.

Nonsense, Leda, said Miss Grier, firmly in Italian. Be quiet a moment. Then turning to me: Would you like to pass a week end at the Villa Colonna-Stiavelli, or not? There's no stipulation about lecturing the Prince. If you like him, you'll feel like talking to him anyway, and if you don't like him, you're welcome to leave him alone.

Two Cabalists were begging me to take a glimpse of the most famous of Renaissance villas, one moreover that was

obstinately closed to the public and that had to be peered at from the road half a mile away. I turned to the Duchess and bowing low accepted her invitation. Whereupon she kissed the shoulder of my coat, murmured with a beautiful smile: Cristiano! Cristiano! and bidding us good night, passed bowing from the room.

I shall see you Sunday at Tivoli, said Miss Grier, and tell you all about it there.

During the next few days my mind lay under the dread of the two engagements that lay ahead of me: the week end at the Villa Horace and the missionary enterprise at the Villa Colonna. I stayed in my rooms, depressed, reading a little, or took long walks through the Trasteverine under-world, thinking about Connecticut.

The car that called for me Saturday morning already contained a fellow guest. He introduced himself as M. Léry Bogard, adding that Mlle. de Morfontaine had offered to send for us separately, but that he had taken the liberty of requesting that we be called for together, not only because any company in crossing the Campagna is better than none, but because he had heard many things of me that led him to believe that we would not be uncongenial. I replied in that language wherein all courtesy sounds sincere, that the possibility of being congenial to so distinguished a member of the French Academy and to so profound a scholar was a greater honor than I dared hope for. These overtures did not tend to chill the encounter. M. Bogard was a fragile elderly gentleman, immaculately dressed. His face was delicately tinted by exquisite reading and expensive food, russet and violet about the eyes, his cheeks a pale plum from which rose the ivory-white of his nose and chin. His manner was soft and conciliatory, expressed for the most part in the play of his eyelids and hands both of which fluttered in unison like petals about to fall upon the breeze. I spoke hesitantly of the pleasure I had derived from his works, especially from those pages, so faintly tinctured

with venom, on Church History. But now he cried out at
once: Do not mention them! My early indiscretions! Horri-
ble! What would I not give to withdraw them. Can that
nonsense have reached as far as America? You must let
your friends know, young man, that those books no longer
represent my attitude. Since then I have become an obedi-
ent son of the Church and nothing would give me greater
comfort than to hear that they had been burned.

What may I tell my friends now represents your real
views? I asked.

Why read me at all? he cried in mock grief. There are too
many books in the world already. Let us read no more, my
son. Let us seek out some congenial friends. Let us sit
about a table (well-spread, pardi!) and talk of our church
and our king and perhaps of Virgil.

My face must have shown a trace of the suffocation I ex-
perienced at this plan of life, for M. Bogard became at once
more impersonal. The country we are traversing now, he
said, has known stirring times . . . and he began an instruc-
tive travelogue, as though I were some stupid acquaintance,
his hostess' son, and as though he were not, nor ever had
been, a distinguished scholar.

On arriving at the Villa we were met by the steward and
shown to our rooms. The Villa had been a monastery for
many years and in purchasing it Mlle. de Morfontaine had
obtained likewise the adjoining church which still served
the peasants of the hillside. She claimed that the Villa was
the very one that Maecenas had given to Horace: local
tradition affirmed it; the foundations were of the best opus
reticulatum; and the location fulfilled the rather vague re-
quirements of classical allusion; even onomatopoeia testi-
fied, declared our hostess, asserting that from her window
the waterfall could be literally heard to lisp

"*. . . domus Albuniae resonantis*
Et praeceps Anio ac Tiburni locus et uda
Mobilibus pomaria rivis."

In furnishing her monastery our hostess had combined, as best she could, a delight in aesthetic effects and a longing for severity. A long low rambling plaster building, without grace of line, was the Villa Horace. Disordered rose gardens surrounded it, with intentionally neglected gravel paths, and chipped marble benches. One entered a long hall at the end of which several steps descended to a library. The hall was lined with doors at regular intervals on both sides, doors to what had once been cells now thrown together into reception rooms. Many of these doors stood open during the day and the long corridor, paved with russet tile, was striped with the sunshine that fell across it. The ceiling had been coffered, and like the doors touched with dark green and gilt, and with that rich wasted brick-red that is the color of Neapolitan tiles. The walls were yellow white, of caked and crumbling plaster, and the beauty of the view with the optical illusion of distance and the depth and the lightness of the library seen like some great green-golden well at the further end, appealed to that sense of balance and one's tactile imagination as do the vistas in the paintings of Raphael, whose spell is said to reside in that secret. To the left lay the reception rooms, carpeted in one color, hung with tabernacles and Italian primitives, while huge candelabra, pots of flowers and tables covered with brocades and crystals and uncut jewels, relieved the severity of unfreshened walls. Toward the end of the hall at the right one ascended a few steps to the refectory, the barest room in the house. By day the refectory was a meaningless casual clubroom. Luncheon was a negligible affair at the Villa; one's conversation must be saved for dinner; at luncheon one barely looked at one another, one talked about the last rains and the next drought, or any subject that did not faintly allude to the devouring passions of the house, religion, and aristocracy and literature. The beauty of the refectory was purely a matter of lighting and at eight o'clock the greatness of the room lay in the pool of wine-yellow light that was shed on the red table cloth, the

dark green crested plates, the silver and the gold, the wine-
glasses, the gowns and decorations of the guests, the ambas-
sadorial ribbons, the pontifical violets, and the little army of
satin-clad footmen that suddenly appeared from nowhere.

On the night of my arrival the Cardinal was the last to
appear at dinner, and entered directly into the refectory
where we stood waiting for him. His expression was be-
nignant, even beaming. While he blessed the meal, Mlle.
de Morfontaine knelt on her admirable yellow gown, and
M. Bogard dropped on one knee and shaded his eyes. The
grace was in English, a strange affair discovered by our
erudite guest among the literary remains of some disap-
pointed Cambridge parson.

> *Oh, pelican of eternity,*
> *That piercest thy heart for our food,*
> *We are thy fledglings that cannot know thy woe.*
> *Bless this shadowy and visionary food of substance,*
> *Whose last eater shall be worm,*
> *And feed us rather with the vital food of*
> *Dreams and grace.*

The Cardinal, though unimpaired in mind and body,
looked all of his eighty years. The expression of dry serenity
that never left his yellow face with its drooping moustache
and pointed beard gave him the appearance of a Chinese
sage that has lived a century. He was born of peasants on
the plain between Milan and Como, and had begun his
education at the hands of the local priests, who soon discov-
ered in him a veritable genius for Latinity. He was passed
upward from school to school, gaining in his progress all the
prizes the Jesuits had to offer. The attention of a large body
of influential churchmen was gradually drawn to him, and
at the time of his graduation from the great college on the
Piazza Santa Maria sopra Minerva (presenting a thesis of
unparalleled brilliance and futility on the forty-two cases
in which suicide is permissible and the twelve occasions on

which a priest may take up arms without danger of homicide) a choice between three great careers was offered to him. The details of each had been prepared under the highest patronage: he might become a fashionable preacher; or one of the courtier-secretaries of the Vatican; or a learned teacher and disputant. To the amazement and grief of his professors he suddenly announced his intention of following a road that to them meant ruin; he declared for Missions. His foster fathers raged and wept and called on heaven to witness his ingratitude; but the boy would hear of nothing less than the Church's most dangerous post in western China. Thither in due time he departed with scarcely a blessing from his teachers, who had already turned their attention to more docile if less brilliant pupils. Through fire, famine, riots, and even torture, the young priest labored for twenty-five years in the province of Szechwan. This missionary fever however did not entirely spring from piety. The boy, conscious of the great powers raging within him, had been throughout his youth insolent, contemptuous of his teachers and of his companions. He knew and despised every type of a churchman to be found in Italy; never had he seen a thing adequately done by them, and now he dreamed of a field of work where he would be answerable to no fool. In the whole realm of the Church there was only one region that filled his requirements; a month's traveling by crude wagon separates one from the next priest in Szechwan. There, then, after a shipwreck, some months of slavery, and other experiences that he never related, but which reached the world from his native helpers, he settled in an inn, dressed as a native, grew a pigtail, and lived among the villagers for six years without mentioning his faith. He passed the time studying the language, the classics, the manners, ingratiating himself with the officials and so perfectly identifying himself with the daily life of the city that in time he all but lost the odor of foreignness. When at last he began to declare his mission to those merchants and officials in whose homes he

had become an almost nightly visitor, his work was rapid.
Perhaps the greatest of all the Church's missionaries since
the Middle Ages, he turned many a compromise that was
destined to shock Rome profoundly. He somehow achieved
a harmonization of Christianity and the religions and ac-
cepted ideas of China that had its parallel only in those
daring readings that Paul discovered in his Palestinian cult.
So subtle were the priest's adaptations that it never occurred
to his first converts to be even conscious of repudiating their
old faith until at last after twenty lectures he showed them
how far they had gone and how charred were the bridges
that lay behind them. Once he had them baptized how-
ever, he could give them only the bitterest bread to eat: the
foundations of his cathedral lay squarely on a score of
martyrs' graves, but once built suffered no further assault
and grew slowly and irresistibly. Finally sheer statistics did
what envy could not prevent and he was made a bishop.
At the end of his fifteenth year in the East he returned to
Rome for the first time and was received with cold dislike.
His health had been partly undermined, and he was granted
a year's repose, during which he worked in the Vatican li-
brary on a thesis relative to nothing in China, the donation
of Constantine. This was considered shocking in a missionary,
and when it was published its learning and impersonality
won it the neglect of the ecclesiastical reviewers. He was
treated with condescension by the courtiers of the Palace;
by implication they described to him their idea of his great
creation in western China: a low mud-brick meetinghouse
and a congregation of beggars who pretended to a conver-
sion in order to be fed. He did not trouble to describe to
them the stone cathedral with two awkward but lofty
towers, the vast porch, the schools and library and hospital;
the processions on Feast days carrying garish but ardent
banners entering the great cavern of the Church and sing-
ing the correctest Gregorian; nor of the governmental
honors, the tax exemptions, the military respect during rev-
olutions, the co-operation of the city.

At last he returned, willingly enough, to sink himself for another ten years into the remote interior. His visit to Rome had not altered his boyish attitude toward his fellowmen. He had heard strange tales about himself—how he had amassed a huge fortune by taking bribes from the Chinese merchants, how he had interpreted the atonement in Buddhist terms and had allowed pagan symbols to be stamped upon the Host itself.

The ecclesiastical honors that eventually arrived must have been extravagantly deserved, for they came without his or any friend's negotiation. Sheer accomplishment must so have stared the Vatican in the face that it had felt torn from its hands the trophies it was accustomed to relinquish only on the receipt of petitions bearing ten thousand signatures or at the instance of wealth or power. To receive these new distinctions, the Bishop returned to Rome again after an absence of ten years. This time he meant to remain in Italy, having decided that henceforth his work would be better in the hands of natives. The ecclesiastics viewed this return with considerable trepidation, for if he returned as a scholar eager for doctrinal debates they dreaded seeing exposed their lack of interest or equipment; if he came as a critic of the Propaganda, they were all in danger. They watched him settle down with two Chinese servants and an absurd peasant woman whom he insisted on referring to as his sister, in a tiny villa on the Janiculum, join the Papal Archaeological Society and apply himself to reading and gardening. Within five years his retirement had become a greater embarrassment to the Church than his pamphlets might have been. His fame among Romanists outside Rome was unbounded; every distinguished visitor rushed from the station to get an introduction to the recluse of Janiculum; the Pope himself was a little tried by the zeal of visitors who imagined that His Holiness enjoyed nothing better than discussing the labors, the illness, and the modesty of the Cathedral Builder of China. English Catholics and American Catholics and Belgian Catholics who did not un-

derstand the exquisite subtlety of these matters and should let them alone, kept crying: Why isn't something being done for him? He humbly refused a high honorary librarianship in the Vatican, but his refusal was not accepted and his name crowned the stationery; the same thing happened with the great committees on Propaganda; he did not appear at the meetings, but no speech was so influential as the report of chance words let fall in conversation with disciples at the Villino Wei Ho. His very lack of ambition frightened the churchmen; they supposed it must arise from a similar emotion to that which kept Achilles sulking in his tent, and dreaded the moment when he would ultimately arise, swinging his mighty prestige and crush them for the honors they begrudged him; finally he was offered the Hat, by a committee from the College all in a perspiration lest he refuse it. This time he accepted their offer and went through the forms with a rigid decorum and with an observance of traditional minutiae that had to be elaborately explained to his Irish-American colleagues.

It would be hard to say what his thoughts were those clear mornings as he sat among his flowers and rabbits, a volume of Montaigne fallen on to the gravel path from the tabouret beside him, what were his thoughts as he gazed at his yellow hands and listened to the hushed excitement of the Aqua Paola exclaiming in eternal praise of Rome. He must surely have asked himself often in what year his faith and joy had fled. Some said that he had become attached to a convert who had relapsed into paganism; some said that one day under torture he had renounced Christianity to save his life from the hands of brigands. Perhaps it was only that he had attempted the hardest task in the world and found it not so difficult after all; and reflecting that he could have built up a huge fortune in the financial world with half the energy and one-tenth the gifts; that he was the only person living who could write a Latin that would have entranced the Augustans; that he was the last man who would be able to hold in his

head at one moment all the learning of the Church; and that to become a Prince of the Church required nothing but a devoted indifference to its workings—reflecting on these things he may well have felt the world not to be worth the thunder of admiration and applause that was so continually mounting to Heaven in its praise. Perhaps one of the other stars is more worthy of one's best efforts.

Grace concluded, the meal could not be begun until the Cardinal was informed as to Alix. But where's Alix?

Alix is always late.

Are you sure she's coming?

She telephoned this afternoon, that. . . .

Now isn't that too bad of her! She's coming in panting when the dinner's half over. Then apologies. Father, you're too kind to her. You always forgive her directly. You must act cross.

We must all act cross.

Everybody look angry when Alix comes in.

I had assumed that the conversation of the Cabala *in camera* would be vertiginous. If I anticipated the wit and eloquence of its table talk I dreaded their gradual discovery that I was tongue-tied or doltish. When, therefore, the conversation at last broke forth I had the mixed sensation of discovering that it was not unlike that of a house party on the Hudson. Wait, I told myself, they will warm up. Or perhaps it is my presence here that prevents them from being at their best. I recalled the literary tradition that the gods of antiquity had not died but still drifted about the earth shorn of the greater part of their glory—Jupiter and Venus and Mercury straying through the streets of Vienna as itinerant musicians, or roaming the South of France as harvesters. Casual acquaintances would not be able to sense their supernaturalism; the gods would take good care to dim their genius but once the outsider had gone would lay aside their cumbersome humanity and relax in the reflections of their ancient godhead. I told myself that I was the obstacle, that these Olympians chattered and chaffed for a

season until my departure, when the air would change—
what divine conversation. . . .

Presently in burst their Alix, the Princess d'Espoli, pant-
ing and aflutter with apologies. She knelt to the Cardinal's
sapphire. No one looked the least bit cross. The very serv-
ants beamed. We are to know a great deal about the Prin-
cess later; suffice it to say that she was a Frenchwoman of
the utmost smallness and elegance, sandy-haired, pretty,
and endowed with a genius for conversation in which every
shade of wit, humor, pathos and even tragic power fol-
lowed in close succession. Within a few moments she was
enchanting the company with a lot of nonsense about a
horse who had started talking on the Pincian Hill and the
efforts of the police force to suppress such an aberration of
nature. As I was presented to her she murmured quickly:
Miss Grier told me to tell you that she will be here at about
ten-thirty.

After dinner Madame Bernstein played the piano for a
time. She was still the power behind the great German
banking house. Without ever venturing into her sons' offices
or directors' meetings she yet disposed of all the larger de-
cisions of the firm by curt remarks at their dinner tables, by
postscripts to her letters and by throaty injunctions at the
moment of saying good night. She wanted the sensation of
having retired from its direction, her whole middle life have
been expended in a magnificent display of generalship and
financial imagination, yet she could not keep her mind off
its problems. The friendship of the Cabala was beginning
to reconcile her to advancing age, and was drawing her
further and further into her love for music.

As a girl she had often heard Liszt and Tausig in her
mother's home; by dint of never playing Schumann or
Brahms she had kept her fingers all silver and crystal, and
even now, practically in her old age, she evoked the great
era of virtuosi, a time when the orchestra had not led piano
technique into a desperate imitation of brass and strings.
Mlle. de Morfontaine sat holding in the cup of her hand the

muzzle of one or other of her splendid dogs. Her eyes were filled with tears, but whether they were the facile tears of her half-mad nature or the witness of memories brought back on the tide of Chopin's sonata, we cannot know. The Cardinal had retired early and the Princess sat in the shadows, not listening to the music, but pursuing some of the phantoms of her most secretive mind.

Barely had the army with banners ceased drilling in the wintry sunlight of the last movement when a servant whispered to me that the Cardinal wished to see me.

I found him in the first of the two small rooms that had been set aside for him at the Villa. He was writing a letter, standing up to it at one of those high desks known to the clerks of Dickens and the illuminators of the Middle Ages. I was later to receive many of those famous letters, never more nor less than four pages long, never falling short of their amazing suavity, never very witty nor vivid yet never untouched from beginning to end by the quality of their composer's mind. Whether he declined an invitation or suggested a reading of Freud's book on Leonardo, or gave suggestions on the feeding of rabbits, always from the first sentence he foresaw his last and always like a movement from Mozart's chamber music the whole unit lay under one spirit and the perfection of details played handmaid to the perfection of the form. He seated me in a chair that suffered all the light that was in the room, treating himself to a fine shadow.

He began by saying that he had heard that I was to keep an eye on Donna Leda's son for a while.

I became warm and unintelligible in an effort at protesting that I could guarantee nothing; that I was most reluctant; and that I still reserved the right to withdraw at any moment.

Let me tell you about him, he began. Perhaps I should say first that I am a sort of old uncle in the family, and their confessor for many years. Well—this Marcantonio. What shall I say? Have you seen him?

No.

The boy is full of good things. He . . . he . . . full of good things. Perhaps that's his trouble. You say you haven't met him yet?

No.

Everything seemed to start well. He was good in his studies. He made a lot of friends. He was particularly good in the ceremonial that his rank requires, his attendance at Court and at the Vatican. His mother was a little anxious about his boyish dissipations. She had his father in mind, I suspect, and wanted the boy to get over them as soon as possible. Donna Leda is a more than usually foolish woman. She was very pleased when he set up his own apartment off on the Via Po and became very secretive about it.

Here the Cardinal began to grope about again, perhaps surprised at his own awkwardness. Presently however he gathered up the reins with new determination and said: And then, my dear young man, something went wrong. We thought he would go through the usual experience of a Roman young man of his class and come out. But he has never come out. Perhaps you can tell me why this young fellow couldn't have had his five or six little affairs and gotten over it?

I showed myself as quite unequal to answering this question. In fact I was so amazed at the five or six little liaisons for a boy of sixteen, that it was all I could do to keep my face casual. I wanted badly not to appear shocked and endeavored by a lift of an eyebrow to imply that the boy might have a score if he liked.

Marcantonio, continued the priest, went around with a group of boys older than himself. His greatest wish was to be like them. You could see them at the races, in the music halls, at Court, in the tearooms and hotel lobbies. They wore monocles and American hats, and all they talked about was women and their own successes. Euh . . . perhaps I should begin at the beginning.

There was a pause.

He was first initiated—perhaps I should use a stronger word—on Lake Como. He used to play tennis with some very warm little South American girls, heiresses from Brazil, I believe, from whom no secrets were hid. I fancy our Tonino merely meant to pay them a shy compliment or two, a sudden kiss under the laurel bushes. But he soon found himself with a little . . . a sort of Rubens riot on his hands. Well, it began in imitation of his older friends. From imitation it went to an exercise of vanity. What was Vanity became Pleasure. Pleasure became a Habit. Habit became a Mania. And that's where he is now.

There was another pause.

You must have heard of how certain insane persons become enormously intelligent—that is, they become sly and secretive—trying to conceal their delusion from their guards? Yes; and I am told that vicious children perform feats of duplicity worthy of the most expert criminals, in an effort to conceal their tricks from their parents. You have heard of such things? Well, that is where Marcantonio is now. What can be done? Some people would say that we should let him go and make himself thoroughly sick. Perhaps they are right, but we should like to step in before that, if possible. Especially since there has come a new development into the story.

My mood at that moment was overwhelmingly against new developments. In the distance I could hear that Madame Bernstein had resumed her Chopin. I would have given a lot for the power of being rude enough to leap for the doorknob and bid my host good night, a long good night to the wallowing little prince and his mother.

Yes, continued the Cardinal, his mother has at last found a marriage for him. To be sure she does not believe there is a house in the world that can bring any new distinction to her own, but she has found a girl with an old name and some money and expects me to do the rest. But the girl's brothers know Marcantonio. They are in the group I de-

scribed to you. They refuse to permit the marriage until
Marcantonio has, well—been quiet for a while.

Now my face must have shown a rich mixture of horror
and amusement and anger and astonishment, for the Car-
dinal became perplexed. You never can tell what will sur-
prise an American, he probably said to himself.

No, no. Excuse me, Father. I can't, I can't.

What do you mean?

You want me to go to the country to hold him down to
a few weeks of temperance. I don't understand how you
can mean such a thing, but you do. He's a sort of Strass-
bourg goose whom you want to stuff with virtue, don't you,
against his marriage. Don't you see . . . ?

You exaggerate!

Excuse me if I sound rude, Father. No wonder you
couldn't make an impression on the boy—you didn't be-
lieve in what you were saying. You don't really believe in
temperance.

Believe in it. Of course I do. Am I not a priest?

Then why not make the boy . . . ?

But after all, *we are in the world.*

I laughed. I shouted with a laughter that would have
been insulting, if it hadn't contained a touch of hysteria.
Oh, I thank thee, dear Father Vaini, I said to myself. I
thank thee for that word. How clear it makes all Italy, all
Europe. *Never try to do anything against the bent of human
nature.* I came from a colony guided by exactly the opposite
principle.

Excuse me, Father, I said at last. I can't go on with it.
Under any conditions I should feel an awful hypocrite talk-
ing to the boy. But if I knew it were only a measure to keep
him good a month or two I should feel ten times more so.
It can't be argued; it's just a matter one feels. I must tell
Miss Grier I cannot visit her friend. She is driving out here
at ten-thirty. If you will excuse me I shall go and find her
in the music room now.

Do not be angry with me, my son. Perhaps you are right. Probably I do not believe these things.

Hardly had I re-entered the music room with my revolt written all over me when the Princess d'Espoli came forward. By that telepathy which the Cabala employed in its affairs she already knew that I had to be persuaded all over again. She made me sit down beside her, and with the briefest outlay of those gifts of suppliance and enchantment of which she held the secret, she won my promise. In two minutes she had made it seem the most natural thing in the world that I should play stern older brother to a gifted drifting friend of hers.

As by the click of some invisible stage manager, Miss Grier entered.

How are you, how are you? she said, trailing her russet draperies across the tiles toward me. You can't guess who drove me out. I must hurry back. The Lateran choir is coming to sing Palestrina to me about twelve—perhaps you know the motets from the Song of Songs? No? Marcantonio brought me here. He loves high-powered cars, and as his mother can't give him one I let him play with mine. Can you come out and meet him now? You'd better get your coat. Do you like night rides?

She led me out to the road where behind two blinding headlights a motor was humming impatiently. Antonino, she called. This is an American friend of your mother's. Do show him the car for half an hour, will you? Don't kill anybody.

An incredibly slight and definite little elegant, looking exactly his sixteen years, with sparklike black eyes bowed stiffly to me in the faint light over the wheel. Italian princes do not rise at the approach of ladies.

Don't hurt my car or my friend, Marcantonio.

No.

Where are you going?

But he did not choose to answer and the aroused motor drowned out the lady's questions. For ten minutes we sat

in silence while the road rose to the headlights. After a harrowing struggle with his own selfishness Don Marcantonio asked me if I wanted to take the wheel. Assured that nothing would alarm me more, he settled down to driving with an almost voluptuous application. He made nice distinctions with grades and corners, took long descents cantabilemente, and played scherzi on cobblestones. The outlines of the Alban hills stood out against the stars that like a swarm of golden bees recalled that haughty Barberini who had declared that the sky itself was the scutcheon of his house. All lights were out on the farms, but occasionally we passed through a village whose francobollo shop showed a lantern and a group of card players. Many a wakeful soul in those enormous family beds must have turned over, crossing himself, at the sighing whistle of our flight.

Presently however the driver wanted to talk. He asked a great many questions about the United States. Could one plunge into the life of the Wild West any minute? Were there many big cities as big as Rome? What language was spoken in San Francisco? in Philadelphia? Where did our athletes train for the Olympic games? Was the public allowed to watch them? Did I know about such things? I replied that at school and college one couldn't help picking up hints on form and training. He then disclosed the fact that at the Villa Colonna he had directed the gardeners to make a running track, cinders and hurdles and pit and shed and embanked corners. And that we were to use it every morning. He dreamed of himself doing incredible distances in incredible time. He outlined a plan to me whereby under my direction he would begin by running a mile every morning, and should add a half-mile daily for weeks. This would go on for years and then he would be ready to enter the Paris Olympics of 1924.

In my head the nerves of astonishment had been a little fatigued lately, what with Mlle. de Morfontaine and her Ecumenical Council, the Cardinal and his tolerances, Miss Grier and her cereals. But I confess they received no small

twinge when this frail and emptied spirit announced his candidacy for a world's record in long runs. Not without sly intention I began to outline the sacrifices that such an ambition would entail. I touched on diet and early hours and early rising; he accepted them eagerly. I then skirted those self-denials that would touch him more particularly, and now with a mounting exaltation, with an almost religious fire, he pledged himself to all temperance. The fact that I was astonished shows my immaturity. I thought I was witness to a great conversion. I told myself that he wanted to be saved; that he was rolling up outside forces that might protect himself from his weakness; and that he hoped to find in athletics a deliverance from despair.

Returning to the Villa we found the company still listening to music. As we entered the room all eyes were turned toward us and I knew that for the present the Cabala had laid aside all activity and was brooding over one thing, the rescue of Donna Leda's son.

On arriving at my rooms in Rome I found several notes from a Mr. Perkins of Detroit, a successful manufacturer who had crossed with me. Mr. Perkins, descending upon Italy for the first time, was resolved to see it at its best. There were no collections so private but that he was able to secure letters of admittance; no servants too occupied but that he obtained their services as ciceroni; audiences he obtained with the Pope were, as he called them, "superspecial"; excavations not yet open to the public suffered his disappointed peerings. Some secretary at the Embassy must have mentioned that I had already made some Italian acquaintances, for there were these notes from him reminding me that he wanted to know some real Italians. He wanted to see what they were like in their homes, and he expected me to show him some. Mind, real Italians. I wrote him at once that all the Italians I knew were half French or half American, but assured him that when I had actually isolated a native I would bring them together. I added that I

was leaving for the country, but would return in a week or two and see what could be done.

To the country then I went, being driven for the greater part of a day by Marcantonio himself. His enthusiasm for running had by no means abated; in fact it seemed to have gone from strength to strength, probably because of some lapses from strict training in the interval. It was late afternoon and a red sunset was filtering through a blue dusk when we entered the great gates of the park. There was first a forest of oaks; then a mile of open lawn with some hurrying sheep; then a pineta with a brook; the farmhouses in a cloud of doves; the upper terrace with a perspective of fountains; and at last the casino with the Black Queen trailing her garments of dusty serge across the driveway of powdered shell. There was little time to admire the orange-brown front of the villa roughened with wreaths and garlands that were crumbling away before the sun and rain, or the famous frieze of the women in Ariosto's poems, recalling the days when Pope Sylvester Lefthand held here his academy and invented the Sylvestrian sonnet form. All I could do was to conceal my pleasure at the discovery that I was to live by candlelight in rooms that though the originals of hundreds of bad copies on Long Island, were here the secret shame of their owners. My hosts' ideal of residence was a hotel on the Embankment and they all but breathed an apology for the enormous rooms to which I was conducted, and in which I stood transfixed, lost in antiquarian dreams until Marcantonio knocked on the door to call me to supper.

At table I was presented to Donna Julia, Marcantonio's half-sister, and to a spinster cousin of the family, always present, always silent and whose lips never ceased moving, as solitaires' must, to the measure of her inner thoughts. Like all girls of her class, Donna Julia had never been alone for more than a half-hour in all her life. Her immense talents for being bad had been balked at every turn; they had been

forced to take refuge in her eyes. She had never even been allowed to read anything more inflammatory than the comedies of Goldoni and I Promessi Sposi, but she guessed at a criminal world and presently when marriage suddenly opened up to her every freedom she played her part in it. Donna Julia was a little stiff, almost ugly with her level baleful regard. She kept silent most of the time, was utterly incurious of me, and seemed chiefly occupied in angling for her brother's evasive glance so as to plant into it a triumphant significant idea.

One retired early at the Villa Colonna. But Marcantonio, for whom my simplest remarks were astonishing, would stop in at my room and talk for hours over some glasses of Marsala. No doubt his mother, noting the visits through her half-opened door down the hall, assumed with great satisfaction that I was reading lectures on hygiene. But, especially as the week advanced, we were chiefly taken up with a diagram that showed day by day how the little champion had run and in what time.

It must have been at the end of a week of this that in one of our late conversations his friendliness suddenly turned into contempt. A week's preoccupation with unsentimental matters now took its revenge. Back into his mind flooded the images of passion, and he wanted to boast. Perhaps he saw that prowess on the field was not to be his, and his egoism being athirst for all possible superlatives, he must replace it with a catalogue of the first prizes he had won in another arena. He recalled the Brazilian girls under the arbors of Como. He described how he had returned to Rome after that initiation bent on seeing whether the game was as easy as it had seemed. Suddenly his eyes had been opened to a world he had not dreamed of. So it was true that men and women were never really engaged in what they appeared to be doing, but lived in a world of secret invitations, signals and escapes! Now he understood the raised eyebrows of waitresses and the brush of the usher's hand as she unlocks the loge. It is not an accident that the

wind draws the great lady's scarf across your face as you emerge from the door of the hotel. Your mother's friends happen to be passing in the corridor outside the drawing room, but not by chance. Now he discovered that all women were devils, but foolish ones, and that he had entered into the true and only satisfactory activity in living—the pursuit of them. One minute he was exclaiming at the easiness of it; the next he described its difficulties and subtlety. Now he sang the uniformity of their weakness and now the endless variety of their temperaments. Next he boasted of his utter indifference and his superiority to them; he knew their tears but he did not believe they really suffered. He doubted whether they had souls.

To incidents that were true he added others that he wished had been true. To his acquaintance with a corner of Rome he added a fourteen-year-old's vision of a civilization where no one thought about anything but caresses. This fantasy took him about two hours. I listened without a word. It must have been this that undermined his exhilaration. He had been talking to impress me. Impressed I certainly was; no New Englander could help it; but I knew that a great deal depended on my not showing it. Perhaps it was his sudden realization that, seen through my eyes, these adventures were not enviable; perhaps it was that the black tide of reaction licked close on the heels of such pride; perhaps it was just truth finding room for utterance in his mounting fatigue—at all events, there was strength left for one more outburst: I hate them all! I hate it. There's no end to it all. What shall I do? And he fell on his knees beside the bed and buried his face in the side of the mattress, his hands feverishly pulling at the cover.

Priests and doctors must often hear the cry, Save me! Save me! I was destined to hear it from two other souls before my Roman year was over. Who now thinks it uncommon?

I scarcely know what I said when my turn at last came around. All I know is that my mind whipped up to its sub-

ject with a glee. Heaven only knows what New England divines lent me their remorseless counsels. I became possessed with the wine of the Puritans and alternating the vocabulary of the Pentateuch with that of psychiatry I showed him where his mind was already slipping; I pointed out wherein he already resembled his uncle Marcantonio, no mean warning; I made him see that even his interest in athletics was a symptom of his disintegration; how that he was incapable of fixing his mind on the general interests of man, and how everything he thought and did—humor, sports, ambition, presented themselves to him as symbols of lust.

My little tirade was effective beyond all expectation and for a number of reasons. In the first place, it had the energy and sincerity which the Puritan can always draw upon to censure those activities he cannot permit himself—not a Latin demonstration of gesture and tears, but a cold hate that staggers the Mediterranean soul. Again, all my words had already their dim counterpart in the boy's soul. It is the libertine and not the preacher who conceives most truly of the ideal purity and soundness, because he pays it out, coin by coin, regretfully, knowingly, unpreventably. All my words went to rejoin their prototypes in Marcantonio's mind. Again, how could I know that he had arrived but recently at that stage of failure when one's whole being reverberates, as with some bell of despair, with the words: I shall never get out of this. I am lost. Again, I found out later that Marcantonio had a streak of religious frenzy in him, that for a year he had watched himself alternating communion and dissipation, the exaltation of the former itself betraying him into the latter and the despair of the latter driving him in anguish to the former. At last in sheer cynicism, after watching himself fail so often, he had missed Mass for several months. All these reasons go toward explaining the prostrating effect my brief and vindictive speech had. He cowered against the carpet, begging me to stop, gasping out his promises of reform. But having brought

him to a conviction he might never attain again, I thought it unwise to let go. I had reserves of indignation left. But now he knelt crying on the carpet, covering his ears with his hands and shaking his wet face at me with all its terror and suppliance. I stopped and we stared at one another, darkly, trembling under our several headaches. Then he went to bed.

The next morning he seemed etherialized, made almost transparent by his new resolutions. He walked lightly and with an air of humility. No reference was made to the scene of the evening before, but his glances over the tennis net implied an obedience and a deference that were more annoying than impudence. After two sets we wandered over to the lower fountain, and here stretched out on the semicircular bench he slept for three hours. It seemed to me as I watched morning advance to noon and the sun penetrate his thin body in the delicious fatigues that follow hysterical outbursts, it seemed that it would not be rash to wonder if possibly we may have succeeded. I daydreamed. From the formal terrace below the casino came the click of topiary shears; from the field where the ancient altar had been placed, drum-shaped and bearing an almost effaced frieze, came the shouts of some divinity students (to whom a little villa on the estate had been offered as a vacation house) playing football, their cassocks tucked up about their knees; from the pine wood the exclamations of two shepherds who sat whittling while their flock drifted almost imperceptibly to the road beyond. The fountain before me gave forth its varied sounds: the whir of its initial jet and the tinkle as it fell back into the first bowl; the drum taps as this overflowed and slipped into the second; and the loud loquacity with which the lowest basin received all that came to it from every level. Tacitus lay unread upon my knee while my eyes followed the lizards that flashed in and out of the brilliant sunshine on the gravel, noting their confusion when a sudden breeze bent the poised veil of the fountain and swept us all with a fine mist. The monotony of light and the

noise of water, of insects, and of doves in the farmhouses behind me, combined to recall those tremulous webs of sound that modern composers set shimmering above their orchestra, to draw across it presently on the oboes their bleating melody in thirds.

While I sat there a note was brought me from the house. Mr. Perkins of Detroit had heard I was at the Villa and from the hotel in the nearby town announced his intention of calling on me—lucky to have a pretext for entering the most inaccessible villa in Italy. I scribbled on the back of his envelope that an unfortunate event in the family prevented my asking him to the house at present.

The hot sunlight of the morning had gathered its storm and all afternoon we sat indoors. Marcantonio and Donna Julia attempted teaching me the Neapolitan dialect, while the silent cousin sat by, deeply shocked. But my lesson soon descended into a subtle and barbed quarrel between the teachers. It was conducted for the most part in rapid and hate-laden parentheses, far above my head, in their thick *argot*. What she taunted him about I can only guess. He was invariably beaten; he grew loud and angry. Twice he leaped around the table to strike her; she waited for the blow, stretching herself sleekly and looking up at him from her magnetic eyes. At length he urged me to come away from her and to go upstairs, and the two parted much as children of seven would with a bout of grimaces and a competition to have the last ugly word.

After dinner the war was resumed. The Duchess was nodding by the fire; the cousin was mumbling opposite her. And the two children sat in the shadows exchanging invective. I was made strangely uneasy by their curious quarreling. I excused myself and went to bed. The last thing I saw was an infuriated blow that Marcantonio directed at his sister's shoulder and the last sound I heard was the tremolo of her provocative laughter as they tussled on the carved wooden chest in the corner. I debated with myself on the stairs: surely I had imagined it; my poor sick head was so

full of the erotic narratives of the week; surely I imagined
the character of mixed love and hate in those blows that
were savage caresses, and that laughter that was half sneer
and half invitation.

But I had not imagined it.

At about three I was awakened by Marcantonio. He was
still dressed. He poured at my drowsy head a torrent of
whirling words in which I distinguished nothing but a fever-
ish reiteration of the phrase: You were right. Then he left
the room as abruptly as he had come.

What luck Mr. Perkins had always had! Even now when
he brought to bear all his American determination and broke
into the gardens of the forbidden Villa, what guardian angel
arranged that he should see the Villa at its most character-
istic? Surely a rich old Italian villa is at its most characteris-
tic when a dead prince lies among the rosebushes. When
Frederick Perkins of Detroit leaped the wall in the crystal
airs of seven in the morning, he discovered at his feet the
body of Marcantonio d'Aquilanera, fourteenth prince and
fourteenth duke of Aquilanera and Stoli, twelfth duke of
Stoli-Roccellina, marquis of Bugnaccio, of Tei, etc., baron of
Spenestra, of Gran-Spenstra, seigneur of the Sciestrian
Lakes; patron of the bailli of the order of San Stephano;
likewise prince of Altdorf-Hotenlingen-Craburg, intendant
elector of Altdorf-H.-C.; prince of the Holy Roman Empire,
etc., etc.; chamberlain of the court of Naples; lieutenant and
cousin of the Papal Familia; order of the Crane (f. class);
three hours cold, and with a damp revolver clutched in his
right hand.

Book Three: Alix

THE Cabalists received the news of Marcantonio's death philosophically. The account of it which the bereaved mother gave to Miss Grier was a miracle of misunderstanding. According to her I had done wonders; in fact it was the suddenness and thoroughness of the boy's reformation that had broken his health. She, *she*, was to blame. She should have foreseen that continence was not to be expected of a mere lad; he had gone insane from an excess of virtue and shot himself from too much sanctity. These things are out of our hands, dear Leda, murmured Miss Grier. The Cardinal made no comment.

The Cabala went back to its usual occupations. Being the biographer of the individuals and not the historian of the group I shall not take up much space here with details of the discomfiture of Mrs. Pole (she had been impudent to Miss Grier), nor of the Renan performance (*L'Abbesse de Jouarre* was effectively not given as a benefit at the Constanzi). From a purely disinterested love of Church tradition they blocked the canonization of several tiresome non-entities that had been proposed to gratify the faithful in Sicily and Mexico. They saved the taxpayers of Rome the purchase of hundreds of modern Italian paintings, and the

establishment of a permanent museum for them. They in-
terested public opinion in the faint smell of drains that is
wafted through the Sistine Chapel. When an oak forest fell
ill in the Borghese Gardens no one but the Cabala had the
sense to send to Berlin for a doctor. To tell the truth their
achievements were not very considerable. I soon saw that I
had arrived on the scene in the middle of the decline of
their power. At first they thought they could do something
about the strikes, and about the Fascismo, and the blas-
phemies in the Senate; and it was only after a great deal of
money had been spent and hundreds of persons ineffec-
tually goaded that they realized that the century had let
loose influences they could not stem, and contented them-
selves with less pretentious assignments.

I came to see more and more of them. My youth and
foreignness never ceased to amuse them and they were
made almost uncomfortable by the knowledge that I so
liked them. They thought they had outgrown being suscep-
tible to being liked. From time to time they would point
their fingers to where I sat staring at them in sheer wonder.

He's like an eager dog with his tongue out of his mouth,
Alix d'Espoli would cry. What does he see in us?

He never loses hope that we will suddenly say something
memorable, said the Cardinal looking at me musingly—the
look of a great talker who knows that for lack of a Boswell
his greatness must die with him.

He comes from the rich new country that will grow more
and more splendid while our countries decline to ruins and
rubbish heaps, said Donna Leda. That's why his eyes shine
so.

Why, no, cried Alix. I believe he loves us. Just simply
loves us in a disinterested new world way. Once I had a
most beautiful setter, named Samuele. Samuele spent all his
life sitting around on the pavement watching us with a look
of most intense excitement.

Did he bite? asked Donna Leda who had a literal mind.

You didn't have to give Samuele a sandwich to win his

devotion. He liked to like. You won't be angry with me if every now and then I call you Samuele to remind me of him?

You mustn't talk about him in front of him, muttered Mme. Bernstein who was playing solitaire. Young man, get me my furs from the piano until these people remember themselves.

The Princess explained me. What fairer service can one render another? How could I do other than attach myself to one with so quick and gracious an interpretation.

The Princess was not really modern. As scientists gazing at certain almost extinct birds off Australia are able to evoke a whole lost era, so in the person of this marvelous princess we felt ourselves permitted to glimpse into the seventeenth century and to reconstruct for ourselves what the aristocratic system must have been like in its flower.

The Princess d'Espoli was exceedingly pretty in a fragile Parisian way; her vivacious head, surmounted by a mass of sandy reddish hair was forever tilted above one or other of her thin pointed shoulders; her whole character lay in her sad laughing eyes and small red mouth. Her father came of the Provençal nobility and she had spent her girlhood partly in provincial convent schools and partly climbing like a goat the mountains that surrounded her father's castle. At eighteen she and her sister had been called in from the cliffs, dressed up stiffly and hawked like merchandise through the drawing rooms of their more influential relatives in Paris, Florence, and Rome. Her sister had fallen to an automobile manufacturer and was making the good and bad weather of Lyons; Alix had married the morose Prince d'Espoli, who had immediately sunk into a profounder misanthrophy. He remained at home sunk in the last dissipations. His wife's friends never saw or referred to him; occasionally we became aware of him, we thought, in her late arrivals, hurried departures and harassed air. She had lost two children in infancy. She had no life, save in other peoples' homes. Yet the sum of her sufferings had been the production of the

sweetest strain of gaiety that we shall ever see, a pure well of heartbroken frivolity. Wonderful though she was in all the scenes of social life, she certainly was at her finest at table, where she had graces and glances that the most gifted actress would fall short of conceiving for the Millamants, and Rosalinds and Célimènes; nowhere has been seen such charm, such manners, and such wit. She would prattle about her pets, describe a leave-taking seen by chance in a railway station, or denounce the Roman fire department with a perfection of rendering of Yvette Guilbert, a purer perfection in that it did not suggest the theater. She possessed the subtlest mimicry, and could sustain an endless monologue, but the charm of her gift resided in the fact that it required the collaboration of the whole company; it required the exclamations, contradictions, and even the concerted shouts as of a Shakespearean mob, before the Princess could display her finest art. She employed an unusually pure speech, a gift that went deeper than a mere aptitude for acquiring grammatical correctness in the four principal languages of Europe; its source lay in the type of her mind. Her thought proceeded complicatedly, but not without order, in long looping parentheses, a fine network of relative clauses, invariably terminating in some graceful turn by way of climax, some sudden generalization or summary surprise. I once accused her of speaking in paragraphs and she confessed that the nuns to whom she had gone to school in Provence had required of her every day an oral essay built on a formula derived principally from Madame de Sévigné and terminating in a *concetto*.

Such rare personalities are not able to derive nourishment from ordinary food. Rumors of the Princess's strange stormy loves reached us continually. It seems that she was doomed to search throughout the corridors of Rome a succession of attachments as brief and fantastic as they were passionate and unsatisfied. Nature had decided to torment this woman by causing her to fall in love (that succession of febrile interviews, searches, feints at indifference, nightlong

solitary monologues, ridiculous visions of remote happiness)
with the very type of youth that could not be attracted by
her, with cool impersonal learned or athletic young North-
erners, a secretary at the British Embassy or a Russian vio-
linist or a German archæologist. As though these trials were
not sufficient, society had added to them this aggravation,
that her Roman hostesses, conscious of this failing and wish-
ing to make sure that at their tables the Princess would dis-
play her finest flights, would intentionally include among
their guests the Princess's latest infatuation to whom
throughout the evening she would sing, like a swan, her
song of defeated love.

As a mere girl, if I may presume to reconstruct the
growth of her personality, she sensed the fact that there
was in her something that a little prevented her making
friends, namely, intelligence. The few intelligent people
who truly wish to be liked soon learn, among the disap-
pointments of the heart, to conceal their brilliance. They
gradually convert their keen perceptions into more practical
channels—into a whole technique of implied flattery of
others, into felicities of speech, into the euphemisms of
demonstrative affection, into softening for others the crude
lines of their dullness. All the Princess's perfection was an
almost unconscious attempt at making friends of those who
would first be her admirers, yet realizing that if she were
too artistic they would be dazzled but repelled, and that if
she were less than perfect they would dismiss her as a trivial
bright hysteric. For many years she had practiced this bab-
bling speech on her friends, unconsciously noting on their
faces which tones of the voice, which appropriate fleck of
the hands, which delayed adjectives were more and which
less successful. In other words she had achieved mastery of
a fine art, the all but forgotten art of conversation, under the
impetus of love. Like some panic-stricken white mouse in
the trap of a psychologist's experiment she had been seek-
ing her ends by the primitive rules of trial and error, only
to learn that at the last one is too bruised by the mistakes

to enjoy the successes. The exquisite and fragile mechanism of her temperament had not been able to stand the strain laid upon it, the double exhaustion of inspiration and woe; and the lovely being was already slightly mad. She grew daily more lightheaded and could be caught from time to time in moods that were variously foolish and pathetic. But her deepest wound was still to come.

James Blair and his notebooks were staying over in Rome after all. He had come upon some new veins of research. For him ten lifetimes would be all too short to pursue the horizons of one's curiosity. Think, he would say, it would take about ten years to work up the full critical apparatus to attack the historical problems surrounding the life of St. Francis of Assisi. It would take almost as many to get up the Roman road system, the salt roads and the wheat roads —God, the whole problem as to how the Rome of the Republic was fed. Another day he would be dreaming about starting on the eight or ten books in French and German on Christina of Sweden and her life in Rome; then one studied up Swedish and read the diaries and the barrels-full of notes; when one knew more about her than did anyone alive one passed on to her father and buried oneself for months in libraries to master the policies and the military genius of Gustavus Adolphus. Thus life stretched . . . bindings . . . bindings . . . catalogues . . . footnotes. One studied the saints and never thought about religion. One knew everything about Michelangelo yet never felt deeply a single work. James spent weeks of fascinated attention on the women of the Caesars and yet could scarcely be dragged to dinner at the Palazzo Barberini. He found all moderns trivial, and was the dupe of the historians' grand style which fails to convey the actuality (for Blair, the triviality) of their heroes. The present casts a veil of cheapness over the world: to look into any face, however beautiful, is to see pores and the folds about the eye. Only those faces not present are beautiful.

The fact is that quite early James Blair had been fright-

ened by life (in a way which the Princess, in a moment of
misery and inspiration, was to divine later with the cry:
What kind of a stupid mother could he have had?) and had
forever after bent upon books the flood tides of his energy.
At times his scholarship resembled panic; he acted as
though he feared that raising his eyes from the page he
would view the world, or his share in the world, dissolving
in ruin. His endless pursuit of facts (which had no fruit in
published work and brought no intrinsic aesthetic pleasure)
was not so much the will to do something as it was the will
to escape something else. One man's release lies in dreams,
another's in facts.

All this resulted in a real unworldliness, which with his
youth and learning and faintly *distrait* courtesy especially
endeared him to older women. Both Miss Grier and Mme.
Agaropoulos hovered about him with mothering delight and
sighed with vexation at his obstinate refusal to come and
see them. He reminded me of the lions that stare, unwink-
ing and unseeing, at the crowd about their cage, the crowd
that grimaces and waves admiring parasols, though the
beast disdains to pick up even a biscuit from such vulgar
givers.

At the time that the Princess's story begins he was en-
gaged in establishing the exact location of the ancient cities
of Italy. He was reading medieval descriptions of the Cam-
pagna and tracing through place names, through dried
watercourses, through cracked old paintings the exact posi-
tion of disused roads and abandoned towns. He was learn-
ing about the country's former plants and animals: he was
quite happy. Sometimes he made notes of all this, but for
the most part he preferred to learn the truth and then for-
get it.

When it began to get cold in his room he serenely made
use of mine, covering my tables with his vellum-bound
folios, standing his pictures against my wall, and strewing
my floors with his maps. He had dazzled one of the librar-

ians at the Collegio Romano with his allusions and had obtained the privilege of bringing the material home.

One day the Princess d'Espoli came to see me. Ottima admitted her. She came in upon James Blair who was kneeling on the floor crawling from city to city on some yellow crested maps. His coat was off; his hair was in a tangle, and his hands were gray with dust. He had never met her and did not like her clothes. He did not want to be drawn into a conversation and stood, handsome and sulky, his glances stealing to the maps on the floor. Explained that I was out. Might not be back before. Would not forget to tell that.

Alix didn't mind. She even asked for some tea.

Ottima had just come in to begin thinking about dinner. While tea was making Alix asked to have the maps explained to her. Now the Princess was more capable of entering into an enthusiasm for old cities than most of the several hundred women of her acquaintance; but short of a doctorate in archæology one does not enter upon such ground with James Blair. Coldly, haughtily, and with long quotations from Livy and Virgil, he harangued my guest. He dragged her remorselessly up and down the seven hills; he wrung her in and out of all the shifting beds of the Tiber. When I finally returned I found her sitting gazing at him over the edge of her teacup with a faintly mocking expression. She had not known that such a man was possible. Throughout the whole episode Blair had acted like nothing so much as a spoiled boy of seven interrupted in a game about Indians. It would be hard to say what had most captivated the Princess, but it was probably that trace of sturdy spoiled egotism. It might have been, in part, the cold douche of being unwelcome—she who was the delight of the most delightful people in Europe, who had never entered a door without arousing a whirlpool of welcome, who had never come too early nor left too late—suddenly she had tasted the luxury of being resented.

As soon as I arrived Blair took a swift and awkward departure.

But he's charming! He's charming! she cried. Who is he?

I told her briefly of his home, his progress through the universities, and his habits of study.

But he's extraordinary. Tell me: is he—shy, is he *boudeur* with everybody? Now perhaps I did something to annoy him? What could I have said, Samuele?

I hastened to reassure her. He's that way with everyone. And most people like him all the more for it. Especially older women. For example, Miss Grier and Mme. Agaropoulos adore him and all he does is to sit on their chairs inventing excuses for not coming to dinner.

Well, I'm not old and I like him. Oh, he is so rude! I could have slapped him. And he only looked at me once. He will have a hard time in life, Samuele, unless he learns to be more gracious. Isn't there anybody he likes, no? besides you?

Yes, he's engaged to a girl in the United States.

Dark hair or light?

I don't know.

Mark my words, he will be very unhappy, unless he learns to be more amiable. But think! what intelligence, what an eye! And how wonderful it is to see such an absence of trickery, you know, such simplicity. Does he live here?

No, he just brings his books in here when it's too cold in his own room.

He is poor?

Yes.

He is poor!

Not very poor, you know. When he really gets down to his last cent he can always find things to do at once. He's happy to be poor.

And he lives quite alone?

Yes. Oh, yes.

And he is poor. This caused her a moment's astonished reflection, until she burst out: But you know, that is not

right! It is society's duty . . . that is, society should be proud
to protect such people. Someone very gifted should be ap-
pointed to watch over such people.

But, Princess, James Blair values his independence above
everything. He doesn't want to be watched over.

They should be watched over in spite of themselves.
Look, you will bring him to tea some day. I am sure my
husband's library has some more old maps of the Campagna.
We have the bailiff's reports of the Espoli back into the
sixteenth century. Wouldn't that bring him?

Even surprised at herself, the Princess tried for a time to
talk of other things, but presently she returned to praise
what she called Blair's single-mindedness; she meant his
self-sufficiency, for while we are in love with a person our
knowledge of his weaknesses lies lurking in the back of our
minds and our idealization of the loved one is not so much
an exaggeration of his excellences as a careful "rationaliza-
tion" of his defects.

When next I saw Blair he wasted two or three hours be-
fore he got up courage to ask me who she was. He listened
darkly while I spoke my enthusiasm. At last he showed me
a note in which she asked him to drive with her to Espoli,
look over the estate, and to examine the archives. He was
to bring me if I wanted. James wished greatly to go; but he
was suspicious of the lady. He liked her and yet he didn't.
He was trying to tell me that he only liked ladies who didn't
like him first. He twisted the letter about trying to decide,
then going to the table wrote a note of refusal.

Then began what it is merely brutal to call a siege. Driv-
ing in the Corso, Alix would say to herself: There's nothing
unconventional in my stopping at his room to see if he
wants to drive in the Gardens. I could do as much for a
dozen men and it would be perfectly natural. I am much
older than he is, so much so that it would merely be an act
of . . . thoughtfulness. When she stood on the platform be-
fore his door (for she was not content to send up the
chauffeur) she would experience a moment of panic, wish-

ing to recall her ring, imagining when no one answered
that he was in hiding behind the closed door, listening, who
knows, in anger or contempt to her loud heartbeats. Or she
would debate all evening among the gilt chairs of her little
salon as to whether she might drop him a note. She would
count the days since last she had spoken to him and gauge
the propriety (the inner, the spiritual propriety, not the
worldly propriety: for the Cabalists the latter had ceased to
exist) of a new meeting. She was always coming upon him
by accident in the city (she called it her proof of the exist-
ence of guardian angels) and it was with these chance
meetings that she had generally to content herself. She
would attract his attention the length of the Piazza Venezia
and carry him to whatever destination he confessed to. No
one has ever been happier than Alix on these few occa-
sions when she sat beside him in her car. How docilely she
sat listening to his lecture; with what tenderness she se-
cretly noticed his tie and shoes and socks: and with what
intensity she fixed her gaze upon his face trying to imprint
upon her memory the exact proportions of his features, the
imprint that indifference retains so much better than the
most passionate love. There was a possibility that they
might have become the most congenial of friends, for he
dimly sensed that there was something in her that allied
her to the great ladies of his study, if she had only suc-
ceeded in concealing her tenderness. At the first signs of his
liking for her she would become so intoxicated with the in-
timation of cordiality that she would make some shy little
remark with a faintly sentimental implication; she would
comment on his appearance or ask him to lunch. And lose
him.

One day he gave her a book that had been mentioned in
their conversations. He did not stop to think that it was
the first move he had made spontaneously in the whole rela-
tion. Hitherto every suggestion, every invitation, had pro-
ceeded from her (from her, trembling, presuffering a re-
buff, lightly) and she longed for a first sign of his interest.

When this book was brought to her, then, she lost her balance; she thought it justified her in pushing the friendship on to new levels, to almost daily meetings, and to long comradely lazy afternoons. She never realized that in his eyes she was, first, an enemy to his studies, and second, that strange, hedged monster which all his wide reading had not been able to humanize: a married woman. She called once too often. Suddenly he changed; he became rude and abrupt. When she climbed his stairs he *did* hide behind the door and the bell rang in vain and with a menacing sound, though she had her ways of knowing he was in. She became terrified. Again she confronted that cavern of horror in her nature: she seemed always to be loving those that did not love her. She came to me, distraught. I was cautious and offered her philosophy until I could sound Blair in the matter.

Blair came to me of his own accord. He paced up and down the room, bewildered, revolted, enraged. His stay in Rome had become impossible. He no longer dared remain in his room and when he was out he clung to the side streets. What should he do?

I advised him to leave town.

But how could he? He was in the middle of some work that. Some work that. Damn it all. All right, he'd go.

I begged him before he went to come to dinner with me once when the Princess would be present. No, no. Anything but that. I, in turn, became angry. I analyzed the different kinds of fool he was. An hour later I was saying that the mere fact of being loved so, whether one could return it or not, put one under an obligation. More than an obligation to be merely kind, an obligation to be grateful. Blair did not understand, but consented at last on the difficult condition that I was not to reveal to the Princess that he was leaving for Spain on the very night of the dinner.

Of course, the Princess arrived early, so enchantingly dressed that I fairly floundered in admitting her. She held tickets for the opera; one no longer cared to hear *Salome,*

but *Petrushka* was being danced after it, at ten-thirty. Blair's train left at eleven. He arrived and played his most gracious. We were really very happy, all of us, as we sat by the open window, smoking and talking long over Ottima's excellent *zabiglione* and harsh Trasteverine coffee.

It was a continual surprise to me to see that in Blair's presence she was always a proud detached aristocrat. Even her faintly caressing remarks were such as would not be noticed if one had let them fall to someone with whom one was not secretly in love. Her fastidious pride even drove her to exaggerating her impersonality; she teased him, she pretended she did not hear when he addressed her, she pretended she was in love with me. It was only when he was not present that she became humble, even servile; only then could she even imagine calling on him unasked. At last she rose: It's time to go to the Russian Ballet, she said.

Blair excused himself: I'm sorry I must go back and work.

She looked as though a sword had gone through her. But surely, three-quarters of an hour with Stravinsky is a part of your work. My car's right here.

He remained firm. He too had a ticket for that night.

For a moment she looked blank. She had never met obstinacy under such conditions and did not know what to do next. After a moment she bent her head and pushed back her coffee cup. Very well, she said lightly. If you can't, you can't. Samuele and I shall go.

Their parting was grim. During the drive to the Constanzi she remained silent, fingering the folds of her coat; during the ballet she sat at the back of the box thinking, thinking, thinking, with staring dry eyes. At the close scores of friends pressed about her in the corridor. She became gay: Let's go to the cabaret run by the Russian refugees, she said. At the door of the cabaret she dismissed her chauffeur, telling him that her maid need not sit up for her. We danced for a long time in silence, her depression stealing back upon her.

When we left the hall the unfriendliest moonlight in the

world was flooding the street. We found a carriage and
started toward her home. But falling into the most earnest
conversation in all our acquaintance we failed to notice that
the carriage had reached her door and had been standing
there for some time.

Look, Samuele, do not make me go to bed now. Let me
go in and change my clothes quickly. Then let us drive
about and watch the sun come up over the Campagna.
Would that make you angry with me?

I assured her that it was just what I wanted and she
hurried into the house. I paid off the driver who was drunk
and quarrelsome and when she rejoined me we strolled
through the streets talking and gradually inviting a resigned
drowsiness. We had experimented with vodka at the cabaret
and the alcohol conferred upon our minds the same mood
that the moonlight was shedding upon the icy bubble of the
Pantheon. We strayed into the courtyard of the Cancelleria
and criticized the arches. We returned to my rooms for
cigarettes.

Last night I wasn't at all brave, she said, lying back in
the darkness on the sofa. I was desperate. That was before
I received your invitation. Could I go to see him or couldn't
I? A week had gone by. I asked myself would he feel . . .
well, insulted, if a lady knocked on his door at ten o'clock.
It was about ten o'clock. Really, there's nothing peculiar
about a lady's paying a perfectly impersonal call at about
nine-thirty. There's nothing self-conscious, Samuele, about
my being here now, for instance. Besides I had a perfectly
good reason for going. He asked me what I thought of La
Villegiatura, and since then I had read it. Now tell, my dear
friend, would it have been ridiculous from the American
point of view if I had . . . ?

Beautiful Alix, you are never ridiculous. But wasn't your
meeting with him tonight all the fresher, all the happier,
just because you hadn't seen him for so long?

Oh, how wise you are! she cried. God has sent you to
me in my trouble. Come by me and let me hold your hand.

Are you ashamed of me when you have seen me suffer so?
I suppose I should be ashamed. You see me without any
dignity. You have kind eyes and I am not ashamed in front
of you. I think you must have loved too, for you take all my
foolishness as a matter of course. Oh, my dear Samuele,
every now and then the thought comes over me that he
despises me. I have all the faults that he hasn't. When I
have this nightmare that he not only dislikes me but laughs
at me, yes, laughs at me, my heart stops beating and I blush
for hours at a time. The only way I can save myself then is
by remembering that he has said many kind things to me;
that he sent me that book; that he has asked after me. And
then I pray God very simply to put into his mind just a bit
of regard for me. Just a bit of respect for those things . . .
those things that other people seem to like in me.

We sat in silence for a time, her feverish hand plunged
deep into mine and her bright eyes gazing into the darkness.
At last she began speaking again in a lower voice:

He is good. He is reasonable. When I am analytical this
way I unfit myself for his loving me. I must learn to be sim-
ple. Yes. Look, you have done so much for me, may I ask
for one more favor. Play to me. I must get out of my mind
that wonderful music where Petrushka wrestles with him-
self.

I felt ashamed of playing before her who played far
better than any of us, but I drew out my folios and started
right through Gluck's *Armide*. I had hoped that the inept
performance would awaken an esthetic annoyance and so
shake her out of her dejection, but I presently saw that she
had fallen asleep. After a long and adroit diminuendo I left
the piano, turned on a shaded light near her, and stole off
into my own room. I changed my clothes and lay down
ready for the walk in which we were to see the sun rise. I
was trembling with a strange happy excitement, made up
partly of my love and pity for her, and partly from the mere
experience of eavesdropping on a beautiful spirit in the last
reaches of its pride and suffering. I was lying thus, proud

and happy in the role of guardian, when my heart suddenly stopped beating. She was weeping in her sleep. Sighs welled up from the depths of her slumber, hoarse protests, obstinate denials and moans followed one upon another. Suddenly her broken breathing ceased and I knew she was awake. There was a half-minute of silence; then a low call: Samuele.

Hardly had I appeared at the door before she cried: I know he despises me. He runs away from me. He thinks me a foolish woman who pursues him. He tells the servant to tell me he is out, but he stands behind the door and hears me go away. What shall I do? I'd better not live. I'd better not live any more. It's best, dear Samuele, that I go out right now, in my own way, and stop all this mistaken, this, this, futile suffering of mine. Do you see?

She had arisen and was groping for her hat. I really have courage enough tonight, she muttered. He is too good and too simple for me to worry him as I do. I'll just slip out. . . .

But Alix, I cried. We love you so. So many people love you.

You can't say that people love me. They like to greet me on the stairs. They like to listen and smile. But no one has ever watched under my window. No one has secretly learned what I do every hour of the day. No one has. . . .

She lay back on the sofa, her cheeks flushed and wet. I talked to her for a long time. I said that her genius was social, that she was made for the delight of company, that she relieved others of the weight of their own boredom, their disguised self-hatred. I promised her that she could find happiness in the exercise of her gift. I could see by a glimpse of her wet cheek turned away, that it calmed her to be told so, for she possessed the one form of genius that is almost never praised to its face. She grew more tranquil. After a pause she began talking in a dreamy tone:

I will leave him alone. I will never see him again, she began. When I was a girl and we lived on the mountains, Samuele, I had a pet goat named Tertullian that I loved

very much. One day Tertullian died. I would not be comforted. I was hateful and obstinate. The nuns with whom I went to school could do nothing with me and when it was my turn to recite I refused to speak. At last my dear Mother Superior called me into her room and at first I was very bad, even with her. But when she began to tell me of her losses I flung my arms about her and wept for the first time. As a punishment she made me stop everyone I met and say to them twice: *God is sufficient! God is sufficient!*

After a pause she added: I know that it can be true for other people, but I still wanted Tertullian. When is your patience with me coming to an end, Samuele?

Never, I said.

The windows were beginning to show the first light of dawn. Suddenly a little bell rang out nearby, a tinkle of purest silver.

Hush, she said. That's the earliest Mass at some church. Santa Maria in Trastevere is just around the corner. Hurry!

We let ourselves out of the palace and breathed the cold gray air. A mist seemed to hang low about the street; puffs of blue smoke lay in the corners. A cat passed us. Shivering but elated we entered the church joining two old women in wadded clothes and a laborer. The basilica loomed above, the candles of our side chapel picking out reflections in the curious marbles and the gold of the mosaics in the vast black cave. The service of the Mass was enrolled with expedition and accuracy. When we came out a milky light had begun to fill the square. The shutters of several shops were being lowered; drowsy passers-by made the diagonals, staggering; a woman was lowering her chickens in a basket from the fifth story for a long day's scratching.

We walked over to the Aventine, crossing the Tiber which twisted like a great yellow rope under a delicate fume. We stopped for a glass of sour blue-black wine and a paper bag of peaches.

For the time at least the Princess seemed to herself to

have forever closed her mind to even the remotest hope that she would ever see Blair again. Sitting on a stone bench on the gloomy Aventine while the sun shouldered its way up through plunging orange clouds, we mused. She seemed for a time to have fallen back into her old despondency; I resumed the arguments that spoke more glowingly of her gifts.

Suddenly she straightened up. All right. I will try it for you. I must do something. Where are you going today?

I murmured that Mme. Agaropoulos was giving a sort of a musicale: that she was introducing a young compatriot who claimed to have discovered the secret of ancient Greek music.

Write her a note. Telephone her. Ask her if I may come. I too shall learn about ancient Greek music. I shall be introduced to everyone there. I shall be asked to everyone's house. Listen, Samuele, since you say it is my talent I shall get to know everyone in Rome. I shall die of social engagements: Here lies the woman who never refused an invitation. I shall meet two thousand people in ten days. I shall lay myself out to please anybody on earth. And mind you, Samuele, if that does not nourish me, we shall have to finish trying, you know. . . .

Mme. Agaropoulos was staggered with joy when she discovered that the unhoped for, the improcurable Princess was coming to her house. Mme. Agaropoulos was not the slave of social categories, but she longed to frequent the Cabala, as some long for the next world. She assumed that in that company all was wit and love and peace. There one would find no silly people, none envious, none quarrelsome. She had met the Princess d'Espoli once and had ever since taken her as the type of person she would herself have been if she had been better looking, thinner and had had more time to read, little realizing that all these had been more in her power than in Alix', and that she had spoiled her own progress by a lazy kindliness, great kindliness but lazy.

The Princess called for me in her car at five o'clock. It

would be impossible for me to describe her clothes; it is enough to say that she had the most incredible power of supplying new angles, shades, lines, that interpreted her character. This aptitude received added éclat from her residence in Italy, for Italian women, though often more beautiful, lack both figure and judgment. They anxiously spend enormous sums in Paris and achieve nothing but bundles of rich stuffs that bulge or trail or blow about them in effects they half guess to be unsuccessful, and seek to repair with a display of stones.

We pursued the Via Po for a mile or two and alighted at the ugliest of its houses, an example of that modern German architecture that has done so much for factories. As we mounted the stairs she kept muttering. Watch me! Watch me! In the hall we found a host of late-comers standing with their fingers on their lip while from the drawing rooms there issued the sound of passionate declamation accompanied by the plucking of a lyre, the desolate *moto perpetuo* of an oriental flute and a rhythmic clapping of hands. In other words we had arrived too early; our campaign for meeting two thousand souls in ten days was being balked at the outset. Fretted we pushed on into the garden behind the house. Sitting down on a stone bench, with the tragic ode still faintly sounding in our ears, we gave our attention to the spectacle in the middle distance of a white-haired gentleman in a wheel chair overflowing with brightly colored shawls. This was Jean Perraye; I told the Princess of how Mme. Agaropoulos had found the saintly old French poet at the point of death, wrapped in shawls in a wretched little hotel at Pisa, and how by supplying him with tender interest, whole milk and a group of pet animals she had restored his muse, comforted his last years and effected his entrance into the French Academy. At this moment he was engaged in addressing a circle of attentive cats. These six cats, intermittently licking the fine silk of their shoulders, and casting polite glances at their patron, were gray angoras, the color of cigarette ash. We had read the poet's

latest book and knew their names: six queens of France. We practically dozed on the bench—the hot sunlight, the choruses of the *Antigone* behind and Jean Perraye's exordium to the queens of France and Persia before, would have made drowsy even those who had not passed a night of confession and tears.

When we came to ourselves the audition was over and the company, doubly noisy after music, was shouting its appreciation. We re-entered the house, hungry for pastry and encounters. A sea of hats, with scores of self-conscious eyes staring about in perpetual search of new salutations, marking down the Princess for their own; occasionally the large stomach of a senator or an ambassador swathed in serge and bound with a golden chain.

Who's the lady in the black hat? whispered Alix.

Signora Daveni, the great engineer's wife.

Fancy! Will you bring her to me or should you take me to her. No, I'll go to her. Take me.

Signora Daveni was a plain little woman presenting the high lifted forehead and fresh eyes of an idealistic boy. Her husband was one of Italy's foremost engineers, an inventor of many tremendous trifles in airplane construction and a bulwark of conservative methods in the rising storm of labor agitation. The Signora was on every philanthropic committee of any importance in the whole country and during the War had directed incalculable labors. The consciousness of her responsibilities combined with a touch of brusqueness from her humble extraction had brought her into many a short triumphant struggle with cabinets and senates and there are stories of her having sharply rebuked the vague, well-intentioned interferences of the royal ladies of Savoy. Yet these distinctions had only made her manners the simpler and her quick cordiality was continually deflating the deference that was paid to her. She dressed badly; she walked badly, her large feet pushing before her like those of some jar carrier in an upland village. It had been rather fine in uniform, but now that she must return to hats

and gowns and rings the consciousness of her lack of grace caused her much depression. Her home was in Turin, but she lived a great deal in Rome out among the open lots of the Via Nomentana and knew everyone. The Princess with the unexpectedness that lies in the very definition of genius turned the conversation upon the use of sphagnum moss as a surgical dressing. The diverse excellence of the two women glimpsed one another; the Princess was astonished to find such quiet mastery in a woman without a *de* and the Signora was amazed to find the same quality in a noblewoman.

I drifted off, but presently the Princess rejoined me. She is real, that woman. I am going to dinner with her Friday; so are you. Find me some more. Who is that blonde with the voice?

You don't want to know her, Princess.

She must be important with that voice; who is she?

She is the woman in the whole world who is most your opposite.

Then I must know her. Will she give me tea and introduce me to a dozen people?

Oh, yes, she'll do that. But you haven't a thing in common. She is a narrow British woman, Princess. Her only interest is in the Protestant Church. She lives in a little British hotel. . . .

But where does she get that *authority*—and the Princess made a gesture of perfect mimicry.

Well, I admitted, she has received the highest honors an Englishwoman can receive. She wrote a hymn and they made her a Dame of the British Empire.

You see I must be caught out of myself. I must meet her right now.

So I led her up to Dame Edith Steuert, Mrs. Edith Foster Prichard Steuert, author of "Far From Thy Ways, I Strayed," the greatest hymn since Newman's. Daughter, wife, sister, what not, of clergymen, she lived in the most exciting currents of Anglicanism. Her conversation ran on vacant liv-

ings and promising young men from Shropshire, and on the editorials in the latest *St. George's Banner* and *The Anglican Cry*. She sat on platforms and raised subscriptions and got names. She seemed to be forever surrounded by a ballet of curates and widows who at her word, rose and swayed and passed the scones. For she was the author of the greatest hymn of modern times and gazing at her one wondered when the mood could have struck this loud conceited woman, the mood that had prompted those eight verses of despair and humility. The hymn could have been written by Cowper, that gentle soul exposed to the flame of an evangelism too hot even for Negroes. For one minute in her troubled girlhood all the intermittent sincerity of generations of clergymen must have combined in her, and late at night, full of dejections she could not understand, she must have committed to her diary that heartbroken confession. Then the fit was over, and over forever. It was a telling example of that great mystery in religious and artistic experience: the occasional profundity of nobodies. Dame Edith Steuert on being presented, straightened visibly to show that she was not impressed by the title. With a candor that was another surprise, Alix asked her if she might use her name as reference on her nephew's application for entrance into Eton College. To be sure the nephew was in Lyons, but if Dame Edith would permit the Princess to call upon her some afternoon she would bring some of the boy's letters, photographs and sufficient apparatus to convince her that he was a student recommendable. Friday afternoon was agreed upon, and the Princess rejoined me for new introductions.

So it went on for an hour. The Princess had no method; each new encounter was a new problem. Within three minutes the meeting became an acquaintance, and the acquaintance a friendship. Little did the new friends guess how strange it was to her. She kept asking me what their husbands "did." It delighted her to think that their husbands did anything; she had never guessed that one could meet

such people and smiled amazedly like a girl about to meet a real, printed poet. A doctor's wife, the wife of a man in rubber, fancy. . . . Toward the end of the afternoon her enthusiasm waned. I feel a little dusty, she whispered. I feel very Bovary. To think that all this has been going on in Rome without my knowing it. I'll go and say good-bye to Mme. Agaropoulos—*tiens,* who is that beautiful lady? That is an American, isn't it? Quick.

For the only time in my life I saw the beautiful and unhappy Mrs. Darrell who had come to take leave of her Roman friends. As she entered the room a silence fell upon the company; there was something antique, something Plato would have seized upon in the effect of her beauty. She made much of it, with that touch of conceit that we allow to a great musician listening exaggeratedly to his own perfect phrasing, or to the actor who sets aside author, fellow players and the fable itself, in order to improvize the last excessive moments of a death scene. She dressed, she glanced, she moved and spoke as only uncontested beauties may: she too revived a lost fine art. To this virtuosity of appearing, her illness and suffering had added a quality even she could not estimate, a magic of implied melancholy. But all this perfection of hers was unapproachable; none of her dearest friends, not even Miss Morrow, dared to kiss her. She was like a statue in a solitude. She pre-suffered her death, and her spirit was set in defiance. She hated every atom of a creation where such things were possible. The next week she was to retire to her villa at Capri with her collection of Mantegnas and Bellinis and to live through four months with their treacherous love affair and to die. But this day in the serenity of the selfishness that was her perfection and the selfishness that was her illness she effaced the room.

He would have loved me if I had looked like that, breathed Alix into my ear, and sinking into a retired chair covered her mouth with her hand.

Mme. Agaropoulos took Helen Darrell's fingertips a little

timidly and led her to the finest chair. No one seemed able
to say anything. Luigi and Vittorio, sons of the house, went
up and kissed her hand; the American ambassador ap-
proached to compliment her.

She is beautiful. She is beautiful, muttered Alix to her-
self. The world is hers. She will never have to suffer as I
must. She is beautiful.

It would not have consoled the Princess if I had explained
to her that Helen Darrell, having been admired extrava-
gantly from the cradle had never been obliged to cultivate
her intelligence to retain her friends and that, if I may say
it respectfully, her mind was still that of a schoolgirl.

Fortunately the flutist was still there to play and during
the performance of the Paradise music from Orpheus
scarcely a pair of eyes in the room left the newcomer's face.
She sat perfectly straight, allowing herself none of the be-
coming attitudes which music suggests to her kind, no ardent
attention, no starry-eyed reverie. I remember thinking she
marked too deliberately the antisentimental. When the
music was over she asked to be taken to say good-bye, for
the present, to Jean Perraye. From the window I could see
them alone together, with the gray cats, queens of France,
moving meaninglessly about them. One wonders what they
said to one another as she knelt beside his chair: as he said
later, they loved one another because they were ill.

Alix d'Espoli would not stir until she knew that Mrs.
Darrell had left the house and garden. All her suffering had
rushed back upon her. She pretended to be sipping a cup
of tea while she gathered herself together. I understand
now, she murmured hoarsely. God has never meant me to
be happy. Others may be happy with one another. But I
shall never be. I know that now. Let us go.

Then began what was ever after known to the Cabala as
Alix aux Enfers. She would lunch at a tiny pension with
some English spinsters; stop in at some studio in the Via
Margutta, pass through a reception at an Embassy; dance
till seven at the Hotel Russie as the guest of some cosmetic

manufacturer's wife; dine with the Queen Mother; hear the last two acts of the opera in Marconi's box. Even after that she might feel the need of finishing the day at the Russian cabaret, perhaps contributing herself a monologue to the program. She no longer had any time to see the Cabala and it watched her progress with terror. They begged her to come back to them, but she only laughed at them with her bright febrile eyes and dashed off into her new-found whirlpools. Long after when some Roman name arose in their conversation they would all cry: Alix knows them! To which she would reply coolly: Of course I know them, and a roar would arise from the table. The acquaintances she was now pursuing for distraction, I had long since pursued for study or from simple liking; but she soon outstripped me by the hundreds. I went to a few engagements with her, but often enough we would come upon one another in ludicrous situations; whereupon we would retire behind a door and compare notes as to how we got there. Did Commendatore Boni ask a few people to the Palatine? she was there. Did Benedetto Croce give a private reading of a paper on George Sand? we glimpsed one another gravely in that solemn air. She lost a comb in defense of Reality at the stormy opening of Pirandello's Sei Personaggi in Cerca d'Autore; at Casella's party for Mengelberg, who had been surpassing himself at the Augusteo, dear old Bossi stood on her train and the sound of ripping satin caught the enraptured ear of a dozen organists.

When the bourgeoisie discovered that she was accepting invitations there was a tumult as of many waters. Most of her hostesses assumed that she would not have come to them were it not for the fact that better doors were beginning to be closed against her, but fair or foul they would accept her. And they had her at her best; the faint touch of frenzy that was driving her on only rendered her gift the more dazzling. People who had spent their lives laughing at tiresome jokes were now given something to laugh at. She would be begged to do this or that "bit" which had become

famous. Have you heard Alix do the Talking Horse? No, but she did the Kronprinz in Frascati for us last Friday. Oh, aren't you lucky!

For the first time she was seeing something of artists and among them she was enjoying her liveliest successes. The underpainting of her misery which especially these days rendered her wit so magical was much clearer to them than to the manufacturers. They never failed to mention it and their love led them to paying her the strangest tributes which at the time she was in too great a daze to stop and value.

For a while I thought she was enjoying all this. She would laugh so naturally over some of the accidents of the days. Moreover I noticed that she was forming some very rare attachments and I hoped that the friendship of Signora Daveni or of Duse or of Besnard would be able to comfort and finally reconcile her. But one evening I was suddenly shown how utterly ineffectual this plunging about the jungle was.

After a month's absence James Blair wrote me from Spain that he had to come back to Rome, even if it were only for a week. He promised to see no one, to keep up side streets and to get out as soon as it was possible.

I wrote him back in the strongest profanity that it was impossible. Go anywhere else. Don't fool with such things.

He replied, no less angry, that he could move about the earth as freely as everybody else. Whether I liked it or not he was coming to Rome the following Wednesday and nothing would stop him. He was on the traces of the Alchemists. He wanted to know all that was left of the old secret societies and his search was leading to Rome. Since I could do nothing to prevent his coming I could at least devote my energies to concealing it. I took almost ridiculous precautions. I even saw to it that Mlle. de Morfontaine had Alix in Tivoli over the week-end and that Besnard had her sitting for a portrait most of the mornings. But there is a cer-

tain spiritual law that requires our tragic coincidences. Which of us has not felt it? Take no precautions.

The seer whom Blair had returned to visit, Sareptor Basilis, lived in three rooms on the top floor of an old palace in the Via Fontanella di Borghese. Rumor had it that he could make lightning play about his left hand and that when his meditations approached ecstasy he could be seen sitting among the broken arcs of a dozen rainbows; and that as you mounted the dark stairs you fought your way through the welcoming ghosts as through a swarm of bees. In the front room where the meetings were held (Wednesdays for adepts, Saturdays for beginners) one was awed by discovering a circular hole in the roof that was never closed. Under it had been laid a zinc-lined depression that carried off the rain water and in this depression stood the master's chair.

Long meditation and ecstatic trances had certainly beautified his face. His blue-green eyes, not incapable of sudden acuteness, drifted vaguely about under a smooth pink forehead; he had the bushy white eyebrows and beard of Blake's Creator. Except for his long walks he seemed to have no private life, but sat all day and night under the hole in the roof, lending an ear to a whispering visitor, writing slowly with his left hand, or gazing up into the sky. A host of people from every walk of life sought him out and held him in reverence. He gave no thought to practical necessities, for his admirers, spiritually prompted, were continually leaving significant looking envelopes beside him on the zinc-lined depression. Some left bottles of wine and bars of bread, and brown silk shirts. The only human occupation that arrested his attention was music, and it is said that he would stand by the door of the Augusteo on the afternoon of a symphony concert and wait for some passer-by, spiritually prompted, to buy him a ticket. If none came, he would continue on his way without bitterness. He composed music himself, hymns for unaccompanied voices which he affirmed he had heard in dreams. They were written in a notation resembling our own, but not sufficiently so to allow

of transcription. I have puzzled for hours over the score of a certain *Lo, where the rose of dispersion empurples the dawn*. This motet for ten voices, a chorus of angels on the last day, began plainly enough with the treble clef on five staves, but how was one to interpret a sudden shrinkage of the horizontal lines to two in all parts? I humbly approached the master on this subject. He replied that the effect of the music at that point could only be expressed by a radical departure from standard notation; that the economy of staves denoted an acuity of pitch; that the note on which my thumb was reposing was an E, a violet E, and E of the quality of a lately warmed amethyst . . . music powerless to express . . . ah . . . the rose of dispersion empurples. At first the nonsense in which he moved and thought enraged me. I invented opportunities for provoking his absurdity. I improvised a story about a pilgrim who had come up to me in the nave of the Lateran and told me it was God's will that I should return with him to a leper colony in Australia. Dear Master, I cried, how shall I know if this be my real vocation? His answer was not clear. I was told that destiny herself was the mother of decision, and that my vocation would be settled by events not by consideration. In the next breath I was bidden to do nothing rashly; to lay my ear over the lute of eternity and to plan my life in harmony with the cosmic overtones. During the course of a year thousands of women visited him, of every rank, and in every sort of perplexity, and to each one he offered the comforts of metaphor. They came away from him with shining faces; these phrases were beautiful and profound to them; they wrote them in their diaries and murmured them over to themselves when they were tired.

Basilis was attended by two homely sisters, the Adolfini girls. Lise must have been thirty and Vanna about twenty-eight. They say that he ran across them in the Italian quarter of London where they were serving as attendants in a ballet school. Penury and abuse had left them scarcely the human semblance. Every evening at eleven when they had

unlaced the last slipper of the night class, treated the floor
with tallow, polished the bars and tied up the chandelier,
they went around the corner to the Café Roma for a thim-
bleful of coffee to sip with their bread. Here Basilis was to
be found, a photographer's assistant with grandoise preten-
sions. He was vice-president of the Rosicrucian Mysteries,
Soho Chapter, a group of clerks, waiters and idealistic bar-
bers who found compensation for the humiliations they un-
derwent by day in the glories they ascribed to themselves
by night. They met in darkened rooms, took oaths with one
hand resting on the works of Swedenborg, read papers on
the fabrication of gold and its metaphysical implications,
and elected one another with great earnestness to the offices
of arch-adept and *magister hieraticorum*. They corresponded
with similar societies in Birmingham, Paris and Sydney, and
sent sums of money to the last of the magi, Orzinda-Mazda
of Mount Sinai. Basilis first discovered his power over the
minds of women when he fell into the habit of talking to
the two mute sisters in the café. They listened wide-eyed
to his stories of how some workmen near Rome, breaking
by chance into the tomb of Cicero's daughter, Tulliola, dis-
covered an ever-burning lamp suspended in mid-air, its
wick feeding on Perpetual Principle; of how Cleopatra's
son Cæsarion was preserved in a translucent liquid "oil of
gold," and could be still seen in an underground shrine at
Vienna; and of how Virgil never died, but was alive still on
the Island of Patmos, eating the leaves of a peculiar tree.
The wonder stories, the narrator's apocalyptic eyes, the ex-
citement of being spoken to without anger, and the occa-
sional offer of vermouth bewitched the sisters. They be-
came his unquestioning slaves; with the money they had
saved up he opened a temple where his gift met extraordi-
nary success. The girls left the ballet school and became
doorkeepers in the house of their lord. The new leisure
into which they entered, the sufficient food, the privilege of
serving Basilis, his confidence and his love, combined to

constitute a burden of happiness almost too great to be
borne. Happiness is in proportion to humility: the humility
of the Adolfini girls was so profound that there was in it no
room for the expression of gratitude or surprise; in the face
of it food could not fatten them nor love soften their bony
features; not even when after some altercation with the
London police Basilis and his handmaidens removed to their
native Rome. To be sure the master in turn never confessed
his indebtedness to the girls for their silent and skillful min-
istration. Even in love he was impersonal; they merely pro-
vided him with that mood of gentle satiety of the senses
which is an indispensable element of the philosopher's
meditation.

It was under this skylight then that Blair and I sat at
about eleven-thirty, waiting for the public séance to begin.
We were early, and leaning back against the wall we
watched the little group of visitors that one by one moved
up to the unboxed confessional that was the master's ear. A
clerk with watery eyes and trembling hands; a stout lady
of the middle class, gripping a large shopping purse and
talking with great rapidity about her *nepote;* a trim little
professional woman, probably a lady's maid, stuffing a tiny
handkerchief into her mouth as she sobbed. Basilis' eyes
seldom strayed to his visitors' faces, while he dismissed
them with a few measured grave sentences his glance
revealed nothing but its serene abstraction. Presently a
younger woman, heavily veiled, crossed the floor swiftly to
the empty chair beside him. She must have been there
before, for she lost no time in greetings. Under deep emo-
tion she pleaded with him. A little surprised by her vehe-
mence he interrupted her several times with the words *Mia
figlia.* The reproaches only increased her energy, and brush-
ing back her veil with her hand in order to thrust her face
into the sage's she revealed herself as Alix d'Espoli. Terror
went through me; I seized Blair's arm and made signs that
we were to escape. But at that moment the Princess with a

gesture of anger, as though she had come, not so much to ask the sage's counsel, as to announce a determination, rose and turned to the door. Unerringly her eyes met ours, and the rebellious light died out, to be replaced by fear. For a moment the three of us hung suspended on one cord of horror. Then the Princess collected herself long enough to tincture the despairing contraction of her mouth with a smile; she bowed to us deliberately in turn and passed almost majestically from the room.

At once I returned home and wrote her a long letter, using the whole truth as a surgeon in an extremity would resort to a wholesale guesswork with the knife. I never received an answer. And our friendship was over. I had often to meet her again, and we even came finally to have agreeable conversations together, but we never mentioned the affair and there was a glaze of impersonality over her eyes.

From the night she had seen us in Basilis' rooms the Princess gave up her social researches as abruptly as she had begun them. Nor did she ever go to the Rosicrucian again. I heard that she was attempting the few remaining consolations that lie open to affliction: she took to the fine arts; she climbed up ladders respectfully placed for her in the Sistine Chapel and stared at the frescos through magnifying glasses; she resumed the culture of her voice and even sang a little in public. She started off on a trip to Greece, but came back without any explanations a week later. There was a hospital phase during which she cut off her hair and tiptoed about among the wards.

At last the beating of the wings, the darting about the cage, subsided. She had come to the second stage of convalescence: the mental pain that had been so great that it had to be passed into the physical and that expressed itself in movement, had now sufficiently abated to permit her to think. All her vivacity left her and she sat about in her friends' homes listening to their visitors.

Little by little then her old graces began to reappear.

First a few wry sarcasms, gently slipping off her tongue; then some rueful narratives in which she appeared in a poor light; then ever so gradually the wit, the energy, and last of all the humor.

The whole Cabala trembled with joy, but pretended to have noticed nothing. Only one night when for the first time at table she had returned to her gorgeous habit of teasing the Cardinal on his Chinese habits, only once on leaving the table did he take her two hands and gaze deep into her eyes with a significant smile that both reproached her for her long absence and welcomed her back. She blushed slightly and kissed the sapphire.

I, who know nothing about such things, assumed that the grand passion was over and dreaded any moment seeing her interesting herself in some new Northerner. But one little incident taught me how deep a wound may be.

One afternoon at the villa in Tivoli we were standing on the balcony overlooking the falls. Whenever she was left alone with me her charm abated; she seemed to be fearing that I might attempt a confidence; the muscles at the coi ners of her mouth would tighten. We were joined from the house by a well-known Danish archæologist who began to discourse upon the waterfall and its classical associations. Suddenly he stopped and turning to me, cried:

Oh, I have a message for you. How could I have forgotten that! I met a friend of yours in Paris. A young American named Blair—let me see, was it Blair?

Yes, Doctor.

What a young man! How many of you Americans are like that? I suppose you never met him, Princess . . . ?

Yes, replied Alix, I knew him too.

Such intelligence! He is surely the greatest instinctive scholar I have ever met, and, believe me, perhaps he is all the greater for never putting anything down on paper. And such modesty, Princess—the modesty of the great scholar that knows that all the learning one human head can hold is but a grain of dust. I spent two whole nights over his

notebooks and I honestly felt as though I had brushed against a Leonardo, really, a Leonardo.

We both stood rapt, listened to the waves of happy praise when suddenly I became aware that the Princess had fainted beside me with a happy smile upon her face.

Book Four: Astrée-Luce and the Cardinal

THERE was a vague understanding among the members of the Cabala that I was engaged upon the composition of a play about Saint Augustine. None of my friends had ever seen the manuscript (even I was surprised to come upon it every now and then at the bottom of my trunk), but it was treated with enormous respect. Mlle. de Morfontaine especially kept asking about it, kept walking about on tiptoes and glancing at it sideways. It was to this that she was alluding in the note I received soon after Blair's frightened departure: Try and arrange to come up to the Villa for a few weeks. It is perfectly quiet until five o'clock every afternoon. You can work on your poem.

It was my turn for a little peace. I had so recently passed through the desperations of Marcantonio and Alix. I sat holding the note for a long while, my wary nervous system begging me to be cautious, begging me to make sure that no hysterical evenings could possibly lie behind it. Here was a place where it was perfectly quiet until five o'clock every afternoon. It was five o'clock every morning that I wanted to be reassured about. You can work on your poem. Surely the only vexation that could proceed from that wonderful lady lay exactly there—she would be asking me every

111

morning about the progress on the Third Act. It would be good for me to be hectored about my play. And what wonderful wines she stored. To be sure, the lady was mad, indubitably mad. But mad in a nice way, with perfect dignity; decently mad on a million a year. I wrote her I would come.

What could have been more reassuring than the first days? Mornings of sunlight when the dust settled thicker on the olive leaves; when the terraced hillside seemed to be powdering away; when no sound reached the garden but the cry of a carter in the road, the cooing of doves stepping high along the eaves of the gardener's shed, and the sound of the waterfall with its mysterious retardations, a sound of bronze. I ate luncheon alone under a grape arbor. The rest of the day was spent in roaming over the hills or among the high chairs of Astrée-Luce's rich and curious library.

From the middle of the afternoon one sensed the approach of dinner. One felt the gradual tightening of the chord of formality until, like the bursting of some pyrotechnical bomb, full of dazzling lights and fascinating detail, the ceremony began. For hours there had come a hum as of bees from the wing of the house that contained the kitchen; there followed the flights of maids and hairdressers through the corridors, the candlelighter, the flower-bearers. The crushing of gravel under the window announces the arrival of the first guests. The major-domo clasps on his golden chain and takes his place with the footmen at the door. Mlle. de Morfontaine descends from her tower kicking her train about to teach it its flexibility. A string quartet on the balcony begins a waltz by Glazounov as subdued as a surreptitious rehearsal. The evening takes on the air of a pageant by Reinhardt. One passes to the salon. At the head of the table behind peaks of fruits and ferns, or cascades of crystal and flowers, sits the hostess, generally in yellow satin, her high ugly face lighted with its half-mad surprise. She generally supports a headdress of branching feathers and looks like nothing so much as a bird of the Andes blown to that bleakness by the coldest Pacific breezes.

I have described how Miss Grier brooded over her table and placed herself to hear every word whispered by her remotest guest. Astrée-Luce followed a contrary procedure and heard so little of what was said that her very guest of honor was often obliged to resign all hope of engaging her attention. She would seem to have been caught up into a trance; her eyes would be fixed on some corner of the ceiling as though she were trying to catch the distant slamming of a door. Generally some Cabalist held the opposite end of the table: Mme. Bernstein, huddled up in her rich fur cape, looking like an ailing chimpanzee and turning from side to side the encouraging amiability of her grimace; or the Duchess d'Aquilanera, a portrait by Moroni, her dress a little spotty, her face a little smudged, but somehow evoking all the passionate dishonest splendid barons of her line; or Alix d'Espoli making passes with her exquisite hands and transforming the guests into witty and lovable and enthusiastic souls. Miss Grier seldom came, having festivals of her own to direct. Nor was it often possible to invite the Cardinal, since any company to meet him must be chosen with infinite discretion.

Almost every evening after the last guest had left the hill or retired to bed, and the last servant had finished finding little things to adjust, Astrée-Luce and I would descend into the library and have long talks over a drop of *fine*. It was then that I began to understand the woman and to see where my first judgments had been wrong. This was not a silly spinster of vast wealth nourishing a Royalist chimera; nor the sentimental half-wit of the philanthropic committees; but a second century Christian. A shy religious girl so little attached to the things about her that she might awake any day and discover that she had forgotten her name and address.

Astrée-Luce has always illustrated for me the futility of goodness without intelligence. The dear creature lived in a mist of real piety; her mind never drifted long from the contemplation of her creator; her every impulse was good-

ness itself: but she had no brains. Her charities were immense but undigested; she was the prey of anyone who wrote her a letter. Fortunately her donations were small, for she lacked the awareness to be either avaricious or prodigal. I think she would have been very happy as a servant; she would have understood the role, have seen beauty in it, and if her position had been full of humiliation and trials it would have deeply nourished her. Sainthood is impossible without obstacles and she never could find any. She had heard over and over again of the sins of pride and doubt and anger, but never having felt even the faintest twinge she had passed through the earlier stages of the spiritual life in utter bewilderment. She felt sure that she was a wicked sinful woman, but did not know how to go about her own reform. Sloth? She had been on her knees an hour every morning before her maid appeared. So difficult, so difficult is the process of making oneself good. Pride? At last after intense self-examination she thought she had isolated in herself some vestiges of pride. She attacked them with fury. She forced herself to do appalling things in public in order to uproot the propensity. Pride of appearance or of wealth? She soiled her sleeves and bodice intentionally and suffered the silent consternation of her friends.

She read the lessons so literally that I have seen her give away her coat time after time. I have seen her walk miles with a friend who asked her to go as far as the road. Now I was to learn that her fits of abstraction were withdrawals into herself for prayer and adoration, and often caused by almost ludicrous incidents. I was no longer left to wonder why all references to fish and fishing sent her off into the clouds; I realized that the Greek word for fish was the monogram of her Lord and acted upon her much as a muezzin's call acts upon a Mohammedan. A traveler spoke flippantly of the pelican; at once Mlle. de Morfontaine repaired to her mental altar and besought its guest not to grieve at the disrespect paid to one of His most vivid symbols. Strangest illustration of all was shown me a little later. One

day she chanced to notice on my hall table an envelope
which I had addressed to Miss Irene H. Spencer, a teacher
of Latin in the high schools at Grand Rapids, who had
come over to put her hand on the Forum. At once Astrée-
Luce insisted on meeting her. I never told Miss Spencer
why she had been tendered so amazing a luncheon, why
her hostess had listened so breathlessly to her trivial trave-
logues, nor why on the following day a golden chain hung
with sapphires had been left at the pension for her. In fact
Miss Spencer was a devout Methodist and would have been
shocked to learn that IHS meant anything.

Strange though Mlle. de Morfontaine was, she was never
ridiculous. Such utter refusal of self can by sheer excess be-
come a substitute for intelligence. Certainly she was able
to let fall remarkable penetrating judgments, judgments that
proceeded from the intuition without passing through the
confused corridors of our reason. Though she was exasperat-
ing at times, at others she would abound in almost mirac-
ulous perceptions of one's needs. People as diverse as Donna
Leda and myself had to love her, one moment almost with
condescension as to an unreasonable child, and the next
with awe, with fear in the presence of something of infinite
possibility. Whom were we entertaining unawares? Might
this, oh literally! be an . . . ?

This then was the being whom I came to know during
those late conversations in the library over a drop of *fine*.
The talk was leisurely, full of pauses and to no point, but
my bruised instinct could no longer escape the conviction
that there was some deeply important matter that she
wished to submit to me. I soon foresaw that I was not to
rest. My dread of the revelation however was heightened by
the obvious difficulty Astrée-Luce found in coming to the
point. Finally instead of trying to avoid the discussion I
tried to provoke it; I thought I could help here and there
by opening veins of conversation that might surprise her
problem. But no. The happy moment hung off.

One evening, she asked me abruptly whether it would

greatly interfere with my work if we were to move to Anzio
for a few days. I replied that I should like nothing better.
All I knew of Anzio was that it was one of the resorts on the
sea, a few hours from Rome, the site of one of Cicero's villas,
and near Nettuno. She added a little anxiously that we
should have to go to a hotel, a very poor hotel at that, but
that it was out of season and there were ways in which she
could supply some of the deficiencies of the service. A little
foresight could prevent my being too uncomfortable.

So one morning we climbed into the large plain car she
reserved for traveling and drove westward. The back seat
served as a warehouse. One glimpsed a maid, a prie-dieu,
a cat, a real panel by Fra Angelico, a box of wines, fifty
books and some window curtains. I found out later that
there had been a lavish assortment of caviar, paté, truffles
and ingredients for rare sauces by which, with a discourag-
ing failure to understand me, she intended to supplement
the resources of a tourists' hotel. She drove, herself, and in
nothing did Heaven's interest in her reveal itself more
clearly. First we stopped at Ostia so that I might see the
veritable spot where the last scene of my wretched play
took place. We read aloud the page of Augustine and I si-
lently vowed to renounce forever any notion of rephrasing
it.

On our first evening at Anzio a cold wind blew in from
the sea. The vines and shrubs whipped the houses; the
lamps of the cafés about the square swung cheerlessly over
wet tables; one could not escape the desolate slap-slap of
the waves against the sea wall. But we both had a taste for
such weather. We decided at about six o'clock to walk
to Nettuno, returning for dinner at half-past nine. We
wrapped ourselves in rubber and started off, leaning against
the wind and spray and feeling strangely exhilarated. For
a time we walked in silence, but entering at last that por-
tion of the road that lies between the high walls of the
villas, Astrée-Luce began to talk:

I have told you before, Samuele (the whole Cabala had

followed the Princess in calling me Samuele), that the hope
of my life is to see a king reigning in France. How impossi-
ble such a thing seems now! No one knows it better than I.
But everything I love most is improbable. And it is the
fact that it seems so untimely that will help us most when
we come to prepare the Divine Right of Kings as a dogma
of the Church. What anger there will be, what sneers! Even
important churchmen will rush down to Rome and beg us
not to upset the progress of Catholicism by such a move.
There will be controversies. All the newspapers and the
reviews will be shouting and weeping and laughing and the
whole basis of democratic government, the folly of repub-
lics, will be aired. Europe will be cleansed of the poison in
its side. We have nothing to fear from debates. The people
will turn to God and ask to be ruled by those houses of His
choosing. —However, I am not trying to convince you of it
now, Samuele; I am only stating it so as to lead up to some-
thing else. You are a Protestant; does this make you impa-
tient? Are you tired of me?

No, no, please. I am very interested, I replied.

At that moment our road brought us again to the water's
edge. We stood for a moment on a parapet looking down
on the loud sea that plunged about on the washing stones
of a village. It began to rain. Astrée-Luce was gripping the
iron railing watching the steam that rose from the waves;
she was crying silently.

Perhaps, she continued, as we returned to our journey,
you can imagine the tenth part of my disappointment as I
watch the Cardinal getting older, and myself, and the na-
tions falling deeper and deeper into error, and so little done.
He can help us. He seems to me to have been especially
created to help us. I do not forget his work in China. It was
heroic. But what a greater work remains for him in Europe.
Year follows year and still he sits up there on the Janiculum,
reading and walking in the garden. Europe is dying. He will
not stir.

At the time I was deeply moved. The rains and her tears

and the puddles and the slapping noises of the water against
the sea wall had begun to affect me. All the voices of nature
kept repeating: Europe is Dying. I would have liked to stop
and have a good meaningless cry myself, but I had to listen
to the voice beside me:

I cannot understand why he does not write. Perhaps I am
not meant to understand. I know he believes that the uni-
versality of the Church is imminent. I know that he believes
that a Catholic Crown is the only possible rule. But he does
not stir to help us. All we ask from him is a book on the
Church and the States. Think, Samuele, his learning, his
logic, his style—but you have never heard him preach? His
irony in controversy and his amazing perorations! What
would be left of Bossuet? The constitutions of the re-
publics of the world would be tossed about—you will for-
give me if I seem disrespectful to your great country—
tossed about like eggshells. His book would not be just a
book fallen from the press: it would be a force of nature; it
would be the simultaneous birth of an idea in a thousand
minds. It would be placed at once on the canon and bound
up with the Bible. And yet he spends his day among rose-
bushes and rabbits and reading histories of this and that. I
want to do this in my lifetime; I want to arouse this great
man to his task. And you can help me.

I was excited. The air was full of a divine absurdity. Here
was someone who was not afraid of using superlatives. This
was being mad on a great scale. It would be hard to come
down to ordinary living after these intoxicating threats
against the presidents of this world and the binderies of the
British Bible Society. I tried to think of something to say. I
mumbled something about willingness.

She did not notice my inadequacy. It seems to me, she
continued, that I have at last discovered one of the causes
of his reluctance to join us. But first, tell me how he is re-
garded by the various Romans whom you have met. What
is his legend among people who do not know him?

Here I was frightened. Could *she* have heard? How could any of those strange rumors have reached her?

But she would learn nothing from me. I took leave of good faith and told her all the favorable reports I had heard. Simple souls were captivated by the thought that apart from a few major obligations he lived on sixty-five lire a week; that he spoke twelve languages; that he enjoyed polenta; that he visited in certain Roman homes (her own, in particular) without ceremony; that he was translating the Confessions and the Imitation into exquisite Chinese. I knew Romans who so loved the very thought of him that they took walks to the Janiculan Hill solely to peer between his garden gates and lurked about the house in the hope of giving their children an opportunity to kiss his ring.

Astrée-Luce waited in silence. At last she said with only a trace of reproach:

You are trying to spare me, Samuele. But I know. There are other stories about him. His enemies have been at work systematically poisoning his prestige. We know that there is no one in Rome who is kinder, more humble, higher minded; but among the common people he has almost the reputation of a monster. Some people have been at work spreading such rumors deliberately. And the Cardinal has heard of them: through the whispering of servants or by cries in the road, or by anonymous letters, in all sorts of ways. He exaggerates this attitude. He feels that he is in a hostile world. It has made his old age tragic. And that is why he will not write. Yet it is within our power to save him still. —But look! There is a francobollo shop. Let us get some cigarettes and find some place to sit down. It makes me so happy to talk of this!

Provided with cigarettes we looked about for a wineshop. Our wish evoked one at the next curve in the road, a smoky uncordial tunnel, but we sat down before the glasses of sour inky wine and continued our conspiracy. Astrée-Luce confessed that if the ill-odor had become attached to the Cardinal's name through any real delinquencies on his part, we

could not have hoped to dissipate it. Truth in such subtle regions as rumor would be unalterable. But she knew that the aspersions in this case were the result of a clever campaign and she felt sure that a countercampaign could still sweeten his reputation. In the first place our enemies had taken advantage of the Italians' prejudice against the Orient. An Italian enjoys the same delicious shudder at the sight of a Chinese that an American boy does at the mention of a trap door over a river. The Cardinal had returned from the East yellow, unwrinkled. His walk troubled them. It was easy to build upon this, to pass the whisper along the Trasteverine underworld that he kept strange images, that animals (his gardenful of rabbits and ducks and guinea fowl) could be heard shrieking late at night, that his faithful Chinese servant had been seen in all sorts of terrifying attitudes. Next, his frugal life stirred their imaginations. Everyone knew he was fabulously wealthy. Rubies as big as your fist and sapphires like doorknobs, where were they? Did you ever go up to the gate of the Villino Wei Ho? Come with me Sunday. If you sniff hard enough you can get the strangest odor, one that will leave you drowsy for days and give you dreams.

We were to change all this. We sat there choosing a committee of rehabilitation. We were to have magazine articles, newspaper paragraphs. His eightieth birthday was approaching. There would be presentations. Mlle. de Morfontaine was donating a Raphael altarpiece to his titular church. But most of all we would send out agents among the people, telling them of his goodness, his simplicity, his donations to their hospitals, and ever so faintly his sympathy with socialistic ideas; he was to be the People's Cardinal. We had anecdotes of his snubbing the arrogant members of the College, of his defending a poor man who had stolen a chalice from his church. China was to be recreated for the Trasteverines. And so on. We were to prop up the Cardinal so that the Cardinal could prop up Europe.

When we returned to the hotel that night Astrée-Luce

seemed to have grown ten years younger. Apparently I was
the first person to whom she had outlined her vision. She
was so eager to be at work that she suddenly asked me if I
minded packing up again and going back to Tivoli that
night. We could the better start work in the morning. What
she really wanted was the exhilaration and fatigue of driv-
ing (her terrible driving) before she went to bed. So we
put back into the car the maid, the Fra Angelico, the in-
gredients for sauces and the cat, and returned to the Villa
Horace at about two in the morning.

The Cardinal was not to know that we were putting up a
scaffolding about his good name and freshening the colors;
but we were to persuade him not to do some of the things
that particularly antagonized the public. The very next
morning Astrée-Luce shyly begged me to go and see him.
She did not know why, but she had a vague idea that now
I knew her hopes my eyes would be open to significant de-
tails.

I found him as one could find him every sunny day the
year round, seated in the garden, a book on his knee, a
reading glass in his left hand, a pen in his right, a head of
cabbage and a Belgian hare at his feet. A pile of volumes
lay on the table beside him: *Appearance and Reality,*
Spengler, *The Golden Bough, Ulysses,* Proust, Freud. Al-
ready their margins had begun to exhibit the spidery nota-
tions in green ink that indicated a closeness of attention that
would embarrass all but the greatest authors.

He laid aside his magnifying glass as I came up the path
of shells. *Eccolo, questo figliolo di Vitman, di Poe, di Vilson,
di Guglielmo James—di Emerson, che dico!* What do you
want?

Mlle. de Morfontaine wants you to come to dinner Fri-
day night, just the three of us.

Very good. Very nice. What else?

What do you want, Father, for your birthday? Mlle. de
Morfontaine wants me to sound you tactfully. . . .

Tactfully! —Samuelino, walk to the back of the house and

tell my sister you will stay to lunch. I am to have a little Chinese vegetable dish. Will you have that or a little risotto and chestnut paste? You can buy yourself something solid on the way down hill. How is Astrée-Luce?

Very well.

A little illness would be good for her. I am uncomfortable when I am with her. There are certain doctors, Samuele, who are not happy when they are talking to people in good health. They are so used to the supplicating eyes of patients that say: Shall I live? In the same way I am ill at ease in the company of persons who have never suffered. Astrée-Luce has eyes of blue porcelain. She has a fair pure heart. It is sweet to be in the company of a fair pure heart, but what can one say to it?

There was St. Francis, Father . . . ?

But he had been libertine in his youth, or thought he had. —Senta! Who can understand religion unless he has sinned? who can understand literature unless he has suffered? who can understand love unless he has loved without response? *Ecc!* The first sign of Astrée-Luce's being in trouble was last month. There is a certain Monsignor who wants her millions for his churches in Bavaria. Every few days he climbs the hill to Tivoli and breathes into her ear: *And the rich He hath sent empty away.* The poor child trembles and pretty soon Bavaria will have some enormous churches, too ugly for words. Oh, you know, there is for every human being one text in the Bible that can shake him, just as every building has a musical note that can overthrow it. I will not tell you mine, but do you want to know Leda d'Aquilanera's? She is a great hater, and they say that during the Pater Noster she closes her teeth tight upon: *Sicut et nos dimittimus debitoribus nostris.*

At this he laughed for a long time, his body shaking in silence.

But was not Astrée-Luce devoted to her mother? I asked.

No, she has had no losses. That was when she was ten. She has poetized her, that is all.

Father, why did not that literal faith of hers carry her to a convent?

She promised her dying mother she would stay alive to put a Bourbon on the throne of France.

How can you laugh, Father, at her devotion to. . . .

We old men are allowed to laugh at things that you little students may not even smile about. Oh, oh, the house of Bourbon. Would you be surprised if I gave up my life to reviving the royal brother-and-sister marriages of Egypt? Well! It is not more impossible.

Dear Father, won't you write one more book? Look, you have about you all the greatest books of the first quarter of my century. . . .

And very stupid they are, too.

Won't you make us one. Such a great book, Father Vaini. About yourself, essays like Montaigne—about China and about your animals and Augustine. . . .

Stop! No! Stop at once. You frighten me. Do not you see that the first sign of childhood in me will be the crazy notion that I should write a book? Yes, I could write a book better than this ordure that your age has offered us (and with a sharp blow he pushed over the tower of books; the Belgian hare gave a squeal as he barely escaped being pinned under Schweitzer's *Skizze*). But a Montaigne, a Machiavelli . . . a . . . a . . . Swift, I will never be. How horrible, how horrible it would be if you should come here some day and find me writing. God preserve me from the last folly. Oh, Samuele, Samuelino, how bad of you to come here this morning, and awaken all the vulgar prides in an old peasant. No, don't pick them up. Let the animals soil them. What is the matter with this twentieth century of yours . . . ? You want me to compliment you because you have broken the atom and bent light? Well, I do, I do. —You may tell our rich friends, tactfully, that I want for my birthday a small Chinese rug now reposing in the window of a shop on the Corso. It would be unbecoming for me to say more than that it is on the left as you approach

the Popolo. —The floor of my bedroom is getting colder every morning, and I always promised myself that when I became eighty I might have a rug in my bedroom.

What went wrong?

The first hour was delightful. The Cardinal always ate very little (never meat) and that with preposterous slowness. If his soup took him ten minutes his rice required half an hour. To be sure the elements of trouble were present merely in these friends' characters. They were so different that just to hear them talking together had an air of high comedy. First, Astrée-Luce made the mistake of referring to the Bavarian Monsignor. She suspected that the Cardinal was out of sympathy with any plans she might have of helping the Church in that direction; she longed to talk over with him the problem of her wealth and its disposition, but he refused to give her the least advice. He had endless resources of ingenuity in evading the subject. As Rome was arranged at that time it was most important that he should exercise no influence on that aspect of his friend's life. Yet he allowed it to be seen that he knew she would handle the matter foolishly. It ailed him to see such an enormous instrument for progress drift down the wind of ecclesiastical administration.

Now we must remember that it was the eve of his eightieth birthday. We have already seen that the event had precipitated a flood of amused bitterness. As he said later, he should have died at the moment of leaving his work in China. The eight years that had elapsed since then had been a dream of increasing confusion. Living is fighting and away from the field the most frightening changes were taking place in his mind. Faith is fighting, and now that he was no longer fighting he couldn't find his faith anywhere. This vast reading was doing something to him. . . . But most of all we must remember his terror at the thought that the people of Rome hated him. He would leave, in dying, a memory without affection and without dignity. An anony-

mous letter had told him that even in Naples children were
kept in good behavior with threats that the Yellow Cardinal
would skin them. If one were young one would laugh at
such a rumor, but being old one grew cold. He was leaving
a world where he was shuddered at for a world that was no
longer as distinct as it had been, but which might yet have
this consolation that he would not be able to look down
from it and see the people surreptitiously spitting on the
endings in *issimus* that would compose his epitaph.

Before I knew it we were in the middle of a wrangle
about prayer. Astrée-Luce had always longed to hear the
Cardinal discourse upon abstract matters. She had often
tried to draw him into arguments on the frequent com-
munion and on the invocation of the saints. He had once
whispered to me that she was trying to extract from him
the materials for a calendar, such sweet manuals as she
could buy in the Place Saint Sulpice. Every word of his
was sacred. She would not have hesitated to put him in a
Church window with St. Paul. It was only after a few mo-
ments that she became aware that he was saying some
rather strange things. Could that be Doctrine? If anything
he said was difficult all she had to do was to try hard to
grasp it. Truth, new truth. So she listened, first with sur-
prise, then with mounting terror.

He was launched upon the paradox that in prayer one
should never ask for anything. His dialectic was doing an
incredible work. He had decided to be Socratic and was
asking Astrée-Luce questions. He wrecked her on several
orthodox assumptions. Twice she fell into heresy and was
condemned by the councils. She seized hold of St. Paul but
the epistle broke in her hand. She came to the surface for
the third time but was struck by a Thomist fragment. The
previous week the Cardinal had been called to the death-
bed of a certain Donna Matilda della Vigna, and it was
poor Donna Matilda who was now dragged forth to point
the argument. Exactly what had the survivors been praying

for? Astrée-Luce was easily routed from the more obvious positions. She became frightened. Presently she rose:

I don't understand. I don't understand. You are joking, Father. Aren't you ashamed of saying such things to bewilder me, when you know how I value everything you say.

Look, then, continued the Cardinal. I shall ask Samuele about this. As he is only a Protestant it will be very easy to entangle him. Samuele, may I assume that God may have intended Donna Matilda to die before long anyway?

Yes, Father, for she died that very night.

But we thought that if we prayed very sincerely we might change His mind.

Why . . . there is authority for our hoping that in extremities our prayer may. . . .

But she died. Then we were not sincere enough! Or persevering enough! Good! Sometimes He grants and sometimes He doesn't, and Christians are expected to pray hard on the chance that this is one of the times He might relent. What a notion! Astrée-Luce, what a thought!

Father, I can't stay and hear you talk this way.

What a view of these things. Listen. It is incredible that He should change His mind. Because we frightened mortals are on the carpet? Oh! You are a slave to the idea of bargain. The money changers are still in the temple!

Here Astrée-Luce, gone quite white, returned to the arena with one more brave venture: But, Father, you know He answers the requests of a good Catholic. Then she added in a lower voice with tears in her eyes. But you were there, dear Father. If you had deeply wished it you could have altered the. . . .

Here he half rose from his chair, crying with terrible eyes: Insane child! What are you saying? I? *Have I no losses?*

Now she flung herself upon the floor before him. You have been saying these things to prove me. What is the answer? I will not let you go until you tell me. Dear Father, you know that prayer is answered. But your clever ques-

tions have upset all my old . . . old. . . . What is the answer?

Come, sit down, my daughter, and tell me yourself. Think!

This went on for another half-hour. I grew more and more astonished. Mere prayer as a problem was soon left far behind. It was the idea of a benignant power behind the world that was being questioned now. For the Cardinal it was an exercise in rhetoric, sharpened by his temperamental skepticism on the one hand and by his latent resentment against Astrée-Luce on the other. It was a kind of questioning that would have had no effect on sound intellectual believers. It was disastrous for Astrée-Luce because she was a woman without a reason who just this once was trying to reason. She would so have liked to have been a deep thinker, and when she fell it was through her desire to be a different person.

It went on and on. At every fresh proposal he would now cry Bargain! A Bargain! and point out that her prayers sprang from fear or the greed for comfort. Astrée-Luce was going to pieces. I moved over behind her chair and pleaded with the Cardinal by gesture. Was he tormenting her out of caprice? Did he realize her devotion to himself?

At last she seemed to have a light:

My head is in a whirl. But I know now what you mean me to answer. We may not ask for things, or people, or relief from sickness, but we may ask for spiritual qualities; for instance for the advancement of the Church . . . ?

Vanity! Vanity! How many years have we been praying for a certain good thing? What have statistics shown us?— I refer to the conversion of France.

With a cry Astrée-Luce rose and left the room. I took upon myself to protest to him.

She is foolish, Samuelino. You cannot call those convictions deep that were overturned with straws. No, trust me. This is for her good. I have been a confessor too long to go astray here. She has the spiritual notions of a schoolgirl.

She must be fed on some harsher bread. Understand that she has never suffered. She is good. She is devout. But as I told you the other day, just by accident she has never known trouble.

Just the same, Eminence, I know her well enough to know that this very moment she is in her chapel, clinging to the altar rails. She will be depressed for weeks.

But just at that moment Astrée-Luce returned. Her manner was agitated and artificially gracious. Will you excuse me if I go to bed now? she asked. (She never called him Father again.) Please stay and talk with Samuele.

No, no. I must be going. But before I go let me tell you one thing. The real truths are difficult. At first they are forbidding. But they are worth all the others.

I shall be thinking over what we have said. I . . . I . . . excuse me, if I ask you something?

Yes, my child, what is it?

Promise me you weren't joking.

I wasn't joking at all.

Did I really hear you say that the prayers of good men are of no . . . ? However. Good night. You will forgive my slipping away now?

So they took their leaves.

I went to bed worried. I was worrying about Astrée-Luce. Was she going to lose her faith? What do bystanders do in such a case? The loss of one's faith is always comic to outsiders, especially when the loser is in fine health, wealth, and of a fairly sound mind. The loss of any one or all of these has a sort of grandeur; Astrée-Luce should have the loss of her faith depend on one of the others. It's not a thing one loses in fine weather.

I was wakened from a troubled sleep by a discreet but continuous knocking upon my door. It was Alviero, the major-domo.

Madame says will you please dress and come to her in the library, please.

What's the matter, Alviero?

I do not know, Signorino. Madame have not slept all night. She have been in the church hitting the floor.

All right, Alviero, I'll be there in a minute. What time is it?

Three o'clock and one-half, Signorino.

I dressed rapidly and hurried to the library. Astrée-Luce was still in her gown. Her face was white and drawn; her hair was disheveled. She came toward me with both hands extended: You will forgive my sending for you, won't you? I want you to help me. Tell me: were you made unhappy by the strange things Cardinal Vaini said after dinner?

Yes.

Have you Protestants ideas on these things?

Oh, yes, Mlle. de Morfontaine.

Were his ideas new? Is that what everyone is thinking?

No.

Oh, Samuele, what has happened to me! I have sinned. I have sinned the sin of doubt. Shall I ever have peace again? Can the Lord take me back after I have had such thoughts? Of course, of course, I believe that my prayers are answered, but I have lost . . . the . . . the reason why I believe it. Surely, there is a key here. Perhaps it's just one word. All you have to do is find the one little argument that makes the whole thing natural. Isn't it strange! I've been looking here (and she pointed at the table which was covered with open books, the Bible, Pascal, the Imitation) but I don't seem to be able to put my finger on the right place. Sit down and try and tell me, my dear friend, what arguments there are that God hears us speak and will answer us.

I talked to her for quite a long while, but achieved nothing. Perhaps I even made it worse. I told her that I was sure that she still believed. I showed her that the very fact that she was distressed about it proved that she was furiously believing. After an hour of this wrestling she seemed a little comforted, however, and picking up a fur coat went back to her cold chapel and prayed diligently for faith until the morning.

At about ten she appeared in the garden and asked me to read a note that she was sending to the Cardinal. I was to pass on it. Dear Cardinal Vaini, I will always honor you above all my friends. I think you love me and wish me well. But in your great learning and multiple interests you have forgotten that we who are not brilliant must cling to our childhood beliefs as best we may. I have been inexpressibly troubled since yesterday evening. I want to ask a favor of you: that you indulge my weakness to the extent of not touching upon matters of belief when I am with you. It gives me great pain to have to ask you this. I beg of you to understand it as apart from any personal feelings of un-friendliness. I hope that I may grow strong enough to talk of these matters with you again.

It was a very bad letter, but that was perhaps due to the content. I suggested shyly that she omit the last sentence. So she copied it and sent it off by a special messenger.

Soon the day came for the end of my stay in the Villa. She came up to my room for a last talk.

Samuele, you have been with me during the saddest days of my life. I cannot deny that all interest has gone out of living for me. I still believe, but I don't believe as I used to. Perhaps it was not right that I went through life as I did. Now I know that I rose up every morning full of unspeakable happiness. It seldom left me. I had never thought before that my beliefs in themselves were unbelievable. I used to boast that they were, but I did not know what I was saying. Now hours come to me when I hear a voice saying: There is no prayer. There is no God. There are people and trees, millions of them both, every moment dying. —You will come and see me again, won't you, Samuele? Have I made it very unpleasant for you in the house?

When I reached my rooms in Rome I found three letters from the Cardinal asking me to come and see him at once. As I entered the gate he came toward me eagerly:

How is she? Is she well?

No, Father, she is in great trouble.

Come inside, my son. I must speak to you.

When we entered his study, he closed his door behind him, and said with great emotion: I want to say to you that I have sinned, greatly sinned. I cannot rest until I have tried to repair the harm I have done. Look, look at this letter she has written me.

Yes, I have seen it.

Her letter forbids my explaining what I meant. Is there no way I can reassure her?

There is only one way now. You must regain all her confidence before you touch on such matters again. You must come and go about her house as though nothing had happened—

Oh, but she will never ask me again!

Yes, she is having you all to dinner quite soon, Alix, Donna Leda, and M. Bogard.

Thanks be to God! I thank Thee, I thank Thee, I thank Thee, I thank Thee. . . .

May I speak quite boldly, Eminence?

Yes. I am a poor old man, all mistakes. Speak to me as you like.

If you go, take great care not to let slip any remark on religious matters. I beg of you, do *not* try to reinstate yourself with some orthodox comments. She might misunderstand one little word and think you were attacking her faith again. It is very serious. Your ideas are not orthodox, Father, and if you said an orthodox thing it would not sound sincere and that would be worst of all. But if you come and go simply and affectionately, she will lose her horror of you—

Horror of me!

Yes, and very gradually, perhaps after a year, you may be able—

But I may not live a year!

Es muss sein!

This struck him as humorous and ruefully he sang Beethoven's phase, adding: All the avenues of life lead to that.

Es muss sein. I should have stayed in China. (Here he fell
silent for a while, heaving deep sighs and staring at his
yellow hands.) God has chosen to take away my reason. I
am an idiot, falling into every ditch. Oh, that I had died
long ago—and yet I cannot die until I have righted myself.
Hand me that red book behind you. There are two plays
about old men, Samuelino, that grow dearer every day to
an old man. There is your Lear, and—and opening *Oedipus
at Colonus* he translated slowly:

Generous son of Aegeus, to the gods alone old age and
death come never. But all else is confounded by all-master-
ing time. The strength of earth decays and the strength of
the body. Faith dies. Distrust is born. Among friends the
same spirit does not last true . . . and bowing his head he
let the book fall to the floor. *Es muss sein.*

I did not go to that dinner. I dined alone with Miss Grier
in the city, but at about ten we drove out to Tivoli to sit
with the company. As we went I outlined to her discreetly
the relations that now existed between two of her best
friends: Oh, how stupid he is, she cried. How cruel! What
a lot he has forgotten. Don't you see that the whole thing
rests, not on the abstract question as to whether her prayers
may be answered, but on the question as to whether ONE
prayer may be answered? Her prayer for France. . . .
Doesn't he believe such things are real to other people?

He thinks that a little doubt will be good for her. He de-
scribes her as the woman who has never suffered.

He is in his dotage. I am so angry I am ill.

At this moment our car drew aside to let pass another

hurrying by toward Rome. This was Mlle. de Morfontaine's great ugly traveling car and the Cardinal was in it.

There he is now, cried Miss Grier. They must have broken up early.

Something's happened, I said.

Yes, something has very likely happened, God forgive us. If everything were all right, Alix would be driving back with him. Our wonderful company is dissolving. Alix no longer trusts us. Leda is losing her good old common sense. Astrée-Luce has quarreled with the Cardinal. I'd better leave Rome and go back to Greenwich.

As we approached the Villa we became aware that something indeed must have happened. The front door was open. The servants were gathered in the hall whispering in front of the closed doors of the drawing rooms. As we entered these opened and Alix, Donna Leda and Mme. Bernstein appeared supporting a sobbing Astrée-Luce. They led her up the stairs to her tower. Miss Grier, without questioning the servants as to what had happened, gently urged them to return to their rooms. We passed into the drawing room just in time to see M. Bogard leaving by another door and looking considerably shaken. We sat down in silence, our thoughts full of foreboding. Simultaneously we became aware of a faint odor of powder and smoke and glancing about my eye fell upon a rent near the ceiling beneath which a little pile of white dust had collected on the floor. Mme. Bernstein hurried in and, after closing the door carefully behind her, came toward us:

Not a soul must hear of this. Oh, this must be kept so quiet. What a thing to happen! Anything is possible after this. What a blessing that no servants were in the room when. . . .

Miss Grier asked her several times what had happened.

I know nothing. I can hardly believe my own senses, she cried. Astrée-Luce must have gone mad. Elizabeth, will you believe me when I tell you that we were sitting here quietly

over our coffee— Look, look! I didn't see that hole in the ceiling before!—Isn't it all frightful?

Please, Anna, please tell us what happened!

I am. —There we were sitting over our coffee, talking in low voices of this and that, when suddenly Astrée-Luce went over to the piano, picked up a revolver from among the flowers and shot at the good Cardinal.

Anna! is he hurt?

No. It didn't even come near him. But what a thing to happen! What on earth could have made her do such a thing! We were friends—we were all such good friends. I do not understand anything.

Try and think, Anna: did she say anything when she fired at him, or before she fired?

That's the strangest of all. You won't believe me. She called out: The devil is here. The devil has come into this room. At the Cardinal!

What had he been saying?

Nothing! Merely everyday things. We had been telling stories about the peasants. He had been telling us about some peasants he had come across on his walks outside S. Pancrazio.

Suddenly Alix appeared: Elizabeth, go to her quickly. She wants to see you. She is alone.

Miss Grier hurried out.

Alix turned to me:

Samuele, you know the major-domo better than we do. Will you go and tell him that Astrée-Luce has had a nervous breakdown. That she thought she saw a burglar at the window, and that she fired at him. It is so important for the dear Father's sake that no hint of this gets about.

I went out and found Alviero. He knew the explanation was insufficient, but utterly devoted to the whole Cabala he could be trusted to dress the story at exactly the points that would most convince the other servants.

Alix did not understand what lay back of the shot, but she was able to recall the conversation that had led up to

it. The Cardinal had told the following simple story, an in-
cident he had witnessed in one of his walks outside the city
wall:

A farmer wished to break his six-year-old daughter of
crying. One afternoon he led her by the hand to the center
of a marshy waste, thickly grown with wiry reeds well
above the child's head. There he had suddenly flung away
her hand, saying: Now are you going to cry any more? The
child, with a last rush of contrary pride and with a begin-
ning of fear, started to cry. All right, shouted the father,
we don't want any bad children in our house. I'm going to
leave you here with the tigers. Good-bye. And jumping out
of the child's sight, he repaired to a wineshop at the edge of
the waste and sat down for an hour's card playing. The
child strayed about from hummock to hummock, wailing.
In due time the father reappeared and taking her affec-
tionately by the hand led her home.

That was all.

But Astrée-Luce had never learned, as the rest of us have,
to harden her heart slightly before stories of cruelty or in-
justice. She may have had no losses of her own, but she had
always been ready to expose her imagination to the full
force of other people's wrongs. Such an anecdote would
have drawn from others a sigh, a swift protective contrac-
tion of the lips and a smile of gratitude for its safe conclu-
sion. But to Astrée-Luce it was the vividest reminder that
the God, whose business it was to brood over the world
ministering to the discouraged and the mistreated, was no
more. The Cardinal had killed him. There was no one left
to soothe the horse that has been beaten to death. The
kittens that the boys fling against the wall have no one to
speak for them. The dog in torment that keeps his eyes upon
her face, and licks her hands even while his eyes grow dim,
shall have no comforter but her. This was not a casual story
the Cardinal was telling: it concealed a covert allusion to
their conversation of the preceding week. It was a taunt.
It was a sort of curse. Look at the world without God, he

was saying. Get used to it. If she had lost God, oh how clearly she had gained the Devil. Here he was triumphing in this lacerating story. Astrée-Luce went over to the piano, picked up a revolver from the flowers and shot at the Cardinal, crying: The Devil has come into this room!

As the Cardinal drove back that night he kept repeating to himself the words: Then these things are real! It had required Astrée-Luce's shot to show him that belief had long since become for him a delectable game. One piled syllogism on syllogism, but the foundations were diaphanous. He strained to remember what faith was like when he had had it. He kept dragging before his mind's eye the young priest in China exhorting the families of the Mandarins. That was himself. Oh, to retrace the way. He would go back to China. If he could look again on the faces that were serene with a serenity he had given them, perhaps he could steal it back. But side by side with this hope was a terrible knowledge: no words could describe the conviction with which he saw himself guilty of the greatest of all sins. Murder was child's play compared to what he had done.

The firing of the shot had done as much for Astrée-Luce. On awakening, her terror lest she had harmed him, later her fear that she had fallen out of reach of his forgiveness was greater than had been her misery in a world without faith. It was given to me to carry from each to the other the first messages of anxious affection. When Astrée-Luce and the Cardinal discovered that they were living in a world where such things could be forgiven, that no actions were too complicated but that love could understand, or dismiss them, on that day they began their lives all over again. This reconciliation was never put into words, in fact it remained to the end merely in a state of hope. They longed to see one another again, but it would have been impossible. They dreamed of one of those long conversations that one never has on earth, but which one projects so easily at midnight,

alone and wise; words are not rich enough nor kisses suffi-
ciently compelling to repair all our havoc.

He received permission to return to China, and sailed
within a few weeks. Several days after leaving Aden he fell
ill of a fever and knew that he was to die. He called the
Captain and the ship's doctor to him and told them that if
they buried him at sea they would have to face the indigna-
tion of the Church, but that they would be fulfilling his
dearest wish. He took what measures he could to shift upon
himself the blame for such an irregularity. Better, better to
be tossing in the tides of the Bengal Sea and to be nosed by
a passing shark, than to lie, a sinner of sinners, under a
marble tomb with the inevitable *insignis pietate,* the in-
escapable *ornatissimus.*

Book Five: The Dusk of the Gods

WHEN my time came to leave Rome I set aside several days for the last offices of piety, piety in the Roman sense. I wrote a note to Elizabeth Grier arranging for a long late talk on the eve of my departure. There are some questions I want to ask you, I said, which no one can answer. Then I went to the Villino Wei Ho and sat for an hour with the Cardinal's sister. The guinea fowl were less vocal than formerly and the rabbits were still hobbling about the garden looking for a gleam of violet. I went to Tivoli and peered through the iron gates of the Villa Horace. Already it looked as though no one had lived there for years. Mlle. de Morfontaine had returned to her estates in France and was living in the closest retirement. They said that she opened no letters, but I wrote her a note of farewell. I even spent an afternoon in the stifling rooms of the Palazzo Aquilanera, where Donna Leda imparted to me in great confidence the news of her daughter's engagement. Apparently the young man was unable to produce any cousins from among the draughty courts of Europe; his family was merely Italian; but he owned a modern palace. At last a bathroom was to make its appearance in the house of Aquilanera. How time flies.

My most considerable observance was a trip to Marc-
antonio's grave. I found it by the village cemetery near
the Villa Colonna-Stiavelli. Consecrated ground had been
denied the boy, but in her bewilderment and love the
mother had contrived a false wall of stones and briars that
seemed to include his grave among those of souls that the
Church felt safe in recommending at the Judgment Day.
Here I sat down and prepared to think about him. I was
perhaps the only person in the world who understood what
had brought him there. The last office of friendship would
be to think about him. But some birds were singing; a man
and his wife were cultivating the ground in the next field;
the sunlight was heavy. Hard as I tried I could not keep my
thoughts on my friend; it was not difficult to recall his fea-
tures or to meditate about dissipation; but really elegiac re-
flection escaped me, Marcantonio. I drove back to Rome
ashamed of myself. But it had been a delightful day in the
country, unforgettable June weather.

There was one association I could not renew; I could not
go to see Alix. Whenever I met her by chance the barrier
of her lowered eyelids told me that we would never have
long talks again.

Closing the apartment was melancholy enough. Ottima
and I spent hours in packing, our heads bent over our boxes
and full of our imminent farewells. She was going back to
her wineshop at the corner. Long before I bought a ticket
she had begun to pray for those in peril on the sea and to
notice the windy days. After an exhausting struggle with
myself I decided to give her the police dog. Kurt's affections
were equally divided between us; in Europe or in America
he would pine for an absent friend. Ottima and Kurt would
grow old together in a life filled with exquisite mutual at-
tentions. I could swear that before I went to the hotel on
that last night Kurt knew I was taking leave of him. There
was a grandeur I fell short of in the way he faced an inevi-
table situation. He placed one paw on my knee and looked
to the right and left in deep embarrassment. Then lying

down he placed his muzzle between his paws and barked twice.

I found Elizabeth Grier at midnight sitting in the library that Blair had catalogued. Her small neat head looked tired and after some desultory conversation I made a move to go. She reminded me that I had intended asking her some questions.

My questions are harder to put than to answer.

Try.

Miss Grier, did you know that you and your friends were called the Cabala?

Yes, of course.

I shall never know such a company again. And yet there seems to be some last secret about you that I've never been able to seize. Haven't you anything to tell me that will show me what you all meant, how you found one another, and what made you so different from anyone else?

Miss Grier took a few minutes off to think this over. She sat smiling strangely and stroking with her fingertips the roots of her hair beside her left temple. Yes, she said, but it will only make you angry if I tell you. Besides it's very long.

It's not long, Miss Grier, but you will insist on making it long because you hate to have your guests leave before dawn. However, I shall listen to you for hours if you promise to throw some light on the Cabala and the dinners at the Villa Horace.

Well, first you must know, Samuele, that the gods of antiquity did not die with the arrival of Christianity. —What are you smiling at?

You're adorable. You have resolved to make your explanation last forever. I asked about the Cardinal and you have gone back to Jupiter. What became of the gods of antiquity?

Naturally when they began to lose worshipers they began to lose some of their divine attributes. They even found themselves able to die if they wanted to. But when one of them died his godhead was passed on to someone else; no

sooner is Saturn dead than some man somewhere feels a
new personality descending upon him like a strait jacket,
do you see?

Now, Miss Grier!

I told you it would make you angry.

You don't pretend this is true?

I won't tell you whether this is true, or an allegory, or
just nonsense. —Next, I am going to read you a strange
document that came into my hands. It was written by a
certain Hollander who became the god Mercury in 1912.
Will you listen?

Has it anything to do with the Cabala?

Yes. And with you. For I sometimes think that you are
the new god Mercury. Take some of that claret and listen
quietly.

I was born in a Dutch parsonage in 1885. I was the de-
spair of my home and the terror of the village, a little liar
and thief in the full enjoyment of my health and wit. My
real life began one morning of my twenty-seventh year
when I experienced the first of a series of violent pains in
the center of my head. This was my deification. Some un-
tender hand was emptying the cup of my skull of its silly
gray brains and filling it with the divine gas of instinct. My
body too had its part in this; each microscopic cell had to be
transformed; I was not to fall sick or grow old or die, save
when I chose. As historian of the gods I have to keep record
of an accident whereby, through some monstrosity in spir-
itual law, an Apollo of the seventeenth century failed to
completely deify: one arm remained corruptible.

It was then that I discovered the first great attribute of
our nature, namely that to wish for a thing is to command
it. It does not suddenly fall into your hand or descend in a
rosy mist upon your carpet. But circumstances start a dis-
creet ballet about you and the desired thing comes your
way through the neatest possible imitation of natural law
and probability. Scientists will tell you that they have never

seen the sequence of cause and effect interrupted at the instance of prayer or of divine reward or retribution. Do they think, the fools, that their powers of observation are cleverer than the devices of a god? The poor laws of cause and effect are so often set aside that they may be said to be the merest approximations. I am not merely a god but a planet and I speak of things I know. So I stole my mother's savings from under her pillow and went to Paris.

But it is at Rome that we were last worshiped under our own names, and it is thither that we are irresistibly called. During the journey I gradually discovered further traits of my new being. I woke up mornings to discover that bits of information had been deposited in my mind overnight, the enviable knowledge, for instance, that I had the power of "sinning" without remorse. I entered the Porta del Popolo one midnight in June, 1912. I ran the length of the Corso, leaped the fence that surrounds the Forum, and flung myself upon the ruins of my temple. All night in the fine rain I tore my clothes in joy and anguish, while up the valley came an interminable and ghostly procession singing my hymns and hiding me in a tower of incense. With the coming of dawn my worshipers vanished and wings no longer fluttered at my heels. I climbed out of the sunken ruins and went out into the misty streets in search of some coffee.

Godlike I never reflect; all my actions arrive of themselves. If I pause to think I fall into error. During the next year I made a great deal of money on the races at Parioli. I speculated in motion pictures and African wheat. I went into journalism and the misrepresentations I sowed will have deferred Europe's recovery from the War many scores of years. I love discord among gods and men. I have always been happy. I am the happiest of the gods.

I had been called to Rome to serve as the gods' messenger and secretary, but more than a year had passed before I recognized even one. The Church of Santa Maria sopra Minerva is built over an ancient temple to that goddess and there one day I found her. So impatient was I to discover

the others that I disobeyed the laws of my nature and went hunting for them. I spent hours hanging about the station in search of newly arrived divinities. One night I strode the platform waiting for the Paris Express. I was trembling with premonition. I had donned a silk hat and its complements, a coral camellia, and a little blond mustache. Plumed with blue smoke and uttering splendid cries the train rushed into the station. The travelers descended from their compartments into a sea of *fachini* and relatives. I bowed to a Scandinavian diplomat and a Wagnerian prima donna. They returned my greeting hesitantly; a glance into their eyes showed me that they were brilliant but not supernatural. There was no incipient Bacchus among the Oxford students on vacation; the Belgian nuns on pilgrimage discovered me no Vesta. I scanned faces for half an hour until the length of pavement was deserted and a long line of old women with pails appeared. I stopped by the engine to ask a guard if another section of the train was to follow. I turned to see a strange face looking at me from the small window of the locomotive—misshapen, black with coal dust, gleaming with perspiration and content, and grinning from ear to ear, was Vulcan.

Here Miss Grier raised her head: There follow fifty pages describing his encounters with the others. Have you anything to say? Do you recognize anything?

But, Miss Grier, I've had no headaches! I don't receive what I want!

No?

What am I to understand? You've made it twice as confused. Explain some more.

He goes on to say that the gods were afraid of being laughed at for what they had lost. Flight, for instance, and invisibility, and omniscience and freedom from care. People would forget that they still had a few enviable powers: their strange elation; their command over matter; their abil-

ity to live or die when they chose and to live beyond good and evil. And so on.

What became of him?

Finally he decided to die, as they all do. All gods and heroes are by nature the enemies of Christianity—a faith trailing its aspirations and remorses and in whose presence every man is a failure. Only a broken will can enter the Kingdom of Heaven. Finally tired out with the cult of themselves they give in. They go over. They renounce themselves.

I was astonished at the desolation in her voice. It held me back from eagerly demanding of her the application to the Cabala of all these principles. We went into the next room where her musicians were waiting to offer us some English madrigals. The applications still occur to me, especially when I am depressed. They give in. They go over.

On the night that my steamer left the bay of Naples I lay sleepless in my deck chair until morning. Why was I not more reluctant at leaving Europe? How could I lie there repeating the Aeneid and longing for the shelf of Manhattan? It was Virgil's sea that we were crossing; the very stars were his: Arcturus and the showery Hyades, the two Bears and Orion in his harness of gold. All these passed before me in a cloudless sky and in the water, murmuring before a light wind, the sliding constellations were brokenly reflected.

Mercury is not only the messenger of the gods; he is the conductor of the dead as well. If in the least part his powers had fallen to me I should be able to invoke spirits. Perhaps Virgil could read my mood for me, and raising my two palms I said in a low voice (not loud enough to reach the open portholes behind me):

Prince of poets, Virgil, one of your guests and the last of barbarians invokes you.

For an instant I thought I saw the shimmer of a robe and the reflection of the starlight on the shiny side of a laurel leaf. I pressed my advantage:

O anima cortese mantovana, greatest of all Romans, out of the eternity of that limbo to which the Florentine, perhaps wrongly, consigned you, grant me a crumb of time.

Now indeed the shade stood in mid-air just above the handrail. The stars were glittering and the water was glittering, and the great shade, picked out in sparks, was glittering furiously. But the image must become clearer. There was one title that might avail more with him than those of poet or Roman.

Oh, greatest spirit of the ancient world and prophet of the new, by that fortunate guess wherein you foretold the coming of Him who will admit you to His mountain, thou first Christian in Europe, speak to me!

Now indeed the gracious spirit became completely visible with pulsations of light, half silver and half gold, and spoke:

Be brief, importunate barbarian. Except for this last salutation wherein you have touched my only pride, I would not delay here. Detain me not from the absorbing games of my peers. Erasmus is in debate with Plato, and Augustine has descended from the hill and sits among us, though the air is gray. Be brief, I pray you and give heed to your Latin.

At this I realized that I had no definite question to put to my guest. In order to mark time and prolong so uncommon an interview, I engaged him in conversation:

Was I then right, Master, in assuming that Dante was not completely in God's confidence?

Indignation infused a saffron stain into the noble figure in silver-gold: where, where is he, that soul of vinegar, that chose to assign the souls of the dead more harshly than God? Tell him that though a pagan I too shall see bliss. It is nothing that I must first pay the penalty of ten thousand years. Behold this moment I exhibit the sin of anger; where is *he* in pain for the sin of pride?

I was a little shocked to discover that neither genius nor death removed us beyond the temptation to asperity, but

said: Master, have you met the poets of the English tongue
that have come into your groves?

Let us be brief, my friend. —One came that had been
formerly blind and did me much honor. He spoke a noble
Latin. Those that stood by assured me that in his lines mine
were not seldom reflected.

Milton was indeed your son. . . .

But before him came another, greater than he, a writer
of pieces for a theater. He was proud and troubled and
strode among us unseeing. He made me no salutation.
Vanity no longer exists among us, but it is sweet to ex-
change greetings among the poets.

He knew but little Latin, Master, and perhaps had never
read your page. Moreover in life he was neither the enemy
nor advocate of grace and being arrived in your region his
whole mind may well have been consumed with anxiety as
to his eternal residence. Is he among you still?

He sits apart, his hand over his eyes, and only raises his
head when, in the long green evenings, Casella sings to us,
or when on the wind there drifts from Purgatory the chorus
that one Palestrina prepares.

Master, I have just spent a year in the city that was your
whole life. Am I wrong to leave it?

Let us be brief. This world where Time is, troubles me.
My heart has almost started beating again—what horror!
Know, importunate barbarian, that I spent my whole life-
time under a great delusion—that Rome and the house of
Augustus were eternal. Nothing is eternal save Heaven.
Romes existed before Rome and when Rome will be a waste
there will be Romes after her. Seek out some city that is
young. The secret is to make a city, not to rest in it. When
you have found one, drink in the illusion that she too is
eternal. Nay, I have heard of your city. Its foundations have
knocked upon our roof and the towers have cast a shadow
across the sandals of the angels. Rome too was great. Oh,
in the pride of your city, and when she too begins to pro-
duce great men, do not forget mine. When shall I erase from

my heart this love of her? I cannot enter Zion until I have forgotten Rome. —Dismiss me now, my friend, I pray thee. These vain emotions have shaken me. . . . (Suddenly the poet became aware of the Mediterranean:) Oh, beautiful are these waters. Behold! For many years I have almost forgotten the world. Beautiful! Beautiful! —But no! what horror, what pain! Are you still alive? Alive? How can you endure it? All your thoughts are guesses, all your body is shaken with breath, all your senses are infirm, and your mind ever full of the fumes of one passion or another. Oh, what misery to be a man. Hurry and die!

Farewell, Virgil!

The shimmering ghost faded before the stars, and the engines beneath me pounded eagerly toward the new world and the last and greatest of all cities.

The
BRIDGE
of
SAN LUIS REY

To my Mother
T. W.

Part One: Perhaps an Accident

ON FRIDAY noon, July the twentieth, 1714, the finest bridge in all Peru broke and precipitated five travelers into the gulf below. This bridge was on the highroad between Lima and Cuzco and hundreds of persons passed over it every day. It had been woven of osier by the Incas more than a century before and visitors to the city were always led out to see it. It was a mere ladder of thin slats swung out over the gorge, with handrails of dried vine. Horses and coaches and chairs had to go down hundreds of feet below and pass over the narrow torrent on rafts, but no one, not even the Viceroy, not even the Archbishop of Lima, had descended with the baggage rather than cross by the famous bridge of San Luis Rey. St. Louis of France himself protected it, by his name and by the little mud church on the further side. The bridge seemed to be among the things that last forever; it was unthinkable that it should break. The moment a Peruvian heard of the accident he signed himself and made a mental calculation as to how recently he had crossed by it and how soon he had intended crossing it again. People wandered about in a trancelike state, muttering; they had the hallucination of seeing themselves falling into a gulf.

There was a great service in the Cathedral. The bodies of the victims were approximately collected and approximately separated from one another, and there was great searching of hearts in the beautiful city of Lima. Servant girls returned bracelets which they had stolen from their mistresses, and usurers harangued their wives angrily, in defense of usury. Yet it was rather strange that this event should have so impressed the Limeans, for in that country those catastrophes which lawyers shockingly call the "acts of God" were more than usually frequent. Tidal waves were continually washing away cities; earthquakes arrived every week and towers fell upon good men and women all the time. Diseases were forever flitting in and out of the provinces and old age carried away some of the most admirable citizens. That is why it was so surprising that the Peruvians should have been especially touched by the rent in the bridge of San Luis Rey.

Everyone was very deeply impressed, but only one person did anything about it, and that was Brother Juniper. By a series of coincidences so extraordinary that one almost suspects the presence of some Intention, this little red-haired Franciscan from northern Italy happened to be in Peru converting the Indians and happened to witness the accident.

It was a very hot noon, that fatal noon, and coming around the shoulder of a hill Brother Juniper stopped to wipe his forehead and to gaze upon the screen of snowy peaks in the distance, then into the gorge below him filled with the dark plumage of green trees and green birds and traversed by its ladder of osier. Joy was in him; things were not going badly. He had opened several little abandoned churches and the Indians were crawling in to early Mass and groaning at the moment of miracle as though their hearts would break. Perhaps it was the pure air from the snows before him; perhaps it was the memory that brushed him for a moment of the poem that bade him raise his eyes to the helpful hills. At all events he felt at peace. Then his

glance fell upon the bridge, and at that moment a twang-
ing noise filled the air, as when the string of some musical
instrument snaps in a disused room, and he saw the bridge
divide and fling five gesticulating ants into the valley below.

Anyone else would have said to himself with secret joy,
"Within ten minutes myself . . . !" But it was another
thought that visited Brother Juniper: "Why did this happen
to *those* five?" If there were any plan in the universe at all,
if there were any pattern in a human life, surely it could be
discovered mysteriously latent in those lives so suddenly
cut off. Either we live by accident and die by accident, or we
live by plan and die by plan. And on that instant Brother
Juniper made the resolve to inquire into the secret lives of
those five persons, that moment falling through the air, and
to surprise the reason of their taking off.

It seemed to Brother Juniper that it was high time for
theology to take its place among the exact sciences and he
had long intended putting it there. What he had lacked
hitherto was a laboratory. Oh, there had never been any
lack of specimens; any number of his charges had met
calamity: spiders had stung them; their lungs had been
touched; their houses had burned down and things had
happened to their children from which one averts the mind.
But these occasions of human woe had never been quite fit
for scientific examination. They had lacked what our good
savants were later to call *proper control*. The accident had
been dependent upon human error, for example, or had
contained elements of probability. But this collapse of the
bridge of San Luis Rey was a sheer Act of God. It afforded
a perfect laboratory. Here at last one could surprise His
intentions in a pure state.

You and I can see that coming from anyone but Brother
Juniper this plan would be the flower of a perfect skepti-
cism. It resembled the effort of those presumptuous souls
who wanted to walk on the pavements of Heaven and built
the Tower of Babel to get there. But to our Franciscan there

was no element of doubt in the experiment. He knew the answer. He merely wanted to prove it, historically, mathematically, to his converts—poor obstinate converts, so slow to believe that their pains were inserted into their lives for their own good. People were always asking for good sound proofs; doubt springs eternal in the human breast, even in countries where the Inquisition can read your very thoughts in your eyes.

This was not the first time that Brother Juniper had tried to resort to such methods. Often on the long trips he had to make (scurrying from parish to parish, his robe tucked up about his knees, for haste) he would fall to dreaming of experiments that justify the ways of God to man. For instance, a complete record of the Prayers for Rain and their results. Often he had stood on the steps of one of his little churches, his flock kneeling before him on the baked street. Often he had stretched his arms to the sky and declaimed the splendid ritual. Not often, but several times, he had felt the virtue enter him and seen the little cloud forming on the horizon. But there were many times when weeks went by . . . but why think of them? It was not himself he was trying to convince that rain and drought were wisely apportioned.

Thus it was that the determination rose within him at the moment of the accident. It prompted him to busy himself for six years, knocking at all the doors in Lima, asking thousands of questions, filling scores of notebooks, in his effort at establishing the fact that each of the five lost lives was a perfect whole. Everyone knew that he was working on some sort of memorial of the accident and everyone was very helpful and misleading. A few even knew the principal aim of his activity and there were patrons in high places.

The result of all this diligence was an enormous book, which as we shall see later, was publicly burned on a beautiful spring morning in the great square. But there was a secret copy and after a great many years and without much notice it found its way to the library of the University of

San Marco. There it lies between two great wooden covers
collecting dust in a cupboard. It deals with one after an-
other of the victims of the accident, cataloguing thousands
of little facts and anecdotes and testimonies, and conclud-
ing with a dignified passage describing why God had set-
tled upon that person and upon that day for His demonstra-
tion of wisdom. Yet for all his diligence Brother Juniper
never knew the central passion of Doña María's life; nor of
Uncle Pio's, not even of Esteban's. And I, who claim to
know so much more, isn't it possible that even I have missed
the very spring within the spring?

Some say that we shall never know and that to the gods
we are like the flies that the boys kill on a summer day, and
some say, on the contrary, that the very sparrows do not
lose a feather that has not been brushed away by the finger
of God.

Part Two: The Marquesa de Montemayor

ANY Spanish schoolboy is required to know today more about Doña María, Marquesa de Montemayor, than Brother Juniper was to discover in years of research. Within a century of her death her letters had become one of the monuments of Spanish literature and her life and times have ever since been the object of long studies. But her biographers have erred in one direction as greatly as the Franciscan did in another; they have tried to invest her with a host of graces, to read back into her life and person some of the beauties that abound in her letters, whereas all real knowledge of this wonderful woman must proceed from the act of humiliating her and of divesting her of all beauties save one.

She was the daughter of a cloth merchant who had acquired the money and the hatred of the Limeans within a stone's throw of the Plaza. Her childhood was unhappy: she was ugly; she stuttered; her mother persecuted her with sarcasms in an effort to arouse some social charms and forced her to go about the town in a veritable harness of jewels. She lived alone and she thought alone. Many suitors presented themselves, but as long as she could she fought against the convention of her time and was determined to

156

remain single. There were hysterical scenes with her mother, recriminations, screams and slamming of doors, At last at twenty-six she found herself penned into marriage with a supercilious and ruined nobleman and the Cathedral of Lima fairly buzzed with the sneers of her guests. Still she lived alone and thought alone, and when an exquisite daughter was born to her she fastened upon her an idolatrous love. But little Clara took after her father; she was cold and intellectual. At the age of eight she was calmly correcting her mother's speech and presently regarding her with astonishment and repulsion. The frightened mother became meek and obsequious but she could not prevent herself from persecuting Doña Clara with nervous attention and a fatiguing love. Again there were hysterical recriminations, screams and slamming of doors. From the offers of marriage that fell to her, Doña Clara deliberately chose the one that required her removal to Spain. So to Spain she went, to that land from which it takes six months to receive an answer to one's letter. The leave-taking before so long a voyage became in Peru one of the formal services of the Church. The ship was blessed and as the space widened between the vessel and the beach both companies knelt and sang a hymn that never failed to sound weak and timid in all that open air. Doña Clara sailed with most admirable composure, leaving her mother to gaze after the bright ship, her hand pressing now her heart and now her mouth. Blurred and streaked became her view of the serene Pacific and the enormous clouds of pearl that hang forever motionless above it.

Left alone in Lima the Marquesa's life grew more and more inward. She became increasingly negligent in her dress and like all lonely people she talked to herself audibly. All her existence lay in the burning center of her mind. On that stage were performed endless dialogues with her daughter, impossible reconciliations, scenes eternally recommenced of remorse and forgiveness. On the street you beheld an old woman, her red wig fallen a little over one

ear, her left cheek angry with a leprous affection, her right
with a complementary adjustment of rouge. Her chin was
never dry; her lips were never still. Lima was a city of ec-
centrics, but even there she became its jest as she drove
through the streets or shuffled up the steps of its churches.
She was thought to be continuously drunk. Worse things
were said of her and petitions were afloat that she be locked
up. She had been denounced three times before the Inqui-
sition. It is not impossible that she might have been burned
had her son-in-law been less influential in Spain and had
she not somehow collected a few friends about the viceregal
court who suffered her for her oddity and her wide reading.

The distressing character of the relations between mother
and daughter were further embittered by misunderstand-
ings over money. The Condesa received a handsome allow-
ance from her mother and frequent gifts. Doña Clara soon
became the outstanding woman of intelligence at the Span-
ish court. All the wealth of Peru would have been insuffi-
cient to maintain her in the grandiose style she fancied for
herself. Strangely enough her extravagance proceeded from
one of the best traits in her nature: she regarded her friends,
her servants and all the interesting people in the capital, as
her children. In fact there seemed only one person in the
world toward whom she did not expend herself in kind
offices. Among her *protégés* was the cartographer De Blasiis
(whose *Maps of the New World* was dedicated to the
Marquesa de Montemayor amid the roars of the courtiers
at Lima who read that she was the *"admiration of her city
and a rising sun in the West"*); another was the scientist
Azuarius whose treatise on the laws of hydraulics was sup-
pressed by the Inquisition as being too exciting. For a dec-
ade the Condesa literally sustained all the arts and sciences
of Spain; it was not her fault that nothing memorable was
produced in that time.

About four years after Doña Clara's departure, Doña
María received her permission to visit Europe. On both
sides the visit was anticipated with resolutions well nour-

ished on self-reproach: the one to be patient, the other to be undemonstrative. Both failed. Each tortured the other and was on the point of losing her mind under the alternations of self-rebuke and the outbursts of passion. At length one day Doña María rose before dawn, daring no more than to kiss the door behind which her daughter was sleeping, took ship and returned to America. Henceforth letter writing had to take the place of all the affection that could not be lived.

Hers were the letters that in an astonishing world have become the textbook of schoolboys and the anthill of the grammarians. Doña María would have invented her genius had she not been born with it, so necessary was it to her love that she attract the attention, perhaps the admiration, of her distant child. She forced herself to go out into society in order to cull its ridicules; she taught her eye to observe; she read the masterpieces of her language to discover its effects; she insinuated herself into the company of those who were celebrated for their conversation. Night after night in her baroque palace she wrote and rewrote the incredible pages, forcing from her despairing mind those miracles of wit and grace, those distilled chronicles of the viceregal court. We know now that her daughter barely glanced at the letters and that it is to the son-in-law that we owe their preservation.

The Marquesa would have been astonished to learn that her letters were immortal. Yet many critics have accused her of keeping one eye on posterity, and point to a number of letters that have all the air of being bravura pieces. To them it seems impossible that Doña María should have put herself to the same pains to dazzle her daughter that most artists expend on dazzling the public. Like her son-in-law they misunderstood her: the Conde delighted in her letters, but he thought that when he had enjoyed the style he had extracted all their richness and intention, missing (as most readers do) the whole purport of literature, which is the notation of the heart. Style is but the faintly contempt-

ible vessel in which the bitter liquid is recommended to the world. The Marquesa would even have been astonished to learn that her letters were very good, for such authors live always in the noble weather of their own minds and those productions which seem remarkable to us are little better than a day's routine to them.

This was the old woman who hour by hour would sit upon her balcony, her odd straw hat casting a purple shadow across her lined and yellow face. How often as she turned her pages with her gemmed hands, she would ask herself, almost with amusement, whether the constant pain at her heart had an organic seat. She wondered whether a subtle doctor cutting through to that battered throne could at last discover a sign and lifting his face to the amphitheater cry out to his students, "This woman has suffered, and her suffering has left its mark upon the structure of her heart." This idea had so often visited her that one day she wrote it into a letter and her daughter scolded her for an introspective and for making a cult of sorrow.

The knowledge that she would never be loved in return acted upon her ideas as a tide acts upon cliffs. Her religious beliefs went first, for all she could ask of a god, or of immortality, was the gift of a place where daughters love their mothers; the other attributes of Heaven you could have for a song. Next she lost her belief in the sincerity of those about her. She secretly refused to believe that anyone (herself excepted) loved anyone. All families lived in a wasteful atmosphere of custom and kissed one another with secret indifference. She saw that the people of this world moved about in an armor of egotism, drunk with self-gazing, athirst for compliments, hearing little of what was said to them, unmoved by the accidents that befell their closest friends, in dread of all appeals that might interrupt their long communion with their own desires. These were the sons and daughters of Adam from Cathay to Peru. And when on the balcony her thoughts reached this turn, her mouth would contract with shame for she knew that she too sinned and

that though her love for her daughter was vast enough to include all the colors of love, it was not without a shade of tyranny: she loved her daughter not for her daughter's sake, but for her own. She longed to free herself from this ignoble bond; but the passion was too fierce to cope with. And then on that green balcony a strange warfare would shake the hideous old lady, a singularly futile struggle against a temptation to which she would never have the opportunity of succumbing. How could she rule her daughter when her daughter saw to it that four thousand miles lay between them? Nevertheless Doña María wrestled with the ghost of her temptation and was worsted on every occasion. She wanted her daughter for herself; she wanted to hear her say, "You are the best of all possible mothers"; she longed to hear her whisper, "Forgive me."

About two years after her return from Spain there took place a series of inconspicuous events that had a great deal to tell about the inner life of the Marquesa. Only the faintest allusion to them occurs in the Correspondence, but as that is found in Letter XXII which contains other signs I shall do my best to give a translation and commentary of the first part of the letter:

"*Are there no doctors in Spain? Where are those good men from Flanders that used to help you so? Oh, my treasure, how can we punish you enough for letting your cold endure so many weeks? Don Vicente, I implore you to make my child see reason. Angels of Heaven, I implore you to make my child see reason. Now that you are better, I beg of you, resolve that when the first warning of a cold comes you will steam yourself well and go to bed. Here in Peru I am helpless; I can do nothing. Do not be self-willed, my beloved. God bless you. I am enclosing in today's packet the gum of some tree which the sisters of San Tomás peddle from door to door. Whether it be of much use I know not. It can do no harm. I am told that in the convent the silly sisters inhale it so diligently that one cannot smell the incense at Mass. Whether it be worth anything I know not; try it.*

"*Rest easy, my love, I am sending His Most Catholic Majesty the perfect gold chain.*" (Her daughter had written her: "*The chain arrived in good condition and I wore it at the christening of the Infante. His Most Catholic Majesty was gracious enough to admire it and when I told Him that you had given it me He sent you His compliments upon your taste. Do not fail to send Him one as like it as possible; send it at once, by way of the Chamberlain.*") "*He need never know that in order to obtain it I had to walk into a picture. Do you remember that in the sacristy of San Martín there is a portrait by Velasquez of the Viceroy who founded the monastery and of his wife and brat? and that his wife is wearing a gold chain? I resolved that only that chain would do. So one midnight I slipped into the sacristy, climbed upon the robing table like a girl of twelve and walked in. The canvas resisted for a moment, but the painter himself came forward to lift me through the pigment. I told him that the most beautiful girl in Spain wished to present the finest gold chain that could be found to the most gracious king in the world. It was as simple as that, and there we stood talking, we four, in the gray and silvery air that makes a Velasquez. Now I keep thinking about a more golden light; I keep looking at the Palace: I must pass the evening in a Titian. Would the Viceroy let me?*

"*But His Excellency has the gout again. I say 'again' because the flattery of the court insists that there are times when he is free of it. This being Saint Mark's day His Excellency started out to visit the University where twenty-two new doctors were being brought into the world. He had hardly been carried from his divan to his coach when he screamed and refused to go any farther. He was carried back to his bed where he broke a most delicious cigar and sent for the Perichole. And while we listened to long doctrinal addresses, more or less in Latin, he heard all about us, more or less in Spanish, from the reddest and cruellest lips in town.*" (Doña María permitted herself this passage, although she had just read in her daughter's last letter:

"How many times must I tell you to be more cautious in the things you say in your letters? They often show signs of having been opened on the journey. Nothing could be more ill-judged than your remarks on the you-know-what-I-mean at Cuzco. Such remarks are not funny, even though Vicente did compliment you upon them in his postscript, and they might get us into a great deal of trouble with Certain Persons here in Spain. I continue to be astonished that your indiscretions have not long since led to your being ordered to retire to your farm.")

"There was a great press at the Exercises and two women fell from the balcony, but God in His goodness saw that they fell on Doña Merced. All three are badly hurt, but will be thinking of other things within a year. The President was speaking at the moment of the accident and being short-sighted could not imagine what the disturbance of cries and talk and falling bodies could be about. It was very pleasant to see him bowing, under the impression that he was being applauded.

"Speaking of the Perichole, and of applause, you should know that Pepita and I decided to go to the Comedia this evening. The public still idolizes its Perichole; it even forgives her her years. We are told that she saves what she can, every morning, by passing alternate pencils of ice and fire across her cheeks." (Translation falls especially short of this conceit which carries the whole flamboyance of the Spanish language. It was intended as an obsequious flattery of the Condesa, and was untrue. The great actress was twenty-eight at this time; her cheeks had the smoothness and polish of dark yellow marble and would certainly have retained that quality for many years. Apart from the cosmetics required by her performances the only treatment Camila Perichole afforded her face was to throw cold water at it twice a day, like a peasant woman at a horse trough.) *"That curious man they call Uncle Pio is by her all the time. Don Rubio says that he cannot make out whether Uncle Pio is her father, her lover, or her son. The Perichole gave a won-*

*derful performance. Scold me all you like for a provincial
ninny, you have no such actresses in Spain."* And so on.

It is on this visit to the theater that further matter hangs.
She decided to go to the Comedia where the Perichole was
playing Doña Leonor in Moreto's *Trampa Adelante;* per-
haps some material could be derived from the visit for her
daughter's next letter. She took with her Pepita, a little girl
about whom later we shall learn much. Doña María had
borrowed her from the orphanage connected with the Con-
vent of Santa María Rosa de las Rosas to be her companion.
The Marquesa sat in her box gazing with flagging attention
at the brilliant stage. Between the acts it was the Perichole's
custom to lay aside the courtly role and appear before the
curtain to sing a few topical songs. The malicious actress
had seen the Marquesa arrive and presently began impro-
vising couplets alluding to her appearance, her avarice, her
drunkenness, and even to her daughter's flight from her.
The attention of the house was subtly directed to the old
woman and a rising murmur of contempt accompanied the
laughter of the audience. But the Marquesa, deeply moved
by the first two acts of the comedy, scarcely saw the singer
and sat staring before her, thinking about Spain. Camila
Perichole became bolder and the air was electric with the
hatred and glee of the crowd. At last Pepita plucked the
Marquesa's sleeve and whispered to her that they should
go. As they left the box the house arose and burst into a roar
of triumph; the Perichole flung herself into a frenzied
dance, for she saw the manager at the back of the hall and
knew that her salary had been increased. But the Marquesa
remained unaware of what had taken place; in fact she was
quite pleased, for during the visit she had contrived a few
felicitous phrases, phrases (who knows) that might bring a
smile to her daughter's face and might make her murmur,
"Really, my mother is charming."

In due time the report reached the Viceroy's ears that
one of his aristocrats had been openly baited in the theater.
He summoned the Perichole to the Palace and ordered her

to call upon the Marquesa and to apologize. The trip was to be made barefoot and in a black dress. Camila argued and fought, but all she gained was a pair of shoes.

The Viceroy had three reasons for insisting. In the first place the singer had taken liberties with his court. Don Andrés had contrived to make exile endurable by building up a ceremonial so complicated that it could be remembered only by a society that had nothing else to think about. He nursed his little aristocracy and its minute distinctions and any insult paid to a Marquesa was an insult to His Person. In the second place, Doña María's son-in-law was an increasingly important personage in Spain, laden with possibilities of injury to the Viceroy, nay with the possibility of supplanting him. The Conde Vicente d'Abuirre must not be vexed, even through his half-wit mother-in-law. Finally, the Viceroy was delighted to humble the actress. He suspected that she was deceiving him with a matador, perhaps with an actor—between the flattery of the court and the inertia of gout he could not quite make out who it was; at all events, it was clear that the singer was beginning to forget that he was one of the first men in the world.

The Marquesa, beside not having heard the scurrilous songs, was in other ways unprepared for the actress's visit. You should know that after the departure of her daughter, Doña María had lighted upon a certain consolation: she had taken to drinking. Everyone drank *chicha* in Peru and there was no particular disgrace in being found unconscious on a feast day. Doña María had begun to discover that her feverish monologues had a way of keeping her awake all night. Once she took a delicate fluted glassful of *chicha* on retiring. Oblivion was so sweet that presently she stole larger amounts and tried dissimulating their effects from Pepita; she hinted that she was not well, and represented herself as going into a decline. At last she resigned all pretense. The boats that carried her letter to Spain did not leave oftener than once a month. During the week that preceded the making of the packet she observed a strict

regimen and cultivated the city assiduously for material. At last on the eve of the post she wrote the letter, making up the bundle toward dawn and leaving it for Pepita to deliver to the agent. Then as the sun rose she would shut herself up in her room with some flagons and drift through the next few weeks without the burden of consciousness. Finally she would emerge from her happiness and prepare to go into a state of "training" in preparation for the writing of another letter.

Thus on the night following the scandal in the theater she wrote Letter XXII and retired to bed with a carafe. All next day Pepita moved about the room, glancing anxiously at the figure on the bed. The next afternoon Pepita brought her needlework into the room. The Marquesa lay staring at the ceiling with wide-open eyes, talking to herself. Toward dusk Pepita was called to the door and informed that the Perichole had come to see the mistress. Pepita remembered the theater very well and sent back word angrily that the mistress refused to see her. The man carried the message to the street door, but returned awe-struck with the news that the Señora Perichole was armed with a letter from the Viceroy presenting her to the lady. Pepita tiptoed to the bed and started talking to the Marquesa. The glazed eyes moved to the girl's face. Pepita shook her gently. With great effort Doña María tried to fix her mind on what was being said to her. Twice she lay back, refusing to seize the meaning, but at last, like a general calling together in a rain and by night the dispersed division of his army she assembled memory and attention and a few other faculties and painfully pressing her hand to her forehead she asked for a bowl of snow. When it was brought her, she long and drowsily pressed handfuls of it against her temples and cheeks; then rising she stood for a long time leaning against the bed and looking at her shoes. At last she raised her head with decision, she called for her fur-trimmed cloak and a veil. She put them on and tottered into her handsomest reception room where the actress stood waiting for her.

Camila had intended to be perfunctory and if possible impudent, but now she was struck for the first time with the dignity of the old woman. The mercer's daughter could carry herself at times with all the distinction of the Monte-mayors and when she was drunk she wore the grandeur of Hecuba. For Camila the half-closed eyes had the air of weary authority and she began almost timidly:

"I come, señora, to make sure that you could not have misunderstood anything I said on the evening that Your Grace did me the honor to visit my theater."

"Misunderstood? Misunderstood?" said the Marquesa.

"Your Grace might have misunderstood and thought that my words were intended to be disrespectful to Your Grace."

"To me?"

"Your Grace is not offended at her humble servant? Your Grace is aware that a poor actress in my position may be carried beyond her intentions . . . that it is very difficult . . . that everything. . . ."

"How can I be offended, señora? All that I can remember is that you gave a beautiful performance. You are a great artist. You should be happy, happy. My handkerchief, Pepita. . . ."

The Marquesa brought out these words very rapidly and vaguely, but the Perichole was confounded. A piercing sense of shame filled her. She turned crimson. At last she was able to murmur:

"It was in the songs between the acts of the comedy. I was afraid Your Grace. . . ."

"Yes, yes. I remember now. I left early. Pepita, we left early, did we not? But, señora, you are good enough to for-give my leaving early, yes, even in the middle of your ad-mirable performance. I forget why we left. Pepita . . . oh, some indisposition. . . ."

It was impossible that anyone in the theater could have missed the intention of the songs. Camila could only assume that the Marquesa, out of a sort of fantastic magnanimity, was playing the farce of not having noticed it. She was al-

most in tears: "But you are so good to overlook my childishness, señora—I mean Your Grace. I did not know. I did not know your goodness. Señora, permit me to kiss your hand."

Doña María held out her hand, astonished. She had not for a long time been addressed with such consideration. Her neighbors, her tradespeople, her servants—for even Pepita lived in awe of her—her very daughter had never approached her thus. It induced a new mood in her; one that must very likely be called maudlin. She became loquacious:

"Offended, offended at you, my beautiful . . . my gifted child? Who am I, a . . . an unwise and unloved old woman, to be offended at you? I felt, my daughter, as though I were—what says the poet?—*surprising through a cloud the conversation of the angels.* Your voice kept finding new wonders in our Moreto. When you said:

> 'Don Juan, si mi amor estimas,
> Y la fe segura es necia,
> Enojarte mis temores
> Es no quererme discreta.
> ¿Tan seguros. . . . ?'

and so on—that was true! And what a gesture you made at the close of the First Day. There, with your hand *so.* Such a gesture as the Virgin made, saying to Gabriel, *How is it possible that I shall have a child?* No, no, you will begin to have resentment at me, for I am going to tell you about a gesture that you may remember to use someday. Yes, it would fit well into that scene where you forgive your Don Juan de Lara. Perhaps I should tell you that I saw it made one day by my daughter. My daughter is a very beautiful woman . . . everyone thinks. Did . . . did you know my Doña Clara, Señora?"

"Her Grace often did me the honor of visiting my theater. I knew the Condesa well by sight."

"Do not remain so, on one knee, my child. —Pepita, tell Jenarito to bring this lady some sweet cakes at once. Think,

one day we fell out, I forget over what. Oh, there is noth-
ing strange in that; all we mothers from time to time. . . .
Look, can you come a little closer? You must not believe
the town that says she was unkind to me. You are a great
woman with a beautiful nature and you can see further than
the crowd sees in these matters. —It is a pleasure to talk
to you. What beautiful hair you have! What beautiful hair!
—She had not a warm impulsive nature, I know that. But,
oh, my child, she has such a store of intelligence and gra-
ciousness. Any misunderstandings between us are so plainly
my fault; is it not wonderful that she is so quick to forgive
me? This day there fell one of those little moments. We
both said hasty things and went off to our rooms. Then each
turned back to be forgiven. Finally only a door separated
us and there we were pulling it in contrary ways. But at
last she . . . took my . . . face . . . thus, in her two white
hands. So! Look!"

The Marquesa almost fell out of her chair as she leaned
forward, her face streaming with happy tears, and made
the beatific gesture. I should say the mythical gesture, for
the incident was but a recurring dream.

"I am glad you are here," she continued, "for now you
have heard from my own lips that she is not unkind to me,
as some people say. Listen, señora, the fault was mine.
Look at me. Look at me. There was some mistake that made
me the mother of so beautiful a girl. I am difficult. I am
trying. You and she are great women. No, do not stop me:
you are rare women, and I am only a nervous . . . a foolish
. . . a stupid woman. Let me kiss your feet. I am impossible.
I am impossible. I am impossible."

Here indeed the old woman did fall out of her chair and
was gathered up by Pepita and led back to her bed. The
Perichole walked home in consternation and sat for a long
time gazing into her eyes in the mirror, her palms pressed
against her cheeks.

But the person who saw most of the difficult hours of the
Marquesa was her little companion, Pepita. Pepita was an

orphan and had been brought up by that strange genius of Lima, the Abbess Madre María del Pilar. The only occasion upon which the two great women of Peru (as the perspective of history was to reveal them) met face to face was on the day when Doña María called upon the directress of the Convent of Santa María Rosa de las Rosas and asked if she might borrow some bright girl from the orphanage to be her companion. The Abbess gazed hard at the grotesque old woman. Even the wisest people in the world are not perfectly wise and Madre María del Pilar who was able to divine the poor human heart behind all the masks of folly and defiance, had always refused to concede one to the Marquesa de Montemayor. She asked her a great many questions and then paused to think. She wanted to give Pepita the worldly experience of living in the palace. She also wanted to bend the old woman to her own interests. And she was filled with a somber indignation, for she knew she was gazing at one of the richest women in Peru, and the blindest.

She was one of those persons who have allowed their lives to be gnawed away because they have fallen in love with an idea several centuries before its appointed appearance in the history of civilization. She hurled herself against the obstinacy of her time in her desire to attach a little dignity to women. At midnight when she had finished adding up the accounts of the House she would fall into insane vision of an age when women could be organized to protect women, women traveling, women as servants, women when they are old or ill, the women she had discovered in the mines of Potosí, or in the workrooms of the cloth merchants, the girls she had collected out of doorways on rainy nights. But always the next morning she had to face the fact that the women in Peru, even her nuns, went through life with two notions: one, that all the misfortunes that might befall them were merely due to the fact that they were not sufficiently attractive to bind some man to their maintenance and, two, that all the misery in the world was worth his

caress. She had never known any country but the environs of Lima and she assumed that all its corruption was the normal state of mankind. Looking back from our century we can see the whole folly of her hope. Twenty such women would have failed to make any impression on that age. Yet she continued diligently in her task. She resembled the swallow in the fable who once every thousand years transferred a grain of wheat, in the hope of rearing a mountain to reach the moon. Such persons are raised up in every age; they obstinately insist on transporting their grains of wheat and they derive a certain exhilaration from the sneers of the bystanders. "How queerly they dress!" we cry. "How queerly they dress!"

Her plain red face had great kindliness, and more idealism than kindliness, and more generalship than idealism. All her work, her hospitals, her orphanage, her convent, her sudden journeys of rescue, depended upon money. No one harbored a fairer admiration for mere goodness, but she had been obliged to watch herself sacrificing her kindliness, almost her idealism, to generalship, so dreadful were the struggles to obtain her subsidies from her superiors in the church. The Archbishop of Lima, whom we shall know later in a more graceful connection, hated her with what he called a Vatinian hate and counted the cessation of her visits among the compensations for dying.

Lately she had felt not only the breath of old age against her cheek, but a graver warning. A chill of terror went through her, not for herself, but for her work. Who was there in Peru to value the things she had valued? And rising one day at dawn she had made a rapid journey through her hospital and convent and orphanage, looking for a soul she might train to be her successor. She hurried from empty face to empty face, occasionally pausing more from hope than conviction. In the courtyard she came upon a company of girls at work over the linen and her eyes fell at once upon a girl of twelve who was directing the others at the trough and at the same time recounting to them with great dra-

matic fire the less probable miracles in the life of Saint Rose
of Lima. So it was that the search ended with Pepita. The
education for greatness is difficult enough at any time, but
amid the sensibilities and jealousies of a convent it must be
conducted with fantastic indirection. Pepita was assigned
to the most disliked tasks in the House, but she came to
understand all the aspects of its administration. She accom-
panied the Abbess on her journeys, even though it was in
the capacity of custodian of the eggs and vegetables. And
everywhere, by surprise, hours would open up in which the
directress suddenly appeared and talked to her at great
length, not only on religious experience, but on how to
manage women and how to plan contagious wards and how
to beg for money. It was a step in this education for great-
ness that led to Pepita's arriving one day and entering upon
the crazy duties of being Doña María's companion. For the
first two years she merely came for occasional afternoons,
but finally she came to the palace to live. She never had
been taught to expect happiness, and the inconveniences,
not to say terrors, of her new position did not seem to her
excessive for a girl of fourteen. She did not suspect that the
Abbess, even there, was hovering above the house, herself
estimating the stresses and watching for the moment when
a burden harms and not strengthens.

A few of Pepita's trials were physical: for example, the
servants in the house took advantage of Doña María's in-
disposition; they opened up the bedrooms of the palace to
their relatives; they stole freely. Alone Pepita stood out
against them and suffered a persecution of small discomforts
and practical jokes. Her mind, similarly, had its distresses:
when she accompanied Doña María on her errands in the
city, the older woman would be seized with the desire to
dash into a church, for what she had lost of religion as faith
she had replaced with religion as magic. "Stay here in the
sunlight, my dear child; I shall not be long," she would say.
Doña María would then forget herself in a reverie before
the altar and leave the church by another door. Pepita had

been brought up by Madre María del Pilar to an almost
morbid obedience and when after many hours she ventured
into the church and made sure that her mistress was no
longer there, still she returned to the street corner and
waited while the shadows fell gradually across the square.
Thus waiting in public she suffered all the torture of a little
girl's self-consciousness. She still wore the uniform of the
orphanage (which a minute's thoughtfulness on the part
of Doña María could have altered) and she suffered hallu-
cinations wherein men seemed to be staring at her and
whispering—nor were these always hallucinations. No less
her heart suffered, for on some days Doña María would
suddenly become aware of her and would talk to her cor-
dially and humorously, would let appear for a few hours all
the exquisite sensibility of the Letters; then, on the morrow
she would withdraw into herself again, and, while never
harsh, would become impersonal and unseeing. The begin-
nings of hope and affection that Pepita had such need to
expend would be wounded. She tiptoed about the palace,
silent, bewildered, clinging only to her sense of duty and
her loyalty to her "mother in the Lord," Madre María del
Pilar, who had sent her there.

Finally a new fact appeared that was to have considera-
ble effect on the lives of both the Marquesa and her com-
panion: "*My dear mother,*" wrote the Condesa, "*the weather
has been most exhausting and the fact that the orchards
and gardens are in bloom only makes it the more trying. I
could endure flowers if only they had no perfume. I shall
therefore ask your permission to write you at less length
than usual. If Vicente returns before the post leaves he will
be delighted to finish out the leaf and supply you with those
tiresome details about myself which you seem to enjoy so.
I shall not go to Grignan in Provence as I expected this Fall,
as my child will be born in early October.*"
What child? The Marquesa leaned against the wall. Doña
Clara had foreseen the exhausting importunities that this

news would waken in her mother and had sought to miti-
gate them by the casualness of her announcement. The ruse
did not succeed. The famous Letter XLII was the answer.

Now at length the Marquesa had something to be anx-
ious about: her daughter was to become a mother. This
event, which merely bored Doña Clara, discovered a whole
new scale of emotions in the Marquesa. She became a mine
of medical knowledge and suggestion. She combed the city
for wise old women and poured into her letters the whole
folk wisdom of the New World. She fell into the most
abominable superstition. She practiced a degrading system
of taboos for her child's protection. She refused to allow a
knot in the house. The maids were forbidden to tie up their
hair and she concealed upon her person ridiculous symbols
of a happy delivery. On the stairs the even steps were
marked with red chalk and a maid who accidently stepped
upon an even step was driven from the house with tears and
screams. Doña Clara was in the hands of malignant Nature
who reserves the right to inflict upon her children the most
terrifying jests. There was an etiquette of propitiation which
generations of peasant women had found comforting. So
vast an army of witnesses surely implied that there was
some truth in it. At least it could do no harm, and Perhaps
it did good. But the Marquesa did not only satisfy the rites
of paganism; she studied the prescriptions of Christianity
as well. She arose in the dark and stumbled through the
streets to the earliest Masses. She hysterically hugged the
altar rails trying to rend from the gaudy statuettes a sign,
only a sign, the ghost of a smile, the furtive nod of a waxen
head. Would all be well? Sweet, sweet Mother, would all be
well?

At times, after a day's frantic resort to such invocations, a
revulsion would sweep over her. Nature is deaf. God is in-
different. Nothing in man's power can alter the course of
law. Then on some street corner she would stop, dizzy with
despair, and leaning against a wall would long to be taken
from a world that had no plan in it. But soon a belief in the

great Perhaps would surge up from the depths of her nature
and she would fairly run home to renew the candles above
her daughter's bed.

At last the time came to satisfy the supreme rite of Peru-
vian households looking forward to this event: she made the
pilgrimage to the shrine of Santa María de Cluxambuqua.
If there resided any efficacy in devotion at all, surely it lay
in a visit to this great shrine. The ground had been holy
through three religions; even before the Incan civilization,
distraught human beings had hugged the rocks and lashed
themselves with whips to wring their will from the skies.
Thither the Marquesa was carried in her chair, crossing the
bridge of San Luis Rey and ascending up into the hills to-
ward that city of large-girdled women, a tranquil town,
slow-moving and slow-smiling; a city of crystal air, cold as
the springs that fed its many fountains; a city of bells, soft
and musical, and tuned to carry on with one another the
happiest quarrels. If anything turned out for disappoint-
ment in the town of Cluxambuqua the grief was somehow
assimilated by the overwhelming immanence of the Andes
and by the weather of quiet joy that flowed in and about
the side streets. No sooner did the Marquesa see from a dis-
tance the white walls of this town perched on the knees of
the highest peaks than her fingers ceased turning the beads
and the busy prayers of her fright were cut short on her lips.

She did not even alight at the inn, but leaving Pepita to
arrange for their stay she went on to the church and knelt
for a long time patting her hands softly together. She was
listening to the new tide of resignation that was rising
within her. Perhaps she would learn in time to permit both
her daughter and her gods to govern their own affairs. She
was not annoyed by the whispering of the old women in
padded garments who sold candles and medals and talked
about money from dawn to dark. She was not even dis-
tracted by an officious sacristan who tried to collect a fee
for something or other and who, from spite, made her
change her place under the pretext of repairing a tile on the

floor. Presently she went out into the sunshine and sat on the steps of the fountain. She watched the little processions of invalids slowly revolving about the gardens. She watched three hawks plunging about the sky. The children who had been playing by the fountain stared at her for a moment, and went away alarmed, but a llama (a lady with a long neck and sweet shallow eyes, burdened down by a fur cape too heavy for her and picking her way delicately down an interminable staircase) came over and offered her a velvet cleft nose to stroke. The llama is deeply interested in the men about her, is even fond of pretending that she too is one of them and of inserting her head into their conversations as though in a moment she would lift her voice and contribute a wan and helpful comment. Soon Doña María was surrounded by a number of these sisters who seemed on the point of asking her why she clapped her hands so and how much her veiling cost a yard.

Doña María had arranged that any letters arriving from Spain should be brought to her at once by a special messenger. She had traveled slowly from Lima and even now as she sat in the square a boy from her farm ran up and put into her hand a large packet wrapped in parchment and dangling some nuggets of sealing wax. Slowly she undid the wrappings. With measured stoic gestures she read first an affectionate and jocose note from her son-in-law; then her daughter's letter. It was full of wounding remarks rather brilliantly said, perhaps said for the sheer virtuosity of giving pain neatly. Each of its phrases found its way through the eyes of the Marquesa, then, carefully wrapped in understanding and forgiveness it sank into her heart. At last she arose, gently dispersed the sympathetic llamas, and with a grave face returned to the shrine.

While Doña María was passing the late afternoon in the church and in the square, Pepita was left to prepare their lodging. She showed the porters where to lay down the great wicker hampers and set about unpacking the altar, the brazier, the tapestries and the portraits of Doña Clara.

She descended into the kitchen and gave the cook exact instructions as to the preparations of a certain porridge upon which the Marquesa principally subsisted. Then she returned to the rooms and waited. She resolved to write a letter to the Abbess. She hung for a long time over the quill, staring into the distance with trembling lip. She saw the face of Madre María del Pilar, so red and scrubbed, and the wonderful black eyes. She heard her voice as at the close of supper (the orphans sitting with lowered eyes and folded hands) she commented on the events of the day, or as, by candlelight, she stood among the beds of the hospital and announced the theme for meditation during the night. But most clearly of all Pepita remembered the sudden interviews when the Abbess (not daring to wait until the girl was older) had discussed with her the duties of her office. She had talked to Pepita as to an equal. Such speech is troubling and wonderful to an intelligent child and Madre María del Pilar had abused it. She had expanded Pepita's vision of how she should feel and act beyond the measure of her years. And she had unthinkingly turned upon Pepita the full blaze of her personality, as Jupiter had turned his upon Semele. Pepita was frightened by her sense of insufficiency; she hid it and wept. And then the Abbess had cast the child into the discipline of this long solitude, where Pepita struggled, refusing to let herself believe that she had been abandoned. And now from this strange inn in these strange mountains, where the altitude was making her lightheaded, Pepita longed for the dear presence, the only real thing in her life.

She wrote a letter, all ink stains and incoherence. Then she went down stairs to see about fresh charcoal and to taste the porridge.

The Marquesa came in and sat down at the table. "I can do no more. What will be, will be," she whispered. She unbound from her neck the amulets of her superstition and dropped them into the glowing brazier. She had a strange sense of having antagonized God by too much prayer and

so addressed Him now obliquely. "After all it is in the hands of another. I no longer claim the least influence. What will be, will be." She sat for a long time, her palms against her cheeks, making a blank of her mind. Her eyes fell on Pepita's letter. She opened it mechanically and started to read. She had read a full half of it before her attention was aware of the meaning of the words: ". . . *but all this is nothing if you like me and wish me to stay with her. I oughtn't to tell you but every now and then the bad chambermaids lock me up in rooms and steal things and perhaps My Lady will think that I steal them. I hope not. I hope you are well and not having any trouble in the hospital or anywhere. Though I never see you I think of you all the time and I remember what you told me, my dear mother in God. I want to do only what you want, but if you could let me come back for a few days to the convent, but not if you do not wish it. But I am so much alone and not talking to anyone, and everything. Sometimes I do not know whether you have forgotten me and if you could find a minute to write me a little letter or something, I could keep it, but I know how busy you are. . . ."*

Doña María read no further. She folded the letter and put it aside. For a moment she was filled with envy: she longed to command another's soul as completely as this nun was able to do. Most of all she longed to be back in this simplicity of love, to throw off the burden of pride and vanity that hers had always carried. To quiet the tumult in her mind she picked up a book of devotion and tried to fix her attention upon the words. But after a moment she suddenly felt the need to reread the whole letter, to surprise, if possible, the secret of so much felicity.

Pepita returned bringing the supper in her hands, followed by a maid. Doña María watched her over the top of her book as she would have watched a visitor from Heaven. Pepita tiptoed about the room laying the table and whispering directions to her assistant.

"Your supper is ready, My Lady," she said at last.

"But, my child, you are going to eat with me?" In Lima, Pepita generally sat down at the table with her mistress.

"I thought you would be tired, My Lady. I had my supper downstairs."

"She does not wish to eat with me," thought the Marquesa. "She knows me and has rejected me."

"Would you like me to read aloud to you while you are eating, My Lady?" asked Pepita, who felt that she had made a mistake.

"No. You may go to bed, if you choose."

"Thank you, My Lady."

Doña María had risen and approached the table. With one hand on the back of the chair she said haltingly, "My dear child, I am sending off a letter to Lima in the morning. If you have one you can enclose it with mine."

"No, I have none," said Pepita. She added hastily, "I must go downstairs and get you the new charcoal."

"But, my dear, you have one for . . . Madre María del Pilar. Wouldn't you . . . ?"

Pepita pretended to be busy over the brazier. "No, I'm not going to send it," she said. She was aware during the long pause that followed that the Marquesa was staring at her in stupefaction. "I've changed my mind."

"I know she would like a letter from you, Pepita. It would make her very happy. I know."

Pepita was reddening. She said loudly, "The innkeeper said that there would be some new charcoal ready for you at dark. I'll tell them to bring it up now." She glanced hastily at the old woman and saw that she had not ceased from staring at her with great sad inquiring eyes. Pepita felt that these were not things one talked about, but the strange woman seemed to be feeling the matter so strongly that Pepita was willing to concede one more answer: "No, it was a bad letter. It wasn't a good letter."

Doña María fairly gasped. "Why, my dear Pepita, I think it was very beautiful. Believe me, I know. No, no; what could have made it a bad letter?"

Pepita frowned, hunting for a word that would close the matter.

"It wasn't . . . it wasn't . . . brave," she said. And then she would say no more. She carried the letter off into her own room and could be heard tearing it up. Then she got into bed and lay staring into the darkness, still uncomfortable at having talked in such a fashion. And Doña María sat down to her dish amazed.

She had never brought courage to either life or love. Her eyes ransacked her heart. She thought of the amulets and of her beads, her drunkenness . . . she thought of her daughter. She remembered the long relationship, crowded with the wreckage of exhumed conversations, of fancied slights, of inopportune confidences, of charges of neglect and exclusion (but she must have been mad that day; she remembered beating upon the table). "But it's not my fault," she cried. "It's not my fault that I was so. It was circumstance. It was the way I was brought up. Tomorrow I begin a new life. Wait and see, oh my child." At last she cleared away the table, and sitting down, wrote what she called her first letter, her first stumbling misspelled letter in courage. She remembered with shame that in the previous one she had piteously asked her daughter how much she loved her, and had greedily quoted the few and hesitant endearments that Doña Clara had lately ventured to her. Doña María could not recall those pages, but she could write some new ones, free and generous. No one else has regarded them as stumbling. It is the famous letter LVI, known to the Encyclopedists as her Second Corinthians because of its immortal paragraph about love: "Of the thousands of persons we meet in a lifetime, my child . . ." and so on. It was almost dawn when she finished the letter. She opened the door upon her balcony and looked at the great tiers of stars that glittered above the Andes. Throughout the hours of the night, though there had been few to hear it, the whole sky had been loud with the singing of these constellations. Then she took a candle into the next

room and looked at Pepita as she slept, and pushed back the damp hair from the girl's face. "Let me live now," she whispered. "Let me begin again."

Two days later they started back to Lima, and while crossing the bridge of San Luis Rey the accident which we know befell them.

Part Three: Esteban

ONE morning twin boys were discovered in the found-
lings' basket before the door of the Convent of Santa María
Rosa del las Rosas. Names were found for them almost be-
fore the arrival of the wet nurse, but the names were not
as useful to them as our names are to most of us, for no one
ever succeeded in telling the boys apart. There was no way
of knowing who their parents were, but Limean gossips,
noticing as the boys grew older how straight they held
themselves and how silent and somber they were, declared
them to be Castilian and laid them in turn at all sorts of
crested doorways. The person in the world who came near-
est to being their guardian was the Abbess of the Convent.
Madre María del Pilar had come to hate all men, but she
grew fond of Manuel and Esteban. In the late afternoon
she would call them into her office, send for some cakes
from the kitchen, and tell them stories about the Cid and
Judas Maccabeus and the thirty-six misfortunes of Harle-
quin. She grew to love them so, that she would catch her-
self gazing deep into their black and frowning eyes, looking
for those traits that would appear when they grew to be
men, all that ugliness, all that soullessness that made hide-
ous the world she worked in. They grew up about the con-

vent until they were a little past the age when their pres-
ence began to be a slight distraction to the dedicated sisters.
From thence they became vaguely attached to all the sacris-
ties in town: they trimmed all the cloister hedges; they pol-
ished every possible crucifix; they passed a damp cloth once
a year over most of the ecclesiastical ceilings. All Lima
knew them well. When the priest rushed through the streets
carrying his precious burden into a sickroom either Esteban
or Manuel was to be seen striding behind him, swinging a
censer. As they grew older, however, they showed no desire
for the clerical life. They gradually assumed the profession
of the scribe. There were few printing presses in the New
World and the boys soon made a fair living transcribing
comedies for the theater, ballads for the crowds, and adver-
tisements for the merchants. Above all they were the copy-
ists of the choirmasters and made endless parts of the
motets of Morales and Vittoria.

Because they had no family, because they were twins,
and because they were brought up by women, they were
silent. There was in them a curious shame in regard to their
resemblance. They had to live in a world where it was the
subject of continual comment and joking. It was never
funny to them and they suffered the eternal pleasantries
with stolid patience. From the years when they first learned
to speak they invented a secret language for themselves,
one that was scarcely dependent on the Spanish for its vo-
cabulary, or even for its syntax. They resorted to it only
when they were alone, or at great intervals in moments of
stress whispered it in the presence of others. The Arch-
bishop of Lima was something of a philologist; he dabbled
in dialects; he had even evolved quite a brilliant table for
the vowel and consonant changes from Latin into Spanish
and from Spanish into Indian-Spanish. He was storing up
notebooks of quaint lore against an amusing old age he
planned to offer himself back on his estates outside Segovia.
So when he heard one day about the secret language of the
twin brothers, he trimmed some quills and sent for them.

The boys stood humiliated upon the rich carpets of his study while he tried to extract from them their *bread* and *tree* and their *I see* and *I saw*. They did not know why the experience was so horrible to them. They bled. Long, shocked silences followed each of the Archbishop's questions, until finally one or the other mumbled an answer. The priest thought for a while that they were merely in awe before his rank and before the luxury of his apartment, but at last, much perplexed, he divined the presence of some deeper reluctance and sadly let them go.

This language was the symbol of their profound identity with one another, for just as resignation was a word insufficient to describe the spiritual change that came over the Marquesa de Montemayor on that night in the inn at Cluxambuqua, so *love* is inadequate to describe the tacit almost ashamed oneness of these brothers. What relationship is it in which few words are exchanged, and those only about the details of food, clothing and occupation; in which the two persons have a curious reluctance even to glance at one another; and in which there is a tacit arrangement not to appear together in the city, and to go on the same errand by different streets? And yet side by side with this there existed a need of one another so terrible that it produced miracles as naturally as the charged air of a sultry day produces lightning. The brothers were scarcely aware of it themselves, but telepathy was a common occurrence in their lives, and when one returned home the other was always aware of it when his brother was still several streets away.

Suddenly they discovered that they were tired of writing. They went down to the sea and found an occupation in loading and unloading vessels, not ashamed of working side by side with Indians. They drove teams across the provinces. They picked fruit. They were ferrymen. And always they were silent. Their somber faces took on from these labors a male and gypsy cast. Their hair was seldom cut and under the dark mat their eyes looked up suddenly surprised and a

little sullen. All the world was remote and strange and hostile except one's brother.

But at last the first shadow fell across this unity and the shadow was cast by the love of women. They had returned to the city and resumed the copying of parts for the theater. One night the manager, foreseeing a thinning house, gave them a free admission. The boys did not like what they found there. Even speech was for them a debased form of silence; how much more futile is poetry which is a debased form of speech. All those allusions to honor, reputation, and the flame of love, all the metaphors about birds, Achilles and the jewels of Ceylon were fatiguing. In the presence of literature they had the same darkling intelligence that stirs for a time behind the eyes of a dog, but they sat on patiently, gazing at the bright candles and the rich clothes. Between the acts of the comedy the Perichole stepped out of her role, put on twelve petticoats and danced before the curtain. Esteban had some copying still to do, or pretended so, and went home early; but Manuel stayed on. The red stockings and shoes of the Perichole had made their impression.

Both brothers had fetched and carried their manuscripts up and down the dusty stairs behind the stage. There they had seen an irritable girl in a soiled bodice mending her stockings before a mirror while her stage director read aloud her lines for memorization. She had let fall upon the boys for a moment the detonation of her amazing eyes, immediately dissipated in her amused recognition that they were twins. Forthwith she had dragged them into the room and placed them side by side. Carefully, amusedly and remorselessly she had peered into every square inch of their faces, until finally laying one hand on Esteban's shoulder she had cried out, "This one is the younger!" That had been several years before and neither brother had thought of the episode again.

Henceforth all Manuel's errands seemed to lead him past the theater. Late at night he would drift about among the

trees beneath her dressing room window. It was not the first time that Manuel had been fascinated by a woman (both brothers had possessed women, and often, especially during their years at the waterfront; but simply, Latinly), but it was the first time that his will and imagination had been thus overwhelmed. He had lost that privilege of simple nature, the dissociation of love and pleasure. Pleasure was no longer as simple as eating; it was being complicated by love. Now was beginning that crazy loss of one's self, that neglect of everything but one's dramatic thoughts about the beloved, that feverish inner life all turning upon the Perichole and which would so have astonished and disgusted her had she been permitted to divine it. This Manuel had not fallen in love through any imitation of literature. It was not of him, at all events, that the bitterest tongue in France had remarked only fifty years before: that many people would never have fallen in love if they had not heard about it. Manuel read little; he had only been once to the theater (where above all there reigns the legend that love is a devotion) and the Peruvian tavern songs that he might have heard, unlike those of Spain, reflected very little of the romantic cult of an idealized woman. When he said over to himself that she was beautiful and rich and fatiguingly witty and the Viceroy's mistress, none of these attributes that made her less obtainable had the power to quench his curious and tender excitement. So he leaned against the trees in the dark, his knuckles between his teeth, and listened to his loud heartbeats.

But the life that Esteban was leading had been full enough for him. There was no room in his imagination for a new loyalty, not because his heart was less large than Manuel's, but because it was of a simpler texture. Now he discovered that secret from which one never quite recovers, that even in the most perfect love one person loves less profoundly than the other. There may be two equally good, equally gifted, equally beautiful, but there may never be two that love one another equally well. So Esteban sat up in their

room by a guttering candle, his knuckles between his teeth, and wondered why Manuel was so changed and why the whole meaning had gone out of their life.

One evening Manuel was stopped on the street by a small boy who announced to him that the Perichole wished him to call upon her at once. Manuel turned in his path and went to the theater. Straight, somber and impersonal, he entered the actress's room and stood waiting. Camila had a service to ask of Manuel and she thought a few preliminary blandishments were necessary, but she scarcely paused in combing a blond wig that was dressed upon the table before her.

"You write letters for people, don't you? I want you to write a letter for me, please. Please come in."

He came forward two steps.

"You never pay me the least visit either of you. That's not Spanish of you" (meaning 'courteous'). "Which are you, Manuel or Esteban?"

"Manuel."

"It doesn't matter. You are both unfriendly. Neither of you ever comes to see me. Here I sit learning stupid lines all day and no one ever comes to see me but a lot of peddlers. It is because I am an actress, no?"

This was not very artful, but for Manuel it was unspeakably complicated. He merely stared at her from the shadows of his long hair and left her to improvise.

"I am going to engage you to write a letter for me, a very secret letter. But now I can see that you don't like me and that to ask you to write a letter would be as good as reading it aloud in all the wineshops. What does that look mean, Manuel? Are you my friend?"

"Yes, señora."

"Go away. Send me Esteban. You do not even say *Yes, señora* as a friend would say it."

Long pause. Presently she raised her head: "Are you still there, Unfriendly?"

"Yes, señora . . . you can trust me to do anything for you . . . you can trust. . . ."

"If I ask you to write one letter for me, or two letters, you promise never to mention to a human being what is in them, or even that you wrote them?"

"Yes, señora."

"What do you promise by?—by the Virgin Mary?"

"Yes, señora."

"And by the heart of Saint Rose of Lima?"

"Yes, señora."

"Name of the Name, Manuel, anyone would think you were stupid as an ox. Manuel, I am very angry with you. You are not stupid. You don't look stupid. Please don't say just *Yes, señora* again. Don't be stupid or I'll send for Esteban. Is anything the matter with you?"

Here Manuel cast himself upon the Spanish language and exclaimed with unnecessary vigor, "I swear by the Virgin Mary and the heart of St. Rose of Lima that all that has to do with the letter will be secret."

"Even from Esteban," prompted the Perichole.

"Even from Esteban."

"Well, that's better." She motioned him to sit down at a table where writing materials were already laid out. As she dictated she strode about the room, frowning, swinging her hips. With her arms akimbo, she hugged her shawl about her shoulders defiantly.

"*Camila Perichole kisses the hands of Your Excellency and says*—No, take another piece of paper and begin again. *The señora Micaela Villegas, artist, kisses the hands of Your Excellency and says that, being the victim of the envious and lying friends that Y. E.'s goodness permits about Him, she can no longer endure Y. E.'s suspicions and jealousy. Y. E.'s servant has always valued Y. E.'s friendship and has never committed, nor even thought, an offense against it, but she can no longer fight against the calumnies that Y. E. believes so readily. Señora Villegas, artist, called the Perichole, therefore returns herewith such of Y. E.'s gifts as*

have not been placed beyond recall, since without Y. E.*'s
confidence,* Y. E.*'s servant can take no pleasure in them."*

Camila continued walking about the room for several
minutes, consumed by her thoughts. Presently without so
much as glancing at her secretary, she commanded, "Take
another leaf. *Have you gone mad? Do not ever think of
dedicating another bull to me again. It has caused a fright-
ful war. Heaven protect you, my colt. Friday night, the
same place, the same time. I may be a little late, for the fox
is wide-awake.* That will be all."

Manuel rose.

"You swear that you have made no errors?"

"Yes, I swear."

"There is your money."

Manuel took the money.

"I shall want you to write me more letters from time to
time. My uncle Pio generally writes my letters; these I do
not wish him to know about. Good night. Go with God."

"Go with God."

Manuel descended the stairs and stood for a long time
among the trees, not thinking, not moving.

Esteban knew that his brother was continually brooding
over the Perichole, but he never suspected that he saw her.
From time to time during the next two months a small boy
would approach him in great haste and ask whether he
were Manuel or Esteban, and being informed that he was
only Esteban, the boy would add that Manuel was wanted
at the theater. Esteban assumed that the call was for copy-
ist's work and was therefore utterly unprepared for a visit
that they received one night in their room.

It was almost midnight. Esteban had gone to bed, and lay
gazing out from under the blanket at the candle beside
which his brother was working. There was a light tap at
the door and Manuel opened to admit a lady heavily veiled,
out of breath and nervous. She threw back the scarf from
her face and said hurriedly:

"Quick, ink and paper. You are Manuel, yes? You must do a letter for me at once."

For a moment her glance fell on the two bright eyes that glared at her from the edge of the cot. She murmured, "Eu . . . you must excuse me. I know it is late. It was necessary . . . I must come." Then turning to Manuel, she whispered into his ear: "Write this, *I, the Perichole, am not accustomed to wait at a rendezvous.* Have you finished that? *You are only a cholo, and there are better matadors than you, even in Lima. I am half Castilian and there are no better actresses in the world. You shall not have the opportunity*—Have you got that?—*to keep me waiting again, cholo, and I shall laugh the last, for even an actress does not grow old as fast as a bullfighter.*"

To Esteban in the shadows the picture of Camila leaning over his brother's hand and whispering into his ear was complete evidence that a new congeniality had formed such as he would never know. He seemed to shrink away into space, infinitely tiny, infinitely unwanted. He took one more glance at the tableau of love, all the paradise from which he was shut out, and turned his face to the wall.

Camila seized the note the moment it was done, pushed a coin along the table and in a last flurry of black lace, scarlet beads and excited whispers left the room. Manuel turned from the door with his candle. He sat down, put his hand over his ears, his elbows on his knees. He worshiped her. He murmured to himself over and over again that he worshiped her, making of the sound a sort of incantation and an obstacle to thought.

He emptied his mind of everything but a singsong, and it was this vacancy that permitted him to become aware of Esteban's mood. He seemed to hear a voice that proceeded from the shadows saying, "Go and follow her, Manuel. Don't stay here. You'll be happy. There's room for us all in the world." Then the realization became even more intense and he received a mental image of Esteban going a long way off and saying good-bye many times as he went. He was filled

with terror; by the light of it he saw that all the other at-
tachments in the world were shadows, or the illusions of
fever, even Madre María del Pilar, even the Perichole. He
could not understand why Esteban's misery should present
itself as demanding a choice between him and the Peri-
chole, but he could understand Esteban's misery, as misery.
And at once he sacrificed everything to it, if it can be said
we ever sacrifice anything save what we know we can never
attain, or what some secret wisdom tells us it would be un-
comfortable or saddening to possess. To be sure, there was
nothing on which Esteban could base a complaint. It was
not jealousy, for in their earlier affairs it had never occurred
to either of them that their loyalty to one another had been
diminished. It was merely that in the heart of one of them
there was left room for an elaborate imaginative attachment
and in the heart of the other there was not. Manuel could
not quite understand this and, as we shall see, he nourished
a dim sense of being accused unjustly. But he did under-
stand that Esteban was suffering. In his excitement he
groped for a means of holding this brother who seemed to
be receding into the distance. And at once, in one unhesitat-
ing stroke of the will, he removed the Perichole from his
heart.

He blew out the candle and lay down on his bed. He was
trembling. He said aloud with exaggerated casualness,
"Well, that's the last letter I write for that woman. She can
go and find a pander somewhere else. If ever she calls here
or sends for me when I'm out, tell her so. Make it plain.
That's the last I have to do with her," and with that he be-
gan reciting his evening psalm aloud. But he had hardly
reached *A sagitta volante in die* when he became aware
that Esteban had risen and was lighting the candle.

"What's the matter?" he asked.

"I'm going out for a walk," replied Esteban somberly,
fastening his belt. After a moment, he broke out with an
assumption of anger, "You don't have to say . . . what you
just said, for me. I don't care whether you write her letters

or not. You don't have to change for me. I haven't anything to do with that."

"Go to bed, you fool. God, you're a fool, Esteban. What made you think I said that, for you? Don't you believe I mean it when I say I'm through with her? Do you think I want to write any more of her dirty letters and get paid for them like that?"

"It's all right. You love her. You don't have to change because of me."

"'*Love* her?' *Love* her? You're crazy, Esteban. How could I love her? What chance would there be for me? Do you suppose she'd give me those letters to write if there were any chance? Do you suppose she'd push a piece of money across the table every time. . . . You're crazy, Esteban, that's all."

There was a long pause. Esteban would not go to bed. He sat by the candle in the middle of the room, tapping with his hand on the edge of the table.

"Go to bed, you fool," shouted Manuel, rising on one elbow under the blanket. He was talking in their secret language and the new pain at his heart gave a greater ring of reality to his assumption of rage. "I'm all right."

"I won't. I'm going out for a walk," replied Esteban picking up his coat.

"You can't go out for a walk. It's two o'clock. It's raining. You can't go and walk about for hours like that. Look, Esteban, I swear to you there's nothing left to all that. I don't love her. I only did for a time."

By now Esteban stood in the dark of the open door. In the unnatural voice with which we make the greatest declarations of our lives, he muttered: "I'm in your way," and turned to go.

Manuel leaped out of his bed. His head seemed to be full of a great din, a voice crying out that Esteban was going away forever, was leaving him alone forever. "In the name of God, in the name of God, Esteban, come back here."

Esteban came back and went to bed and the matter was

not mentioned again for many weeks. The very next eve-
ning Manuel had an opportunity of declaring his position.
A messenger arrived from the Perichole and was told
harshly to inform the actress that Manuel would write no
more letters for her.

One evening Manuel tore open the flesh on his knee
against a piece of metal.

Neither brother had ever been ill for as much as a day
in his life, and now Manuel, utterly bewildered, watched
his leg swell and felt the waves of pain rise and fall in his
body. Esteban sat by and stared at his face trying to imagine
what great pain was. At last one midnight Manuel remem-
bered that the signboard of a certain hairdresser in the city
described the proprietor as an experienced barber and sur-
geon. Esteban ran through the streets to fetch him. He
pounded on the door. Presently a woman leaned out of a
window and announced that her husband would be back
in the morning. During the fearful hours that followed they
told one another that when the doctor had seen the leg all
would be well. He would do something about it, and
Manuel would be out around the town in a day or two,
even in a day perhaps, even less than a day.

The barber arrived and prescribed various draughts and
ointments. Esteban was instructed to lay cold cloths on his
brother's leg every hour. The barber withdrew and the
brothers sat down to wait for the pain to subside. But
while they continued staring into one another's face wait-
ing for the miracle of science the pain grew worse. Hour
after hour Esteban approached with his dripping towel
and they discovered that the moment of its application was
the worst of all. With all the fortitude in the world Manuel
could not prevent himself from shouting and from flinging
himself about upon the bed. Night came on and still Esteban
stolidly waited and watched and worked. Nine, ten, eleven.
Now when the time drew near to apply the cloths (the hour
struck so musically from all those towers) Manuel would

plead with Esteban not to do his work. He would resort to guile and declare that he scarcely felt it. But Esteban, his heart bursting with pain and his lips a line of iron, would roll back the blanket and bind the towel fiercely in its place. Manuel gradually became delirous and under this application all the thoughts he did not permit himself in his right mind would burst magnified from his mouth.

Finally at two o'clock, out of his mind with rage and pain, and flinging himself half out of the bed until his head struck the floor, Manuel cried, "God condemn your soul to the hottest hell there is. A thousand devils torture you forever, Esteban. God condemn your soul, do you hear?" At first, the air gone out of his body, Esteban went out into the hall and leaned against the door, his mouth and eyes wide open. Still he heard from within, "Yes, Esteban, may God damn your beastly soul forever, do you hear that? For coming between me and what was mine by right. She was mine, do you hear, and what right had you. . . ." and he would go off into an elaborate description of the Perichole.

These outbursts recurred hourly. It was some time before Esteban was able to realize that his brother's mind was not then clear. After some moments of horror, in which his being a devout believer had its part, he would return to the room and go about his duties with bent head.

Toward dawn his brother became serener. (For what human ill does not dawn seem to be an alleviation?) It was in one of these intervals that Manuel said quite calmly:

"God's son! I feel better, Esteban. Those cloths must be good after all. You'll see. I'll be up and around tomorrow. You haven't slept for days. You'll see I won't cause you any more trouble, Esteban."

"It's no trouble, you fool."

"You mustn't take me seriously when I try and stop you putting on the old cloths, Esteban."

A long pause. At last Esteban brought out, barely audible:

"I think . . . don't you think it would be fine if I sent for

the Perichole? She could just come and see you for a few
minutes, I mean. . . ."

"Her? You still thinking about her? I wouldn't have her
here for anything. No."

But Esteban was not content yet. He dragged up a few
more phrases from the very center of his being:

"Manuel, you still feel, don't you, that I came between
you and the Perichole and you don't remember that I told
you it was all right with me. I swear to you I'd have been
glad if you'd gone away with her, or anything."

"What are you bringing that up for, Esteban? I tell you,
in God's own name, I never think of that. She's nothing to
me. When are you going to forget that, Esteban? I tell you
I'm glad things are as they are. Look, I got to get angry
when you keep going back to that."

"Manuel, I wouldn't speak of it again, only when you get
angry at me about the cloths . . . you, you get angry at me
about that, too. And you talk about it and you. . . ."

"Look, I'm not responsible what I say. My old leg hurts
then, see."

"Then you don't damn me to hell because . . . it looks like
I came between you and the Perichole?"

"Damn you to . . . ? What makes you say that? You're
going crazy, Esteban; you're imagining things. You haven't
had any sleep, Esteban. I've been a curse to you and you're
losing your health because of me. But you'll see, I won't
trouble you much more. How could I damn you to hell,
Esteban, when you're all I've got? Understand, see, that
when the cold cloths go on, I just lose myself, see. You
know. Don't think about it twice. It's time to put them on
now. I won't say a word."

"No, Manuel, I'll skip this time. It won't do you any
harm, I'll just skip this time."

"I've got to get well, Esteban. I've got to get up soon,
you know. Put them on. But one minute—give me the
crucifix. I swear by the blood and body of Christ that if I
say anything against Esteban, I don't mean it and it's just

the foolish words when I'm dreaming because of the pain in my leg. God make me well again soon, amen. Put it back. There. Now I'm ready."

"Look, Manuel, it won't hurt if I skip just this once, see. It'll be good for you, sure, to not get it all stirred up just this once."

"No, I've got to get well. The doctor said it had to be done. I won't say a word, Esteban."

And it would begin all over again.

During the second night a prostitute in the next room started beating on the wall, outraged at such language. A priest in the room on the other side would come out into the hall and beat on the door. The whole floor would gather before the room in exasperation. The innkeeper came up the stairs, loudly promising his guests that the brothers would be dumped into the street the very next morning. Esteban, holding his candle, would go into the hall and permit them to rage at him for as long as they pleased; but after that he took to pressing his hand firmly over his brother's mouth during the moments of greatest stress. This increased Manuel's personal rage at him and he would babble all through the night.

On the third night, Esteban sent for the priest, and amidst the enormous shadows Manuel received the sacrament, and died.

Thereafter, Esteban refused to come near the building. He would start off upon long walks, but presently drifting back, would hang about, staring at passers-by, within two streets of where his brother lay. The innkeeper failing to make any impression upon him and remembering that the boys were brought up at the Convent of Santa María Rosa de las Rosas, sent for the Abbess. Simply and soundly she directed all that was to be done. At last she went down to the street corner and spoke to Esteban. He watched her approach him, a glance mixed of longing and distrust. But when she stood near him he turned sideways and looked away.

"I want you to help me. Won't you come in and see your brother? Won't you come in and help me?"

"No."

"You won't help me!" A long pause. Suddenly as she stood there full of her helplessness there flashed through her mind an incident of many years before: the twin brothers about fifteen years old were sitting at her knee and she was telling them the story of the crucifixion. Their large grave eyes were fixed upon her lips. Suddenly Manuel had cried out loudly, "If Esteban and I had been there we would have prevented it."

"Well, then, if you won't help me, will you tell me which you are?"

"Manuel," said Esteban.

"Manuel, won't you come and sit with me up there for just a short time?"

After a long pause: "No."

"But Manuel, dear Manuel, can't you remember as children how you did so many things for me? You were willing to go across the town on some little errand. When I was ill you made the cook let you bring me my soup?" Another woman would have said, "Do you remember how much I did for you?"

"Yes."

"I, too, Manuel have lost. I too . . . once. We know that God has taken them into His hands. . . ." But this did not do at all. Esteban turned vaguely and walked away from her. When he had gone about twenty paces he stopped and stared down a side street, like a dog who wants to go away, but is reluctant to offend the master who calls him back.

That was all they could get out of him. When the fearful procession passed through the city, with its black hoods and masks, its candles in broad daylight, its display of heaped-up skulls, its terrifying psalms, Esteban followed it in the parallel streets, catching glimpses of it from a distance, like a savage.

All Lima was interested in this separation of the brothers.

Housewives whispered together sympathetically about it as they unfurled their carpets from the balconies. The men in the wineshops, alluding to it, shook their heads and smoked in silence for a while. Travelers from the interior told of seeing Esteban as he strayed with eyes like coals along the dried-up beds of rivers or through the great ruins of the old race. A herder of llamas had come upon him standing upon a hilltop, asleep or dazed, wet with dew under the stars. Some fishermen surprised him swimming far out from shore. From time to time he would find work to do, he would become a shepherd or a carter, but after a few months he would disappear and stride from province to province. But he always returned to Lima. One day he appeared at the door of the Perichole's dressing room; he made as though to speak, gazed earnestly at her and vanished. One day a sister came running into the office of Madre María del Pilar with the news that Esteban (whom the world called Manuel) was lingering about the door of the convent. The Abbess hurried out into the street. For months she had been asking herself what strategy could reconcile this half-demented boy to living among them again. She assembled as grave and calm a manner as she was able and appearing at the street door murmured "My friend" and looked at him. He gazed back at her with the same glance of longing and distrust that he had shown her before, and stood trembling. Again she whispered "My friend" and moved a step forward. Suddenly Esteban turned and breaking into a run disappeared. Madre María del Pilar rushed stumbling back to her desk and fell upon her knees, exclaiming angrily, "I have prayed for wisdom and You have given me none. You have not chosen to give me the least grace. I am a mere scrubber of floors. . . ." But during the penance she set herself for this impudence the thought came to her to send for Captain Alvarado. Three weeks later she had a ten-minute conversation with him. And the next day he started for Cuzco where, it was said, Esteban was doing some copying for the University.

There was this strange and noble figure in Peru during these years, the Captain Alvarado, the traveler. He was blackened and cured by all weathers. He stood in the square with feet apart as though they were planted on a shifting deck. His eyes were strange, unaccustomed to the shorter range, too used to seizing the appearances of a constellation between a cloud and a cloud, and the outline of a cape in rain. His reticence was sufficiently explained for most of us by his voyages, but the Marquesa de Montemayor had other light on the matter. *"Captain Alvarado is bringing you this letter in person,"* she wrote to her daughter. *"Introduce him to some of your geographers, my treasure, though it may make them a little uncomfortable, for he is the diamond of sincerity. They will never see anyone who has traveled so far. Last night he described to me some of his voyages. Imagine him pushing his prow through a sea of weeds, stirring up a cloud of fish like grasshoppers in June; or sailing between islands of ice. Oh, he has been to China and up the rivers of Africa. But he is not merely an adventurer and he seems to take no pride in discovering new places; nor is he a mere merchant. One day I asked him narrowly why he lived so, and he avoided my question. I found out from my laundress what I think is the reason of his wandering: My child, he had a child; my daughter, he had a daughter. She was just old enough to cook a holiday meal, and do a little sewing for him. In those days he merely sailed between Mexico and Peru and hundreds of times she waved him farewell or welcome. We have no way of knowing whether she was more beautiful or intelligent than the thousands of other girls that lived about him, but she was his. I suppose it seems ignoble to you that a great oak of a man should go about the world like a blind man about an empty house merely because a chit of a girl has been withdrawn from it. No, no, you cannot understand this, my adored one, but I understand and grow pale. Last night he sat with me and talked of her. He laid his cheek against his hand and looking into the fire, he said, 'It sometimes seems*

*to me that she is away upon a voyage and that I shall see
her again. It seems to me that she is in England.' You will
laugh at me, but I think he goes about the hemispheres to
pass the time between now and his old age."*

The brothers had always entertained a great respect for
Captain Alvarado. They had worked for him a short time
and the silence of the three of them had made a little kernel
of sense in a world of boasting, self-excuse and rhetoric. So
now when the great traveler came into the dark kitchen
where Esteban was eating, the boy drew his chair farther
into the shadow, but at a distance, he was glad. The Cap-
tain gave no sign of recognizing or even of seeing him until
he had finished his meal. Esteban had finished long before,
but not wishing to be spoken to, waited until the Captain
should have left the cave. At last the Captain walked over
to him and said:

"You are Esteban or Manuel. You helped me once with
some unloading. I am Captain Alvarado."

"Yes," said Esteban.

"How are you?"

Esteban muttered something.

"I am looking for some strong fellows to go on my next
trip with me." Pause. "Would you like to come?" Longer
pause. "England. And Russia. . . . Hard work. Good wages.
. . . A long way from Peru. —Well?"

Apparently Esteban had not been listening. He sat with
his eyes on the table. At last the Captain raised his voice,
as to a deaf person:

"I said: Do you want to go on my next trip with me. . . ."

"Yes, I'll go," answered Esteban suddenly.

"Fine. That's fine. I want your brother, too, of course."

"No."

"What's the matter? Wouldn't he want to come?"

Esteban mumbled something, looking away. Then half
rising, he said, "I got to go now. I've got to see somebody
about something."

"Let me see your brother myself. Where is he?"

". . . 'dead," said Esteban.

"Oh, I didn't know. I didn't know. I'm sorry."

"Yes," said Esteban. "I got to go."

"Hmm. —Which are you? What's your name?"

"Esteban."

"When did Manuel die?"

"Oh, just a . . . just a few weeks. He hit his knee against something and . . . just a few weeks ago."

They both kept their eyes on the floor.

"How old are you, Esteban?"

"Twenty-two."

"Well, that's settled then, you're coming with me?"

"Yes."

"You may not be used to the cold."

"Yes, I'm used to it. —I've got to go now. I got to go in the city and see somebody about something."

"Well, Esteban. Come back here for supper and we'll talk about the trip. Come back and have some wine with me, see. Will you?"

"Yes, I will."

"Go with God."

"Go with God."

They had supper together and it was arranged that they were to start for Lima the next morning. The Captain got him very drunk. At first they poured and drank and poured and drank in silence. Then the Captain began to talk about ships and their courses. He asked Esteban questions about tackle and about the guide stars. Then Esteban began to talk about other things, and to talk very loudly:

"On the ship you must give me something to do all the time. I'll do anything, anything. I'll climb up high and fix ropes; and I'll watch all night—because, you know, I don't sleep well anyway. And, Captain Alvarado, on the ship you must pretend that you don't know me. Pretend that you hate me the most. So that you'll always give me things to do. I can't sit still and write at a table any more. —And don't tell the other men about me . . . that is, about. . . ."

"I hear you went into a burning house, Esteban, and pulled someone out."

"Yes. I didn't get burned or anything. You know," cried Esteban, leaning across the table, "you're not allowed to kill yourself; you know you're not allowed. Everybody knows that. But if you jump into a burning house to save somebody, that wouldn't be killing yourself. And if you became a matador and the bull caught you that wouldn't be killing yourself. Only you mustn't put yourself in the bull's way on purpose. Did you ever notice that animals never kill themselves, even when they're sure to lose? They never jump into a river or anything, even when they're sure to lose. Some people say that horses run into bonfires. Is that true?"

"No, I don't think that's true."

"I don't think it's true. We had a dog once. Well, I mustn't think of that. —Captain Alvarado, do you know Madre María del Pilar?"

"Yes."

"I want to give her a present before I go away. Captain Alvarado, I want you to give me all my wages before I start—I won't need any money anywhere—and I want to buy her a present now. The present isn't from me only. She was . . . was. . . ." Here Esteban wished to say his brother's name, but was unable to. Instead he continued in a lower voice, "She had a kind of a . . . she had a serious loss, once. She said so. I don't know who it was, and I want to give her a present. Women can't bear that kind of a thing like we can."

The Captain promised him that they would choose something in the morning. Esteban talked about it at great length. At last the Captain saw him slip under the table, and himself, rising up, went out into the square before the inn. He looked at the line of the Andes and at the streams of stars crowding forever across the sky. And there was that wraith hanging in mid-air and smiling at him, the wraith with the silvery voice that said for the thousandth time,

"Don't be gone long. But I'll be a big girl when you get back." Then he went within and carried Esteban to his room and sat looking at him for a long while.

The next morning he was waiting at the bottom of the stairs when Esteban appeared:

"We're starting when you're ready," said the Captain.

The strange glitter had returned to the boy's eyes. He blurted out, "No, I'm not coming. I'm not coming after all."

"Aïe! Esteban! But you have promised me that you would come."

"It's impossible. I can't come with you," and he turned back up the stairs.

"Come here a moment, Esteban, just a moment."

"I can't come with you. I can't leave Peru."

"I want to tell you something."

Esteban came down to the foot of the stairs.

"How about that present for Madre María del Pilar?" asked the Captain in a low voice. Esteban was silent, looking over the mountains. "You aren't going to take that present away from her? It might mean a lot to her . . . you know."

"All right," murmured Esteban, as though much impressed.

"Yes. Besides, the ocean's better than Peru. You know Lima and Cuzco and the road. You have nothing more to know about them. You see it's the ocean you want. Besides on the boat you'll have something to do every minute. I'll see to that. Go and get your things and we'll start."

Esteban was trying to make a decision. It had always been Manuel who had made the decisions and even Manuel had never been forced to make as great a one as this. Esteban went slowly upstairs. The Captain waited for him and waited so long that presently he ventured half the way up the stairs and listened. At first there was silence; then a series of noises that his imagination was able to identify at once. Esteban had scraped away the plaster about a beam and was adjusting a rope about it. The Captain stood on the

stairs trembling: "Perhaps it's best," he said to himself. "Perhaps I should leave him alone. Perhaps it's the only thing possible for him." Then on hearing another sound he flung himself against the door, fell into the room and caught the boy. "Go away," cried Esteban. "Let me be. Don't come in now."

Esteban fell face downward upon the floor. "I am alone, alone, alone," he cried. The Captain stood above him, his great plain face ridged and gray with pain; it was his own old hours he was reliving. He was the awkwardest speaker in the world apart from the lore of the sea, but there are times when it requires a high courage to speak the banal. He could not be sure the figure on the floor was listening, but he said, "We do what we can. We push on, Esteban, as best we can. It isn't for long, you know. Time keeps going by. You'll be surprised at the way time passes."

They started for Lima. When they reached the bridge of San Luis Rey, the Captain descended to the stream below in order to supervise the passage of some merchandise, but Esteban crossed by the bridge and fell with it.

Part Four: Uncle Pio

IN ONE of her letters (the XXIXth) the Marquesa de Montemayor tries to describe the impression that Uncle Pio "*our aged Harlequin*" made upon her: "*I have been sitting all morning on the green balcony making you a pair of slippers, my soul,*" she tells her daughter. "*As the golden wire did not take up my whole attention I was able to follow the activity of a coterie of ants in the wall beside me. Somewhere behind the partition they were patiently destroying my house. Every three minutes a little workman would appear between two boards and drop a grain of wood upon the floor below. Then he would wave his antennae at me and back busily into his mysterious corridor. In the meantime various brothers and sisters of his were trotting back and forth on a certain highway, stopping to massage one another's heads, or if the messages they bore were of first importance, refusing angrily to massage or to be massaged. And at once I thought of Uncle Pio. Why? Where else but with him had I seen that very gesture with which he arrests a passing abbé or a courtier's valet, and whispers, his lips laid against his victim's ear? And surely enough, before noon I saw him hurry by on one of those mysterious errands of his. As I am the idlest and silliest of*"

205

women I sent Pepita to get me a piece of nougat which I placed on the ant's highway. Similarly I sent word to the Café Pizarro asking them to send Uncle Pio to see me if he dropped in before sunset. I shall give him that old bent salad fork with the turquoise in it, and he will bring me a copy of the new ballad that everyone is singing about the d–q–a of Ol–v–s. My child, you shall have the best of everything, and you shall have it first."

And in the next letter: *"My dear, Uncle Pio is the most delightful man in the world, your husband excepted. He is the second most delightful man in the world. His conversation is enchanting. If he weren't so disreputable I should make him my secretary. He could write all my letters for me and generations would rise up and call me witty. Alas, however, he is so moth-eaten by disease and bad company, that I shall have to leave him to his underworld. He is not only like an ant, he is like a soiled pack of cards. And I doubt whether the whole Pacific could wash him sweet and fragrant again. But what divine Spanish he speaks and what exquisite things he says in it! That's what one gets by hanging around a theater and hearing nothing but the conversation of Calderón. Alas, what is the matter with this world, my soul, that it should treat such a being so ill! His eyes are as sad as those of a cow that has been separated from its tenth calf."*

You should know first that this Uncle Pio was Camila Perichole's maid. He was also her singing master, her coiffeur, her masseur, her reader, her errand boy, her banker; rumor added: her father. For example, he taught her her parts. There was a whisper around town that Camila could read and write. The compliment was unfounded; Uncle Pio did her reading and writing for her. At the height of the season the company put on two or three new plays a week, and as each one contained a long and flowery part for the Perichole the mere task of memorization was not a trifle.

Peru had passed within fifty years from a frontier state

to a state in renaissance. Its interest in music and the the-
ater was intense. Lima celebrated its feast days by hearing
a Mass of Tomás Luis de Victoria in the morning and the
glittering poetry of Calderón in the evening. It is true that
the Limeans were given to interpolating trivial songs into
the most exquisite comedies and some lachrymose effects
into the austerest music; but at least they never submitted
to the boredom of a misplaced veneration. If they had dis-
liked heroic comedy the Limeans would not have hesitated
to remain at home; and if they had been deaf to polyphony
nothing would have prevented their going to an earlier
service. When the Archbishop returned from a short trip to
Spain, all Lima kept asking, "What has he brought?" The
news finally spread abroad that he had returned with tomes
of masses and motets by Palestrina, Morales and Vittoria,
as well as thirty-five plays by Tirso de Molina and Ruiz de
Alarçon and Moreto. There was a civic fete in his honor.
The choirboys' school and the greenroom of the Comedia
were swamped with the gifts of vegetables and wheat. All
the world was eager to nourish the interpreters of so much
beauty.

This was the theater in which Camila Perichole gradually
made her reputation. So rich was the repertory and so de-
pendable the prompter's box that few plays were given
more than four times a season. The manager had the whole
flowering of the seventeenth century Spanish drama to draw
upon, including many that are now lost to us. The Perichole
had appeared in a hundred plays of Lope de Vega alone.
There were many admirable actresses in Lima during these
years, but none better. The citizens were too far away
from the theaters of Spain to realize that she was the best
in the Spanish world. They kept sighing for a glimpse of
the stars of Madrid whom they had never seen and to whom
they assigned vague new excellences. Only one person knew
for certain that the Perichole was a great performer and
that was her tutor, Uncle Pio.

Uncle Pio came of a good Castilian house, illegitimately.

At the age of ten he ran away to Madrid from his father's hacienda and was pursued without diligence. He lived ever after by his wits. He possessed the six attributes of the adventurer—a memory for names and faces, with the aptitude for altering his own; the gift of tongues; inexhaustible invention; secrecy; the talent for falling into conversation with strangers; and that freedom from conscience that springs from a contempt for the dozing rich he preyed upon. From ten to fifteen he distributed handbills for merchants, held horses, and ran confidential errands. From fifteen to twenty he trained bears and snakes for traveling circuses; he cooked, and mixed punches; he hung about the entries of the more expensive taverns and whispered informations into the travelers' ears—sometimes nothing more dubious than that a certain noble house was reduced to selling its plate and could thus dispense with the commission of a silversmith. He was attached to all the theaters in town and could applaud like ten. He spread slanders at so much a slander. He sold rumors about crops and about the value of land. From twenty to thirty his services came to be recognized in very high circles—he was sent out by the government to inspirit some half-hearted rebellions in the mountains, so that the government could presently arrive and wholeheartedly crush them. His discretion was so profound that the French party used him even when they knew that the Austrian party used him also. He had long interviews with the Princesse des Ursins, but he came and went by the backstairs. During this phase he was no longer obliged to arrange gentlemen's pleasures, nor to plant little harvests of calumny.

He never did one thing for more than two weeks at a time even when enormous gains seemed likely to follow upon it. He could have become a circus manager, a theatrical director, a dealer in antiquities, an importer of Italian silks, a secretary in the Palace or the Cathedral, a dealer in provisions for the army, a speculator in houses and farms, a merchant in dissipations and pleasures. But there seemed

to have been written into his personality, through some ac-
cident or early admiration of his childhood, a reluctance to
own anything, to be tied down, to be held to a long engage-
ment. It was this that prevented his thieving, for example.
He had stolen several times, but the gains had not been
sufficient to offset his dread of being locked up; he had suffi-
cient ingenuity to escape on the field itself all the police in
the world, but nothing could protect him against the tale-
bearing of his enemies. Similarly he had been reduced for a
time to making investigations for the Inquisition, but when
he had seen several of his victims led off in hoods he felt
that he might be involving himself in an institution whose
movements were not evenly predictable.

As he approached twenty, Uncle Pio came to see quite
clearly that his life had three aims. There was first this
need of independence, cast into a curious pattern, namely:
the desire to be varied, secret and omniscient. He was will-
ing to renounce the dignities of public life, if in secret he
might feel that he looked down upon men from a great
distance, knowing more about them than they knew them-
selves; and with a knowledge which occasionally passed
into action and rendered him an agent in the affairs of states
and persons. In the second place he wanted to be always
near beautiful women, of whom he was always in the best
and worst sense the worshiper. To be near them was as
necessary to him as breathing. His reverence for beauty
and charm was there for anyone to see and to laugh at, and
the ladies of the theater and the court and the houses of
pleasure loved his connoisseurship. They tormented him
and insulted him and asked his advice and were singularly
comforted by his absurd devotion. He suffered greatly their
rages and their meannesses and their confiding tears; all he
asked was to be accepted casually, to be trusted, to be al-
lowed like a friendly and slightly foolish dog to come and
go in their rooms and to write their letters for them. He was
insatiably curious about their minds and their hearts. He
never expected to be loved by them (borrowing for a mo-

ment another sense of that word); for that, he carried his
money to the obscurer parts of the city; he was always des-
perately unprepossessing, with his wisp of a mustache and
his wisp of a beard and his big ridiculous sad eyes. They
constituted his parish; it was from them that he acquired
the name of Uncle Pio and it was when they were in trou-
ble that he most revealed himself; when they fell from
favor he lent them money, when they were ill he outlasted
the flagging devotion of their lovers and the exasperation
of their maids; when time or disease robbed them of their
beauty, he served them still for their beauty's memory; and
when they died his was the honest grief that saw them as
far as possible on their journey.

In the third place he wanted to be near those that loved
Spanish literature and its masterpieces, especially in the
theater. He had discovered all that treasure for himself,
borrowing or stealing from the libraries of his patrons,
feeding himself upon it in secrecy—behind the scenes, as
it were, of his mad life. He was contemptuous of the great
persons who for all their education and usage, exhibited no
care nor astonishment before the miracles of word order in
Calderón and Cervantes. He longed himself to make verses.
He never realized that many of the satirical songs he had
written for the vaudevilles passed into folk music and have
been borne everywhere along the highroads.

As the result of one of those quarrels that arise so nat-
urally in brothels his life became too complicated and he
removed to Peru. Uncle Pio in Peru was even more versa-
tile than Uncle Pio in Europe. Here too he touched upon
real estate, circuses, pleasures, insurrections and antiques. A
Chinese junk had been blown from Canton to America; he
dragged up the beach the bales of deep-red porcelain and
sold the bowls to the collectors of virtu. He traced down
the sovereign remedies of the Incas and started a smart
trade in pills. Within four months he knew practically every-
one in Lima. He presently added to this acquaintance the
inhabitants of scores of seacoast towns, mining camps and

settlements in the interior. His pretensions to omniscience became more and more plausible. The Viceroy discovered Uncle Pio and all this richness of reference; he engaged his services in many affairs. In the decay of his judgment Don Andrés had retained one talent, he was a master of the technique of handling confidential servants. He treated Uncle Pio with great tact and some deference; he understood which errands the other should not be asked to undertake and he understood his need for variety and intermission. Uncle Pio in turn was perpetually astonished that a prince should make so little use of his position, for power, or for fantasy, or for sheer delight in the manipulation of other men's destinies; but the servant loved the master because he could quote from any of Cervantes' prefaces and because his tongue had a little Castilian salt about it still. Many a morning Uncle Pio entered the Palace through corridors where there was no one to cross but a confessor or a confidential bully and sat with the Viceroy over his morning chocolate.

But for all his activity nothing made Uncle Pio rich. One would have said that he abandoned a venture when it threatened to prosper. Although no one knew it, he owned a house. It was full of dogs that could add and multiply, and the top floor was reserved for birds. But even in this kingdom he was lonely, and proud in his loneliness, as though there resided a certain superiority in such a solitude. Finally he stumbled upon an adventure that came like some strange gift from the skies and that combined the three great aims of his life: his passion for overseeing the lives of others, his worship of beautiful women, and his admiration for the treasures of Spanish literature. He discovered Camila Perichole. Her real name was Micaela Villegas. She was singing in cafés at the age of twelve and Uncle Pio had always been the very soul of cafés. Now as he sat among the guitarists and watched this awkward girl singing ballads, imitating every inflection of the more experienced singers who had preceded her, the determination

entered his mind to play Pygmalion. He bought her. Instead
of sleeping locked up in the wine bin, she inherited a cot
in his house. He wrote songs for her, he taught her how to
listen to the quality of her tone, and bought her a new
dress. At first all she noticed was that it was wonderful not
to be whipped, to be offered hot soups, and to be taught
something. But it was Uncle Pio who was really dazzled.
His rash experiment flourished beyond all prophecy. The
little twelve-year-old, silent and always a little sullen, de-
voured work. He set her endless exercises in acting and
mimicry; he set her problems in conveying the atmosphere
of a song; he took her to the theaters and made her notice
all the details of a performance. But it was from Camila as
a woman that he was to receive his greatest shock. The
long arms and legs were finally harmonized into a body of
perfect grace. The almost grotesque and hungry face be-
came beautiful. Her whole nature became gentle and mys-
terious and oddly wise; and it all turned to him. She could
find no fault in him and she was sturdily loyal. They loved
one another deeply but without passion. He respected the
slight nervous shadow that crossed her face when he came
too near her. But there arose out of this denial itself the
perfume of a tenderness, that ghost of passion which, in the
most unexpected relationship, can make even a whole life-
time devoted to irksome duty pass like a gracious dream.

They traveled a great deal, seeking new taverns, for the
highest attribute of a café singer will always be her novelty.
They went to Mexico, their odd clothes wrapped up in the
selfsame shawl. They slept on beaches, they were whipped
at Panama and shipwrecked on some tiny Pacific islands
plastered with the droppings of birds. They tramped
through jungles delicately picking their way among snakes
and beetles. They sold themselves out as harvesters in a
hard season. Nothing in the world was very surprising to
them.

Then began an even harder course of training for the girl,
a regimen that resembled more the preparation for an acro-

bat. The instruction was a little complicated by the fact that her rise to favor was very rapid; and there was some danger that the applause she received would make her content with her work too soon. Uncle Pio never exactly beat her, but he resorted to a sarcasm that had terrors of its own.

At the close of a performance Camila would return to her dressing room to find Uncle Pio whistling nonchalantly in one corner. She would divine his attitude at once and cry angrily:

"Now what is it? Mother of God, Mother of God, what is it now?"

"Nothing, little pearl. My little Camila of Camilas, nothing."

"There was something you didn't like. Ugly faultfinding thing that you are. Come on now, what was it? Look, I'm ready."

"No, little fish. Adorable morning star, I suppose you did as well as you could."

The suggestion that she was a limited artist and that certain felicities would be forever closed to her never failed to make Camila frantic. She would burst into tears: "I wish I had never known you. You poison my whole life. You just think I did badly. It pleases you to pretend that I was bad. All right then, be quiet."

Uncle Pio went on whistling.

"The fact is I know I was weak tonight, and don't need you to tell me so. So there. Now go away. I don't want to see you around. It's hard enough to play that part without coming back and finding you this way."

Suddenly Uncle Pio would lean forward and ask with angry intensity, "Why did you take that speech to the prisoner so fast?"

More tears from the Perichole: "Oh, God, let me die in peace! One day you tell me to go faster and another to go slower. Anyway I shall be crazy in a year or two and then it won't matter."

More whistling.

"Besides the audience applauded as never before. Do you hear me? *As never before.* There! Too fast or too slow is nothing to them. They wept. I was divine. That's all I care for. Now be silent. Be silent."

He was absolutely silent.

"You may comb my hair, but if you say another word I shall never play again. You can find some other girl, that's all."

Thereupon he would comb her hair soothingly for ten minutes, pretending not to notice the sobs that were shaking her exhausted body. At last she would turn quickly and catching one of his hands would kiss it frantically: "Uncle Pio, was I so bad? Was I a disgrace to you? Was it so awful *that you left the theater?*"

After a long pause Uncle Pio would admit judiciously, "You were good in the scene on the ship."

"But I've been better, Uncle Pio. You remember the night you came back from Cuzco——?"

"You were pretty good at the close."

"Was I?"

"But my flower, my pearl, *what was the matter in the speech to the prisoner?*"

Here the Perichole would fling her face and arms upon the table amid the pomades, caught up into a tremendous fit of weeping. Only perfection would do, only perfection. And that had never come.

Then beginning in a low voice Uncle Pio would talk for an hour, analyzing the play, entering into a world of finesse in matters of voice and gesture and tempo, and often until dawn they would remain there declaiming to one another the lordly conversation of Calderón.

Whom were these two seeking to please? Not the audiences of Lima. They had long since been satisfied. We come from a world where we have known incredible standards of excellence, and we dimly remember beauties which we have not seized again; and we go back to that world. Uncle Pio and Camila Perichole were tormenting themselves in an

effort to establish in Peru the standards of the theaters in some Heaven whither Calderón had preceded them. The public for which masterpieces are intended is not on this earth.

With the passing of time Camila lost some of this absorption in her art. A certain intermittent contempt for acting made her negligent. It was due to the poverty of interest in women's roles throughout Spanish classical drama. At a time when the playwrights grouped about the courts of England and France (a little later, of Venice) were enriching the parts of women with studies in wit, charm, passion and hysteria, the dramatists of Spain kept their eyes on their heroes, on gentlemen torn between the conflicting claims of honor, or, as sinners, returning at the last moment to the cross. For a number of years Uncle Pio spent himself in discovering ways to interest the Perichole in the roles that fell to her. Upon one occasion he was able to announce to Camila that a granddaughter of Vico de Barrera had arrived in Peru. Uncle Pio had long since communicated to Camila his veneration for great poets and Camila never questioned the view that they were a little above the kings and not below the saints. So it was in great excitement that the two of them chose one of the master's plays to perform before his granddaughter. They rehearsed the poem a hundred times, now in the great joy of invention, now in dejection. On the night of the performance Camila peering out between the folds of the curtain had Uncle Pio point out to her the little middle-aged woman worn with the cares of penury and a large family; but it seemed to Camila that she was looking at all the beauty and dignity in the world. As she waited for the lines that preceded her entrance she clung to Uncle Pio in reverent silence, her heart beating loudly. Between the acts she retired to the dusty corner of the warehouse where no one would find her and sat staring into the corners. At the close of the performance Uncle Pio brought the granddaughter of Vico de Barrera into Camila's room. Camila stood among the clothes that hung upon the

wall, weeping with happiness and shame. Finally she flung
herself on her knees and kissed the older woman's hands,
and the older woman kissed hers, and while the audience
went home and went to bed the visitor remained, telling
Camila the little stories that had remained in the family, of
Vico's work and of his habits.

Uncle Pio was at his happiest when a new actress entered
the company, for the discovery of a new talent at her side
never failed to bestir the Perichole. To Uncle Pio (standing
at the back of the auditorium, bent double with joy and
malice) it seemed that the body of the Perichole had be-
come an alabaster lamp in which a strong light had been
placed. Without any resort to tricks or to false emphasis,
she set herself to efface the newcomer. If the play were a
comedy she became the very abstraction of wit, and (as was
more likely) if it was a drama of wronged ladies and im-
placable hates, the stage fairly smoldered with her emotion.
Her personality became so electric that if she so much as
laid her hand upon that of a fellow actor a sympathetic
shudder ran through the audience. But such occasions of
excellence became less and less frequent. As her technique
became sounder, Camila's sincerity became less necessary.
Even when she was absent-minded the audience did not
notice the difference and only Uncle Pio grieved.

Camila had a very beautiful face, or rather a face beauti-
ful save in repose. In repose one was startled to discover
that the nose was long and thin, the mouth tired and a little
childish, the eyes unsatisfied—a rather pinched peasant girl,
dragged from the cafés-chantants and quite incapable of
establishing any harmony between the claims of her art, of
her appetites, of her dreams, and of her crowded daily rou-
tine. Each of these was a world in itself, and the warfare
between them would soon have reduced to idiocy (or trivi-
ality) a less tenacious physique. We have seen that in spite
of her discontent with her parts, the Perichole knew very
well the joy that might reside in acting and warmed her-
self from time to time at that flame. But that of love at-

tracted her more often, though with no greater assurance of happiness, until Jupiter himself sent her some pearls.

Don Andrés de Ribera, the Viceroy of Peru, was the remnant of a delightful man, broken by the table, the alcove, a grandeeship and ten years of exile. As a youth he had accompanied embassies to Versailles and Rome; he had fought in the wars in Austria; he had been in Jerusalem. He was a widower, and childless, of an enormous and wealthy woman; he had collected coins a little, wines, actresses, orders and maps. From the table he had received the gout; from the alcove a tendency to convulsions; from the grandeeship a pride so vast and puerile that he seldom heard anything that was said to him and talked to the ceiling in a perpetual monologue; from the exile, oceans of boredom, a boredom so persuasive that it was like pain—he woke up with it and spent the day with it, and it sat by his bed all night watching his sleep. Camila was passing the years in the hard-working routine of the theater, savored by a few untidy love affairs, when this Olympian personage (for he had a face and port fit to play gods and heroes on the scene) suddenly transported her to the most delicious midnight suppers at the Palace. Contrary to all the traditions of the stage and state she adored her elderly admirer; she thought she was going to be happy forever. Don Andrés taught the Perichole a great many things and to her bright eager mind that was one of the sweetest ingredients of love. He taught her a little French; to be neat and clean; the modes of address. Uncle Pio had taught her how great ladies carry themselves on great occasions; he taught her how they relax. Uncle Pio and Calderón had trained her in beautiful Spanish; Don Andrés furnished her with the smart slang of *El Buen Retiro*.

Uncle Pio was made anxious by Camila's invitation from the Palace. He would have much preferred that she continue with her little vulgarian love affairs in the theatrical warehouse. But when he saw that her art was gaining a new finish he was well content. He would sit in the back of

the theater, rolling about in his seat for sheer joy and amusement, watching the Perichole intimate to the audience that she frequented the great world about whom the dramatists wrote. She had a new way of fingering a wineglass, of exchanging an adieu, a new way of entering a door that told everything. To Uncle Pio nothing else mattered. What was there in the world more lovely than a beautiful woman doing justice to a Spanish masterpiece?—a performance (he asks you), packed with observation, in which the very spacing of the words revealed a comment on life and on the text—delivered by a beautiful voice—illustrated by a faultless carriage, considerable personal beauty and irresistible charm. "We are almost ready to take this marvel to Spain," he would murmur to himself. After the performance he would go around to her dressing room and say "Very good!" But before taking his leave he would manage to ask her where, in the name of the eleven thousand virgins of Cologne, she had acquired that affected way of saying *Excelencia*.

After a time the Viceroy asked the Perichole whether it would amuse her to invite a few discreet guests to their midnight suppers, and he asked her whether she would like to meet the Archbishop. Camila was delighted. The Archbishop was delighted. On the eve of their first meeting he sent the actress an emerald pendant as big as a playing card.

There was something in Lima that was wrapped up in yards of violet satin from which protruded a great dropsical head and two fat pearly hands; and that was its archbishop. Between the rolls of flesh that surrounded them looked out two black eyes speaking discomfort, kindliness and wit. A curious and eager soul was imprisoned in all this lard, but by dint of never refusing himself a pheasant or a goose or his daily procession of Roman wines, he was his own bitter jailer. He loved his cathedral; he loved his duties; he was very devout. Some days he regarded his bulk ruefully; but the distress of remorse was less poignant than the distress of fasting and he was presently found deliberating over the

secret messages that a certain roast sends to the certain salad that will follow it. And to punish himself he led an exemplary life in every other respect.

He had read all the literature of antiquity and forgotten all about it except a general aroma of charm and disillusion. He had been learned in the Fathers and the Councils and forgotten all about them save a floating impression of dissensions that had no application to Peru. He had read all the libertine masterpieces of Italy and France and reread them annually; even in the torments of the stone (happily dissolved by drinking the water from the springs of Santa María de Cluxambuqua), he could find nothing more nourishing than the anecdotes of Brantôme and the divine Aretino.

The Archbishop knew that most of the priests of Peru were scoundrels. It required all his delicate Epicurean education to prevent his doing something about it; he had to repeat over to himself his favorite notions: that the injustice and unhappiness in the world is a constant; that the theory of progress is a delusion; that the poor, never having known happiness, are insensible to misfortune. Like all the rich he could not bring himself to believe that the poor (look at their houses, look at their clothes) could really suffer. Like all the cultivated he believed that only the widely read could be said to *know* that they were unhappy. On one occasion, the iniquities in his see having been called to his notice, he almost did something about it. He had just heard that it was becoming a rule in Peru for priests to exact two measures of meal for a fairly good absolution, and five measures for a really effective one. He trembled with indignation; he roared to his secretary and bidding him bring up his writing materials, announced that he was going to dictate an overwhelming message to his shepherds. But there was no ink left in the inkwell; there was no ink left in the next room; there was no ink to be found in the whole palace. This state of things in his household so upset the

good man that he fell ill of the combined rages and learned
to guard himself against indignations.

The addition of the Archbishop to the suppers was so
successful that Don Andrés began to think of new names.
He had grown increasingly dependent upon Uncle Pio, but
waited until Camila should propose his inclusion of her
own accord. And in due time Uncle Pio brought with him
that courser of the seas, the Captain Alvarado. Generally
the reunion had been several hours under way. before Ca-
mila was able to join them after her performance at the
theater. She would arrive toward one o'clock, radiant and
bejeweled and very tired. The four men received her as
they would a great queen. For an hour or so she would
carry the conversation, but gradually reclining more and
more against Don Andrés' shoulder she would follow the
talk as it flitted from one humorous lined face to the other.
All night they talked, secretly comforting their hearts that
longed always for Spain and telling themselves that such a
symposium was after the manner of the high Spanish soul.
They talked about ghosts and second sight, and about the
earth before man appeared upon it and about the possibility
of the planets striking against one another; about whether
the soul can be seen, like a dove, fluttering away at the
moment of death; they wondered whether at the second
coming of Christ to Jerusalem, Peru would be long in re-
ceiving the news. They talked until the sun rose, about wars
and kings, about poets and scholars, and about strange
countries. Each one poured into the conversation his store
of wise, sad anecdotes and his dry regret about the race of
men. The flood of golden light struck across the Andes and
entering the great window fell upon the piles of fruit, the
stained brocade upon the table, and the sweet thoughtful
forehead of the Perichole as she lay sleeping against the
sleeve of her protector. There would ensue a long pause,
no one wishing to make the first move to go, and the glances
of them all would rest upon this strange beautiful bird who
lived among them. But Uncle Pio's glance had been upon

her all night, a quick glance from his black eyes, full of tenderness and anxiety, resting on the great secret and reason of his life.

But Uncle Pio never ceased watching Camila. He divided the inhabitants of this world into two groups, into those who had loved and those who had not. It was a horrible aristocracy, apparently, for those who had no capacity for love (or rather for suffering in love) could not be said to be alive and certainly would not live again after their death. They were a kind of straw population, filling the world with their meaningless laughter and tears and chatter and disappearing still lovable and vain into thin air. For this distinction he cultivated his own definition of love that was like no other and that had gathered all its bitterness and pride from his odd life. He regarded love as a sort of cruel malady through which the elect are required to pass in their late youth and from which they emerge, pale and wrung, but ready for the business of living. There was (he believed) a great repertory of errors mercifully impossible to human beings who had recovered from this illness. Unfortunately there remained to them a host of failings, but at least (from among many illustrations) they never mistook a protracted amiability for the whole conduct of life, they never again regarded any human being, from a prince to a servant, as a mechanical object. Uncle Pio never ceased watching Camila because it seemed to him that she had never undergone this initiation. In the months that followed her introduction to the Viceroy he held his breath and waited. He held his breath for years. Camila bore the Viceroy three children, yet remained the same. He knew that the first sign of her entrance into the true possession of the world would be the mastery of certain effects in her acting. There were certain passages in the plays that she would compass some day, simply, easily, and with secret joy, because they alluded to the new rich wisdom of her heart; but her treatment of such passages became more and more cursory, not to say embarrassed. He presently saw that she had tired of

Don Andrés and had returned to a series of furtive love
affairs with the actors and matadors and merchants of the
town.

She became more and more impatient of acting and an-
other parasite found its way into her mind. She wanted to
be a lady. She slowly contracted a greed for respectability
and began to refer to her acting as a pastime. She acquired
a duenna and some footmen and went to church at the fash-
ionable hours. She attended the prize days at the Univer-
sity and appeared among the donors of the great charities.
She even learned to read and write a little. Any faint dis-
crimination against her as a Bohemian she challenged with
fury. She led the Viceroy a horrible life with her passion for
concessions and her gradual usurpation of privileges. The
new vice displaced the old and she became noisily virtuous.
She invented some parents and produced some cousins. She
obtained an undocumented legitimatization of her children.
In society she cultivated a delicate and languid magdaele-
nism, as a great lady might, and she carried a candle in the
penitential parades, side by side with ladies who had noth-
ing to regret but an outburst of temper and a furtive glance
into Descartes. Her sin had been acting and everyone
knows that there were even saints who had been actors—
there was Saint Gelasius and Saint Genesius and Saint Mar-
garet of Antioch and Saint Pelagia.

There was a fashionable watering place in the hills not
far from Santa María de Cluxambuqua. Don Andrés had
traveled in France and had thought to build himself a little
mock Vichy; there was a pagoda, some drawing rooms, a
theater, a little arena for bullfights and some French gar-
dens. Camila's health had never known a shadow, but she
built herself a villa in the vicinity and sipped the hateful
waters at eleven o'clock. The Marquesa de Montemayor
has left a brilliant picture of this *opéra bouffe* paradise
with the reigning divinity parading her fierce sensitiveness
along the avenues of powdered shell and receiving the
homage of all those who could not afford to offend the

Viceroy. Doña María draws a portrait of this ruler, stately and weary, gambling all through the night in sums that would have raised another Escurial. And beside him she sets the portrait of his son, Camila's little Don Jaime. Don Jaime, at seven years, was a rachitic little body who seemed to have inherited not only his mother's forehead and eyes, but his father's liability to convulsions. He bore his pain with the silent bewilderment of an animal, and like an animal he was mortally ashamed when any evidences of it occurred in public. He was so beautiful that the more trivial forms of pity were hushed in his presence and his long thoughts about his difficulties had given his face a patient and startling dignity. His mother dressed him in garnet velvet, and when he was able he followed her about at a distance of several yards, extricating himself gravely from the ladies who tried to detain him in conversation. Camila was never cross to Don Jaime and she was never demonstrative. When the sun was shining the two could be seen walking along those artificial terraces in silence, Camila wondering when the felicity would begin that she had always associated with social position, Don Jaime rejoicing merely in the sunlight and anxiously estimating the approach of a cloud. They looked like figures that had strayed there from some remote country, or out of an old ballad, that had not yet learned the new language and had not yet found any friends.

Camila was about thirty when she left the stage and it required five years for her to achieve her place in society. She gradually became almost stout, though her head seemed to grow more beautiful every year. She took to overdressing and the floors of the drawing rooms reflected a veritable tower of jewels and scarves and plumes. Her face and hands were covered with a bluish powder against which she drew an irritable mouth in scarlet and orange. The almost distraught fury of her temper was varied by the unnatural sweetness of her address in the company of the dowagers. In the earliest stages of her progress upward she had intimated

to Uncle Pio that he was not to be seen with her in public,
but finally she became impatient even of his discreeter
visits. She conducted the interviews with formality and
evasion. Her eyes never crossed his and she angled for pre-
texts to quarrel with him. Still he ventured out once a
month to try her patience and when the call had become
impossible he would climb the stairs and finish the hour
among her children.

One day he arrived at her villa in the hills and, through
her maid, begged for an opportunity to talk with her. He
was told that she would see him in the French gardens a
little before sunset. He had come up from Lima on a strange
sentimental impulse. Like all solitary persons he had in-
vested friendship with a divine glamor: he imagined that
the people he passed on the street, laughing together and
embracing when they parted, the people who dined to-
gether with so many smiles—you will scarcely believe me,
but he imagined that they were extracting from all that
congeniality great store of satisfaction. So that suddenly he
was filled with the excitement of seeing her again, of being
called "Uncle Pio," and of reviving for a moment the trust
and humor of their long vagabondage.

The French gardens were at the southern end of the
town. Behind them rose the higher Andes and before them
there was a parapet overlooking a deep valley and over-
looking wave after wave of hills that stretched toward the
Pacific. It was the hour when bats fly low and the smaller
animals play recklessly underfoot. A few solitaries lingered
about the gardens, gazing dreamily into the sky that was
being gradually emptied of its color, or leaned upon the
balustrade and looked down into the valley, noting in which
village a dog was barking. It was the hour when the father
returns home from the fields and plays for a moment in the
yard with the dog that jumps upon him, holding his muzzle
closed or throwing him upon his back. The young girls look
about for the first star to fix a wish upon it, and the boys
grow restless for supper. Even the busiest mother stands

for a moment idle-handed, smiling at her dear and exasperating family.

Uncle Pio stood against one of the chipped marble benches and watched Camila coming toward him:

"I am late," she said. "I am sorry. What is it you wish to say to me?"

"Camila—" he began.

"My name is Doña Micaela."

"I do not wish to offend you, Doña Micaela, but when you let me call you Camila for twenty years, I should think——"

"Oh, do as you like. Do as you like."

"Camila, promise me that you will listen to me. Promise me that you will not run away at my first sentence."

At once she burst out with unexpected passion, "Uncle Pio, listen to me. You are mad if you think you can make me return to the theater. I look back at the theater with horror. Understand that. The theater! The theater, indeed! The daily payment of insults in that filthy place. Understand that you are wasting your time."

He answered gently, "I would not have you come back if you are happy with these new friends."

"You don't like my new friends, then?" she answered quickly. "Whom do you offer me in their stead?"

"Camila, I only remember. . . ."

"I will not be criticized. I don't want any advice. It will be cold in a moment, I must go back to my house. Just give me up, that's all. Just put me out of your mind."

"Dear Camila, don't be angry. Let me talk to you. Just suffer me for ten minutes."

He did not understand why she was weeping. He did not know what to say. He talked at random, "You never even come to see the theater, and they all notice it. The audiences are falling away now, too. They only put on the Old Comedy twice a week; all the other nights there are these new farces in prose. All is dull and childish and indecent. No one can speak Spanish any more. No one can even

walk correctly any more. On Corpus Christi Day they gave
Belshazzar's Feast where you were so wonderful. Now it
was shameful."

There was a pause. A beautiful procession of clouds, like
a flock of sheep, was straying up from the sea, slipping up
the valleys between the hills. Camila suddenly touched his
knee, and her face was like her face twenty years before:
"Forgive me, Uncle Pio, for being so bad. Jaime was ill this
afternoon. There's nothing one can do. He lies there, so
white and . . . so surprised. One must just think of other
things. Uncle Pio, it would be no good if I went back to the
theater. The audiences come for the prose farces. We were
foolish to try and keep alive the Old Comedy. Let people
read the old plays in books if they choose to. It is not
worth-while fighting with the crowd."

"Wonderful Camila, I was not just to you when you were
on the stage. It was some foolish pride in me. I grudged you
the praise that you deserved. Forgive me. You have always
been a very great artist. If you come to see that you are
not happy among these people you might think about going
to Madrid. You would have a great triumph there. You are
still young and beautiful. There will be time later to be
called Doña Micaela. We shall be old soon. We shall be
dead soon."

"No, I shall never see Spain. All the world is alike, Madrid
or Lima."

"Oh, if we could go away to some island where the peo-
ple would know you for yourself. And love you."

"You are fifty years old and you are still dreaming of
such islands, Uncle Pio."

He bent his head and mumbled, "Of course I love you,
Camila, as I always must and more than I can say. To have
known you is enough for my whole life. You are a great
lady now. And you are rich. There is no longer any way
that I can help you. But I am always ready."

"How absurd you are," she said smiling. "You said that
as boys say it. You don't seem to learn as you grow older,

Uncle Pio. There is no such thing as that kind of love and that kind of island. It's in the theater you find such things."

He looked shamefaced, but unconvinced.

At last she rose and said sadly, "What are we talking about! It is growing cold. I must be going in. You must be resigned. I have no heart for the theater." There was a pause. "And for the rest? . . . Oh, I do not understand. It is just circumstance. I must be what I must. Do not try to understand either. Don't think about me, Uncle Pio. Just forgive, that's all. Just try to forgive."

She stood still a moment, searching for something deeply felt to say to him. The first cloud reached the terrace; it was dark; the last stragglers were leaving the gardens. She was thinking of Don Jaime, and of Don Andrés and of himself. She could not find the words. Suddenly she bent down and kissed his fingers and went quickly away. But he sat for a long time in the gathering clouds trembling with happiness and trying to penetrate into the meaning of these things.

Suddenly the news was all over Lima. Doña Micaela Villegas, the lady that used to be Camila the Perichole, had the smallpox. Several hundred other persons had the smallpox also, but popular interest and malignity were concentrated upon the actress. A wild hope ran about the town that the beauty would be impaired that had enabled her to despise the class from which she sprang. The news escaped from the sickroom that Camila had become ludicrous in homeliness and the cup of the envious overflowed. As soon as she was able she had herself carried from the city to her villa in the hills; she ordered the sale of her elegant little palace. She returned her jewels to their givers and she sold her fine clothes. The Viceroy, the Archbishop, and the few men at court who had been her sincerest admirers besieged her door still with messages and gifts; the messages were ignored and the gifts were returned without comment. No one but her nurse and maids had been permitted to see her since the commencement of her illness. As an answer to his repeated attempts, Don Andrés received a large sum of

money from her with a letter compounded of all that is possible in bitterness and pride.

Like all beautiful women who have been brought up amid continual tributes to her beauty she assumed without cynicism that it must necessarily be the basis of anyone's attachment to herself; henceforth any attention paid to her must spring from a pity full of condescension and faintly perfumed with satisfaction at so complete a reversal. This assumption that she need look for no more devotion now that her beauty had passed proceeded from the fact that she had never realized any love save love as passion. Such love, though it expends itself in generosity and thoughtfulness, though it give birth to visions and to great poetry, remains among the sharpest expressions of self-interest. Not until it has passed through a long servitude, through its own self-hatred, through mockery, through great doubts, can it take its place among the loyalties. Many who have spent a lifetime in it can tell us less of love than the child that lost a dog yesterday. As her friends continued in their efforts to draw her again into society she grew more and more angry and dispatched insulting messages to the city. It was said for a time that she was retiring into religion. But new rumors that all was fury and despair on the little farm contradicted the old. For those near to her the despair was fearful to behold. She was convinced that her life was over, her life and children's. In her hysterical pride she had given back more than she owed and the approach of poverty was added to the loneliness and the gloom of her future. There was nothing left for her to do but to draw out her days in jealous solitude in the center of the little farm that was falling into decay. She brooded for hours upon the joy of her enemies and could be heard striding about her room with strange cries.

Uncle Pio did not allow himself to be discouraged. By dint of making himself useful to the children, by taking a hand in the management of the farm and by discreetly lending her some money, he obtained his entrance into the

house and even into the presence of its veiled mistress. But even then Camila, convinced in her pride that he *pitied* her, lashed him with the blade of her tongue and derived some strange comfort from heaping him with sneers. He loved her the more, understanding better than she did herself all the stages in the convalescence of her humiliated spirit. But one day an accident befell that lost him his share in her progress. He pushed open a door.

She thought she had locked it. For just one hour a foolish secret hope had come to her; she wondered whether she could make a paste of chalk and cream to spread upon her face. She who had sneered so often at the befloured grandmothers of the court wondered for a few moments whether she had learned anything on the stage that would aid her now. She thought she had locked the door and with hurried hands and beating heart she laid on the coat, the grotesque pallor, and as she gazed into the mirror and recognized the futility of her attempt she caught the image of Uncle Pio standing in the door amazed. She rose from the chair with a cry and covered her face with her hands.

"Go away. Go away out of my house forever," she screamed. "I never want to see you again." In her shame she drove him out with blasphemy and hatred, she pursued him down the corridor and hurled objects down the stairs. She gave her farmer orders that Uncle Pio was forbidden to come into the grounds. But he continued for a week trying to see her again. At last he went back to Lima; he filled in the time as best he could, but he longed to be by her as a boy of eighteen would long. At last he devised a stratagem and returned up into the hills to put it into effect.

One morning before dawn he arose and lay on the ground below her window. He imitated in the darkness the sound of weeping, and, as nearly as he could, of a young girl's weeping. He continued in this for the whole quarter of an hour. He did not let his voice rise above that degree of loudness which Italian musicians would represent by the direction *piano,* but he frequently intermitted the sound trust-

ing that if she were asleep it would insinuate itself into her mind as well by duration as by degree. The air was cool and agreeable. The first faint streak of sapphire was appearing behind the peaks and in the east the star of morning was pulsating every moment with a more tender intention. A profound silence wrapped all the farm buildings, only an occasional breeze set all the grasses sighing. Suddenly a lamp was lighted in her room and a moment later the shutter was thrown back and a head wrapped in veils leaned far out.

"Who is there?" asked the beautiful voice.

Uncle Pio remained silent.

Camila said again in a tone edged with impatience:

"Who is there? Who is there weeping?"

"Doña Micaela, my lady, I beg of you to come here to me."

"Who are you and what do you want?"

"I am a poor girl. I am Estrella. I beg of you to come and help me. Do not call your maid. I pray you, Doña Micaela, to come yourself."

Camila was silent a moment, then said abruptly, "Very well," and closed the shutter. Presently she appeared around the corner of the house. She wore a thick cloak that dragged in the dew. She stood at a distance and said, "Come over here to where I am standing,—Who are you?"

Uncle Pio rose up. "Camila, it is I—Uncle Pio. Forgive me, but I must speak to you."

"Mother of God, when shall I be free of this dreadful person! Understand: I want to see no one. I don't want to speak to a soul. My life is over. That is all."

"Camila, by our long life together, I beg of you to grant me one thing. I shall go away and never trouble you again."

"I grant you nothing, nothing. Stay away from me."

"I promise you I shall never trouble you again if you listen to me this once." She was hurrying around to the door on the other side of the house and Uncle Pio was obliged to

run beside her to make sure that she heard what he was saying. She stopped:

"What is it then? Hurry. It is cold. I am not well. I must go back to my room."

"Camila, let me take Don Jaime for a year to live with me in Lima. Let me be his teacher. Let me teach him the Castilian. Here he is left among the servants. He is learning nothing."

"No."

"Camila, what will become of him? He has a good mind and he wants to learn."

"He is sick. He is delicate. Your house is a sty. Only the country is good for him."

"But he has been much better these last few months. I promise you I shall clean out my house. I shall apply to Madre María del Pilar for a housekeeper. Here he is in your stables all day. I shall teach him all that a gentleman should know—fencing and Latin and music. We shall read all. . . ."

"A mother cannot be separated from her child like that. It is impossible. You are crazy to have thought of it. Give up thinking of me and of everything about me. I no longer exist. I and my children will get on as best we can. Do not try to disturb me again. I do not want to see any human being."

Now it was that Uncle Pio felt obliged to use a hard measure. "Then pay me the money that you owe me," he said.

Camila stood still, confounded. To herself she said, "Life is too fearful to bear. When may I die?" After a moment she answered him, in a hoarse voice, "I have very little money. I will pay you what I can. I will pay you now. I have a few jewels here. Then we need never see one another again." She was ashamed of her poverty. She took a few steps, then turned and said, "Now I see that you are a very hard man. But it is right that I pay you what I owe you."

"No, Camila, I only said that to enforce my request. I

shall take no money from you. But lend me Don Jaime for one year. I shall love him and take every care of him. Did I harm you? Was I a bad teacher to you in those other years?"

"It is cruel of you to keep urging gratitude, gratitude, gratitude. I was grateful—good, good! But now that I am no longer the same woman there remains nothing to be grateful for." There was a silence. Her eyes were resting on the star that seemed to be leading forth the whole sky in its wonder. A great pain lay at her heart, the pain of a world that was meaningless. Then she said, "If Jaime wishes to go with you, very well. I shall talk to him in the morning. If he wishes to go with you, you will find him at the Inn about noon. Good night. Go with God."

"Go with God."

She returned to the house. The next day the grave little boy appeared at the Inn. His fine clothes were torn and stained now and he carried a small bundle for change. His mother had given him a gold piece for spending money and a little stone that shone in the dark to look at in his sleepless nights. They set off together in a cart, but soon Uncle Pio became aware that the jolting was not good for the boy. He carried him on his shoulder. As they drew near to the bridge of San Luis Rey, Jaime tried to conceal his shame for he knew that one of those moments was coming that separated him from other people. He was especially ashamed because Uncle Pio had just overtaken a friend of his, a sea captain. And just as they got to the bridge he spoke to an old lady who was traveling with a little girl. Uncle Pio said that when they had crossed the bridge they would sit down and rest, but it turned out not to be necessary.

Part Five: Perhaps an Intention

A NEW bridge of stone has been built in the place of the old, but the event has not been forgotten. It has passed into proverbial expressions. "I may see you Tuesday," says a Limean, "unless the bridge falls." "My cousin lives by the bridge of San Luis Rey," says another, and a smile goes around the company, for that also means: under the sword of Damocles. There are some poems about the accident, classics to be found in every Peruvian anthology, but the real literary monument is Brother Juniper's book.

There are a hundred ways of wondering at circumstances. Brother Juniper would never have arrived at his method had it not been for his friendship with a certain master in the University of San Martín. This student's wife had stolen away one morning on a boat for Spain, following a soldier, and had left him the care of two daughters in their cradle. He was possessed of all the bitterness that Brother Juniper lacked and derived a sort of joy from the conviction that all was wrong in the world. He whispered into the Franciscan's ear such thoughts and anecdotes as belied the notion of a guided world. For a moment a look of distress, almost of defeat, would come into the Brother's eyes; then he would begin patiently explaining why such stories held no diffi-

233

culty for a believer. "There was a queen of Naples and Sicily," the student would say, "who discovered that she was carrying an angry tumor in her side. In great dismay she commanded her subjects to fall to their prayers and ordered that all the garments in Sicily and Naples be sewn with votive crosses. She was well loved by her people and all their prayers and embroideries were sincere, but ineffectual. Now she lies in the splendor of Monreale, and a few inches above her heart may be read the words: *I shall fear no evil.*"

It was by dint of hearing a great many such sneers at faith that Brother Juniper became convinced that the world's time had come for proof, tabulated proof, of the conviction that was so bright and exciting within him. When the pestilence visited his dear village of Puerto and carried off a large number of peasants, he secretly drew up a diagram of the characteristics of fifteen victims and fifteen survivors, the statistics of their value *sub specie aeternitatis.* Each soul was rated upon a basis of ten as regards its goodness, its diligence in religious observance, and its importance to its family group. Here is a fragment of this ambitious chart:

	GOODNESS	PIETY	USEFULNESS
Alfonso G.	4	4	10
Nina	2	5	10
Manuel B.	10	10	0
Alfonso V.	−8	−10	10
Vera N.	0	10	10

The thing was more difficult than he had foreseen. Almost every soul in a difficult frontier community turned out to be indispensable economically, and the third column was all but useless. The examiner was driven to the use of minus terms when he confronted the personal character of Alfonso V., who was not, like Vera N., merely bad: he was a propagandist for badness and not merely avoided church but led others to avoid it. Vera N. was indeed bad, but she

was a model worshiper and the mainstay of a full hut. From all this saddening data Brother Juniper contrived an index for each peasant. He added up the total for victims and compared it with the total for survivors, to discover that the dead were five times more worth saving. It almost looked as though the pestilence had been directed against the really valuable people in the village of Puerto. And on that afternoon Brother Juniper took a walk along the edge of the Pacific. He tore up his findings and cast them into the waves; he gazed for an hour upon the great clouds of pearl that hang forever upon the horizon of that sea, and extracted from their beauty a resignation that he did not permit his reason to examine. The discrepancy between faith and the facts is greater than is generally assumed.

But there was another story of the master of San Martín (not so subversive, this one) that probably gave to Brother Juniper the hint for his procedure after the fall of the bridge of San Luis Rey.

This master was one day walking through the Cathedral of Lima and stopped to read the epitaph of a lady. He read with an increasingly prominent lower lip that she had been for twenty years the center and joy of her home, that she had been the delight of her friends, that all who met her went away in astonishment at her goodness and beauty, and that there she lay awaiting the return of her Lord. Now on the day that he read these words, the master of San Martín had had much to fret him, and raising his eyes from the tablet he spoke aloud in his rage. "The shame of it, the persecution of it! Everyone knows that in the world we do nothing but feed our wills. Why perpetuate this legend of selflessness? Why keep this thing alive, this rumor of disinterestedness?"

And so saying he resolved to expose this conspiracy of the stonecutters. The lady had been dead only twelve years. He sought out her servants, her children and her friends. And everywhere he went, like a perfume, her dear traits had survived her and wherever she was mentioned there

arose a suffering smile and the protest that words could not describe the gracious ways of her. Even the eager youth of her grandchildren, who had never seen her, was made more difficult by the news that it was possible to be as good as that. And the man stood amazed; only at last he muttered, "Nevertheless, what I said was true. This woman was an exception, perhaps an exception."

In compiling his book about these people Brother Juniper seemed to be pursued by the fear that in omitting the slightest detail he might lose some guiding hint. The longer he worked the more he felt that he was stumbling about among great dim intimations. He was forever being cheated by details that looked as though they were significant if only he could find their setting. So he put everything down on the notion perhaps that if he (or a keener head) reread the book twenty times, the countless facts would suddenly start to move, to assemble, and to betray their secret. The Marquesa de Montemayor's cook told him that she lived almost entirely on rice, fish and a little fruit and Brother Juniper put it down on the chance that it would some day reveal a spiritual trait. Don Rubío said of her that she used to appear at his receptions without invitation in order to steal the spoons. A midwife on the edge of the town declared that Doña María called upon her with morbid questions until she had been obliged to order her away from the door like a beggar. The bookseller of the town reported that she was one of the three most cultivated persons in Lima. Her farmer's wife declared that she was absent-minded, but compact of goodness. The art of biography is more difficult than is generally supposed.

Brother Juniper found that there was least to be learned from those who had been most closely associated with the subjects of his inquiry. Madre María del Pilar talked to him at length about Pepita, but she did not tell him of her own ambitions for her. The Perichole was at first difficult of approach, but presently even liked the Franciscan. Her characterization of Uncle Pio flatly contradicted the stores

of unsavory testimonies that he had acquired elsewhere. Her
allusions to her son were few and conceded with pain. They
closed the interview abruptly. The Captain Alvarado told
what he could of Esteban and of Uncle Pio. Those who
know most in this realm, venture least.

I shall spare you Brother Juniper's generalizations. They
are always with us. He thought he saw in the same accident
the wicked visited by destruction, and the good called early
to Heaven. He thought he saw pride and wealth con-
founded as an object lesson to the world, and he thought he
say humility crowned and rewarded for the edification of
the city. But Brother Juniper was not satisfied with his rea-
sons. It was just possible that the Marquesa de Montemayor
was not a monster of avarice, and Uncle Pio of self-indul-
gence.

The book being done fell under the eyes of some judges
and was suddenly pronounced heretical. It was ordered to
be burned in the Square with its author. Brother Juniper
submitted to the decision that the devil had made use of
him to effect a brilliant campaign in Peru. He sat in his cell
that last night trying to seek in his own life the pattern that
had escaped him in five others. He was not rebellious. He
was willing to lay down his life for the purity of the church,
but he longed for one voice somewhere to testify for him
that his intention, at least, had been for faith; he thought
there was no one in the world who believed him. But the
next morning in all that crowd and sunlight there were
many who believed, for he was much loved.

There was a little delegation from the village of Puerto,
and Nina (Goodness 2, Piety 5, Usefulness 10) and others
stood with drawn, puzzled faces while their little friar was
given to the congenial flames. Even then, even then, there
remained in his heart an obstinate nerve insisting that at
least St. Francis would not utterly have condemned him,
and (not daring to call upon a greater name, since he
seemed so open to error in these matters) he called twice

upon St. Francis and leaning upon a flame he smiled and died.

The day of the service was clear and warm. The Limeans, their black eyes wide with awe, poured through the streets into their Cathedral and stood gazing at the mound of black velvet and silver. The Archbishop enclosed in his wonderful and almost wooden vestments perspired upon his throne, lending from time to time a connoisseur's ear to the felicities of Vittoria's counterpoint. The choir had restudied the pages that, as his farewell to music, Tomás Luis had composed for his friend and patron, the Empress of Austria, and all that grief and sweetness, all that Spanish realism filtering through an Italian mode, rose and fell above the sea of mantillas. Don Andrés, under the colors and feathered hangings of his office, knelt, ill and troubled. He knew that the crowd was furtively glancing at him, expecting him to play the father who has lost his only son. He wondered whether the Perichole was present. He had never been obliged to go so long without smoking. The Captain Alvarado pushed in from the sunny square for a moment. He looked across the fields of black hair and lace at the trooping of the candles and the ropes of incense. "How false, how unreal," he said and pushed his way out. He descended to the sea and sat on the edge of his boat, gazing down into the clear water. "Happy are the drowned, Esteban," he said.

Behind the screen the Abbess sat among her girls. The night before she had torn an idol from her heart and the experience had left her pale but firm. She had accepted the fact that it was of no importance whether her work went on or not; it was enough to work. She was the nurse who tends the sick who never recover; she was the priest who perpetually renews the office before an altar to which no worshipers come. There would be no Pepita to enlarge her work; it would relapse into the indolence and the indifference of her colleagues. It seemed to be sufficient for Heaven

that for a while in Peru a disinterested love had flowered
and faded. She leaned her forehead upon her hand, follow-
ing the long tender curve that the soprano lifts in the Kyrie.
"My affection should have had more of that color, Pepita.
My whole life should have had more of that quality. I have
been too busy," she added ruefully and her mind drifted
into prayer.

Camila had started from the farm to attend the service.
Her heart was filled with consternation and amazement.
Here was another comment from the skies; that was the
third time she had been spoken to. Her smallpox, Jaime's
illness, and now the fall of the bridge—oh, these were not
accidents. She was as ashamed as though letters had ap-
peared on her forehead. An order from the Palace an-
nounced that the Viceroy was sending her two daughters
to a convent school in Spain. That was right. She was alone.
She gathered a few things together mechanically and
started to the city for the Service. But she fell to thinking
of the crowds gaping over her Uncle Pio and over her son;
she thought of the vast ritual of the church, like a chasm
into which the beloved falls, and of the storm of the *dies
irae* where the individual is lost among the millions of the
dead, features grow dim and traits fade. At a little more
than half the journey, at the mud church of San Luis Rey
she slipped in and knelt against a pillar to rest. She wan-
dered through her memory, searching for the faces of her
two. She waited for some emotion to appear. "But I feel
nothing," she whispered to herself. "I have no heart. I am a
poor meaningless woman, that's all. I am shut out. I have
no heart. Look, I won't try and think of anything; let me
just rest here." And scarcely had she paused when again
that terrible incommunicable pain swept through her, the
pain that could not speak once to Uncle Pio and tell him
of her love and just once offer her courage to Jaime in his
sufferings. She started up wildly: "I fail everybody," she
cried. "They love me and I fail them." She returned to the
farm and carried for a year the mood of her self-despair.

One day she heard by accident that the wonderful Abbess had lost two persons whom she loved in the same accident. Her sewing fell from her hand: then *she* would know, she would explain. "But no, what would she say to me! She would not even believe that such a person as I could love or could lose." Camila decided to go to Lima and look at the Abbess from a distance. "If her face tells me that she would not despise me, I will speak to her," she said.

Camila lurked about the convent church and fell humbly in love with the homely old face, though it frightened her a little. At last she called upon her.

"Mother," she said, "I . . . I. . . ."

"Do I know you, my daughter?"

"I was the actress, I was the Perichole."

"Oh, yes. Oh, I have wished to know you for a long while, but they told me you did not wish to be seen. You too, I know, lost in the fall of the bridge of San. . . ."

Camila rose and swayed. There! again that access of pain, the hands of the dead she could not reach. Her lips were white. Her head brushed the Abbess's knee. "Mother, what shall I do? I am all alone. I have nothing in the world. I love them. What shall I do?"

The Abbess looked at her closely. "My daughter, it is warm here. Let us go into the garden. You can rest there." She made a sign to a girl in the cloister to bring some water. She continued talking mechanically to Camila. "I have wished to know you for a long while, señora. Even before the accident I had wished much to know you. They told me that in the *autos sacramentales* you were a very great and beautiful acress, in *Belshazzar's Feast*."

"Oh, Mother, you must not say that. I am a sinner. You must not say that."

"Here, drink this, my child. We have a beautiful garden, do you not think so? You will come and see us often and some day you will meet Sister Juana who is our gardener-in-chief. Before she entered religion she had almost never seen a garden, for she worked in the mines high up in the

mountains. Now everything grows under her hand. —A year
has gone by, señora, since our accident. I lost two who had
been children in my orphanage, but you lost a real child of
your own?"

"Yes, Mother."

"And a great friend?"

"Yes, Mother."

"Tell me. . . ."

And then the whole tide of Camila's long despair, her
lonely obstinate despair since her girlhood, found its rest
on that dusty friendly lap among Sister Juana's fountains
and roses.

But where are sufficient books to contain the events that
would not have been the same without the fall of the
bridge? From such a number I choose one more.

"The Condesa d'Abuirre wishes to see you," said a lay
sister at the door of the Abbess's office.

"Well," said the Abbess, laying down her pen, "who is
she?"

"She has just come from Spain. I don't know."

"Oh, it is some money, Inez, some money for my house
for the blind. Quick, bid her come in."

The tall, rather languorous beauty entered the room.
Doña Clara, who was generally so adequate, seemed con-
strained for once. "Are you busy, dear Mother, may I talk
to you for a while?"

"I am quite free, my daughter. You will excuse an old
woman's memory; have I known you before?"

"My mother was the Marquesa de Montemayor. . . ."
Doña Clara suspected that the Abbess had not admired her
mother and would not let the older woman speak until
she herself had made a long passionate defense of Doña
María. The languor fell away in her self-reproach. At last
the Abbess told her of Pepita and Esteban, and of Camila's
visit. "All, all of us have failed. One wishes to be punished.
One is willing to assume all kinds of penance, but do you

know, my daughter, that in love—I scarcely dare say it—but in love our very mistakes don't seem to be able to last long?"

The Condesa showed the Abbess Doña María's last letter. Madre María dared not say aloud how great her astonishment was that such words (words that since then the whole world has murmured over with joy) could spring in the heart of Pepita's mistress. "Now learn," she commanded herself, "learn at last that anywhere you may expect grace." And she was filled with happiness like a girl at this new proof that the traits she lived for were everywhere, that the world was ready. "Will you do me a kindness, my daughter? Will you let me show you my work?"

The sun had gone down, but the Abbess led the way with a lantern down corridor after corridor. Doña Clara saw the old and the young, the sick and the blind, but most of all she saw the tired, bright old woman who was leading her. The Abbess would stop in a passageway and say suddenly, "I can't help thinking that something could be done for the deaf-and-dumb. It seems to me that some patient person could . . . could study out a language for them. You know there are hundreds and hundreds in Peru. Do you remember whether anyone in Spain has found a way for them? Well, someday they will." Or a little later: "Do you know, I keep thinking that something can be done for the insane. I am old, you know, and I cannot go where these things are talked about, but I watch them sometimes and it seems to me. . . . In Spain, now, they are gentle with them? It seems to me that there is a secret about it, just hidden from us, just around the corner. Someday, back in Spain, if you hear of anything that would help us, you will write me a letter . . . if you are not too busy?"

At last after Doña Clara had seen even the kitchens, the Abbess said, "Now will you excuse me, for I must go into the room of the very sick and say a few words for them to think about when they cannot sleep. I will not ask you to come with me there, for you are not accustomed to such . . . such sounds and things. And besides I only talk to them as

one talks to children." She looked up at her with her modest rueful smile. Suddenly she disappeared a moment to return with one of her helpers, one who had likewise been involved in the affair of the bridge and who had formerly been an actress. "She is leaving me," said the Abbess, "for some work across the city and when I have spoken here I must leave you both, for the flour broker will not wait for me any longer, and our argument will take a long time."

But Doña Clara stood in the door as the Abbess talked to them, the lamp placed on the floor beside her. Madre María stood with her back against a post; the sick lay in rows gazing at the ceiling and trying to hold their breaths. She talked that night of all those out in the dark (she was thinking of Esteban alone, she was thinking of Pepita alone) who had no one to turn to, for whom the world perhaps was more than difficult, without meaning. And those who lay in their beds there felt that they were within a wall that the Abbess had built for them; within all was light and warmth, and without was the darkness they would not exchange even for a relief from pain and from dying. But even while she was talking, other thoughts were passing in the back of her mind. "Even now," she thought, "almost no one remembers Esteban and Pepita, but myself. Camila alone remembers her Uncle Pio and her son; this woman, her mother. But soon we shall die and all memory of those five will have left the earth, and we ourselves shall be loved for a while and forgotten. But the love will have been enough; all those impulses of love return to the love that made them. Even memory is not necessary for love. There is a land of the living and a land of the dead and the bridge is love, the only survival, the only meaning."

The
WOMAN
of
ANDROS

The first part of this novel is based upon the Andria, a comedy of Terence who in turn based his work upon two Greek plays, now lost to us, by Menander.

THE earth sighed as it turned in its course; the shadow of night crept gradually along the Mediterranean, and Asia was left in darkness. The great cliff that was one day to be called Gibraltar held for a long time a gleam of red and orange, while across from it the mountains of Atlas showed deep blue pockets in their shining sides. The caves that surround the Neapolitan gulf fell into a profounder shade, each giving forth from the darkness its chiming or its booming sound. Triumph had passed from Greece and wisdom from Egypt, but with the coming on of night they seemed to regain their lost honors, and the land that was soon to be called Holy prepared in the dark its wonderful burden. The sea was large enough to hold a varied weather: a storm played about Sicily and its smoking mountains, but at the mouth of the Nile the water lay like a wet pavement. A fair tripping breeze ruffled the Aegean and all the islands of Greece felt a new freshness at the close of day.

The happiest, and one of the least famous of the islands, Brynos, welcomed the breeze. The evening was long. For a time, the sound of the waves, briskly slapping against the wall of the little harbor, was covered by the chattering of women, by the shouts of boys, and by the crying of lambs.

As the first lights appeared, the women retired; as the air was filled with the clamor of the shop fronts being put into place, the boys' voices ceased; and finally only the murmur of the men in the wineshops, playing at games with ivory counters, mingled with the sounds from the sea. A confused starlight, already apprehensive of the still unrisen moon, fell upon the tiers of small houses that covered the slope and upon the winding flights of stairs that served as streets between them.

The wineshops stood about the roughly paved square at the water's edge and in one of them the five or six principal fathers of the island sat playing. By the time the moon had risen, two of these, Simo and Chremes, had outstayed their companions. Simo was the owner of two warehouses; he was a trader and had three ships that passed continually to and fro among the islands. The men had finished playing; the counters lay on the table between them and they sighed into their beards as they thought of the long walk through the ghostly olive trees to their homes. Simo was more tired than usual: whereas the law of moderation teaches us that the mind cannot be employed for more than three hours daily over merchandise and numerals without soilure, he had that day spent five hours in argument and traffic.

"Simo," said Chremes suddenly, with the air of a man bracing himself to an unpleasant and long deferred task, "your boy is twenty-five now—"

Simo groaned as he saw the subject arising that he was never able to look in the face.

"It's four years," continued Chremes, "since you first said that a young man mustn't be forced into marriage by his old people. And certainly no one has been trying to force Pamphilus. But what is he waiting for? He helps you in the warehouse; he exercises in the field; he dines at the Andrian's. How many years must that kind of life go on before you agree with me that he would be better off married to my daughter?"

"Chremes, he must come to me of his own accord. I will not be the first one to speak about it to the boy."

"First! It won't be speaking of it first, Simo. It has been understood between our families for years that he will marry Philumena. It's being spoken of all the time. The young people tease him about it from morning to night. He knows perfectly well that my daughter is ready to marry him. It's sheer laziness on his part. It's sheer unwillingness to take on the responsibilities of being a husband and a father and the foremost young householder on the island."

"He's a young man who knows what he means to do. I will not coerce him."

"Then it's settled that he doesn't want to marry my daughter. It's a humiliation for her to be waiting all these years for him to make up his mind, and her mother's been after me to close the matter for a long time. Perhaps I shouldn't say it, but you'll be throwing away a good thing through sheer hesitancy, both of you. Philumena is by far the healthiest and the prettiest girl on any of these islands. And she's clever at everything that is expected of a woman in the home. The uniting of our two families has advantages, Simo, that I don't have to point out to you. But this lapse of time has made it clear that your son is going to wait until his fancy has been caught by some other girl, I suppose. So be it! From this very night my wife is going to start looking about for some other young man."

"Chremes, Chremes, he's only twenty-five. Let him play about a little longer. Why must they become husbands and fathers so soon? He's good and he's happy. So is your daughter. Let them be awhile."

"Grandchildren!—that's what I want to see. There shouldn't be a long step between the generations. It's bad for customs and manners."

"You'll make a greater mistake by hurrying than by delaying."

"Well," Chremes continued, "there's another reason why I want the matter settled soon. And that is this: we don't

like the visits that Pamphilus is paying to the Andrian woman. Naturally, Simo, it's hard for me to be severe about it, because my own son goes there too. But it's natural that a father should be more exacting in regard to his son-in-law than in regard to his son."

Simo looked more uncomfortable than ever and remained silent. Chremes went on:

"I don't think you like this resort to foreign women any more than I do. Our islands have always been famous for strict and good behavior. If the devil was in us as boys we could always follow some shepherdess up a dark road. But this Andrian has brought the whole air of Alexandria to town with her, perfumes and hot baths and late hours."

Simo stroked his cheeks a moment and then replied in a low grunting voice, "Well, if it isn't one thing, it's another, I suppose. I don't know anything about this Andrian. The women seem to talk of nothing else from morning to night, but one can't believe what they say."

Thus invited, Chremes launched into his exposition with considerable relish, examining Simo's face from time to time to see if the details were arousing in him the interest they held for himself. "Her name is Chrysis, and I don't know what she means by calling herself Andrian. The island of Andros was never famous for such airs and graces as she puts on. She's flitted from Corinth and Alexandria, you may be sure. She should have stayed in her cities instead of burying herself in our town and reciting poetry to our young men. Yes, yes, she recites poetry to them like the famous ones. She has twelve or fifteen of them to dinner every seven or eight days—the unmarried ones, of course. They lie about on couches and eat odd food and talk. Presently she rises and recites; she can recite whole tragedies without the book. She is very strict with the young men, apparently. She makes them pronounce all the Attic accents; they eat in the Athenian mode, drinking toasts and wearing garlands, and each in turn is elected King of the Banquet. And at the

close, hot towels are passed around for them to wipe their hands on."

Simo did not concede to Chremes the pleasure of his close interest; his eyes were lowered and his face wore the same bored expression that it brought to all island gossip. Chremes decided to be less expansive, and added with easy indignation, "As for me, Alexandria is Alexandria and Brynos is Brynos. A few more imported notions and our island will be spoiled forever. It will become a mass of poor undigested imitations. All the girls will be wanting to read and write and declaim. What becomes of home life, Simo, if women can read and write? You and I married the finest girls of our time and we've been happy. We can at least provide one more generation of good sense and good manners on this island before the age arrives when all the women will have the airs of dancers and all the men go about waiting on them."

Simo knew the answer to this, but he repressed it. Chremes, more than any man on the island, was ruled by his wife. In fact, from her loom in the shadow, Chremes's wife tried to rule the whole island, using her harassed husband as her legislative and punitive arm. Simo asked:

"What happens after the banquet?"

"Each boy pays for his plate, and pays right smartly too, and from time to time one or another is graciously permitted to stay until morning. That's all I know."

"Is your son at all these dinners?"

"He was quarreling or something—or perhaps he drank too much, I don't know. At all events, he was expelled for a time. Thrown right out into the street, he was, by the other guests. But he's made his peace with her again."

"Do you talk to him about this . . . this Chrysis?"

"Why, no. I pretend to know nothing about it."

"Is my son always there?"

"They say he's practically always there."

There was a long pause. The boy who attended in the wineshop went out into the moonlight and started putting

up the shutters. Presently he returned and whispered to Simo that an old woman was waiting outside to speak to him and that she had been waiting there for some time. This was unusual on Brynos, but Simo took pride in never betraying any surprise. He nodded slightly and continued staring before him.

"Are there any other women at the Andrian's?" he asked.

"I don't know. Some say there are and some say there aren't. But there's a houseful of some sort. In fact it's a kind of hospital for the old and the lame and the . . . all kind of old battered pensioners. The house is way up at the edge of the town. . . ."

"I know where it is."

". . . and the people, whoever they are, never come into town. They never even go out on the road by day. Oh, you can be sure the townspeople talk of nothing else."

Chremes rose and put on his cloak. He saw that Simo was as far as ever from committing himself. "Well, that's how it stands," he said. "I hope that in another ten days you can give me a more definite answer. My wife is after me a good deal, Simo, and she says that I'm to tell you this, that unless Pamphilus stops those visits all idea of a marriage between himself and Philumena is impossible. And that any such marriage must be definitely settled pretty soon or you'll have to start finding some other girl one-tenth as good."

For the first time Simo bestirred himself and said slowly, "You and your wife will be throwing away a good thing too, Chremes. It's precisely because Pamphilus is a great deal more than an ordinary island boy that I can't speak to him as I could to another son. There are more sides to Pamphilus than you imagine."

"Yes, Simo, we know that he's a fine young man. But we also know, if you will forgive me, that there's a strain in Pamphilus of the . . . the undecided, the procrastinating. To do his best and to take his place, Pamphilus must be urged on by someone, like yourself, whom he admires. And

he's not as interested in this island and in what it stands for as he should be. Do you know the young priest of Æsculapius and Apollo? Well, there is something of the priest in Pamphilus. Such people aren't interested in putting their foot forward. They haven't yet come to see what life is about."

Chremes went out and plodded home along the rocky road. Simo sat on a minute longer. What a bad ending to a bad day, he thought. The two men had grown up on the island together. For thirty years they had been its leading citizens. They knew one another too well. In their conversation they had let play the faint antagonism that always lay between them. This boasting about their children—how vulgar, how un-Hellenic. How unphilosophic. Yet that was true: there was something of the priest in Pamphilus.

Simo turned to the old woman who was hiding in the shadow by the door. "You wanted to speak to me?" he asked roughly.

Between fright and suspense—for she had been waiting there for the greater part of two hours—Mysis was barely able to find her voice. "My mistress wishes to speak to you, sir—Chrysis, the Andrian," and she pointed with both hands toward the waterfront.

Simo grunted. Looking up he saw the beautiful woman leaning against the parapet at the water's edge fifteen paces away. Her head and body were wrapped in veils, and she waited calmly and impersonally in the moonlight as though two hours were but a moment in her serenity. Below her in the little protected harbor the boats knocked against one another in friendly fashion, but all else was still under the melancholy and peace of the moon. Simo approached her without deference and said, "Well?"

"I am—" she began.

"I know who you are."

She paused and began again. "I am in an extremity. I am driven to ask a service of you." Simo pushed his lips forward, raised his eyebrows, and lowered his eyes wearily. She continued in an even voice, without anxiety or suppliance, "A friend of mine is very ill on the island of Andros from which I come. Twice I have sent this friend money by the hands of various sea captains going between the islands. I know now that the captains are dishonest and that my money never reaches him. All that I ask is that you put your frank upon the package of money and it will reach him."

Simo did not like to see women carrying themselves, as this Andrian did, with dignity and independence. His antagonism was increased; he asked abruptly, "Who is this friend?"

"He was formerly a sea captain," she replied, still without servility. "But now he is not only ill; he is insane. He is insane by reason of the hardships he endured in the war. I have put him in charge of some people, but they will only be kind to him as long as I send them money for it. Otherwise they will put him away on a small island nearby with the others. You know such islands . . . where basins of food are left for them every few days . . . and where—"

"Well," said Simo harshly, "since your friend has lost the use of his reason and since he cannot realize the conditions under which he lives, it is best that you leave him upon the island with the others. Is that not so?"

Chrysis tightened her lips and looked far out over his head. "I have no answer for that," she replied. "It may be true for you, but it is not true for me. This man was once a very famous sea captain. You may have known him. His name was Philocles. Now I think I am his only friend, unless you choose to help him also."

Simo did not acknowledge having known him, but the tone in his next words was less vindictive. "When would you like this money to go?"

"I . . . I have some money ready now, but I would prefer to send some in ten days."

"What is your name?"

"My name is Chrysis, daughter of Arches of Andros."

"Chrysis, I will do this for you, and I will even add to the sum. In return you will do a favor for me. You will refuse my son entrance into your house."

Chrysis moved slightly to one side, and stretching her arm along the parapet, looked down into the harbor. "Favors cease to be favors when there are conditions attached to them, Simo. Magnanimity does not bargain with its powers." These maxims were almost murmured; then she raised her head and said to him, "I cannot do that, unless I tell your son that it is because you have ordered it."

Simo's slightly cynical superiority over the rest of the world reposed on the fact that he had gone through life without ever having been surprised as unjust, untruthful, or ungenerous. Angry, but with himself for having been caught at this disadvantage, he replied, "That is not necessary. It would be quite simple for your servant to tell him that you do not wish him to come into the house."

"I could not do that. There are several young men on the island to whom my door, for one reason or another, is closed. I cannot do that to Pamphilus without giving him a reason. If you understood the spirit of our group you would not wish me to do that; I think that there we are not lacking in respect for one another. I hardly know your son; I have scarcely exchanged twenty words with him; but I know that he is by far the first young man among my guests." Suddenly the image of Pamphilus rose up before her and she was filled with an excitement and joy in praising him, and for that very reason she subdued herself and added in a lower voice: "He is old enough to make decisions for himself. And if I do this, he must understand."

Simo was aware that some strange, wise praise of his son hovered between them and his heart almost stopped beating for pleasure, but from his lips there rushed the brutal phrase he had prepared a moment before: "Then you must send your money to Andros some other way."

"Very well," she said.

They stood looking at one another. Simo suddenly realized that he lived among people of thin natures and that he was lonely; he was out of practice in conversing with sovereign personalities whose every speech arose from resources of judgment and inner poise. With his wife, with Chremes, with the islanders one could talk with half one's mind and still hold one's authority, but here in a few moments this woman had caught him twice at a disadvantage. Chrysis saw this and came to his aid; she broke the silence that was leaving him obstinate, angry, and small.

"It is perhaps his younger brother whose life can be arranged for him; your Pamphilus deserves to be better understood than that." And her tone implied: "You and he are of one measure and should stand on the same side."

Simo preferred talking about his sons to any other activity in the world, but his emotions were very mixed as he assembled an answer to this remark:

"Well, well . . . Andrian, I will frank your money for you. I have boats going to Andros every twelve days. One went off today."

"I thank you."

"Could I ask you . . . euh . . . not to mention this to Pamphilus?"

"I shall not."

"Well . . . well, good night."

"Good night."

Simo trudged home in an unaccustomed elation. It made him happy to hear Pamphilus praised and "probably this woman was an exceptional judge of persons." He had made a fool of himself, but in good hands one does not mind. "Life . . . life . . ." he said to himself, hunting for a generalization that would describe its diversity, its power of casting up from time to time on the waves of tedious circumstance such starlike persons. The generalization did not arrive, but he walked on in a bright astonishment. How he would like to hear her read a play; he used to be interested in such

things and when his journeys took him to an island that was
large enough to have a theater he never missed an oppor-
tunity to hear a good tragedy.

As he entered the courtyard of his farm he saw Pam-
philus standing alone, looking at the moon.

"Good evening, Pamphilus," he said.

"Good evening, father."

Simo went to bed, deeply moved with pride, but for
form's sake he repeated anxiously to himself: "I don't know
what I'll do with him. I don't know what I'll do with him."

And Pamphilus stood looking at the moon and thinking
about his father and mother. He was thinking about them
in the light of a story that Chrysis had told. As the ban-
quets drew to a close she liked to move the conversation
away from local comment and to introduce some debate
upon an abstract principle. (She cited often the saying of
Plato that the true philosophers are the young men of their
age. "Not," she would add, "because they do it very well;
but because they rush upon ideas with their whole soul.
Later, one philosophizes for praise, or for apology, or be-
cause it is a complicated intellectual game.") Pamphilus
remembered that on one evening the conversation had
turned upon the wrong that poets do in pretending that life
is heroic. And a boy from the other end of the island had
said, half-mockingly and half-hopefully, "Well, you know,
Chrysis . . . you know, life in a family is not in the same
world as life in Euripides."

Chrysis sat a moment searching for her answer, then she
lifted her hand and said: "Once upon a time—"

The table burst out laughing, but with an affectionate
laugh of mock repudiation, because they knew that she
liked to cast her remarks into the form of fables and to
begin them with this childish formula. Pamphilus heard
again her beautiful voice saying:

"Once upon a time there was a hero who had done a
great service to Zeus. When he came to die and was wan-
dering in the gray marshes of Hell, he called to Zeus re-

minding him of that service and asking a service in return: he asked to return to earth for one day. Zeus was greatly troubled and said that it was not in his power to grant this, since even he could not bring above ground the dead who had descended to his brother's kingdom. But Zeus was so moved by the memory of the past that he went to the palace of his brother and clasping his knees asked him to accord him this favor. And the King of the Dead was greatly troubled, saying that even he who was King of the Dead could not grant this thing without involving the return to life in some difficult and painful condition. But the hero gladly accepted whatever difficult or painful condition was involved, and the King of the Dead permitted him to return not only to the earth, but to the past, and to live over again that day in all the twenty-two thousand days of his lifetime that had been least eventful; but that it must be with a mind divided into two persons—the participant and the onlooker: the participant who does the deeds and says the words of so many years before, and the onlooker who foresees the end. So the hero returned to the sunlight and to a certain day in his fifteenth year.

"My friends," continued Chrysis, turning her eyes slowly from face to face, "as he awoke in his boyhood's room, pain filled his heart—not only because it had started beating again, but because he saw the walls of his home and knew that in a moment he would see his parents who lay long since in the earth of that country. He descended into the courtyard. His mother lifted her eyes from the loom and greeted him and went on with her work. His father passed through the court unseeing, for on that day his mind had been full of care. Suddenly the hero saw that the living too are dead and that we can only be said to be alive in those moments when our hearts are conscious of our treasure; for our hearts are not strong enough to love every moment. And not an hour had gone by before the hero who was both watching life and living it called on Zeus to release him from so terrible a dream. The gods heard him, but before he left

he fell upon the ground and kissed the soil of the world that is too dear to be realized."

It was with such eyes that Pamphilus now saw his father pass into the house and that he had seen his mother moving about, covering the fire and going about the last tasks of the day. And it was in the light of that story that his eyes had been opened to the secret life of his parents' minds. It seemed suddenly as though he saw behind the contentment and the daily talkativeness into the life of their hearts—empty, resigned, pathetic and enduring. It was Chrysis' reiterated theory of life that all human beings—save a few mysterious exceptions who seemed to be in possession of some secret from the gods—merely endured the slow misery of existence, hiding as best they could their consternation that life had no wonderful surprises after all and that its most difficult burden was the incommunicability of love. Certainly that explained the humorous sadness of his father and the fretful affection of his mother. And now as his father passed him in the courtyard this interpretation shook him more forcibly than ever. What can one do for them? What—to be equal to them—can one do for oneself? He was twenty-five already, that is—no longer a young man. He would soon be a husband and a father, a condition he did not invest with any glamour. He would soon be the head of this household and this farm. He would soon be old. Time would have flowed by him like a sigh, with no plan made, no rules set, no strategy devised that would have taught him how to save these others and himself from the creeping gray, from the too easily accepted frustration.

"How does one live?" he asked the bright sky. "What does one do first?"

Chrysis' view of human experience expressed itself, as we have seen, in fables, in quotations from literature, in proverbs and in mottoes. Herself she summed up in a word:

she regarded herself as having "died." Dead then as she was, the inconveniences of her profession, the sneers of the villagers, the ingratitude of her dependents no longer had the power to disturb her. The only thing that troubled her in her grave was the recurrence, even in her professional associations, of a wild tenderness for this or that passer-by, brief and humiliating approaches to love. These experiences and any others that were able to depress her she now dismissed as weakness, as pride, as an old, rebellious and unwhipped vanity. The morning after the conversation with Simo at the water's edge she awoke strangly troubled; but she resolved not to examine the new dejection. It floated all day above her head—a voice repeating, "I am alone. Why have I never seen that before? I am alone." Indeed the profession she followed was one of those that emphasize the dim notion that lies at the back of many minds: the notion that we are not necessary to anyone, that attachments weave and unweave at the mercy of separation, satiety and experience. The loneliest associations are those that pretend to intimacy.

But she had discovered two ways of mitigating this unresponsiveness and instability in the world she lived in. The first was the development she brought to the institution of the hetaira's banquet. She took endless pains over these reunions, and to the wide-eyed guests they seemed indeed all that one could conceive of wit and eloquence and aristocratic ease. Great talkers are so constituted that they do not know their own thoughts until, on the tide of their particular gift, they hear them issuing from their mouths. Chrysis gave herself that luxury, the luxury of talking to these young men from her whole mind. Much of it lay beyond their reach; but her refusal to condescend, her assumption that the analysis of ideas and of masterpieces was their natural element, excited them. She knew that apart from her beauty she was not particularly fitted for her calling; she lacked the high spirits that please the customers of middle age; but younger men, who still approach love with a touch of awe,

are not so disappointed with those common exercises when they find them invested with melancholy, dignity and literature. Perhaps the maturity of a civilization can be judged by this trait, by observing whether the young men first fall in love with women older or younger than themselves; if in their youth their imaginations pass their time in hallowing the images of prattling unnourishing girls their natures will be forever after the thinner. But even at their best Chrysis' guests seemed remote and immature to her and finally she discovered a second way of making life more stable and her friends more constant: she adopted stray human beings that needed her.

In the inner monologue of her thoughts Chrysis called these dependents her "sheep." And although they were gathered into her shelter from places and moments of fearful extremity, they became accustomed to their new comfort with extraordinary rapidity. In fact their past trials began to take on a romantic color and when anything in the present situation did not suit them they had been known to regret the lost felicities of the slave markets, the mills and the massacred villages. For Chrysis, human nature no longer had many surprises, and the manner in which the sheep scolded and even condescended to their shepherd did not deject her. She loved them and was sufficiently repaid by occasional hours of a late afternoon when the odd group would sit in the garden, weaving in amity and humor. Such hours almost resembled life in a home.

There was to be a banquet that evening, so shaking her head at the shadow that hovered above her she descended into the town to do the marketing. She was accompanied by Mysis and the porter—Mysis carrying a net to hold the fruit and the salad greens, and the porter a large jar to be filled with salt water and then with fish and shellfish. Chrysis moved slowly down the long twisting flights of stairs. She was wrapped about by a great scarf of antique finely wrinkled material and wore a broad-brimmed Tanagraean hat of woven straw. The one hand that appeared outside the folds

of her scarf carried a small wooden fan. It was her business to be invested with the remoteness and glamour of a legend, for at that time Greek taste turned upon a nostalgia for the antique; it was her business to be as different from other women as possible and to convert that difference into money. The shops and temporary booths were all on the open square at the water's edge and there in the bright sunlight the most excitable and loquacious of races was enjoying its morning tumult; but as this calm and daydreaming figure appeared above them a hush fell upon the bargainers. This was the very deportment the Greek women lacked and sighed for. They were short and swarthy and shrill, and their incessant conversation was accompanied by the incessant play of their hands. The whole race was haunted by a passionate admiration for poise and serenity and slow motion, and now for an hour the Andrian's every move was followed by the furtive glances of the islanders, with mingled awe and hatred. The Brynians, when she appeared, felt themselves to be provincial and commercial. From time to time some of the young men who had been guests at her house approached her and spoke to her. Then it was that the unmarried girls and the young wives of the island gazed with consternation and fallen jaw at the way she smiled and talked and dismissed their brothers and their future husbands. Philumena, in the shadow of an awning, leaned back against a wall and watched the stranger; turning her head slightly she could see Pamphilus at the tally desk in the door of his father's warehouse. Her eyes fell on her rough gown and her red arms and a long slow blush mounted to her face. But all the while Chrysis' heart had been growing heavier. "I have lived alone and I shall die alone," it said, and groaned within her.

As she returned to her house from the market she fell into a feverish monologue. "The fault is in me. It's my lack of perseverance in affection. I know that. Now, Chrysis, you must begin your life over again; you must assemble some plan. You must devote yourself with all your mind to your

sheep. You must break down all their coldness and willful-
ness. You must make yourself love them again. You must
bring back the happiness you felt with each one of them
when you first knew them. It is routine, it is the daily con-
tact that has spoiled all that. It's cowardly of me to be able
to love people only when they are new. Now, now, Chrysis!
—arise!" For the hundredth time she was visited by hope
and courage. She would win in this thing. As she ap-
proached the house she was all but stumbling in her eager-
ness; she would create a home. "If I love them enough, I
can understand them," she muttered. "One never learns how
to live, or one's lights on living arrive too late, when one
has spoiled the surrounding situation, spoiled it beyond
repair. But I am to be on the earth for fifty years, and I
must do it."

Chrysis did not realize what took place in the house dur-
ing her absences, and that when she left it the house was
empty. The personalities of her flock were extinguished.
They fretted; they hovered about the gates peering in the
direction from which she would return, and their minds
ceased to act save in terms of that resentment which is the
complement of devotion. She did not realize that this
wasting of love in fretfulness was one of the principal ac-
tivities on the planet. When she was away fear descended
upon them; their dependence upon her was so great that
even her temporary absences reminded them of the desti-
tution from which they had been lifted—circumstances so
fearful that their conscious minds never revisited them, but
which hovered in the distance enriching their present ease
and hardening their self-centeredness. All this antagonism
therefore met her in a flood as she stumbled across the
threshold of her home. By the middle of the afternoon she
was saying to herself, almost in a panic, "It is impossible. I
can do nothing. They even hate me. But fortunately I am
dead. It is not my pride that is hurt. I am at peace in the
ground. Yet, oh! if only we had some help in these matters.
If only the gods were sometimes present among us. To have

nothing to go by except this idea, this vague idea, that there lies the principle of living!"

During the banquet she looked about her for comfort. "It is also cowardly of me to be happy only at the banquets where I can lead the conversation and display my thoughts and be admired." But tonight even that exhilaration was wanting; her guests seemed younger and remoter than ever, and she in turn was capricious and all but irritable. It was to be expected, therefore, that the conversation would take turns little likely to comfort her.

Niceratus, one of the more assured of her guests, asked her what life would be like in two thousand years.

"Why," she said at once, "there will be no more war."

"I should not wish to be alive in a world where there was no war," he replied. "That would be an age of women."

Now Chrysis was jealous of the dignity of women and lost no occasions to combat such hasty disparagements. She leaned forward and asked encouragingly:

"You wish to serve the state, Niceratus?"

"I do."

"And you admire courage?"

"I do, Chrysis."

"Then go bear children," she replied, turning away.

Niceratus found this remark unseemly and left the house. (He absented himself from the two successive banquets, but later returned and asked her pardon for making a personal grievance out of a difference of opinion. Confessions of error always gave Chrysis great pleasure. "Happy are the associations," she would say, "that have grown out of a fault and a forgiveness.")

The conversation then turned upon the plays concerning Medea and Phaedra, which she had read to them at an earlier banquet, and upon all manifestations of extravagant passion. The young men declared that the problem was not as complicated as it appeared to be and that such women should have been whipped like disobedient slaves and shut

up in a room with a jar of water and a little plain food until
their pride was subdued. They then recounted to her, al-
most in whispers, the story of a girl from a village on the
farther side of the island whose behavior had thrown her
family and her friends into consternation. The girl had con-
tinued for a time, glorying in her disorders, until one morn-
ing, rising early, she had climbed a high cliff near her home
and thrown herself into the sea. A silence fell on the com-
pany as all turned inquiringly to Chrysis asking for the
explanation of such a reversal.

To herself she said, "Do not try to explain to them. Talk
of other things. Stupidity is everywhere and invincible."
But their continued expectancy prevailed upon her. She
seemed to struggle with herself for a moment, deeply trou-
bled, and then began in a low voice, "Once upon a time the
great army of women came together to a meeting. And they
invited to this meeting one man, a tragic poet. They told
him that they wished to send a message to the world of
men and that he was to be their advocate and mouthpiece.
'Tell them,' said the women eagerly, 'that it is only in ap-
pearance that we are unstable. Tell them that this is because
we are hard-pressed and in bitter servitude to nature, but
that at heart, only asking their patience, we are as stead-
fast, as brave and as manly as they.' The poet smiled sadly,
saying that the men who knew this already would merely
be ashamed to be told it again, and the men who did not
know it would learn nothing through the mere telling; but
he consented to deliver the message. The men at first were
silent, then one by one they broke out into laughter. And
they sent the poet back to the army of women with these
words: 'Tell them not to be anxious and not to trouble their
pretty heads with these matters. Tell them that their pop-
ularity is not dying out, and let them not endanger it
through heroics.' When the poet had repeated these words
to the women, some blushed with shame and some with
anger; some rose with a weary sigh: 'We should never have

spoken to them,' they said. They went back to their mirrors and started combing their hair and as they combed their hair they wept."

Chrysis had barely finished this story when a young man who had hitherto taken little part in the conversation suddenly launched into a violent condemnation of her means of livelihood. This youth was of that temper that seeks to mold the lives of others abruptly to certain patterns of its own choosing. He now commanded Chrysis to become a servant or a sempstress. The other guests began to whisper among themselves and to avert their faces from confusion and anger, but Chrysis sat gazing at his flashing eyes and admiring his earnestness. There was a certain luxury in having an external mortification added to an inner despair. She was already troubled by her recent discomfiture of Niceratus and now chose to be magnanimous. She arose and approached the young fanatic; taking his hand she smiled at him with grave affection, saying to the company, "It is true that of all forms of genius, goodness has the longest awkward age."

But these incidents were not of a nature to distract her mind from the protracted oppression of the day. "Vain. Empty. Transitory," the voice within her repeated. But just as she was about to finish the day with the comprehensive summary that she had nothing to lend to life and no place to fill, her eyes fell upon Pamphilus. It was his custom, through lack of self-confidence, to take the last seat at the remote end of the room. The guests acknowledged his pre-eminence among them, but when one evening they had wished to elect him King of the Banquet he had furtively and savagely intimated to them his refusal and the votes had passed to another. But Chrysis' eyes had often, as now, rested upon that head bent forward to receive her every word and that received each one with so earnest a frown.

"That is something!" she said to herself suddenly and for a moment her heart stopped beating.

She had intended to recite to them *The Clouds* of Aristophanes that evening, but she now changed her mind. She felt the need to nourish her heart and those watchful eyes with something lofty and deeply felt. Perhaps what she called the "lofty" was in this world merely a beautiful form of falsehood, cheating the heart. But she would try again tonight and see whether, after so dejected a day, it woke any stir of conviction. "What shall I read?" she asked herself as the tables were being removed. "Something from Homer?—Priam begging of Achilles the body of Hector? No. . . . No. . . . Nor would they understand the *Oedipus at Colonus*. The *Alcestis?* The *Alcestis?*"

One of the shyer guests, seeing her deliberating over the choice of the evening's declamation, timidly asked her to read the *Phaedrus* of Plato.

"Oh, my friend," she said, "I have not seen the book for several years. I should be obliged to improvise long stretches in it. . . ."

"Could you . . . could you read the opening and the close?"

"I shall try it for you," she replied and rising slowly, disposed the folds of her robe about her. The servants withdrew and silence fell upon the company. This was the moment (on happier evenings) that she loved; this hush, this eagerness, this faintly mocking affection. What drives them —she would ask herself—in the next fifteen years to become so graceless . . . so pompous, or envious, or so busily cheerful?

At first all went well. The boys listened with delight to the account of how other young men gathered in the streets and palaestra of Athens to hear the arguments of Socrates. Listening, they agreed that nothing in the world was more to be prized than a beautifully ordered speech. Then followed the description of the walk that Socrates and Phaedrus took into the country. *"This is indeed a rare resting place. This plane tree is not only tall, but thick and*

spreading. And this agnus castus is at the very moment of flowering and its shade and its fragrance will render our stay the more agreeable. These images and these votive offerings tell us that the place is surely sacred to some nymphs and to some river god. . . . Truly, Phaedrus, you are an admirable guide."

From there she passed to the close:

"But let us go now, as the heat of the day is over.

"Socrates: Would it not be well before we go to offer up a prayer to the gods of this place?

"Phaedus: It would, Socrates.

"Socrates: Beloved Pan, and all ye other gods who haunt this place, grant that I may become beautiful in the inner man and may whatever I possess without be in harmony with that which is within. May I esteem the wise men alone to be rich. And may my store of gold be such as none but the good may bear. Phaedrus, need we say anything more? As for myself I have prayed enough.

"Phaedrus: And let the same prayer serve for me, for these are the things friends share with one another."

All went well until this phrase. Then Chrysis, the serene, the happily dead, seeing the tears that stood in the eyes of Pamphilus, could go no further, and before them all she wept as one weeps who after an absence of folly and self-will returns to a well-loved place and an old loyalty. It was true, true beyond a doubt, tragically true, that the world of love and virtue and wisdom was the true world and her failure in it all the more overwhelming. But she was not alone; he too saw the long and failing war as she did, and she loved him as though she were loving for the first time and as one is never able to love again. That was sealed; that was forever assigned.

After a few moments she collected herself and quieted the guests who had risen in concern about her. "Sit down, my friends. I am ready now," she said smiling. "I shall read you *The Clouds* of Aristophanes."

But it was some time before the laughter rose among the couches, the laughter that was a just tribute to the divine wit of the poet of *The Clouds*.

Brynos rose with the dawn, and it was not many hours later that the morning's work was over. Several days after the conversation recorded above, Pamphilus, having helped his father in the warehouse and being in no mood for exercising in the field, started out to walk to the highest point on the island. It was early spring. A strong wind had blown every cloud from the sky and the sea lay covered with flying white-tipped waves. His garments leaped and billowed about him and his very hair tugged at his head. The gulls themselves, leaning upon the gusts, were caught unawares from time to time and blown with ruffled feathers and scandalized cries toward the violet-blue zenith. Pamphilus led his life with much worry and self-examination, and all the exhilaration of wind and sun could not drive from his mind the anxious affection with which he now turned over his thoughts of Chrysis and Philumena and of the four members of his family. He was straying among the rocks and the lizards and the neglected, dwarfed olive trees, when his attention was suddenly caught by an incident on the hillside to his left. A group of boys from the town was engaged in tormenting a young girl. She was retreating backwards up the slope through a disused orchard, shouting haughtily back at her pursuers. The boys' malice had turned to anger; they were retorting hotly and letting fly about her a few harmless stones. Pamphilus strode over to the group and with a gesture ordered the boys down the hill. The girl, her face still flushed and distrustful, stood with her back against a tree and waited for him to come toward her. They looked at one another for a moment in silence. Finally Pamphilus said:

"What is the matter?"

"They're just country fools, that's all. They've never seen anyone before who didn't come from their wretched Brynos." And then from rage and disappointment she began to cry uncontrollably and despairingly.

Pamphilus watched her for a time and then asked her where she had been going.

"Nowhere. I was just going for a walk and they followed me from the town. I can't do anything. I can't go anywhere. . . . I wasn't hurting them. I was just going for a walk alone and they called names after me. They followed me way up here; I called names at them and then they started throwing things at me. That's all."

"I thought I knew everyone on the island," said Pamphilus thoughtfully, "but I have never seen you before. Have you been here long?"

"Yes, I've been here almost a year," she replied, adding indistinctly, ". . . but I hardly ever go out or anything."

"You hardly ever go out?"

"No," and she fumbled with her dress and stared at the sea, frowning.

"You should try to know some of the other girls and go out for walks with them."

This time she turned and looked into his face. "I don't know any of the other girls. I . . . I live at home and they don't let me go out of the house, except when I go out for walks nights with . . . well, with Mysis." She continued to be shaken with sobs, but she was adjusting her hair and the folds of her dress. "I don't see why they have to throw stones at me," she added.

Pamphilus looked at her in silence, gravely. Presently he collected himself and said, "There's a big smooth stone over there. Will you go over there and sit down?"

She followed him to the stone, still busy with her hair and drawing her fingers across her eyes and cheeks.

"I have a sister just about your age," said Pamphilus. "You can begin by knowing her. You can go for walks with her and then you wouldn't be a stranger any more. Her

name is Argo. You'd like one another, I know. My sister is
weaving a large mantle for my mother and she'd like you
to help her with it and she could help you with yours. Are
you making a mantle?"

"Yes."

"That would be fine," said Pamphilus, and from that mo-
ment Glycerium loved him forever.

"I probably know your father, don't I?" he asked.

"I have no father," she replied, looking up at him weakly.
"I am the sister of the woman from Andros."

"Oh . . . oh . . ." said Pamphilus, more astonished than
he had ever been in his life. "I know your sister well."

"Yes," said Glycerium. Her bright wet eyes strayed over
the streaked sea and the blown birds. "She doesn't want
anyone to know that I'm there. All day I stay up on the
top of the house or work in the court. Only at night I'm
allowed to go for a walk with Mysis. Even now I'm sup-
posed to be in the house, but I broke my promise. She has
gone to the market and so I broke my promise. I wanted
to see what the island and the sea look like by day. And I
wanted to look across to Andros where I come from. But
the boys followed me here and threw stones at me and I
can never come again."

Here she fell to weeping even more despairingly than
before and Pamphilus could do nothing but say "Well"
several times and "Yes." At last he asked her what her
name was.

"Glycerium. Chrysis went away from home a long time
ago and I was living with my brother and he died and I
couldn't live with him any more. And I had nowhere to go
or anything, and one day she came back and took me to
live with her. That's all."

"Have you any brothers or sisters?"

"Oh, no."

"Who is Mysis?"

"Mysis isn't Greek. She is from Alexandria. Chrysis found
her. All of them in the house—she just found them some-

where. That's what she does. Mysis was a slave in the cloth mills. Sometimes she tells me about it."

Pamphilus still gazed at her, and bringing back her wandering evasive glance from the sea she looked at him from her thin face and enormous hungry eyes. Even a long glance did not now embarrass them.

"Do you want me to ask Chrysis to let you go about the island by day?" he asked.

"If she doesn't want it, we mustn't change her. Chrysis knows best." She turned away from him and said in a lower voice, dreamy and embittered, "But what can become of me? Am I always to stay locked up? I am fifteen already. The world is full of wonderful things and people that I might never know about. I know it was wrong of me to break my promise; but to live for years without ever knowing new people—to hear them passing the door all day, and to see them a long way off. Do you think I did very wrong?"

"No."

"I don't know anyone. I don't know anyone."

"Well . . . well, you'll come to know my sister. That will be a beginning," he said, taking her fingertips thoughtfully and wonderingly in his.

"Yes," she said.

"Everything is beginning over again. I'm your friend. Then my sister. Soon you will have a great many. You'll see."

"But where will I be five years from now and ten years from now," she cried, staring about her wildly. "I don't know. I'm afraid. I'm unhappy. Everyone in the world is happy except me."

The caress of the hands in first love, and never so simply again, seems to be a sharing of courage, an alliance of two courages against a confusing world. As his hand passed from her hair to her shoulder, she turned to him with parted lips and hesitant eyes, then suddenly bound both her arms about his neck. Into his ears her lips wildly and all but meaninglessly repeated, "Yes. Yes. Yes. I can't stay there

forever. I should never know anyone. I should never see anybody."

"She will let you come to see me," he said.

"No," said Glycerium. "But I'll come by myself. I mustn't ask her. She would not let me come. She always knows best. And the boys can throw their stones. I don't mind, if you're here. What . . . what is your name?"

"My name is Pamphilus, Glycerium."

"Can . . . can I call you by it?"

It was not at this meeting, nor at their next, but at the third, beneath the dwarfed olive trees, that those caresses that seemed to be for courage, for pity and for admiration, were turned by Nature to her own uses.

These conversations took place in the early spring. One afternoon in the late summer, Chrysis slipped out of her house and climbed the hill behind it. She was filled with a great desire to be alone and to think. She looked out over the glittering sea. The winds were moderate on that afternoon and before them the innumerable neat waves hurried toward the shore, running up the sands with a long whisper, or discreetly lifting against the rocks a scarf of foam. In the distance a school of dolphins engaged at their eternal games led the long procession of curving backs. The water was marbled at intervals with the strange fields and roadways of a lighter blue; and behind all she beheld with love the violet profile of Andros. For a time she strayed about upon the crest of the hill, making sure that no one was watching or following her, then descending the further side she sought out her favorite retreats, a point of rock that projected into the sea and a sheltered cove beside it. As she drew near the place, she stumbled forward, almost running, and as she went she murmured soothingly to herself: "We are almost there. Look, we are almost there now." At last, climbing over the boulders she let herself down into an amphitheater of hot dry sand. She started unbinding her hair, but stopped herself abruptly: "No, no. I must think. I should fall asleep here. I must think first. I shall come back

soon," she muttered to the amphitheater, and continuing her journey she reached the furthermost heap of stones and sat down. She rested her chin upon her hand, and fixing her eyes upon the horizon she waited for the thoughts to come.

The first thing to think about was her new illness. Several times she had been awakened by a wild fluttering in her left side that continued, deepening, until it seemed to her as though a great stake were being driven into her heart. And all the day the sensation would remain with her as of a heavy object burdening the place where this trouble lay. "Probably . . . very likely," she said to herself, "the next time I shall die of it." At the thought a wave of anticipation passed over her. "I shall probably die of it," she repeated cheerfully and became interested in some crayfish in the pool at her feet. She plucked some grasses behind her and started dragging them before the eyes of the indignant animals. "Nothing in life could make me abandon my sheep, but if I die they will have to fall back on Circumstance as I did. Glycerium, what will become of you? Apraxine, Mysis . . . ? There are times when we cannot see one step ahead of us, but five years later we are eating and sleeping somewhere." (It was humorous, pretending that one's heart was as hard as that.) "Yes," she said aloud, to the pain that trembled within her, "only come quickly." She leaned forward still dragging the stems before the shellfish: "I have lived thirty-five years. I have lived enough. *Stranger, near this spot lies Chrysis, daughter of Arches of Andros: the ewe that has strayed from the flock lives many years in one day and dies at a great age when the sun sets.*" She laughed at the deceptive comforts of self-pity, and taking off a sandal put her foot into the water. She drew herself up for a moment, asking herself what there was left in the house for the colony's supper; then recollecting some fish and some salad on the shelf, she returned to her thoughts. She repeated her epitaph, making it a song and emphasizing, for self-mockery, its false sentiment. "O Andros, O

Poseidon, how happy I am. I have no right to be happy like this. . . ."

And she knew as she gazed at the frieze of dolphins still playing in the distance that her mind was avoiding another problem that awaited her. "I am happy because I love this Pamphilus—Pamphilus the anxious, Pamphilus the stupid. Why cannot someone tell him that it is not necessary to suffer so about living." And the low exasperated sigh escaped her, the protest we make at the preposterous, the incorrigible beloved. "He thinks he is failing. He thinks he is inadequate to life at every turn. Let him rest some day, O ye Olympians, from pitying those who suffer. Let him learn to look the other way. This is something new in the world, this concern for the unfit and the broken. Once he begins that, there's no end to it, only madness. It leads nowhere. That is some god's business." Whereupon she discovered that she was weeping; but when she had dried her eyes she was still thinking about him. "Oh, such people are unconscious of their goodness. They strike their foreheads with their hands because of their failure, and yet the rest of us are made glad when we remember their faces. Pamphilus, you are another herald from the future. Some day men will be like you. Do not frown so. . . ."

But these thoughts were very fatiguing. She arose, and returning to the amphitheater, laid herself down upon the sand. She murmured some fragments from the Euripidean choruses and fell asleep. She had always been an islander and this hot and impersonal sun playing upon a cold and impersonal sea was not unfriendly to her. And now for two hours the monotony of sun and sea played about her and wove itself into the mood of her sleeping mind. As once the gray-eyed Athena stood guarding Ulysses—she leaning upon her spear, her great heart full of concern and of those long divine thoughts that are her property—even so, now, the hour and the place all but gathered itself into a presence and shed its influence upon her. When her eyes finally opened she listened for a time to the calm in her heart.

"Someday," she said, "we shall understand why we suffer. I shall be among the shades underground and some wonderful hand, some Alcestis, will touch me and will show me the meaning of all these things; and I shall laugh softly for hours as I do now . . . as I do now."

She arose and binding up her hair prepared to ascend the slope. But just as she turned to leave the place, there visited her the desire to do something ceremonial, to mark the hour. She stood up straightly and held out her arms to the setting sun: "If you still hear prayers from the lips of mortals, if our longings touch you at all, hear me now. Give to this Pamphilus some assurance—even some assurance such as you have given to me, unstable though I am—that he is right. And oh! (but I do not say this from vanity or pride, O Apollo—but perhaps this is weak, this is childish of me, perhaps this renders the whole prayer powerless!) if it is possible, let the thought of me or of something I have said be comforting to him some day. And . . . and. . . ."

But her arms fell to her side. The world seemed empty. The sun went down. The sea and sky became suddenly remote and she was left with only the tears in her eyes and the longing in her heart. She closed her lips and turned her head aside. "I suppose there is no god," she whispered. "We must do these things ourselves. We must drag ourselves through life as best we can."

Chrysis had made the mistake of accustoming the members of her household to her invariable presence and now while she slept they became increasingly indignant at the length of her absence. In twos and threes they hovered about the door, peering to the right and to the left with mingled scorn and alarm.

"When she comes in, see that no one says a word to her," directed Apraxine, a tall lame woman whom Chrysis had found beaten and left for dead at the edge of the desert below the terraces of Alexandria.

"Pretend you don't see her."

". . . to go sallying off a whole day without a word to a soul."

"I'm sure I don't wish to stay in a house where I count for nothing."

". . . less than nothing, it seems."

Presently however something happened that distracted their minds from their resentment. A new sheep arrived at the fold.

Simo's frank had carried to Andros the money that Chrysis intended for the support of the stricken sea captain. But Philocles' guardians had long since tired of their charge and become discontented with the intermitten payments. They decided to take advantage of this sum of money to ship him off to Brynos. It was necessary for this purpose to wait for a lucid interval in the patient's condition. Such a moment finally arrived; they hurriedly made up his bundle, brushed his hair, and led him down to the water front, where they found the captain of a boat sailing between the Cyclades who was willing to undertake the commission. And thus it was that on the afternoon of Chrysis' retreat to solitude Philocles arrived on Brynos. A boy who attended at one of the wineshops in the town was directed to escort him to her house, and suddenly the child-like sea captain was thrust into the courtyard among the conspiring pensioners.

Ten years before, Philocles had been the greatest navigator on the Mediterranean, first in skill and experience and first in fame. He had been many times to Sicily and to Carthage; he had passed through the Gates of Hercules and visited the Tyrian mines in Britain. He had sailed westward for months across the great shelf of water, seeking new islands, and had been forced to turn back by the visible anger of the gods. In the present age men were captains or merchants or farmers, but in the great age men had been first Athenians or Greeks, and the islanders regarded Philocles as of that order, a belated giant. He was already in

middle life when Chrysis first knew him—she had been a passenger on one of his trips to Egypt—and it astonished her to find someone laconic in a chattering world and with quiet hands in a gesturing civilization. He was blackened and cured by all weathers. He stood in the squares of the various ports of call, his feet apart as though they were for-ever planted on a shifting deck. He seemed to be too large for daily life; his very eyes were strange—unaccustomed to the shorter range, too used to seizing the appearances of a constellation between a cloud and a cloud, and the out-lines of a headland in rain. Wind, salt and starvation had molded his head, and his mind had been rendered, not buoyant, but rich and concentrated by the enforced asceti-cisms of a prolonged duty and of long sea voyages. He had been one of the persons whom Chrysis had most loved in all her life and it was she who had discovered his secret, the secret that it was neither adventure nor gain that drove him along his adventurous life. He was passing the time and filling the hours in anticipation of release from a life that had lost its savor with the death of his daughter. These two saw in one another's eyes the thing they had in com-mon, the fact that they had both died to themselves. They lived at one remove from that self that supports the gen-erality of men, the self that is a bundle of self-assertions, of greeds, of vanities and of easy offended pride. Three years before, Philocles had been forced to captain some ships of a city at war. He had been captured and mutilated and what was left of so kingly a person was a timorous child.

The sheep examined the newcomer who had been thrust so abruptly into their midst. They questioned him and amused themselves with his answers. Then they gave him a bench in the sunlight where he might whisper to his heart's content.

The sun set and soon after Chrysis came stumbling through the door, laughing apologetically and pushing back her hair. "Forgive me, O my dear friends, forgive me. I fell asleep on the sand and I'm very sorry I'm so late." (The

men and women raised their eyebrows cynically and went on with their work.) "Apraxine, has anything happened?" (Apraxine cleared her throat with Alexandrian hauteur and became absorbed in looking for a thread on the ground.) "Now we must find something particularly rare for supper."

The sheep exchanged pitying glances over all this tawdry artifice and when Chrysis passed into the house they burst into laughter. The laughter was condescending, but the soul had returned to the community. Finally at a signal from Apraxine, Glycerium went to the door and announced to Chrysis that Philocles had arrived from Andros. He had seen her pass and some twinge of memory had set him trembling. He rose and walked unsteadily to the middle of the court. She saw him standing before her, haggard, with hollow puzzled eyes and with untrimmed beard.

She went forward repeating, "My dear friend, my friend!" but as she embraced him a loud voice within her seemed to say: "Something is going to happen. The threads of my life are drawing together."

That night Chrysis was awakened from a light and feverish sleep by the instinctive knowledge that someone was near her. She raised herself on one elbow and peered toward the faint glimmer of the door.

"Who is it? Who is there?" she said.

A figure seemed suddenly to rise from the threshold. "It's I, Chrysis. It's Glycerium."

"Is something the matter? Is someone ill?"

"No . . . it's only. . . ."

"Light a lamp, my child. What do you want?"

"Chrysis, are you angry with me for waking you up? I couldn't sleep, Chrysis, and I had to come into your room."

"But why are you crying, my dear, my dove? Come now and sit on the edge of the bed. Of course I'm not angry with you." Glycerium sank upon the floor beside her. "No,

no—the floor is cold. Come sit up here. Your hair is wet! Tell me now, what is making you unhappy?"

"Nothing."

"What? Then you have something to tell me?"

"No . . . I don't know what . . . I just want you to talk to me."

"Well, I have something to tell you." Chrysis was stroking Glycerium's hair, delicately following with her fingertips the strands as they passed above and behind the ear, when suddenly Glycerium threw her arms about her sister's neck and sobbed uncontrollably. Chrysis continued gravely with her caress, thinking that she was merely dealing with one of the meaningless accesses of despair that descend upon adolescence when the slow ache of existence is first apprehended by the growing mind. "There!" she murmured in a rhythmic undertone, "Sh . . . sh . . . sh . . . sh. . . . We love you. We all love you in this house. Our beautiful Glycerium, our gentle, our very beautiful Glycerium . . . sh . . . sh . . . there! Are you comfortable now? I have some good news for you. (No, no, there is plenty of room.) This is it: Beginning tomorrow you are going to lead an altogether different life. I am going to let you wander all over the island alone. And when Mysis and I go to market you can go with us. You may climb the hills if you like, and you may explore along the water's edge—I shall even show you the secret of the secrets of my heart—a beautiful hidden shelter by the sea where one can be perfectly alone. . . . Well? are you pleased? Doesn't this news make you happy?"

"Yes, Chrysis."

"Now! I thought it would make you very happy and all you say is: Yes, Chrysis!"

"Chrysis, tell me: what will become of me?"

Chrysis changed her position and in the dark shut her eyes a moment. "Oh, my dear, my dear . . . that's what everyone asks, everyone on earth. Well, first you tell me: what do you want to become?"

"I want to marry someone and . . . and be in his home.

Chrysis, tell me: can I marry someone? Without a father
and a mother and without anything, is it possible that I can
marry someone?"

"My dear, there is always . . ."

"Chrysis, I'm grown-up now. I'm fifteen. Please tell me
the truth. I must know. Don't say something merely to quiet
me. I must know the truth. Can a man ever ask me to marry
him? Why are you waiting so long to answer me?"

"I have been planning to have a long talk with you about
all these things. But not now. Wait a short time; wait until
you have had a week, two weeks, of this new life when you
will be free to wander all over the island. Then you will be
able to understand better what I have to say."

Glycerium paused a moment. "I know, I know," she said,
her face against Chrysis' shoulder. "That means that no
one will ever be able to marry me."

"No, no, I don't say that. . . ."

Glycerium rose and stood in the middle of the room. "I
understand," she said in the darkness.

Chrysis raised herself again on one elbow and said slowly,
"We are not Greek citizens. We are not people with homes.
We are considered strange, only a little above the slaves.
All those others live in homes and everyone knows their
fathers and their mothers; they marry one another. They
think we would never fit into their life. Although all that is
true,—"

"But there are stories," said Glycerium, "of men who
even married girls that had been slaves."

"Yes, if a young man should fall in love with you, it is
possible that he would take you into his home. That is why
I have tried to take such care of you and why I have kept
you hidden here in the house. Through the young men who
come to the banquets ,the island knows that you are here
and that you have been carefully protected. And now that
you are to walk about the island freely you must be a hun-
dred times more careful than other girls. You are beautiful
and you are good, and before all their unfriendly eyes you

must show them your modesty and your goodness. That is all there is to say and to hope, my child."

"Perhaps, Chrysis . . . it is best that I do not go about the island freely, after all."

"No, no. You will feel like going out. It will come gradually. But now you must go to bed and to sleep, my darling. All these things will solve themselves as best they can. All you can do for the present is to be yourself, your very self, my Glycerium."

Glycerium moved unsteadily toward the bed: "Chrysis, I must tell you something."

"Yes?"

"You will be angry with me, Chrysis."

"Why. . . ."

"May the gods protect me, I . . . I have been talking with Mysis and now I know that I am going to be the mother of a child."

There was silence for a moment, followed by the sound of Chrysis putting her feet upon the floor. "Where is Mysis? Let me get up."

"It is true, Chrysis. I broke my promise the times when you were away. I used to go out over the hills."

"Oh, my child, my child!"

"But he loves me. He will marry me. He loves me, I know."

"Who is it? What is his name?"

"It is Pamphilus, son of Simo."

Chrysis grew rigid in the darkness. Then she slowly put her feet back into the bed. Glycerium continued wildly, "He loves me. He will take care of me. He has told me so a hundred times. Chrysis, what shall I do? What shall I do? I am afraid."

A low moan at the door revealed the fact that Mysis had accompanied her younger mistress to this interview and was kneeling outside the door without the courage to enter.

After a moment Chrysis said in a light impersonal voice, "Well, you . . . go off to bed now and go to sleep. Yes. We'll

both be catching cold here. It's late. I think it must be al-
most morning."

"I cannot sleep."

"Everything will be all right, Glycerium. I can't talk any
more now. I'm not well. We'll talk about it in the morning."

Glycerium left the room, trembling.

In her darker hours Chrysis carried on what she called
a "dialogue with Fate." And now as she turned to the wall
she said, "I hear you. You have won again."

Before long the pain in her side became fixed and unre-
mitting, and Chrysis knew that her life was drawing to a
close. She took to her bed and her thoughts no longer clung
to the world about her. Now when her courage was being
undermined by her pain she dared not ask herself if she
had lived and if she were dying, unloved, in disorder, with-
out meaning. From time to time she peered into her mind
to ascertain what her beliefs were in regard to a life after
death, its judgments or its felicities; but the most exhaust-
ing of all our adventures is that journey down the long
corridors of the mind to the last halls where belief is en-
throned. She resigned herself to the memory of certain
moments when intuition had comforted her and she quieted
her heart with Andrian cradlesongs and with fragments
from the tragic poets. She saved her strength to fulfill a last
desire, one that may perhaps seem unworthy to persons of
a later age. Her mind had been molded by formal literature,
by epics and odes, by tragedies and by heroic biography,
and from this reading she had been imbued with the super-
stition that one should die in a noble manner, and in this
high decorum even the maintenance of her beauty played a
part. The only terror left in the world was the fear that she
might leave it with cries of pain, with a torn mind, and with
discomposed features.

The news spread about the island that the Andrian was
gravely ill. The young men who had been her guests were
confused by the discrepancy between their mothers' sar-
casms and the respect that Chrysis had inspired in them-

selves, but some brought shy offerings of wine and cheese to her door. For such brief interviews she raised herself on one elbow and sought to recover her light-spoken graciousness. But most of the young men stayed away; it required a maturer mind than they could summon to hold side by side their memories of sensual pleasure and their respect due to the dying.

Pamphilus had other reasons for staying away. It seemed more and more unlikely that he would ever be permitted to marry Glycerium. But one morning he appeared at Chrysis' house and asked to see her. He traversed the court, picking his way among her motley and dismayed pensioners, and his eyes fell upon Glycerium. She was seated beside Philocles at her sister's door, silent and without hope. Pamphilus stopped for a moment on one knee before her and took her hands in his. "Do not be afraid," he said in a low voice. "No harm will come to you." She derived no courage from his words; she lifted her eyes and scanned his face. Her mouth trembled, but no words came and her eyes returned to the ground. Pamphilus passed into the room where Chrysis lay; for a moment he could distinguish nothing in the darkness. Presently he became aware of the priest of Æsculapius and Apollo bending over a brazier in the corner, and finally he saw Chrysis smiling at him gravely from the bed. He sat down beside her in silence; each waited for the other to begin.

"We are sorry, all of us are sorry, Chrysis," he said at last, "to hear that you have been so ill."

"Thank you, Pamphilus. Thank them all."

"There . . . there has been so much rain. When the sunlight returns you will feel better at once."

"Yes, it has always been the sunlight that has done me the most good. You are all well on your farm?"

"Yes, the gods be praised."

"The gods be praised. I shall never forget a favor your father did for me."

Pamphilus was struck with amazement. "My father?"

"Oh, forgive me . . . I remember now I promised him
not to mention it to you. Oh, my illness has made me for-
get that. I am ashamed, I am ashamed. But now I had
better add that it was a small commission he did for me by
one of his boats going to Andros. I would not have him
think me unfaithful to my promise. I beg of you earnestly
not to tell him that I spoke of it."

"Indeed, I shall not tell him, Chrysis."

There fell another pause between them, while her
strengthless hands lightly pressed upon the bed in her
self-reproach.

"Yes," said Pamphilus. "When there is more sunlight you
will feel better at once. The sky has been overcast for a
long time. I cannot remember when it has been overcast so
long."

To themselves they both cried: "How shall we ever get
out of this?"

"We have missed the banquets. I would like to tell you
again, Chrysis, what great pleasure they gave me. I have
been looking forward to the next one when you promised
to read us I forget what play."

"It was to have been the *Ion* of Euripides."

"Yes."

"This," said Chrysis, glancing toward the priest with a
smile, "this is my Ion."

But perhaps the words were ill-chosen. She thought she
saw the priest frowning as he bent over his work. "Forgive
me," she said to him abruptly, "if I have offended you. I
did not mean it ill."

But the tears were rolling down her cheeks. "Life, Pam-
philus," she said, "is full of mistakes, but the wrongs we do
to those we love and honor are more than we can endure."
The priest approached the farther side of the bed and ad-
justed the pillows; he whispered a few words into her ear
and went back to his brazier.

"Am I tiring you?" Pamphilus asked.

"No, no. I am very happy that you have come." To her-

self she thought: "Time is passing, and what are we say-
ing! Is there not something heartfelt that I can find to say
to him, something to remember, for him and for me?" But
she distrusted the emotion that filled her heart. It was per-
haps mere excitement and pain; or a vague and false senti-
ment. Probably the best thing to do was to be stoic; to be
brave and inarticulate; to talk of trivial things. Or was it a
greater bravery to surmount this shame and to say what-
ever obvious words the heart dictated? Which was right?

Pamphilus was thinking, "She is dying. What can I say
to her? But I have never been able to place words rightly.
I am dull. I am nothing to her but the man who has
wronged her sister." Aloud he said in a low voice, "I shall
marry Glycerium if I can, Chrysis. At all events you may
be sure that no harm will come to her."

"Though I love her dearly," replied Chrysis, finding her
words with great difficulty "I shall not urge you. I . . . I
no longer believe that what happens to us is important. You
will marry Glycerium or another. The years will unfold
these things. It is the life in the mind that is important."

"I shall do what I can for her."

"You have only to be yourself without fear, without
doubting, Pamphilus."

"Chrysis, you will forgive me for having spoken to you
so little at the banquets . . . and for having sat at the fur-
ther end and . . . that is the way I am. It was not because
I did not respect you. I cannot talk as those others can. I
am only a listener. Even now I cannot say what I mean.
But I followed all that you said."

The pain in Chrysis' side seemed to increase beyond all
endurance. "Oh, friend," she said, "do not distrust. These
things are not so unsatisfactory . . . so interrupted as they
seem to be." The priest had been watching her; she made a
slight sign to him. "I do not wish you to go away," she
continued to Pamphilus, almost in a whisper, "but it is best
that I sleep now." Then raising herself on one elbow she
breathed in anguish: "Perhaps we shall meet somewhere

beyond life when all these pains shall have been removed. I think the gods have some mystery still in store for us. But if we do not, let me say now . . ." her hands opened and closed upon the cloths that covered her, ". . . I want to say to someone . . . that I have known the worst that the world can do to me, and that nevertheless I praise the world and all living. All that is, is well. Remember someday, remember me as one who loved all things and accepted from the gods all things, the bright and the dark. And do you likewise. Farewell."

Simo arose early to witness Chrysis' funeral. The Greeks, for reasons that lay deep in their sense of the fitness of things and in their superstition, conducted their funerals in the hour before dawn, and it was therefore still profound night when the little procession of her household prepared to pass through the streets of the town. When Simo arrived at the square he found that many of the men of Brynos had already gathered there, and drawing the folds of their rough cloaks about them, were standing talking together in low voices. The men of his own age had brought their curiosity and contempt with them and were congratulating themselves on the island's happy deliverance from the foreign woman; but the younger men who had known Chrysis stood with sullen faces, their throats rigid with antagonism at the glee of their elders. Simo took his place in silence beside Chremes, but refused to respond to the latter's animated comment. Presently as the sounds of the flute and the mourners were heard approaching he discovered Pamphilus standing beside him, as silent as himself.

Mysis herded the shuffling and stumbling company before her as best she could. Philocles walked with lifted knees, as children do in a procession. In one hand he held some grasses and with the other he clutched the mantle of his companion, the old doorkeeper; but he was continually

straying off, or standing still to gaze with wide dazzled eyes at the torches that preceded him or at the laughing bystanders. Behind him the deaf and dumb Ethiopian girl could scarcely be restrained from running forward to walk beside her sleeping friend, Chrysis, whose rebuke had been so terrible when she had done wrong and whose smile had been sufficient compensation for her imprisonment in silence. Glycerium walked with lowered eyes, lost to hope and lost to the decorum that now required of her the wailing and the distraught gestures of a conspicuous mourner. All these passed forward under the bright stars that had received the first intimation of day and shone with a last heightened brilliance, and under the long garlands of smoke that hung above the company in that windless air.

As the onlookers accompanied the procession into the open country, Simo's attention was fixed upon Glycerium, by reason of her condition, which was apparent to all, of her resemblance to her sister, of the dejection that invested her, and of the beauty and modesty of her bearing. And he became aware that his son also was watching the girl. In fact, during the whole journey, Pamphilus bent upon her his burning eyes, trying to intercept her glance and to communicate to her his encouragement and his love. But not until they reached the heaped-up wood whereon the bodies of a goat and a lamb were laid beside that of Chrysis, and not until the fire had touched it, did she raise her eyes. Then as the sound of the wailing increased in shrillness and the sound of the flute floated piercingly above all, she turned to Mysis and began to speak wildly into her ear. But the words of her vehemence were not heard in that din, nor were Mysis' words of encouragement. Glycerium was trying to draw herself away from the supporting arm of the other and the slow faltering struggle of the two women was lighted up by the rising flames. Pamphilus, in the intensity of his concentration upon the suffering of the girl, moved slowly forward, his hands held out before him. And now he heard the words that she was repeating, "It's best. It's best

so!" Suddenly Glycerium pushed the older woman away from her and with a loud cry of "Chrysis!" stumbled forward to fling herself upon the body of her sister.

But Pamphilus had foreseen this attempt. Running across the sand, he seized her by her disheveled hair and drew her back and into his arms. The touch of that encircling arm released her tears. She laid her head against his breast as one who had been there before and was returning home.

The scandal of this embrace was felt at once by all the bystanders and chiefly by Chremes, who turned upon Simo with his protest and astonishment. But Simo had moved away and was walking slowly home through the breaking dawn. Now he understood the Pamphilus of the last months.

The islanders discussed interminably the surprising event that had taken place at Chrysis' funeral. They watched with hushed excitement the chill that had fallen across the relations between the families of Simo and of Chremes. Rumor presently asserted that Pamphilus had promised to acknowledge the child, though no one, naturally, even discussed the possibility of a marriage. Readers of a later age will not be able to understand the difficulties that beset the young man. Marriage was not then a sentimental relation, but a legal one of great dignity, and the bridegroom's share in the contract involved not so much himself as his family, his farm, and his ancestors. Without the support of his parents and without a residence in their home a young man was a mere adventurer without social, economic or civil standing. A marriage was only possible if Simo declared it to be so. The customs of the islands encouraged fathers in the luxuries of blustering and tyranny, but Simo's relations with his son had always been strangely impersonal. He was confused by his own deference for his son, by what he thought was his own weakness. Yet Simo's silence did not have the air of a final refusal; it even seemed to imply that the decision, with all its possibilities of lifetime regret and of a lifetime's contention on the farm, rested with Pamphilus.

One day several months after Chrysis' funeral Pamphilus betook himself to the palaestra for some exercise. He entered the low door and, nodding to a group of friends that sat scuffling under an awning at the edge of the enclosure, he walked across the hot red sand. The old attendant at the door, who had won a laurel wreath in his youth, came trotting across the burning ring after him and as soon as Pamphilus had seated himself on a marble bench began kneading his calves and ankles. In the center of the field Chremes' son was going through the motions of hurling an imaginary discus; thirty and fifty times he turned with lifted knee, trying to fix in his muscular memory the perfect synchronization of the gestures. Two other young men were practicing a festival dance, interrupting their work from time to time to criticize one another's slightest deviation from a harmonious balance. The young priest of Æsculapius and Apollo was running around the course. Pamphilus sent the attendant away and lying down on his cloak let the sunlight beat upon him. He did not think about his problem, but left his mind a blank, suffused with a dull misery that identified itself with the drowsy heat. Presently he placed his elbow on the ground and raising his head rested his cheek upon his hand and watched the priest of Apollo.

The priest never entered the competitive games, but he was undoubtedly first upon the island for endurance and second only to Pamphilus in swiftness. Save on the days of festival he appeared for exercise daily and ran six miles. He preserved a perfect temperance: he drank no wine; he lived on fruit and vegetables; he awoke with the sun and unless there was some call to attend the sick he went to sleep with it. He had taken the vow of chastity, the vow that forever closes the mind to the matter, without wistful back-glancing and without conceding the possibility that circumstance might yet present a harmless deviation, the vow which, when profoundly compassed, fills the mind with such power that it is forever cut off from the unstable tentative sons of men. His office required his passing so much

time among the sick and the distressed that he had become inadequate to the cheerful and the happy and no one on the island knew him very well. But he had a strange power over the sick and the demented and only in their hours of confession and despair was the shutter of his impersonality lifted; such as had known him then followed him ever after with their eyes, in gratitude and in astonishment. He was only twenty-eight, but he had been sent to Brynos by the priests that attended the great mysteries of Athens and Corinth as a signal honor; for the shrine on Brynos was one of particular significance in the legend of Æsculapius and his father Apollo. Pamphilus had never spoken to him beyond the salutations of the field, but he would rather have known him than anyone in the world, and he in turn watched Pamphilus with grave interest. Now Pamphilus lay following him with his eyes and wishing he had his own life to live over again.

Suddenly he became aware that someone was shaking him by the shoulder. It was one of his companions. "Here comes your father," said the boy and went back to the awning. Pamphilus rose to his feet and waited respectfully as Simo approached, preceded by the old attendant.

"Stay where you are. Lie down again," said Simo; "I'll sit here on this bench. I want to talk to you."

Pamphilus lay down, his face turned away toward the track.

Simo wiped his face with the hem of his skirt. "I won't be long, my boy. . . . But we must consider this matter somehow . . . after all." He was not sure of himself. He blew his nose. He coughed several times and roughly adjusted the folds of his gown. He repeated "Very well" and "Now" and waited in vain for Pamphilus to say something. At last he launched forth among his prepared introductions:

"Well now, my boy, I assume you want to marry the girl. Hm. . . ."

Pamphilus put his head down between his folded arms as though he were going to sleep. He sighed in anticipa-

tion of all the irrelevancies he was about to hear. In his
heart he knew he had only to say yes or no and his father
would accede to his wish.

"I don't·wish to coerce you. I think you are old enough
to see the good and the bad for yourself. But for a few mo-
ments now I want to talk all around the matter. I want to
put the other side of the case in its plainest terms and
leave it there for a while. May I do that?"

"Yes," said Pamphilus.

"Well, to begin with, it's only right to face the fact that
there is no outward obligation to marry the girl. I've looked
into the matter. She is not a Greek citizen. She happens to
have been brought up in a sheltered manner, or so I take it.
This Chrysis seems to have tried to prevent the girl's falling
into her way of life; but that does not alter the fact that
she is a mere dancing girl. Now, mind you, I can see that
she is modest and well-mannered. She appears to be just
such a person as our own Argo. But she could never have
hoped for anything above the situation she is now in. The
world is full of just such likable stray girls as this Glycerium,
but we cannot be expected to welcome them into the fabric
of good Greek family life. You may be sure that Chrysis
knew perfectly well that Glycerium must some day become
a hetaira like herself, or a servant."

Simo paused. He could see the back only of his son's
head, but he was able to imagine upon his face the set un-
happy expression they had all been obliged to watch there
for the last weeks. He coughed again and abruptly flung
himself upon another of his openings:

"No doubt you feel yourself fairly bound to her by a
promise—but a promise, Pamphilus, in which you failed to
consider the rest of us, and especially your mother. If you
decided to marry the girl, your mother and sister would
try to live with her as peaceably as possible, we know; but
it would be a good deal to ask of them. You know them.
This girl does not understand the first thing about our island
manners. She doesn't know how simple and monotonous

our women's lives are. I expect that life with the Andrian and with that strange company at the house on the hill was an odd affair. She'd be unhappy with us. And even if she didn't contradict your mother all day . . . and worse . . . she'd become silent and sullen. Pamphilus, they would never grow fond of one another. It would be better to be cruel to her now and let her alone, than to set up discord, a lifetime of discord on our farm."

For a moment his memory failed him, but he rallied and continued:

"Well, even assuming that your mother and sister came to like her and to accept her cordially in the home, all her life she would have to endure something insulting in the manner of the other women on the island. We men do not take that interest in social discrimination, my son, but women . . . women with their few interests and . . . and so on . . . they enjoy having someone to ignore or to stare down. It warms them. Glycerium is not a Greek citizen. Her sister was a hetaira. All her life she would be obliged to endure their looking at her with straight lips and (I can see them) with half-closed eyes. But even that is not the chief thing."

He hoped that the suspense in this splendid transition would be reflected in some change in his son's position, but the young man lay motionless. Simo's weary eyes turned slowly about the palaestra.

"The girl is not strong. The women of the village seem to know something about it. She's a quick nervous high-strung girl and she'd bring you a series of thin and sickly children. You and I know those homes. She's not unlike our neighbor Douro's wife; isn't she? And the uneven health of such women—even though they're often more likable, yes, more likable, than the Philumenas—takes the shape of complaining and quarrelsomeness. And in their children. One has no right to bring into the world those children that cannot join others in their games, silent children who go through life regularly subject to fevers and coughs and pains. The most important thing in life is a houseful of strong healthy

boys. Take Philumena, now. You do not 'love' Philumena,
as the poets use the word. Well, when I married your
mother perhaps I did not 'love' her in that sense. But I
grew to love her and . . . euh . . . now I cannot imagine my-
self as having been married to anyone else, as satisfactorily
married to anyone else. Philumena is handsome. But most
important of all, Philumena is strong. So . . . so, Pam-
philus, does what I am saying seem to have some truth in
it? . . . Pamphilus?"

But Pamphilus had fallen asleep.

His last thought had been the recollection of one of
Chrysis' maxims, an ironic phrase which he had chosen to
take literally: *The mistakes we make through generosity
are less terrible than the gains we acquire through caution.*

Simo was not vexed. He sighed. Looking up he saw the
priest of Æsculapius and Apollo running around the course.
He recalled the day several months before when he and
Sostrata had taken Pamphilus' sister to the temple. For two
days and two nights, Argo had been suffering from an ear-
ache, and although they knew that the priest was often un-
gracious when his attention was asked on smaller ills they
ventured to present her to him. The hour at which he was
accustomed to receive the sick was a little after sunrise and
there they found his colony. There were invalids brought
to him on beds; there were sufferers from tumors, from pro-
tracted languors, from sore eyes; there were the possessed.
Simo and Sostrata had passed their lives without ailments.
They regarded them, like poverty, like uncleanliness, as
mere bad citizenship; they were on the point of returning
home, so great was their distaste for such manifestations.
The priest required that the guardians who had brought
their sick to him should retire to a distance during his in-
terviews, and Simo and Sostrata had withdrawn with an
ill grace to a nearby grove. Argo seemed not to share her
parents' revulsion from these matters; even before she ap-
proached the place (her fingers pressed upon her ear) she
had been subdued to awe and when her turn came she told

her little story with caught breath. The priest gently
touched her ear, reciting a charm. He poured in some oil
and looked deeply into her shy eyes. And gradually as he
gazed at her a smile appeared upon his lips and slowly she
smiled in return. True influence over another comes not
from a moment's eloquence nor from any happily chosen
word, but from the accumulation of a lifetime's thoughts
stored up in the eyes. And there is one thing greater than
curing a malady, and that is accepting a malady and shar-
ing its acceptance. The earache did not abate at once, but
Argo pretended to her parents that it did, for the other
healing they would not have understood; and all night
long instead of complaining she pressed against her ear the
little bag of laurel leaves he had given her and talked to
herself, rehearsing that interview and that glance. There-
after she never had any conversation with the priest, but
when she happened to meet him upon the road, her heart
was filled with excitement; she gave him a shy greeting and
her eyelids fluttered in a quick intimate glance and he in
turn let fall upon her a faint allusion to his smile. Her
parents were amused by this bond; the priest had brought
out in their daughter a side they had never known in her,
and one that sent messages all along her life. Henceforth
she even stood up straighter. One day a cousin who lived
on the other side of the island came to a meal with them
and let fall a remark in disparagement of the priest, saying
that he was a comfort chiefly to old women who imagined
themselves to be ill. Argo's eyes grew dark and her lips
straight with anger. She refused to eat another mouthful
and forever after the poor foolish cousin could never draw
a word from her and never knew why. All this now returned
to Simo's mind as he watched the priest.

"People like that," he thought to himself, "have some
secret about living. Why don't they tell it to us outright,
instead of wrapping it up in mystery and ceremonial? They
know something that prevents their blundering about, as
we do. Yes, what am I doing here," he added, pushing out

his lower lip, "but playing the fool? Blundering, advising in things I know nothing about." He looked long at his sleeping son. "Pamphilus has some of that secret, too. And that woman from Andros had it, too. Chremes was right, though he meant it ill: there is something of the priest in Pamphilus, something of the priest trying to make its way in him. Let me get up and go away before I say anything more."

So he arose and a little guiltily left the field.

Pamphilus's mind was all but made up, yet still under the burden of perplexity and self-reproach, he decided to seek still more light on his problem and a last reassurance by reviving a custom that had been in frequent use among the Greeks of the great age, but which had fallen off at the time of the events of this story. It consisted merely in abstaining from speech and from food from one sunrise to the next and in either passing the night in the temple enclosure or in arriving there before the dawn that closed the watch. There was not thought to be any particular magic in the practice: it cleared the mind of bodily fumes, it removed it from the commerce of the day and prepared it perhaps for a significant dream. The watcher guarded his fast and his silence, but the Greek mind did not approve of heightening the experience by any further self-denial. One moved about the home as usual, exercised in the palaestra or worked at the loom; one slept. If some uninformed person spoke to the watcher, he drew his finger across his lips and the condition of the vow was understood. Athletes still observed it several days before a race; brides on the eve of their wedding; old ladies who hoped to recover some lost trinket, or to recapture in a dream the features of some all-but-forgotten love; and devout soldiers about to set forth upon an expedition. It was indeed little short of odd that a healthy young man in the even current of life should revive this custom, but the islanders were still sufficiently religious to respect the habits that had expressed the spiritual life of their glorious grandfathers, and made no comment.

By midafternoon hunger had gained upon him and his dejection had increased a hundredfold. Whichever choice he made would involve the unhappiness of others. Under the weight of the alternatives even the memory of Glycerium lost for a time any tender association. He climbed over the remoter parts of the island, gazing absently out to sea and idly plucking the grasses among the rocks where he sat. He came to the spot where he had first seen Glycerium and stood for a time, quiet as the stones about him, asking himself whether the associations in life are based upon an accidental encounter or upon a profound and inner necessity. When he returned to the farm his mother and sister felt the desolation that invested him and moved about with hushed steps. The very slaves went about their tasks on tiptoe and finally withdrew in silence and in alarmed interrogation. During the evening meal Pamphilus sat by the door with closed eyes. His brother, returning, stepped over his feet with awed circumspection (he too had made the watch only a few months before, but in pomp, with twelve other youths on the occasion of their enrollment in the League) and held himself at a distance, rendered uncomfortable by so much seriousness in a good athlete. Of her own accord Argo brought Pamphilus a bowl of water which he drank, smiling the while intimately into her grave eyes; she returned to her place at the table with great dignity and with secret excitement, as though she had done something conspicuous. When Simo finally told her and her brother to go to bed she slipped up to her father and laid her lips against his ear: "What is it, father?" she whispered. "No, tell me, what is the matter?" He took her hands and played with them a moment; he raised his eyebrows wisely and told her to go to bed and sleep well. From her bed in the darkness she noted the movements of the family: that her mother took a cloak and went out into the garden by the cliff, and that later her father did the same. With wide eyes and cautious lifted ear she followed this unaccustomed nocturnal roaming. She was filled with loving excitement;

she kissed her doll many times with violence and wept. She became aware that her younger brother was venturing on hands and knees toward the moonlight in the court: she too ventured out and they stared at one another, but Pamphilus suddenly loomed up from the shadows and waved them back to their beds.

Pamphilus wandered about the outer court. Again the moon was at the full, throwing a milky blue mist over the tiers of olive trees that climbed the hill across the road and casting black shadows among the farm buildings. Its serenity contrasted strangely with the mysterious excitement it awakened among the human beings it fell upon. Pamphilus had seen his parents go into the garden, but he saw them now without emotion, without pity. He returned to the house and lay down upon his bed. Never had he been possessed by mood further from illumination. Lying on his face he traced outlines upon the floor with his finger.

The shells gleamed on the path as Simo walked up and down; from time to time he cast a furtive glance at his wife. She was sitting on a bench of chipped and stained marble that had been his mother's favorite seat. It had been placed there generations before, under a fig arbor blown down long since on a night of legendary storm. It stood at the very end of the garden where a cliff broke down to the sea, and from it one could hear forever the long, spreading whispers of the ebbing and the rising waves below. From that seat his mother had directed the bringing up of five children, had dried their tears and listened with nodding head to the absurd procession of their shifting enthusiasms. "Viewed from a distance," Simo said to himself, "life is harmonious and beautiful. No doubt the years when my mother smiled to us from that bench were as full of crossed wills and exasperations as today, but how beautiful they seem in memory! The dead are wrapped in love; in illusion, perhaps. They go underground and slowly this tender light begins to fall upon them. But the present remains: this succession of small domestic vexations. I have lived such a life

for sixty years and I am still upset by its ephemeral decisions. And I am still asking myself which is the real life: the present with its discontent, or the retrospect with its emotion?" He looked again guardedly at Sostrata, who sat fingering the folds of her cloak and expressing in every line of her position her unfriendliness and her rebellion. "The fault is in me," he continued. "If I were wiser, I could do this thing. As the head of the family I should be firmer. I should say 'yes' or 'no' clearly and let Pamphilus bring in his little girl. I should weed out all these hesitations. Even now she is waiting for me to make up her mind for her; if I spoke distinctly, even against her will, she would adjust herself without great effort. The house would find a way of accepting the new member and things would run on smoothly enough." He was thinking of going toward her with smiling affection, suggesting that at sixty they had earned the right to remain tranquil though the house fell; but he foresaw that her pride would not accommodate itself to any such resignation, and he continued up and down the garden.

Indeed Sostrata did not wish Simo to speak to her. Her mind was filled with one long obstinate exclamation at the stupidity of men. Only a woman's mind could foresee all the harm that would result from such a marriage as the one now being weighed. It was the women of the island that had measured all danger that came with the arrival of the Alexandrian woman; and now she, the first matron of Brynos, was being ordered to receive into her home the last offscouring of that dispersed colony. She had anticipated all her life the rich satisfactions of being a mother-in-law and a grandmother, though what she anticipated was a daughter-in-law of straw. A Greek HOME, she knew, was the only breakwater against the tide of oriental manners, of financial fluctuation, and of political chaos. The highest point toward which any existence could aspire was to be a member of an island family, living and dying on one farm, respected, cautious, and secretly wealthy; of a family stretch-

ing into the past as far as the mossy funerary urns could record, and into the future as far as the imagination could reach, that is to one's grandchildren. Society was similarity. These things she repeated to herself, and under the waves of her indignation and self-pity—though the greater part of the time she stood in awe of her husband and her son—all her gracious traits disappeared, her beautiful eyes became harsh that for three days had been bright with the angry tears of her inner monologue.

When after a long stretch of time, Simo paused in his walk and approached her with deferential hesitation, she arose abruptly and walked past him into the house, breathing hard and trembling with excitement.

At last Pamphilus arose, and throwing his fleece-lined cloak over his shoulder, slowly and musingly walked through the little garden in the court and passed through the outer gates of the farm. He was strangely lightheaded from hunger and dejection. He paused for a moment to gaze at the rising hillside before him and its silvered olive trees. To his eyes they seemed to be pulsating in even waves of intensity, as though the whole earth and sky were on fire and burning with a pale slow silver flame, the whole earth and sky, unconsumed yet incessantly feeding the countless tongues of flame. He was gazing at this serene conflagration when he became aware of two dim figures in a pool of profound shadow at his right, leaning against the pillar of the gate. Glycerium was pressing her cheek against the stone and breathing her prayer toward the house within and beside her Mysis, distraught and helpless, stood urging her mistress to return home and to leave the ominous vapors of the night and the jealous chill of the moon.

When Glycerium saw that Pamphilus was standing in the road and that he had recognized her, she drew back into Mysis' arms overcome with shame; but slowly collecting herself she stretched forward a hand to him and fixed her great eyes imploringly on his face.

Mysis whispered to her, "We must go home, my bird, my treasure."

"Pamphilus," said Glycerium, "help me!"

His heart contracted within him as he realized the extremity of suffering that had led her thus far. He laid his finger gravely across his lips. He did not smile, but approaching her he looked down into her face with earnest reassurance and beckoned her to accompany Mysis toward the town.

Glycerium pushed back the scarf from her forehead and fell upon one knee before him, babbling incoherently, "I love you. I love you, Pamphilus. You promised me that you loved me. What am I to do? What is to become of me?"

Pamphilus looked at Mysis and again drew his finger across his mouth.

"Hush, my darling," she said. "You see he has taken the vow and cannot speak to us. And we must not speak to him. Look, he wants you to start home with me." She put her arm about the girl's waist and they began to move slowly toward the road.

"He promised me that he loved me," muttered Glycerium, unable to see for her tears, but permitting herself to be led forward. After a few steps, however, she turned and, pushing Mysis aside, said, "No, no! I wish to see him again." She pressed her scarf against her mouth for a moment and gazed at him, her whole soul in her eyes: "Pamphilus, do not marry me, if it is not right. But do not leave me alone. Do not leave me so long alone. Remember Chrysis. Remember the day you found me being stoned by the boys. No, no, do not marry me, if your father and your mother do not wish it, but let me know that . . . that I am still loved by you."

At last he nodded and smiled and waved to her slowly.

"He is nodding his head, Mysis!" cried Glycerium.

"Yes, my treasure."

"Look, Mysis, he is smiling at me. Can you see? Look very hard, Mysis."

"See, now he is waving to you. Wave to him again."

Glycerium waved eagerly, like a child, until Pamphilus was out of sight. It was a long walk home over uneven stones. Glycerium talked excitedly of the smile, trying to estimate the exact shade of intention and affection that lay in his waving to her and in the nod of his head. They discussed the significance of his taking the vow and they talked in general of the custom of taking the vow and recalled all the occasions they could remember of this usage and the results of each occasion. "All will be well, Mysis," she repeated feverishly. "You will see, believe me, all will be well." But finally they fell silent, and in the silence their fears returned and an overwhelming weariness. As they reached the door of their house, Glycerium paused with tight-drawn lower lip and with fear in her eyes, "There is nothing to hope for," she said. "The gods are angry because I thought for a time that I was happy and that the world was easy to live in. At that time I did not understand anything about life and I said cruel things to Chrysis, because I thought the world was easy to live in. And the gods are right. Oh, if I could speak to her for only one moment and could tell her that now I understand her goodness, her goodness. But Chrysis is dead!" She turned to Mysis, but at these words Mysis had withdrawn from her and, beating upon her forehead with the knuckles of her two hands, had fallen upon the threshold of the house.

Pamphilus continued in the opposite direction. He wandered about the upland pastures as he had done all day, and climbed to the highest point on the island to gaze upon the moon and the sea. He tried to lift his mind out of the narrow situation of his problem by thinking of things not before him. He thought of the ships that under that magical flowing light were making their way from port to port, each

one casting aside at its prow two glistening murmurous waves. It was the hour when the helmsman in the security of the course falls into a reverie, remembers his childhood or reckons up his savings. Pamphilus thought of the thousands of homes over all Greece where sleeping or waking souls were forever turning over the dim assignment of life. "Lift every roof," as Chrysis used to say, "and you will find seven puzzled hearts." He thought of Chrysis and her urn, and remembered her strange command to him that he praise all life, even the dark. And as he thought of her his depression, like a cloud, drifted away from him and he was filled with a tremulous happiness. He too praised the whole texture of life, for he saw how strangely life's richest gift flowered from frustration and cruelty and separation. Chrysis living and Chrysis dying in pain; the thoughtful glance that his father so often let rest upon him and the weary expression on his father's face when he thought himself unobserved; the shy mystery of Glycerium. It seemed to him that the whole world did not consist of rocks and trees and water nor were human beings garments and flesh, but all burned, like the hillside of olive trees, with the perpetual flames of love—a sad love that was half hope, often rebuked and waiting to be reassured of its truth. But why then a love so defeated, as though it were waiting for a voice to come from the skies, declaring that therein lay the secret of the world. The moonlight is intermittent and veiled, and it was under such a light that they lived; but his heart suddenly declared to him that a sun would rise and before that sun the timidity and the hesitation would disappear. And as he strode forward this truth became clearer and clearer to him and he laughed because he had been so long blind to what was so obvious. He strode forward, his arms raised to the sky in joyous gratitude, and as he went he cried, "I praise all living, the bright and the dark."

The exhilaration gave place finally to a tranquil fatigue.

As he entered the shadowy temple he saw the priest sleeping before the altar he tended. The priest opened his eyes a moment, and above the curve of his arm he watched the young man spread his cloak upon the marble pavement and lie down upon it and fall asleep.

Simo was awakened a little before dawn by the sounds of shrill voices and of unaccustomed movement in the outer courtyard. On approaching he discovered that a clamorous old woman had entered the gates and that a number of his slaves were trying in vain to quiet her and to drive her back into the road. He recognized Mysis. With a gesture he commanded the men to release her. "What is the matter?" he asked.

"I must see Pamphilus."

"He is not here."

"I cannot go away until I have seen him," she replied, her voice rising in feverish insistence. "A life depends upon it. I do not care what happens to me, but Pamphilus must know what they have done to us."

Simo said quietly, "I shall have you whipped; I shall have you shut up in a room for three days, if you continue to make this noise. Pamphilus will be able to listen to you later in the morning."

Mysis was silent a moment, then she raised her eyes and said somberly, "Later in the morning will be too late, and all will be lost. I beg of you to let me see him now. He would wish it. He would not forgive you for turning me away now."

"Come, tell me what is the matter and I will help you."

"No, it is you who have done this harm and now he alone can save us."

Simo sent the slaves back to their quarters. Then he turned to her again: "In what way have I harmed you?"

"You do not wish to help us," she said. "The Leno's boat has arrived at the island and my mistress Glycerium and all the household of Chrysis have been sold to him as slaves. We were awakened in the middle of the night by the herald of the village and told to gather our clothes together and to go down to the harbor. Glycerium is not well now; she must not be driven so. I myself escaped through the rows of a vineyard and have come to find Pamphilus. It was you who have done this, for it was the Fathers of the Island who ordered that we should be sold as slaves to pay our debts."

This was true. He remembered having listened without interest to a discussion of the matter, assuming that it would be carried out with sufficient warning and delay to admit of Glycerium's being separated from the rest of the destitute company. The Leno's boat visited Brynos so seldom that it seemed to the Fathers of the Island that they might yet be under the necessity of providing for the household through many months while awaiting the arrival of this purchaser.

Suddenly a light dawned upon Mysis: "He is at the temple! How could I have forgotten that he was under the vow of silence and that he must be there!" And turning, she started to enter the road.

"You must not go to him at the temple," said Simo sharply. "I shall come down to the harbor with you now and buy your mistress from the Leno."

He returned to the house for his cloak, then walked into the town with Mysis hurrying at his heels. Dawn was breaking as he descended the winding stairs to the square. Against the streaked sky he saw the mast of the Leno's boat. The Leno was not only a dealer in slaves; he was a wandering bazaar and sold foreign foods and trinkets and cloths. If an island were large enough he came ashore and conducted a fair and a circus. And now in the first cold light of morning Simo could see on the raised portion of the deck a brightly colored booth, a chained bear, an ape, two parrots, and other samples of the Leno's stock in trade,

including the household of Chrysis. Philocles had remained
on shore and for two hours had been standing at the para-
pet uttering short broken cries toward his companions.
Being a Greek citizen he could not be sold into slavery and
was to be transported later to Andros.

Simo descended the steps of the landing with Mysis and
was rowed out to the boat. While he concluded his trans-
action with the black and smiling Leno, Mysis sank upon
her knees before Glycerium, telling her of this good fortune.
But Glycerium derived no joy from the news. She sat be-
tween Apraxine and the Ethiopian girl, amid the bundles
of their clothes, and for weariness she could scarcely raise
her eyes or move her lips. "No," she said, "I shall stay here
with you. I do not wish to go anywhere."

Simo approached them. "My child," he said to Glycerium,
"you are to come with me now."

"Yes, my beloved," Mysis repeated into her ear, "you
must go with him. All will be well. He is taking you ashore
to Pamphilus."

Still Glycerium remained with bent head. "I do not wish
to move. I do not wish to go anywhere," she said.

"I am the father of Pamphilus. You must come with me
and good care will be taken of you."

At last and with great difficulty she arose. Mysis sup-
ported her to the side of the boat, and there taking her
farewell she whispered to her, "Good-bye, my dear love.
Now may the gods bring you happiness. I shall never see
you again, but I pray you to remember me, for I have loved
you well. And wherever we are, let us remember our dear
Chrysis."

The two women embraced one another in silence, Gly-
cerium with closed eyes. At last she said, "I would that I
were dead, Mysis. I would that I were long dead with
Chrysis, my dear sister."

"You are to come with us too," said Simo to Mysis, who
having known even greater surprises obediently followed

him. The little group was rowed in silence to the shore. The Leno's oarsmen struck the water, his bright colored sails were raised, and his merchandise left the harbor for other fortunes.

The sun had already risen when Pamphilus returned with swift and happy steps to his home. There he discovered Glycerium sleeping peacefully under his mother's care. There was not a sound to be heard on the farm, for his mother, already invested with the dignity of her new duties as guardian and nurse to the outcast girl, had ordered a perfect quiet. Argo was sitting before the gate, her eyes wide with wonder and pleasure at the arrival of this new friend. Simo had gone to the warehouse and when he returned, for all his happiness, he moved about with lowered eyes, driven by the constraint in his nature to act as though nothing had happened.

In the two days that followed, all their thoughts were centered about the room where the girl lay and all their hearts were renewed under the fragile claims that Glycerium's beauty and shyness made upon them. Simo seemed, after Pamphilus, to have best understood her reticence and to have been understood by her; a friendship beyond speech had grown up between them. This flowering of goodness, however, was not to be put to the trial of routine perseverance nor to know the alternations of self-reproach and renewed courage; for on the noon of the third day Glycerium's pains began, and by sunset both mother and child were dead.

That night after many months of drought it began to rain. Slowly at first and steadily, the rain began to fall over all Greece. Great curtains of rain hung above the plains; in the mountains it fell as snow, and on the sea it printed its countless ephemeral coins upon the water. The greater part of the inhabitants were asleep, but the relief of the long-expected rain entered into the mood of their sleeping minds. It fell upon the urns standing side by side in the

shadow, and the wakeful and the sick and the dying heard the first great drops fall upon the roofs above their heads. Pamphilus lay awake, face downward, his chin upon the back of his hand. He heard the first great drops fall upon the roof over his head and he knew that his father and mother, not far from him, heard them too. He had been repeating to himself Chrysis' lesson and adding to it his Glycerium's last faltering words: "Do not be sorry; do not be afraid," and he had been remembering how, with the faintest movement of her eyes to one side, she had indicated her child and said, "Wherever we are, we are yours." He had been asking himself in astonishment wherein had lain his joy and his triumph of the few nights before: how could he have once been so sure of the beauty of existence? And some words of Chrysis returned to him. He recalled how she had touched the hand of a young guest who had returned from an absence, having lost his sister, and how she had said to him in a low voice, so as not to embarrass those others present who had never known a loss, "You were happy with her once; do not doubt that the conviction at the heart of your happiness was as real as the conviction at the heart of your sorrow." Pamphilus knew that out of these fragments he must assemble during the succeeding nights sufficient strength, not only for himself, but for these others—these others who so bewilderingly now turned to him and whose glances tried to read from his face what news there was from the last resources of courage and hope, to live on, to live by. But in confusion and with flagging courage he repeated, "I praise all living, the bright and the dark."

On the sea the helmsman suffered the downpour, and on the high pastures the shepherd turned and drew his cloak closer about him. In the hills the long-dried stream beds began to fill again and the noise of water falling from level to level, warring with the stones in the way, filled the gorges. But behind the thick beds of clouds the moon

soared radiantly bright, shining upon Italy and its smoking mountains. And in the East the stars shone tranquilly down upon the land that was soon to be called Holy and that even then was preparing its precious burden.